Savannah of Williamsburg

Ben Franklin, Freedom & Freedom of the Press
Virginia 1735

Book III in the Savannah Squirrel Series

Jennifer Susannah Devore

Kramerica International Media, LLC.
Williamsburg, Virginia

Savannah of Williamsburg
Ben Franklin, Freedom & Freedom of the Press
Virginia1735

Kramerica International Media, LLC.
P.O. Box 2305
Williamsburg, Virginia 23187

www.kramericamedia.com
www.historysquirrel.com
savannahsquirrel@yahoo.com

Cover art by KIM, LLC
Author photo by KIM, LLC
Library of Congress data available
First edition 2008

Again, forever, for G
"Padua"

Also for Miss Onyx, PB3 and, because he's a key, creative inspiration, Woody Allen.

A special thanks to Seth MacFarlane and Larry David for offering the globe your insane genius. Most of this was written watching your DVDs.

Finally for Mommy and Daddy, Dr. and Mrs. Robert Morris Gerstle. Thank you again for understanding why we do what we do.

CHAPTER ONE

The lightning snapped like a bullwhip on a tin roof. The strike was so sharp, so vicious and terrifying it was as though the misty bowels of the earth thrust it up through the terrain, instead of down from the heavens. Bolts hit close before, but this was wild. This time Samuel was sure it cracked right under Merlin's belly. Merlin thought so, too, and jerked up straight as a board, only his hind legs making contact with the ground. His front hooves punching wildly at invisible offenders, Merlin nearly pitched Samuel clean off his saddle and straight back into the waiting, leafy arms of a huge oak. Samuel held tight, though.

His arms tightened, his hands gripped the reins like roots to soil, his thighs clenched and his knees cleaved to Merlin's sides, determined not to fall. Samuel's face was rain-soaked and he flipped a thick, sticky, blond forelock out of his eyes; but, it was no use as it stayed glued to his left eyelid and all Samuel accomplished was straining a muscle somewhere deep in his neck. Within seconds, gravity and momentum did their jobs and Merlin was pulled safely forward, his hooves hitting the foggy ground at a full gallop.

Merlin accelerated so fast that Samuel lost control of one hand and flew backwards, his tailbone briefly brushing the rise of his worn, leather saddle. In a single motion, Samuel swept the hair out of his eye, pasting it back to his skull and grabbed Merlin's mane, wrapped it once around his fist and pulled himself upright in a rather graceful arc, considering the speed, imbalance and general terror of the moment. Even through his knuckles, Samuel could feel all the muscles and sinews in Merlin's neck stretch, tighten and contract. It felt a little creepy, like he was, at that very moment, morphing from normal, earthly horse to some supernatural steed of the underworld. Dread passed over Samuel's face as he looked at Merlin's face. His eyes were black as onyx but Samuel could swear he saw sparks of sapphire blue, tiny explosions inside his pupils with every hoof beat. Geysers of steam, aerated and expanded by the night's fog, spewed from his great nostrils in exact time with the sapphire explosions. As a fourteen-year old boy, Samuel generally showed very little emotion and very little actually fazed him. This fazed him and he was terrified.

Quickly, he regained his posture, gripped the saddle tightly with his thighs and leaned closer into Merlin's neck, his cheek now feeling the blood and sinews pumping and adding to the fright of the moment. Just as he gained the courage to release his right hand momentarily to give Merlin a hearty, Good Boy-pat, a new bolt came spiking down: cloud-to-ground and louder than ever. The sky flashed completely white, at imperceptible intervals, again and again, outlining every leaf and raindrop in sight with a spooky, silver glow. The thunder shuddered almost simultaneously with each strike.

Samuel tried to count in between lightning strikes and thunderclaps. His father once told him the lower the number, the closer the lightning and if you couldn't get to two, stoop! Currently, he had not gotten to two for well over a mile. It was like the storm was following him, tracking him, keeping pace with him. He contemplated slowing down, maybe even stopping altogether and taking refuge under a tree as the storm passed. However, he had very little say in the matter. Merlin decided long ago the faster and farther from Baltimore, the better. He could sense the storm was moving just slowly enough that they'd have to stay put for about four hours before the storm passed.

Snap! Crack! That one, Samuel could swear, hit Merlin's tail and judging by the accompanying *snap* in the back of Samuel's neck as he was thrust backwards in the saddle, Merlin agreed. A new round of thunder was coming as Samuel straightened. Merlin could sense it before Samuel ever heard it. Merlin's ears twitched back and up, razor sharp as he anticipated the next shudder, rolling up behind them like wine barrels under the road. Samuel scanned the trees as he rode past in a fury. Every once in a while, when the lightning lit up the forest, he could see eyes and small figures deep in the woods. They were certainly just the nocturnal creatures, the raccoons, weasels, cats and owls that waited for nighttime to frolic, work and hunt. At least, that is what he told himself.

There were, of course, legends about these woods, this stretch of the countryside that wound down the coast. The well-travelled roads around New-York, Boston and Philadelphia were one thing. There were plenty of riders, coaches, the general traffic of commerce amongst these towns. Yet, down here was a whole different thing. It was easy to go a full day and see maybe five people. Nighttime was even worse. Plus, Samuel and Merlin were well south of Baltimore now. There was nothing south of Baltimore. Only collections of Indian villages, mostly Mattaponi and Chickahominy tribes, and the odd port or plantation could be found for miles and miles south of Baltimore. Too far south and too close to the water you'd get pyrates, although everyone knew they were pretty harmless on land. Still, as another flash brought the night a moment of noon, Samuel knew he didn't want to see anything but raccoon eyes through those leaves.

Samuel placed a hand on one of the satchels hanging off Merlin's rump. The bag was wet all the way through. Fortunately, in anticipation of just such a storm, he'd wrapped everything inside with nearly a yard of pitch cloth. If pitch could keep a sailor's backside dry in a North Sea tempest, surely it could keep some newspapers and letters dry inside a leather satchel. Whatever the possible water damage, he still had them, they hadn't fallen off and that was what mattered.

Samuel's only job was to deliver the contents of these bags to the Raleigh Tavern down in Williamsburg, Virginia. It was the capital and apparently a pretty important town, but how important could it be, being so far from Boston and New-York? Being fourteen and originally from Boston, Samuel was pretty sure that if he didn't know about something, it might not be too worthy of knowing. He'd never delivered this far south, never wanted to; but, the boy who had normally run this route had fallen seriously ill with a pox and was not expected to recover. Now, the route fell to Samuel whom, whilst worried about his predecessor's health, was at the moment worried about his own well-being.

Crack! "This is it!" Samuel thought. Merlin whinnied and stood so high that his saddle, now loosened by rain and sweat, spun completely around and now hung upside down on his belly. Only the brittle leather reins kept Samuel astride as he hung completely vertical, grasping a slippery combination of mane and leather, his boots dangling and entwined with Merlin's black, silky tail. Samuel just held on and waited for gravity to do its job again and bring Merlin back to all fours safely. After what felt like an eternity, gravity did its job alright. Backwards. Merlin flipped all the way over and came down hard, right on top of Samuel. The last thing Samuel saw was black: Merlin's mane then Merlin's head, then nothingness.

Hours later, as the rain streaming down Samuel's face grew gradually warmer and warmer, he realized it wasn't rain, but blood. He could barely see. Whether it was the rain, the blood or a general failing of his body he was unsure. The fact was he couldn't see well and he needed to know his pal was okay. Samuel strained his neck, tried to lift it but it was too heavy. He went completely limp and his head hit the dirt like a sack of potatoes. His green eyes blinked, his long lashes dripped with salt, blood and rain. His chest was tight beyond description, not painful, just too much pressure to bear much longer. Considering he had a horse on top of him, this made sense. He released one last, great expulsion from his lungs before he shut down completely. As his eyes slowly closed for good, he saw Merlin blink.

That blond strand still stuck to Samuel's forehead, but was now pink with blood. He couldn't move anything except his mouth which sent a quick and quiet smile to his friend. If only he'd listened to his parents. They told him not to go, at least not overnight. He watched Merlin finally close his dark eyes all the way. Samuel's eyes hurt as he stared. The sides of his eyes hurt, the bone above his eyes hurt, his pupils hurt. Then, Samuel began to cry and all of him hurt. He already missed Merlin and though it was an odd time for a craving, he really wanted a piece of his mother's corn bread.

Jennifer Susannah Devore

4

CHAPTER TWO

"Your Excellency," a tiny, nervous man of about fifty ran down the dock, tripping on the boards every few feet, addressing the newest member of the New-York colony, "we are most pleased, yes, the Council and Governor VanDam and I, yes, we all welcome you to New-York. . ." He stopped walking and turned back, realizing his guest had stopped about ten paces ago.

The night was excessively warm, even for August. Fortunately though, it was not too humid. The stars were sprinkled about the black sky like hints of gems in a cave and there was even a very slight breeze, but not enough to quell the warmth. Only the lack of direct sunlight made August nights in New-York better than the days. It was late, nearly midnight and the newly arrived travellers were all restless, irritable, sick and famished. This one, His Excellency, in particular seemed like everything was bothering him. Of course, voyaging is like that; the actual travel days, the frantic and stressful days spent getting to and fro can break even the most charming of folks.

Slowly removing his hat, a richly-hued, purple, velvet tricorn, His Excellency stood back and took a deep breath. He breathed through his nose loudly, turning his face to look at the moonbeam on the harbor and rubbed his face with his open palms, letting all those around him, an entourage of about fifty servants, lackeys, sycophants and family members, know just how very irritated he was. He was so irritated it seemed, that he couldn't even speak. He had to first gather his thoughts. He rolled his neck and sighed with loud exaggeration.

"*Governor* VanDam?" he hissed. "*Governor* VanDam?!" he then bellowed, scaring off a cormorant sitting atop a mast.

"Uh, yes, Your Excellency. Governor VanDam has been, well,

acting-governor while you were, um, yes, well, not here. We knew you would indeed arrive, presently, Sir. We just knew not when, exactly. Heh heh?" the greeter laughed nervously, bowing all the while, his hat behind his back.

Turning his head far to the right, then to the left, making an audible crack each time, His Excellency took six precise and angry steps toward the tiny man from the New-York Provincial Council, a secretary called Phipps, and planted his boots directly in front of him, his silk scarf fluttering in Phipps' nose. Phipps sneezed and casually took one step backwards, politely regaining some of his personal space. His Excellency just stepped forward again, then looked down and spoke into the one-man welcoming committee's bald spot.

"Now you listen to me, little man," he lifted the little man's head with a silk-gloved finger under his chin. "New-York has one and only one governor and *I am he!*" his final three words coming at a full yell. "There is no *Governor* VanDam. VanDam is merely a Council member whom acted in my stead, whom worked *for me* whilst I was away on business so important, a man of your stature and brain could never begin to comprehend. Do you understand? *I* am the governor. *I* am the only governor. I am *the* Royal Governor William Cosby, ruler, by command of His Royal Majesty King George II, of the provinces of New-York and New-Jersey." By now, he was spraying his words directly onto the thick, black curls atop Phipps' head. Phipps was visibly shaken.

"Governor Cosby," an older man, a young seventy years and exquisitely dressed, came striding down the dock through the evening mist, full of genuine kindness and self-confidence. He offered a sincere smile, an outstretched hand and a true happiness in his walk, almost a bouncing stride, the long curls of his black wig bombilating with every silver-buckled step.

"Welcome, welcome!" Arriving late, he missed most of Cosby's assault on Phipps, though his manners probably would have led him to be this gracious anyway. "What a pleasure it is to finally see you! We have been most anxious for your arrival and your home, your offices, everything you could need or want is ready and waiting for you and your fine family!"

Cosby's family stood behind him on the dock. Most of them sneered and none broke a smile. They just looked around at their new home in disgust. Though New-York was much better than Cosby's previous post, Royal Governor of Minorca, one of the Balearic Islands off Spain's east coast, New-York was still, to Cosby's family, a small, dank, dirty and uncivilized island outpost of outlaws, urban scum and country folk.

The new, elegant greeter now bowed deeply to Cosby and stood politely at attention, his hat in his hand behind his back, his other hand flat across his waistcoat.

"I would be most honoured to personally escort you to your new home here within Fort George," he bowed again but his offer was met with a sneer.

"Or, to your offices across the water at City Hall. A ferry is always ready and at your disposal, Your Excellency. Whichever you so choose, Governor Cosby," he smiled still, though his joy was clearly fading.

"Who are you again?" Cosby looked right past the man and at the rather simple, stone structure of Fort George. This was certainly no Windsor Castle.

There was a gentle hush over the crowd gathered at the dock. Besides the town's most important men and their assistants, there were townsfolk, house servants, slaves, children, just about anybody whom wasn't in bed or at a job whom had come to greet the new governor. Everybody there, with the exception of Cosby, knew exactly who the elegant man was. Could this new governor be that out of touch? That obtuse or that stupid? There had been very quiet rumours that Cosby was rather unintelligent, lazy, too. It was a fact that, if not unintelligent, he was certainly uneducated. Uneducated, maybe, but certainly rulers had to be smart, didn't they? Certainly they wouldn't be in power if they weren't some of the smartest men around. Right? Perhaps he was just rude, mean and self-involved. Of course, when meeting someone new, especially fresh off a travel day, most people are forgiving and will tend to ignore the very proof in front of them that speaks otherwise. People are mostly good and want to believe others are, too. Probably, Cosby was just tired and just wasn't up to speed, yet.

"Speak up, man! Who are you and why are you squawking and flustering at me?" Nope. Not tired. Just nasty.

"Your Excellency?" the elegant one stood erect, replaced his hat on his head and adjusted first his vest, then his frock coat, then his overcoat and stared at Cosby until the nasty newcomer was forced to make eye contact.

With more grace and breeding than a king, the polite man held up his chin and chose his words carefully and spoke them with perfect enunciation and speed.

"I, Sir, am your acting-Governor Rip VanDam. I have seen to your provinces and their needs for over a year as we have awaited your arrival. I am a longtime member in unquestionably good standing of your Provincial Council and am now, at your service."

He bowed once more with all propriety and expected genuflection; however, this time there was no ebullience, no friendliness. It was now all business.

"Ah, VanDam," Cosby recalled. "Yes, excellent. I shall require an escort to City Hall in the morning. Nine o'clock. Meet me here, at my fort, at my residence inside. Or, are my family and I to stand here all night and wither in the summer moonlight? I cannot imagine what form of housing could possibly be provided in here for me," he looked with dismay at Fort George.

Around Fort George was even more dismaying. Fort George sat on an island, Governors' Island. Wrapping its arms around the island, the Hudson and East Rivers hugged Cosby's new home. To the west stood New-Jersey and Staten Island, to the east stood Brooklyn. Lighting the direct path between Governors' Island and Manhattan, the moon blanketed Upper New-York Bay. Straight ahead twinkled the very few lights of Manhattan's tip.

Fort George was a wide, low, protective stone structure built by the Dutch some hundred years previously, in the early 1600s. Situated right on the Atlantic, it was a natural place to guard against sea attacks by the French, Spanish, Portuguese, whomever might challenge Holland's authority over *Nieuw Amsterdam*, as it was called by them. It did not, however, protect them very well against the British and in 1664, Britain took control of New Amsterdam from the Dutch and renamed it New-York. The fort itself underwent a number of name changes after that and now it bore the name of England's current monarch, King George II.

On the Island, within the walls of Fort George there stood some commerce, a few taverns and a small number of residences. Like any military fixture, support services and staff needed their own places to live and function and shop. Governor's Island was its own little village. Outside the walls of Fort George though, stood the forests and all the wild animals and Indians one's imagination could muster. Though the Dutch had known it and longtime residents of New-York knew it, the Indians of the area, the original inhabitants, were prosperous and wealthy tribes: the Canarsie, Minetta, Algonquin and Iroquois. Cosby neither knew, nor cared. To him, Indians were as base and uncivilized as the rats that scuttled across the dock that night. Thinking about them, Cosby and his equally ignorant family were getting antsy standing around on an open dock in the middle of the night.

"I assume my residence is ready, and the finest in all of the provinces?" Cosby demanded.

VanDam nodded in the affirmative, his eyes fixed and chilly but nevertheless polite, always polite.

"Nay, make it eleven o'clock. I am absolutely exhausted," Cosby suddenly changed his mind about tomorrow, rolled his head around in a stretch and drew out the final word into a whine.

"Very good, Your Excellency. I shall be at your door at eleven o'clock. These gentlemen shall show you and your family inside," VanDam nodded toward a group of ten soldiers whom all jumped to grab baggage, birdcages, pets, crates, baskets, anything that was to go inside the fort walls. VanDam continued, "Phipps here is prepared to show you the way inside. I think you and your lovely family shall be quite comfortable and quite safe."

"Comfortable? Well, I surely hope we are to be more than comfortable!"

Cosby laughed and twisted around toward his family, half of whom laughed with him and half of whom just stood there dim-witted with their arms crossed and their faces sour.

"Oh, and VanDam?" Cosby closed his eyes and pointed at VanDam, shaking his finger slightly as if trying to remember what he wanted to say, "I think a parade to greet me on Manhattan should be nice. Not like this," he shook his fingers at the late-night assemblage on the dock, dissatisfied and disgusted. "I want a real gathering, a procession. Soldiers, politicians, get the town's most important merchants and their wives," he liked the idea of lots of wealthy wives waving to him. He whipped around and pointed directly at VanDam, "The pretty ones only. I want this town to know the real governor is here and things are about to change. Day one, everything changes."

VanDam looked perplexed, but not thrown off guard at all. "A parade, Governor?"

"Are you deaf as well as stupid? Yes, a pa-ray-duh for me," he sounded out the word for VanDam in such an ill-bred and rude fashion that the whole dock gasped a little.

"I, I am sorry, Governor. Yes, of course, a parade. I shall make the preparations this evening. Presently, of course," he glanced at Phipps whose mind was already a muddle of logistics. A parade? How absurd and probably impossible!

Cosby then gestured to his servants to begin walking with whatever baggage and crates they carried. Within seconds, the ship and the dock were frenetic with the general business of unloading. Phipps scuttled sideways, like a crab, a few feet behind Cosby and to the right, constantly turning straining his neck to be sure the governor was content. He was not. He walked at a slow pace, deliberately because he knew Phipps wished he'd walk faster. The discomfort he knew he was causing Phipps made him smile an evil grin, his thin, pink lips tight as though the skin and muscles were completely unfamiliar with such a motion as a smile. His chin, thin and non-existent, melted into his neck and gave an overall appearance of old butter sliding off an upended plate.

VanDam strode next to Phipps. VanDam's hands were clasped behind his back and his head uncharacteristically low: not hung, just not high.

"Oh, Phipps," VanDam lamented quietly. "'Tis going to be a long night, my friend."

VanDam breathed in a small pleasure this night: the thick, briny, marine smell that forever meant summer.

"Nay, Mr. VanDam," Phipps whispered back. "I have a feeling 'tis going to be a long, royal appointment."

VanDam breathed in again, this time audibly enough to turn Cosby's head and reveal the sneer that was apparently his default face. As small a pleasure as it was, VanDam was going to enjoy every bit of the sea air he could tonight and as he trod the dock behind this new monster of the Crown, VanDam smiled a little, his full lips happy to return to the state which they were most accustomed.

Across the Upper Bay and further up Broadway on the Manhattan mainland, where the smell of brine, fish and seaweed was replaced by that of soot, livestock and dung, Smith Street housed in one of its thin townhouses the offices of a young, German immigrant who went by the name of Herr John Peter Zenger.

"Herr Zenger," a young boy of ten shouted from across the printing office, "I have finished prepping the ink beaters, all the type is organized in the proper spaces and I even swept the floor in the back office. First thing in the morning, I can walk right in and ink all the type. Everything is ready to go."

Zenger stopped writing in his accounts book and looked up at his apprentice and waited for the pitch.

"So, I was wondering," the boy continued, "do you think I might be able to be finished for the night? I heard the new governor is sailing in tonight! Maybe I can get a glimpse of him."

"Of course, Linus. But it is past midnight. The ferries have probably stopped running. Besides, it is dangerous downtown this late. You have worked diligently today and you have earned a good night's rest. Go home and sleep. You will see the new governor sometime soon, I am sure."

Zenger turned back to his accounts and bit his quill pen in mild consternation, then realized he had a bit of goose feather in his mouth and pried it from his teeth. He could feel the boy looking at him. "What about your mother? Surely she would not allow you to go to Governors' Island at midnight."

"She won't know. She's sleeping and always expects me home late the closer we get to final print days."

Zenger admired the boy's dedication to his apprenticeship. Besides, under the contract of an apprenticeship, Zenger was as responsible for the boy as his mother was. He really should forbid him going. Of course, this was a big event and the boy wanted to learn about the news-paper industry. Finding stories first-hand was a good way.

"Go," Zenger relented. "Go see our new governor and take notes. Maybe there's a story in it, but I doubt it. But be careful, the docks are dangerous most times of the day, let alone this late. If you cannot get the ferry to Governors' Island right away, do not wait. Just go home."

Linus straightened a couple of things at his work desk and went to put on his coat.

"I hear he may not be all sausages and roses," Zenger said.

"What?" Linus asked, hearing the odd description. Must be a German saying.

"Cosby. The new governor. I hear he's a bit of trouble, a much greedier sort than our recent governors," he continued to cipher accounts in his head as he talked, then placed the correct numbers in the appropriate rows. "We shall see, Linus. In truth, royal governors are neither here nor there to me. They are politicians with far greater matters to worry about than I care to think on and quite frankly, my life seems to remain basically the same, regardless of whom sleeps in Fort George."

"Still, don't you find it exciting to see this new man, Herr Zenger?" Linus asked hurriedly as he threw his rucksack over his left shoulder and pulled up his socks. "What might he look like? Is he fat or short or skinny or tall? Maybe he has a pretty daughter," Linus's eyebrows shot up at this recent consideration.

"I suppose all that might be true," Zenger was half-listening as he searched for two shillings on paper that could not be accounted for anywhere. "But whether this man is fat or thin, it does not change my life. I have my wife, my beautiful children and my business. I may not be the most successful printer in town, but this shop is mine and I like what I do. How many men get to say that?" Linus shrugged, not really interested anymore and itching to leave.

"Here is what I do say, young Linus. A new governor is okay by me. It matters not and shan't affect me. How could it? Besides imposing higher taxes, which they all bring and always will, how is a British governor going to touch me and my little life? Now go. Gawk at your new governor, take some good notes."

Linus was out the door at the word 'go'. Zenger laughed a bit, shook his head and went back to his figures, certain those shillings would emerge eventually.

CHAPTER THREE

Last night's wind and rain had blown out virtually every speck of dirt and grime from the forest. Leaves sparkled in the sun they were so waxy and spotless. Rocks, still moist, gleamed like pewter plates and the sky itself covered everything like swaths and swaths of billowing French-blue silk. Throughout the trees, all the beauty and happiness this day brought to a little fox could be heard, manifested in song. The stringy strums and plinky plucks of a mandolin drifted through the branches and bounced off the rocks as the little fox named Sterling sang a song of his own composition, sweet of lyrics and vaguely medieval in melody.

She's got a square face,
But I think she's lovely.
I'd go to her place,
But she's not too cuddly.
I love to dine before we say grace,
But she already ate all the bisquits and gravy.

Sterling had such a bad night that no matter what happened, today was bound to be better. Though he had found a small den in which to hide from the storm, it barely helped. In fact, it nearly flooded, leaving his raw silk breeches soaked, his peasant blouse filthy and his red, leather clogs still squishing with dirty water every step he took. Not to worry though. His mandolin and his favourite green hat were safe. As long as those were clean and dry, everything else could be tolerated. Everything else would dry.

Clomp, squish. Clomp, squish. Clomp, squish. Clomp, squish. Sterling's clogs trod their way across the damp forest floor in perfect time with his song. While he was not by nature an exceptionally silly fox, today was definitely what Sterling would call a good day and his mood, pace and melodies reflected this. On occasion, a bluebird or a cardinal would stop their duties and perch on a branch just long enough to listen to the travelling balladeer. On occasion, he would leap at the birds, then apologize for trying to eat them. A very bad habit he'd never been able to shake.

All was right with the world and Sterling had successfully stashed the past horrors of his very short time here in America into the farthest storehouses of his mind. Today was all about sunshine, blue skies, happy, uneaten birds and a quick tempo. *Clomp, squish. Clomp, squish. Clomp, squish. Clomp, squish.* Sterling thought about filling the pewter mug that hung from his suspenders. Ale would be nice, wine even better, but fresh water from a stream would be just fine right now.

About half a mile down the well-worn trail he was travelling, he saw a curve in the path and just overhead, to the right, he saw the tops of a grove of trees. That many trees bundled together, all quite tall, meant there had to be a creek or a stream near them. Trees didn't grow in that tight and tall a fashion unless they were near water.

Sterling picked up his step and his tempo and skipped toward the water source. He could almost taste it as he thought about it: clean, sparkling, crisp and cool. Mmmm. He'd eat some of the berries he had in his satchel and a little piece of bisquit when he got there. A picnic! He would make a picnic for himself! What a perfect idea for such a perfect day. There! Just ahead he could see the grove. He could hear the running water. He could see a boulder up ahead, just obscuring his view of the water. Actually, a picnic atop that boulder might be the perfect spot. It would still be cool and moist from the rain, a good thing on this ever-warming, August day and he'd have a lovely view of the stream, or creek, or whatever it was. Then, he'd play his mandolin and most likely, with his belly full of bisquits and berries, he'd take a nap in the summer sun. Mmmm. A nap sounded fabulous.

Sterling dug in his satchel for the berries and hoped the bisquits weren't too soggy. What fortune! He had wrapped them well enough and since he hung it up high in the den last night, the spray of rain that entered from outside only bathed the top flap of his bag. He then started to untie the ribbon that held his mug to his suspenders. As he untied it, he carefully held the mug in one paw. Pewter can crack easily and if he dropped this mug, he would have nothing until he could get to another town to buy one. Gently, he moved the mug to his other paw as he stuffed the ribbon into a front pocket, careful not to lose it as he picnicked. As he balanced his snacks, vessel and satchel he did not look where he was walking and stumbled right into the large boulder. *Thunk*. Then, *clank!*

Sterling dropped his mug and just as he knew it would, it developed a large crack as it hit a smaller rock near his feet. The berries tumbled out of his paw and rolled like marshmallows into the road, his bisquit dropped, broke in two and each half stopped to lie flat next to the mug. Sterling's mandolin strap, lengths of ribbon and scarves braided together, hung around his body and over his shoulder, the bowl of his instrument clanking as it came to rest atop the pearl buttons of his waistcoat. As he bent to pick up his berries and bisquit his body froze in full arrest. His eyes grew wide and in an instant all he could hear was the running of the creek, or brook or whatever it was and the growing rush of blood in his own head. His heart began to beat so fast he actually covered his chest with both hands in an effort to slow it down. He then moved closer to the boulder, slowly, and with escalating horror came to the very unsavoury realization that this was no boulder.

"It could not have lasted," Sterling whispered to himself and began to shiver in the increasing summer heat. "I thought today would be a good day, all day long. 'Tis not to be."

Sterling stared at the scene in front of him just a bit longer, then took a deep breath. He must do something. Clearly he must help, somehow. As Sterling knelt down and gently pet what was obviously not a boulder, but a horse, he saw that under the great animal was not just a large satchel, similar to his own tiny one, but a human. A young boy who lay lifeless. Sterling would run for help. Someone would have to notify the families and he really hoped it wouldn't have to be him. Never mind that right now. He had to catch his breath for a minute. Then, he would run. He would run and find the proper authorities to help. He leaned against a tree for a second, cleared his mind of any self-pity, stood up, threw his mandolin around his back and told himself to buck up and do this. Then, he heard a rustle. Not in the trees and not near the water, but right at his feet. He looked down to see what it was. Most likely, it was a field mouse happy to find some warm, summer berries. No, it was not a mouse. It was the boy! The boy's hand had moved! He was still alive!

Sterling ran down to the brook, yes, it was definitely a brook, and scooped up water in his cracked mug. It still held water, but leaked all the way back to the boy. Sterling cupped his paw under the boy's chin and poured the cool water on his lips, then helped him part them and poured small amounts into his mouth. He began to sputter little coughs. That was good. He was definitely alive, but not very strong. Worst of all, his legs were pinned under this horse. Sterling pulled and pulled on the boy's arms, but to no avail. A young fox was never going to be strong enough. He'd have to go for help; but, he hated to leave this boy and his horse. The boy would never be free of that horse if he didn't go, though. Once again, Sterling summoned all his courage, re-slung his instrument so it lay flat on his back and gave way to the inner thoughts that told him he could and must do this. As he turned to go, something caught his leg, a berry vine.

This time of year the berries were all gone, picked clean by the birds, mice and young couples in love whom took to the berry picking trails early before the sun became too strong. He swatted at the vine. It swatted back. Spooked and startled as he generally was, Sterling jumped straight up in the air and landed on top of the horse's rump. Startled by that, he leapt again and this time landed on a less corporeal log and stared at what had swatted him. The boy had swung at him. He was conscious!

"Please. Come. I shan't harm you. I need help. I am Samuel, Samuel Woodrow Allen, " he whispered, not forgetting his manners. Samuel whispered, his head lolling back and forth on the mossy trail.

"Yes, yes, but of course," Sterling jumped down from his log and knelt at Samuel's side. "I am just off to find help, Mate. I tried to free your legs," he gestured with his long snout in that direction, "but could not budge him or you. I think we are not far off from a town. The trail is a little wider here and the path a little smoother. That tells me it gets a bit of traffic. We've got to be close to somebody."

Samuel smiled weakly and said, between coughs, "You are a bright fox.

Yes, I am headed for the town of Williamsburg. It is not more than half a day down this path. 'Tis a large town, plenty of folks."

"Yes, I shall bring someone back by nightfall. I can run very fast!" Sterling boasted not in vanity, but in reassurance to the boy. "Be still, breathe slowly and think of something lovely, maybe sing a song. I shall be back with help. Please, worry not."

Sterling looked the boy deep in his eyes and smiled. He pat the boy on the head and turned to leave. Samuel grabbed his leg.

"Merlin. My horse. Is he still alive? I cannot feel him breathe," Samuel's eyes filled with tears as he stared at Merlin's face, the great steed's eyes closed.

"I do not know. Yet, the air seems extra warm and moist around his nose. Of course, who can tell in this weather?" he laughed nervously. Sensing it was no time for a jest, he patted Samuel on the head again. "He must be breathing a little. His belly does not show this, but I just do not sense death," he sniffed the air, his nose twitching rapidly. "He is in bad shape, though. He will die if I do not return soon. Please, I must go now. Sing something sweet to yourself. I shall be back very, very soon."

"No, wait. You must take these with you," Samuel tugged at his satchels, not easily loosened from under his own weight.

Sterling took the cue and helped to pull, freeing the double-pack bag and falling back on his great tail as he did so. Without even looking at it, he fitted the strap over his other shoulder, balancing himself so that the mandolin crossed his body over his right shoulder and the double-satchel over his left, one sack on each hip. "Of course," he politely obliged. "What do I do with it?"

"It is vital, Mister. . .what is your name?"

"Sterling Zanni diPadua," he bowed grandly, his mandolin slipping toward the front, the tuning keys knocking Sterling on the ear.

"Yes, Mr. diPadua, listen. It is vital, beyond vital that you deliver this satchel for me to the Raleigh Tavern in Williamsburg. The Raleigh Tavern," he said the name slowly.

"Yes, yes, Chappie. The Raleigh Tavern, of course. What is it? What is inside? Music sheets?" Sterling thought of the most important thing he could and what could fit into a leather satchel and what could be more important than music sheets?

"No. Well, maybe. I know not. It is the royal mail. Letters, documents from London, Boston, New-York, Philadelphia probably. News-papers. It is all very important correspondence intended for the Virginia capital and the Royal Governor Gooch, probably his Council and magistrates. I know not exactly. I just know they are government papers sent by order of the Crown. I am a royal messenger. Please, you must get them to the Raleigh."

Samuel was exhausted by the time he got out this directive. Every word was an effort and took what little breath he had. He dropped his head with an audible *thunk*.

"Stop worrying, Samuel. Look, I have it securely on my shoulder and it is on its way now. I will find help and then find the tavern."

"No, go directly to the tavern," with struggle, he lifted his head one more time. "These are late already. You will find help at the tavern. Deliver these first. Remember, the Raleigh Tavern in Williamsburg."

Samuel once more dropped his head and in a burgeoning state of delirium, began to laugh and sing a quiet tune his mother used to sing him as a child. Sterling watched him for a moment, listened to the melody and plucked a few notes on his mandolin, just to give the boy some peace. He felt awful leaving him. That laugh did not sound normal. Sterling set a fast pace down the path, plucking his tune as he ran, the notes lingering behind him like incense smoke swirling around Samuel's head.

In short time, Samuel's laughter turned to yawns and he fell to sleep, to dreaming of home and warm bread and cakes. The pain in his legs lessened as they involuntarily shifted under Merlin's weight, the human body at work protecting itself when the conscious mind is at rest. The blood flowed more strongly through his legs and Merlin must have felt the surge. Maybe his subconscious just liked the song, for as Samuel's blood surge began, Merlin's haunches twitched. "A very good sign," Samuel dreamed to himself and smiled a bit broader as he swam about peacefully in a very deep sleep.

CHAPTER FOUR

"Your blues are all wrong," Ichabod advised between sips of wine.

"How so?" Savannah whipped her head around, squinting her huge, black eyes at Ichabod, a portion of her bonnet's huge, ice-pink bow partially covering one eye. Savannah did not like being criticized. As squirrels went, Savannah prided herself in her grasp of high culture that many an average grey squirrel did not possess, especially her knowledge and talents where Fine Art was concerned.

"They just are. Look abofe you," Ichabod nodded upward, pointing to the sky with his tiny, black, shiny nose. "Your skies are almost a turqvoise, far too brilliant for a Villiamsburg sky." Ichabod prided himself on his grasp of high culture that many an average dog, squirrel, cat, human, any mammal really, did not possess.

Although he had lived in Virginia for countless years now, Ichabod had lost neither his thick, German accent, nor his polished sense of aesthetics nor, as some might say, his characteristic snobbery, well-acquired during his days as a court dog, a proud member of the élite Tea-cup Pomeranians at Versailles, in service to Louis XIV. Still, as was most often the case, Ichabod was right.

"I know. You are absolutely correct," Savannah said with a discernible pout and some dejection. She couldn't stand to be wrong, especially where the arts were concerned. "Of course, I am not trying to capture a Williamsburg sky. I am trying to capture that glorious Venetian look," she said dreamily as she looked out onto the James River, nibbling absentmindedly on the end of her paintbrush.

"I think it looks good," Dante leaned back on his thick, tabby paws, drinking in the late-morning, summer warmth as he waited patiently on the riverbank with his fishing pole: three hours into the day and not a single bite. Not very impressive at all for a cat.

Dante enjoyed the arts: plays, dance, music, sculpture, painting. Yet unlike Ichabod, Dante was uninterested in the complexities and academics of it all. He just knew when something was appealing and to him, that was art.

"Vell, I suppose if you are creating a fantasy piece, it is fery lofely. Villiamsburg's James Rifer full of regattas, vater parades, romantic couples in gondolas," Ichabod stood back, squinted one eye shut and examined the painting silently for a few moments as Savannah squinted one eye shut and examined him. "Okay," Ichabod finally declared. "I like it."

"Oh, well I am thrilled you approve," Savannah joked and happily went back to painting her scene. "In fact it is a fantasy: the James River in the style of Canaletto. It is our very own Venetian canal, right here in Williamsburg. Look, I've even put a giant festival barge on the water, right there near Black Point," she pointed with her brush upriver toward the tip of Jamestown Island, a knuckle of land covered with pines that jutted out into the James River. She then pouted for a moment as she saw she'd tinged her lustrous tail with blue.

"Your blues are still wrong. There is no blue like a Fenetian blue. Sky or vater. It is a brilliant, truly fantastic blue. You must fix this. Other than that, *E Molto bello*. It is beautiful," Ichabod concluded and went back to his wine and his book, a pocket collection of animal fables by La Fontaine.

He laughed aloud as he read, reclining comfortably against a tree, his fluffy tail providing an extra cushion to the thick blanket he had propped up against the birch to keep the insects, spiders and other nags of nature away from his lustrous, black fur.

"Well, I am to meet Anthony this week to pick up some new painting supplies and some grocery items. Fresh yummies and teas from the tropics! New wines and teas, I hear," Savannah imagined the dried fruits, bisquits, herbs, teas and wine she would have by week's end.

Savannah liked her teas and her fruit shrubs: marvelous sweet ginger ales mixed with fruit pulp. The thought of a raspberry shrub made her mouth water a little.

"I haf heard from a friend at the Capitol that Anthony has been trying to stock more Firginia wines. I haf had some of these and they are just awful. They are certainly no French wines. Of course, vone does not hafe to vait for them to cross the sea," he took a sip of his current, Virginia wine to make his point and grimaced a bit as it went down. "See, it is not so bad. Fery nice for a day like today. It reminds me of a vine I used to drink vhen I vas in college."

Ichabod laughed to himself as Dante and Savannah looked at each other. It really didn't seem that funny. Ichabod sensed this and laughed again.

"Oh, I am sorry, you two. It is only a little joke my friends and I at the Capitol say sometimes." He sipped once more for full effect, swishing the liquid in his mouth and scrunching his eyes, looking upward as if deep in concern. "Yes," he repeated the line. "It reminds me of a little vine I used to drink vhen I vas in college. It is just something funny ve say vhen a vine is just okay. Not great and clearly not of the best quality."

He went back to his animal stories and giggled to himself. Ichabod found himself to be very good company and enjoyed his own sense of humour unapologetically.

"Anyhoo," Savannah continued her thought aloud.

"Anyhoo?" Dante interrupted. "When did you start saying 'anyhoo'?" He laughed as he crossed his paws behind his head, giving in to the idea of a nap.

"I do not know. I just heard it somewhere. I like it," she flipped her chin up toward the blue sky she was trying to depict on canvas. "Anyhooooo," she dragged out the word at Dante as she lowered her graceful chin and went back to painting, "I suppose I could ask Anthony if he could get me some new, blue paint. Something brighter. Right, Ichabod?" she asked his advice. "Yes. Brighter. Think of sapphires, jewels, the Mediterranean Sea. *That* is the blue you vant. The blue of the Mediterranean."

Ichabod drifted off for a moment, thinking on the holidays spent in the South of France and the coasts of Italy. Mmmm, he would have to make a trip there soon again. He certainly enjoyed the wealth, comfort and quiet of Williamsburg, but he missed the exotic lands and perhaps it was time for a little trip. He would think on it for a while. Dante thought about it, too. Perhaps one day he would travel to the Mediterranean, to Rome, the home of his ancestors: the cats of Julius Caesar. Maybe he would find them someday and with them frolic in and explore *il Colloseo* and all the ancient sites of the world's greatest civilization. Well, at least Dante thought the Romans, the Italians overall, to be the world's greatest civilization. He looked over at Ichabod sipping his wine and reading his fancy, French satire. Ichabod probably thought the French and the Germans were the greatest of all. Dante's gaze then shifted to Savannah: pristine, proper, kind, hyper-polite and educated. Coming from London, the grounds of Eton no less, she probably thought the English were the best.

"Well," Dante thought as he wiggled and nestled deep into the warm grass, keeping one eye half-open to spy on his fishing pole, the sun already growing stronger and sharper, "too bad they are wrong," and his half-opened eye closed and he quickly began to snore a wheezy, happy snore.

CHAPTER FIVE

The burrs had long ago lodged three-, maybe four-deep in between his toes and the pads of his feet were beyond bloodied and raw. The pain was intense, but nothing compared with the piercing ache in his lungs. He had never run so hard in all his life and being forced to do so in the heat of a Virginia summer, he was certain that with each new intake of muggy air his chest might just close up altogether like a cork stuffed back into a wine bottle. Still, he wasn't running fast enough. He had to run faster, farther, quieter. He needed more cover; another thicket or tree grove would be perfect. The dogs were getting closer, their baying growing louder. Surely they were catching more distinct whiffs of his scent as his wounds continued to bleed out more and more profusely. The deepest cuts were now throbbing, bringing tears so thick his vision grew bleary and weak. He had to stop, but he couldn't. He'd have to find a trench or something somewhere; then, he'd stop and tend to his wounds. If he didn't find adequate cover soon though, these wide, open meadows would certainly be his death. It amazed him always that the river could be so close, but totally unseen because of this flat land. He could smell the brine, the sea just beyond the river, to the east. But all he could see were fields and meadows with an occasional line of forest or trees surrounding a small pond. He might as well be in a desert.

Spying just such a line of trees up ahead, he ran toward it like the Devil himself was chasing him, and he was. He hop scotched his way to the treeline, trying in vain to throw the dogs off his scent, and ducked into a cluster of berry vines that bordered a slow running creek that looked like it probably led right to the river. The vines were thin and leafy and the berries had long been picked or fallen away. As late in the season as it was, this was no surprise. It was a pity, however, because Remus thought the tart blackberries and huckleberries that generally grew in this area would have been beyond refreshing right now, maybe revitalizing or enlivening, just what he could use for that extra spurt of energy that could save his life. Sure, they're just berries, but Mother Nature has a way of knowing just what her children need.

Remus rested for a minute inside a particularly large berry bush and whilst he did not find any berries anywhere, not even rotted ones on the ground, he did find hundreds of miniature thorns burying themselves into his skin. Finding their way through his muslin shirt they stung his arms and his back. Even his thick woolen trousers, horrid in this heat, but usually a perfect guard against insects and bramble, were no protection against the ambitious needles of the berry vines. As he shifted around inside the bush, trying to hide himself, the thorny pricks scratched his already torn skin and tugged at his clothes, imploring him to accept the offer of cover within the glade, but for a nominally bloody fee.

Remus dealt with the thorns and took as long as he thought safe to rest and catch his breath. It seemed nearly impossible. With every breath, his intake seemed less and less, but the effort more and more difficult. He picked up his right foot and brought it up to his face for a clear look at the damage. It was very bad indeed.

Some miles back he remembered stepping on a piece of shale or slate, something extremely sharp jutting our from a creek bed. He hadn't a moment to stop back then and now, ever since the initial slice, the cut had become longer, wider and bloodier with every step. Surely, his blood was trailed all over the East Coast by now. Pulling his foot closer to his dusty and gritty eyes, he could see the entire bottom of his foot was pink and feel it was warm to the touch, a different kind of warm than the rest of his body. The same kind of warm as his forehead, he noted. He was having a hard time focusing on the injury because of this pain and heat in his head. It was making his eyes water and this mixed with the dust, giving them a sheer wiping of dirt each time he blinked. Pulling his foot even closer, essentially right up to his eyeball, he could see the wound was stuffed to its brim with pebbles, mud, grass and bits of oyster and clam shells. At least the bleeding had stopped. It had to with all the debris. Yet, now the dried blood had caked around the trash in his wound, forming a black, lumpy tar. Using first his fingernail, then a twig, Remus tried to excavate some of the rubble from his foot; but, the pain was too great and mixed with his headache and fever, he nearly passed out more than once. He stopped digging and stood up straight to hop down to the creek, the berry thorns pleading with him not to go.

Resting against a rock beside the water, he let it rush over his wound, bringing a comforting tingle to his whole body. Maybe the water would wash away his scent and when the dogs arrived here, they'd have finally lost him for good. This sounded like good sense to him and he got to thinking if the water could take the scent off his foot, why not his whole body? He decided that this smart concept and the quick need to wake up and cool off, from the weather as well as this growing fever he could feel in his head, were reasons enough to take the chance of a few minutes to jump in the water. Barely deep enough to cover his head, he stepped in gingerly with his bad foot and walked until his shoulders were covered. He ducked his head under the green water and came up with a layer of algae attached to his head. A nearby turtle saw this and found it very funny and ducked below the surface to tell some friends.

Remus bobbed about for a bit, enjoying the lightness and freedom of it all, carelessly forgetting the chase of his life. Then, he opened his arms like a cross, lay back and allowed the water to buoy him up, flat to the surface. Then, he spun round and round like an otter, cooling and cleansing and playing. It very well might have been one of the worst days of his life, but at that very moment, he was having the time of his life. The water was like a loving hug from a beautiful, cool angel.

Eventually, as he flipped and flopped in the creek, smiling and calling the attention of a few robins, a woodchuck on the shore, a group of five turtles with only their heads poking over the waterline, and a solitary blue heron who found it all very strange, Remus' heartbeat mellowed, his breathing calmed and he no longer felt faint or feverish. He was no longer seeing white flashes and his head didn't feel nearly as light and spacey as it had mere moments earlier. In fact, his foot didn't even hurt that much. The joy and comfort he was feeling was so good, so relaxing he felt he could just float there all day long and fall to sleep.

Jennifer Susannah Devore

He, of course, reminded himself not to go to sleep and to ensure against this he flipped over each time a sleep wave came over him. The movements became harder and harder, though. He was exhausted. He had no more to give. No more air, no more strength, no more spirit. Mother Nature had given him what he needed, but it wasn't enough.

Then all of a sudden, floating there and listening to two robins chatter back and forth, he realized he didn't care anymore. It was all too much: the pain, the humility, the dread. He was not a useless creature, a beast of burden; yet, here he was, being chased and hunted as such. He was a man, but not to those men. He never would be. When they caught him, they would kill him, or worse.

Maybe they would take a foot, maybe a foot and a hand, leaving him just enough appendages to do some work. Probably though, they would kill him and it would take a long time, they would be sure of that. It would be a lesson to all the other slaves on the plantation. "Run away, even think about it and this is what you get!" He would be the enduring lesson to all. He would be dragged back to the plantation, literally dragged behind a horse, then made a spectacle, a carnival for all slaves far and wide. But, he didn't care anymore. Let them catch him. His gods told him he would find peace later and he believed this. Besides, once he reached his next life, he would finally be able to help others. Being dead, becoming a spirit, was maybe the best way to protect the living. He could help the others on the plantation. Death would be a good thing. He finally understood that peace and the end of his suffering, maybe the suffering of others, too, were close. At times like these, individuals tend to look over their lives and, in the span of mere minutes, can sum up and judge their entire lives in just a few words. Remus did this quite easily. "It had not been good." Simple and efficiently stated. "The next life is bound to be better."

Then, he heard the dogs' baying grow closer and he realized he did care, just a little, but he did and it was enough to get him up and running again. They might make an example of him someday, but not today; and, if he died today, it would be by himself or among family. After all, that was why he was running: because of family, toward family.

He had no idea how far he was from this Williamsburg town, but he would get there and then, after his business, he could die with true peace.

Whatever happened he resolved then and there in that creek that he would not give *them* his final moments. *They* would not take his last breath. He would give it to the trees, the earth, family, but not *them*. Not the monsters that took it from him in the first place.

Almost smiling, with the sad solace and bitter cheer that comes to those whom know they are soon to leave this world and are finally okay with it, he sprung from the water, as though reborn from Mother Earth, and took a huge breath and looked around at the animals whom had been watching him. He smiled at them. He had always liked the animals back on the plantation, especially the squirrels. They were so silly and playful. These animals here looked friendly, too. How he wished he could spend the rest of the day swimming and frolicking with them. They seemed so trouble-free. But, he couldn't.

He looked out over the water, whispered some private words to an unknown entity and, taking a huge breath, listened with his ears and his eyes for the exact direction of the dogs. They were very close and just to the west. He would have to stick to the coast. There was no more time for lofty thoughts of life and afterlife, or silly thoughts of swimming and squirrels. It was run now, or die at their hands.

CHAPTER SIX

Linus ran up and down the crowds, squeezing in and out of any space he could find trying to get a good spot. It was already past ten o'clock and people had been lining up along the route from Whitehall Port to City Hall since about seven o'clock that morning. Well, those that could: either solvent enough to have a morning free from work, or unfortunate enough to be out of work all together. Linus fell into neither of these categories: he was working. Although he was apprenticing for Mr. Zenger, learning the mechanics of printing, what he really wanted to do was to write. He had written a few stories about fishing, the weather, a country fair: fluff pieces. This event, the parade of the new governor to his post at City Hall was what might be called hard news. A story like this might even make it into a London news-paper. He had missed the ferries going to Governors' Island last night; but, this was turning out to be a much bigger event anyway.

Mr. Zenger wasn't exactly running a daily, or even weekly, news-paper right now, but he was a printer and printed just about anything people could want to read: pamphlets, court documents, religious material, books, anything readable or saleable. Whilst he personally felt totally unfazed by the arrival, Linus was all together so enthralled that Zenger told him he'd give him a chance to write a story about it. He figured all that enthusiasm had to come through on paper. If it was written well enough and if this month's accounts went well enough that he could spare the time, paper and ink, Zenger told Linus he would print the arrival story on the backside of a brochure, granted Linus could find at least one merchant to advertise somewhere on the page. When Mr. Zenger promised him this chance, Linus went right out to track down advertisers. He found three: VanDerZander's Cabinet Makers; Le Petit Ecrueil Grocers, and;

Snyder and Son Gunsmithing. Now, he just had to write the story.

Linus jumped up on a brick wall that surrounded a small garden near where Wall Street ran into Broadway. Being Swedish, Linus was pretty tall already. With his height, this spot on the wall made for a great viewing platform around. Below him was a woman with a ridiculous wig. It reached nearly up to his own neck as he stood on the wall! He moved over a few inches so as not to touch it. The sugar-flower designs inside it were melting in the early morning heat and had brought a number of flies and one very large bumble bee. Blissfully, she had no idea and was certain everyone was admiring her great taste in fashion. Linus watched as the bee headed into one of the confections and tried to pollinate it. Seconds later the bee emerged feeling foolish and angry at being duped and buzzed off to romance some real flowers.

Linus spent the next hour writing thoughts into his note pad as he waited for the parade to reach his spot: observations about the day like the weather, the crowds, the pretty lady with the sugary, melty hat. The sun was beginning to irritate him and the humidity was rising so quickly that before Linus actually realized anything had changed, he was suddenly unbearably uncomfortable, sticky and hot. Seconds ago he was luxuriating on the wall, basking in the sun like a cat who found a sunlight beam through a window. Yet, summer was suddenly disgusting and intolerable. It was as though his clothes were instantly bound to his skin with wet, warm tape. Linus loosened every string he could find on his clothes: his collar, the knees of his knickers, his waistband. He billowed and fluffed out his huge sleeves and his knickers, in essence doing everything short of stripping down to his birthday suit to keep cool. Then, snapping him out of his misery in a flash, a blast of coronets and sharp drum strikes filled the air and the procession was here.

Sometime after 11:00 a.m., the new royal governor had left his new home at Fort George and crossed the Upper Bay to his new offices at New-York's City Hall. From this point, several cobblestone blocks stretched between Governor Cosby and City Hall.

The first to march down Broadway were the horses. Their hooves and the carriage wheels making far more noise than the din of drums, fifes and horns that followed. The horses numbered six and were as white and lustrous as freshwater pearls. Their hardware, the bits, stirrups, reins, and such, were all made of solid gold. The leather pieces were black and shined like oil. They wore no saddles, but did wear delicate, silk blankets of red and green. Linus was certain they were miserable. Everyone knew silk was one of the worst things to wear in a humid heat. Nevermind, the six royal horses held their chins high and their prances higher, never betraying any hint of discomfort. Atop their heads were small, but intricately detailed gold crowns rimmed with rubies and emeralds and spewing great plumes of red, green and black.

For some reason, Linus looked toward the woman with the sugary wig at this moment. He had a weird feeling she liked the horses' adornments. He was right. Her eyes lit up and her eyebrows arched. He could tell she was already designing a new wig in her head. She'd have to run to her peruke-maker as soon as this was over and tell him all about it. Linus chuckled to himself and was strangely glad this woman seemed so happy about something so silly. With all the misery that was a reality in this day and age, Linus found comfort, not jealousy, in those whose lives appeared pleasant and comfortable. He was also glad he wasn't a girl. He couldn't imagine wearing a huge wig like that on a day like this. Ick!

The horses pulled an open carriage, all trimmed in solid gold and gold leaf, and all painted a bright green. Being a son of Ireland and having served in her Royal Irish Regiment as a young man, Cosby was fond of the colour green and wore just such an ensemble today. He wore an intensely emerald green frock coat with intricate, floral embroidery on the front. Under it he wore a matching waistcoat of equally beautiful design and knickers of the same linen. He also wore a fresh white blouse dripping with Irish lace cuffs. His lace collar, cravate and handkerchief were all of Irish lace, too. All of it made especially for him in Dublin. His shoes were very high, black and polished to a fine shine and his buckles were gold, to match his horses' gear. His wig looked as if it might have been spun of Irish lace, or spiderwebs it was so frothy and delicate. It seemed to sparkle in the morning sun, glimmering like the Atlantic as both he and the sea moved in time through the light, summer wind.

Behind Cosby and his horses were members of the Governor's Council and high-ranking members of the governor's staff. Heading up all of these notable and influential figures were two of the town's most notable: Provincial Councillor Rip VanDam and Chief Justice of the New-York Supreme Court, Lewis Morris. Linus worried a bit about Mr. VanDam. The heat was terrific for himself, let alone a seventy-five year old man. Of course, Mr. VanDam did not look seventy-five, nor did he act seventy-five. He was in fact quite fit and while he did have a hanky out for the length of the walk to City Hall and mopped his face often, so did just about everybody that morning. Linus decided Mr. VanDam would be just fine. The one person he did worry about was that one little man.

He just kept running up and down the parade, checking on the horses, peering into the carriage, making sure the governor looked relatively happy, keeping the musicians in line, shooing children away who kept trying to join the procession. Linus thought that, as energetic as he seemed, he looked like he might pass out at any moment. He looked worse than VanDam, but was easily much younger. This one was so wiry and wore no wig today, so the sun just cooked his balding head like an egg as he ran to and fro, all the while trying to remain discreet and managerial, but being only obvious and frazzled. Linus took notes on him, unsure of whether or not to include him in the story, but prepared just in case.

Next marched the military. Twenty or so men marched in four rows of five wide, their forty-some boots stamping in time to the drumbeat. They were all so young. Some were probably not older than Linus. They wore their best dress uniforms of red, white and green and shouldered rifles. Not a single one smiled. Whether it was the heat or the seriousness of the event, Linus wasn't sure. He was sure, however, that he could think of nothing worse than being a soldier. He was going to be a writer, like Shakespeare or Jonathan Swift or Richard Lovelace who had, ironically, been a soldier for a time. Not him. Linus would never carry a rifle or murder people over a difference of country, king, religion or political opinion. He would let people be and he would write about the differences, never kill over them.

Linus watched the little man some more as he sped by Linus. This time, he was running toward the governor and looked panic stricken. In fact, the whole procession was beginning to back up. Governor Cosby had stopped, even as the horses continued up ahead. As necks stretched to see what was the matter, Linus heard someone in the crowd cry, "It is dung! Dung has been flung into the carriage!"

The thin man heard this and sprinted to the governor, pulling one of the younger soldiers out of line and along with him.

"Phiiiiiiiipps! Phiiiiiiipps! Somebody! Get up here! Someone has flung horse dung onto me!" Cosby screamed like a little girl as he stared in horror at a tiny piece of brown, hay-flecked dung that had indeed made its way to Cosby's lapel.

"Quick! Get in there and clean his coat! Quickly! Go!" Phipps pleaded with the lad he was dragging, stuffing his own handkerchief into the boy's hand.

The young soldier hopped to his duty, stepped into the carriage and did a little bow to the governor who screamed at him to get busy. Without a cringe or a sigh, the boy went to work immediately cleaning the horse manure from Cosby's coat. It was barely visible. Obviously a tiny fleck of horse poo that had been kicked up by one of the horses themselves. The boy was pretty sure he heard the horses laughing and started to smile himself. He quickly stopped smiling as he felt the governor's stern gaze upon him and, using a fingernail wrapped within the hanky, drew out all traces of poo from the seam where the lapel met the body of the coat. After that, he turned the cloth over, manure-free side, and began polishing the nearest button until Cosby got frustrated and pushed him out of his way.

"Alright, alright! Get off me, boy! That is enough!" He pushed the boy so hard he toppled over and landed on the floor of the carriage. "Now go! Get out of my carriage. Get back in formation. You are ruining my parade."

The boy did just that. Linus felt sorry for him, but other people in the audience laughed. Linus would never volunteer to be in a military position whereby he might have to do such a thing; but, he did not fault this young boy for his decision and felt betrayed as a fellow youth that someone old enough to know about good manners would treat another human that way. He turned around and gave a dirty look to the group of men behind him laughing. They were old enough to know better, too. Linus was becoming more and more of the opinion that just because someone was older than he it didn't mean they were automatically a better person. Being older clearly didn't always equal worthiness. Respect your elders? Only if they really deserved it.

Linus watched the boy walk back in line. Phipps walked back down the procession, too and glanced at VanDam as he passed him. They both rolled their eyes. VanDam returned the expression. This was indeed going to be a long governorship. No, Linus did not want anything to do with the military, the government or politics of any kind. Writing was clearly the safest way to go. What kind of trouble could one get into just writing? He scribbled more notes and thoughts into his precious journal and smiled broader and broader as he did so.

Eventually, the festivities faded away. At the parade's end, the town citizenry, mostly very young boys, who found it amusing to pretend they were part of the parade, waved to the thinning crowds and high-stepped in a military mockery. Linus probably would have joined in the silliness when he was younger. But, he was fourteen now. He did not have the time to be silly. He was a journaler, a writer and he had a story to create. He had a head full of images and a pad full of notes. He had far more important things to do than play parade or clean horse poo from a fop's overpriced frock. Yes, Linus was going to be important someday. First, he had to write this account. As he hopped down off the wall and started down the road back to Herr Zenger's print shop, he watched a couple of robins search for insects in the grass. As the robins frantically ran sprints up and down the wide border, their heads bobbing up and down each time they stopped and started, Linus thought about that thin man named Phipps. He wondered what his day was going to be like once he reached City Hall. He wondered what everybody's day was going to be like. Boy, if he could be a fly on the wall in City Hall, what a story that would be!

"Governor Cosby," a rotund man in a mint-green, linen frock coat pleaded, nearly whined, with the new governor. "Please be reasonable."

"Silence!" Cosby's voice bellowed and carried across City Hall's chamber. "I have been reasonable," his voice returned to a standard tone. "I have been reasonable for well over a year. Now it is time to stop messing around and give me my due," he stood and addressed the twenty-six members of the New-

York Assembly gathered here to greet the governor and officially commence the business of New-York under this new man. Cosby extended his arm and pointed rudely, directly at VanDam. "That man owes me my salary," he lowered his arm, but remained standing. "I want fully all of it now!" his voice rose again.

"Fully all?" VanDam repeated with a smile. "Is that proper phrasing? Can something be 'fully all'?"

He was quickly growing tired of Cosby's offensive nature.

"Governor Cosby. Really," the rotund one, who was called Dr. Jacobs, pleaded again. "We have already agreed to a five-year salary for you, plus a bonus of one thousand pounds for your," he cleared his throat, "tiresome efforts for the colonists in front of Parliament, all payable to you immediately. Beyond that, in all fairness we can do no more."

Cosby stamped a foot as he sat and crossed his arms like a child.

"Your Excellency, we have been through all this countless times this morning," Dr. Jacobs continued unswayed. "Mr. VanDam was doing the *full* job of royal governor until you arrived just last night. Fair salary for fair work, Your Excellency."

"I told you I was awaiting instruction!!" Cosby stamped a foot again and whined. "I did not know what to do! I was waiting in London for the Board of Trade to tell me exactly where to go and what to do when I got there!"

He continued to whine at an escalating pitch and it was very unattractive, not at all empowering his image with his new assemblage.

"Besides, I did work whilst I waited for orders! What about that? I have spent the last year in London, fighting for these, these people, these colonists!" The word 'colonists' clearly disgusted him. "I spent nearly a year in front of British Parliament fighting against passage of the Molasses Act! That was hard! Do you all think I have been sitting on my bum and am now just asking for money for nothing?!"

In fact, though no one would dare utter it, yes. Every man in that room thought this and was actually surprised Cosby would have the audacity to even suggest it. Yes, it was documented that Cosby had argued in front of the Parliament against the Molasses Act: a law that would place an exorbitant tax on all molasses and sugars coming to the American colonies from the West Indies, a tax that would just kill businesses both in England and America.

Plainly, the New-York Council did not believe that he worked ardently for a full year on anything. No, it was not worth half a year's salary. Moreover, it was widely-known that during his time as a royal governor of Minorca, an island off the Spanish coast, he illegally seized the property and assets of a wealthy merchant and helped himself to all belongings thereby. Of course, he was eventually ordered to pay all damages and material offenses to the merchant. Thus, he came to be in great debt and it was further widely-known that he had only one intention during his service as the New-York and New-Jersey governor: to re-build his own fortune.

"I shan't argue this any further! Not only do I want my salary from the date of my appointment as governor, I want payment retroactive to the date of the *death* of the previous governor and I expect this to be resolved at my earliest convenience!"

The whining had stopped. Now he was just vicious. Cosby slammed both fists on the thick, oak table in front of him, turned on his shiny heels and left the room. Storming out of City Hall and fuming with anger out onto the front steps, he kicked a small kitten who was trying to sneak in the building.

As summer changed into autumn, the divisive matter of the governor's back-salary demand only became compounded as Cosby time and again proved to the citizens of New-York that he couldn't care less about them and was only concerned with the affairs of his own bank accounts. Besides tax hikes on land ownership that were known to jump straight to his pockets, he decided that every new parcel of land he granted, a royal grant, he would take one-third of it for himself and his family. He also took part in every kind of unscrupulous business from removing judges who didn't rule to his liking to using public funds for personal interests. Cosby severely disliked his New-Yorkers and made no attempt to hide this fact.

From openly turning up his nose at common people on the street to inviting various assemblymen to dinner at his home and then insulting them on every subject from their political beliefs to their wardrobes, these were just some of the ways Cosby's distaste manifested itself. Just two months after his arrival in August of 1732, Cosby wrote to his friend back in London, the

Duke of Newcastle, overseer of all American colonies. In his typical mixture of condescension, arrogance, awful spelling and bad education, he wrote to the Duke stating,

> *I had more trouble to manige these people then I could of imagined, however for this time I have done pritty well with them.*

By November of the same year, Cosby had received no satisfaction on his demands for the retroactive full salary. A compromise was finally made and Cosby now agreed to half of VanDam's salary. VanDam agreed also, sort of. He agreed to share half of his salary from the past year, if Cosby shared half of everything he made in London during the past year. Of course, Cosby became so enraged that some say from that point forward his life became consumed with revenge. The first step in his journey of revenge was to sue VanDam. The next step was to ignore and defy the British rule of a jury tryal for such matters. He next replaced that rightful jury of New-Yorkers with a three-judge panel: a Supreme Court in which two of the three were very, very good friends. Governor William Cosby was the worst kind of governor: naturally unintelligent, no education, no conscience, no ability to foresee consequence, too much power, too much money and too many friends. New-York was in for a fight with a mean and stupid beast. New-York was ready.

CHAPTER SEVEN

Ben closed his eyes, drew in a long whiff through his nose and smiled. "Sublime," he whispered, eyes closed, still smiling. "Andrew, you must indulge. Do yourself a favour and order a large cup of this Turkish blend," he took another whiff. "Not since I was in London, at that tiny, tiny coffeehouse in Oxford, have I tasted coffee this perfect."

"Mmm. I know the spot well. The little stone place wedged betwixt the baker and the tailor?" Ben's friend, Andrew, leaned back in his chair, crossed his arms over his chest and looked at the ceiling as he happily reminisced.

"Yes, that's the one!" Ben's eyes glowed with happy memories.

"All Oxford students, wall to wall. What a wonderful atmosphere for discussion and debate," Andrew continued, happy in his own memories.

Ben watched him over the rim of his mug, his eyebrows arched and eyes wide, nodding vigorously in agreement as his mouth was busy savouring the Oxford-Turkish brew.

"You know, I had a chum in law school," Andrew reminisced as he stirred some cream into his own drink. "A Turkish chap actually. He claimed to have been directly related to the original Turkish gent who opened the place back in 1637."

"Of course," Ben laughed. "Once something is that far in the past, who is to argue? Suddenly, everyone is related to the founder of this or the king of that. Just once, I would like to hear someone say, 'Did you know that my ancestor, Great-great-great Uncle Von Noodlehead was the only fool in all of Germany to patent a brick mortar made out of fish paste and kitten fur. He actually built a small building with it, it collapsed and killed a man who came to see the ridiculous feat. Plus, all the cats in the neighborhood descended upon my ancestor late one night and scratched him terrifically from head to toe. Uncle Von Noodlehead lost in a huge lawsuit over the whole matter, set the whole family into debt and five generations later, I am the direct result of a disgraced and low-bred family.'"

Ben laughed again and turned toward the front door as he heard some familiar voices enter the coffeehouse, Monk's Nervosa Café.

"Gentlemen! Gentlemen! This way! Join us, please. Andrew, help me pull over that table."

Ben and Andrew shuffled a few seats around, pulled over some chairs and stood eagerly to greet their friends and welcome them to their table. Ben lived for days like this. The chance to relax, take a café, have a sweet treat, bump into some friends and spend the rest of the day drinking cup after cup and arguing the merits of some policy, the faults of a certain lawmaker, the curiosity of the latest scientific developments and the ever-rising price of the very drink they so loved.

"Can you believe the price of this swill? 'Tis criminal!" someone would inevitably complain every time. "Oh, while you're up, could you get me another cup?"

The coffeehouse culture had not changed much over the years. First with the Arabians and their *qahveh khaneh* in Mecca, luxurious establishments erected solely for the purpose of making coffee an all day activity: sipping, talking, listening to music. Coffee was the perfect answer to a Moslem culture that forbade wine and found water a more precious commodity than gold.

From its unaccountable origins in Venice and its accompanying rejection by many a Venetian as "the bitter invention of Satan" to the ironic saving graces of a Pope who took a cup and declared it "delightful", coffee began its devilish hold on countless societies of thinking and drinking men and women.

From the opening of Kolschitsky's *Blue Bottle* in Vienna in the late 1600's, the first coffeehouse in Vienna and built from the spoils of war with the Turks (billions of coffee beans nobody wanted except a brilliantly clever Austrian named Franz George Kolschitsky), to seedlings stolen from a single coffee tree belonging to Louis XIV (a gift from the Dutch) that flourished in Martinique under the obsessive care of a French sea captain, coffee's importance to man grew as fast as those seedlings.

With an abundance of coffee supply throughout Dutch and French colonial holdings across Africa, South America and the West Indies, coffeehouses sprouted up across the European continent as meeting places for great and curious minds. So much so that not only did great thoughts flourish, so did great fears.

Fears of sedition, rebellion and revolution became so great that even England's Charles II, the Restoration King and well-known lover of all things mind-expanding, literary and artistic, closed down all English coffeehouses in 1675. Ironically, this hasty action brought about a mass rebellion and, thank Fortuna, he was forced to re-open all coffeehouses as quickly as they had been closed.

Beginning in the earliest days of the Dancing Goat Society (Abyssinian goats and their herders eating the hitherto unknown red, coffee berries that gave them enough energy to dance through the boredom of the day) and with the admiration of a passing monk who witnessed the festive goats, ate a few himself and found he could "pray all night with remarkable clarity", coffee entered civilization as a new religion which would bring energy, confidence, industriousness and dancing of the soul to the masses. This was the stuff Ben lived for; this was where he belonged.

"Ah! Welcome, gentlemen!" Ben ran around the table pulling out all the unused chairs. "An unexpected meeting of the Junto! Why not a Wednesday morning instead of a Friday night?! Yes, we shall have two meetings this week. Excellent! Come, let us share our tales of commerce and gossip."

The young, enterprising Benjamin Franklin referenced the young men's society he personally organized back in 1727, a weekly meeting of young, entrepreneurial, male minds in Philadelphia. The Junto was a meeting of the minds where all members could share what they had learned in business, relate anything remarkable, anyone remarkable, warn others of bad risks and discuss possibilities and propositions for community and self. What better place for such an impromptu gathering than Monk's Nervosa Café?

Jennifer Susannah Devore

40

"Mr. Hamilton, will you have more of the Ethiopian or would you like to try the Oxford Turkish blend?" Ben asked the renowned, Philadelphia attorney and longtime friend.

"Yes, yes, of course. I will try your Oxford blend," Andrew Hamilton accepted as he patted the back of a newcomer to the table, a young lawyer.

Ben walked to the counter and informed the coffeekeep that more mugs and pots of the Oxford Turkish coffee would be required for the gents at the collection of tables by the back window. Niles, the owner and barista nodded, happy to have such good business on a mid-morning.

Ben bounded back to the table and in a loud and jovial tone demanded, "Alright, which man has the most interesting tale to tell today?"

"I've got one!" contributed a talented fellow of twenty-three named Covington and a struggling limner, or portrait painter. "It's quite unreal. Involves that wretched Governor Cosby over in New-York."

Everyone leaned in toward the center of the group. News about Cosby was always juicy.

"Well," he continued, "I was up in Boston last month working on a commission, a portrait of a hideous old woman whom, by the way, refused to pay her bill because I could not turn her into a Venus on canvas," he shuddered and made a face, "what a waste of paint. Horrid, mean, ugly woman. Anyway, whilst up there, I read an old copy of the *Boston News-Letter* that was lying around the tavern where I lodged. Now, keep in mind this news was then a few months old. Nevertheless, what I read was still shocking."

The group leaned in even closer. Two men then leaned away from each other and made an opening for Niles, whom had come to the table with a serving tray full of pots, mugs and a few complimentary treats for his best table. As Covington continued his tale, Niles listened as he placed the items about the table.

"Well, I am sure we all recall the issues betwixt Cosby and VanDam? How Cosby demanded all that money for nothing and then VanDam agreed to share his salary if Cosby coughed up half of his? Remember? It was all over the papers."

"Yessss. *the New-York Gazette*. Verrry unbiased journalism," Franklin chided with great sarcasm, then taking a sip and looking over the rim of his mug at the group. Finishing his sip and seeing that all were awaiting the last half of this remark he happy obliged with, "*the New-York Gazette*, my friends, only happens to be operated by the colony's, and thereby the king's official printer, William Bradford. You know that."

"True, but Bradford's a good man. He does have a family to feed, though. Official Royal Printer is quite a career leap," a banker in the group offered as he poured himself some coffee.

"To be certain," Covington added. "But, Bradford is not the issue here. Cosby is."

"Yes, yes. Back to Cosby," Franklin encouraged.

"Well, you all know that Cosby eventually sued VanDam, right? *The Boston News-Letter* reported that the scoundrel Cosby did away with the traditional jury for that case. He appointed a three-judge Supreme Court to make certain the lawsuit went in his favour!" Covington sat back in his chair, folded his arms and waited for responses.

"I have heard this! Unimaginable!" Hamilton reacted eagerly.

"And, good fellows, he has since fired one of those judges! A Lewis Morris, Sr. for not siding with him in the VanDam matter! It is beyond wrong. A man cannot make such arbitrary changes in policy and the law. It sickens me and makes me wary," Covington looked pensively into his mug and stirred it with a spoon.

"Maybe he had a good reason. Nobody could be that abusive," a cooper, or barrel maker, spoke up in disbelief.

"Oh, but he is. Do not be so naive, friend. Cosby has done worse and I suspect will do further damage to those unsuspecting New-Yorkers. Do you know that Lewis Morris served as a judge for nearly twenty years? Plus, his son is in danger of losing his position. Such a young and influential boy in the New-York Assembly. I fear it is all very bad for anyone under Cosby's rule," Ben responded.

"I read further in *The Boston News-Letter*, at least it was speculated therein, that even if Morris had sided with Cosby on the VanDam ruling, Cosby was going to next sue *Morris* for half of *his* salary while he was acting-governor of New-Jersey in Cosby's absence," Hamilton shared.

"He really is a menace to society!" Covington pounded his fist on the table, shaking all the mugs and calling attention from the whole coffeehouse.

"I imagine that is why he refused to side with Cosby in the first place. Why create a legal precedent that could bring about your own bad ruling?" Hamilton surmised in a purposely soft voice, attempting to bring privacy back to the conversation.

"I tell you what, gentlemen. We ought to count ourselves fortunate we are not under the rule of Governor William Cosby. Surely he is one bad apple in the barrel of British rulers in America. We are Britons, they are Britons. Fear not, friends. With good humour and some tolerance we must trust our royal representatives. With the odd exception like Cosby, they have our best at heart and in mind. After all, what is good for folk here is good for folk there. America and Britain are one and a good mother takes care of her children, even when far away."

Covington shook his head and did not buy Franklin's optimism. Many of the other young men around the table commiserated in quiet tones and furrowed eyebrows. Hamilton watched the twenty-somethings and laughed to himself, nodding sagely.

Andrew Hamilton, Esquire was an attorney of great reputation in this town. Now in his seventies he had experienced enough of mankind in general to know that people were not always what they seem and that no government ever really had anything at heart and mind but riches and power. Still, he admired the positive nature and unwavering ambition of his young friend Benjamin Franklin. They were longtime friends from Ben's teenage days back in London where they were both victims, ironically, of a vindictive and cruel trick played by another petty royal governor, Pennsylvania's William Keith. Though no great damage was done, Keith's nastiness wasted time, money and spirit of both men, mostly the seventeen-year old Ben.

In short, Governor Keith sent Ben to London with what Ben thought was a satchel full of personal references of credit for Ben, from Keith himself. With these letters, Keith sent Ben to London for the sole purpose of purchasing a printing press and supplies. Ben would then return to Philadelphia and become the Official Royal Printer for both Pennsylvania and Delaware. When Ben arrived at the shop where he would purchase these items, he found the letters were nothing more than a complex practical joke: mean lies and nasty tales about Ben. The letters informed the shopkeep that the very boy standing in front of him was a rogue, a scoundrel and not to be trusted. Ben was flabbergasted.

He learned the whole joke was in fact a scheme to embarrass Hamilton, whom was currently in London on business for Keith. Ben never understood the connection, but went straight to Hamilton, through a mutual friend named Thomas Denham, and told him of the bad prank. Secure and confident, Hamilton just laughed and warned Ben that nobody trusted Keith and, furthermore, he was most likely insane. From that day forth, Hamilton served as friend and mentor to the young Franklin.

Tonight at Monk's Nervosa Café, Hamilton watched this enthusiastic group of young professionals, craftsmen, artists and students and smiled. As long as modern, thinking societies continued to give birth to and harbour tireless and energetic minds like these, men like Keith and Cosby would certainly see their days numbered.

CHAPTER EIGHT

Sterling kept a fast pace, enough to keep his breathing laboured. He was too warm and horribly uncomfortable in this coastal heat. It was as though someone had bound him up tightly in leather and sailcloth and set him over a kettle of boiling water. The heat was unbearable and the humidity was stifling and oppressive. There was zero breeze and he hadn't the luxury of stopping for water when he passed the many water sources that freckled the landscape: creeks, brooks, ponds. He found comfort only in his feet. He wore his favourite clogs and he loved them. They kept his paws cool and protected from the debris of rocks and sticks along the path.

Yet, all this discomfort mattered not because Sterling would, in all likelihood, be in Williamsburg early the next morning. Just another few miles down the road, a quick ferry trip across the York River, then across Queen's Creek and he'd be at Queen Mary's Port: one of Williamsburg's main shipping ports. He had been given very specific directions by a travelling silk merchant yesterday, just hours after leaving Samuel. This man assured Sterling he had less than two days' walk to go. Considering the distances Sterling had covered since leaving home a year ago, two days should be no problem.

Upon his arrival in Williamsburg, Sterling would go directly to the Raleigh Tavern, deliver his satchel and be done with this unexpected task. The silk merchant had agreed to send help for Samuel and his horse but Sterling would also report the incident at the Raleigh.

Otherwise, Sterling's life would be his own again. He might even stick around this Williamsburg and check it out for a bit. He was tired and had been on the road for far too long, even before he came across Samuel. Maybe he would find a theatre in this Williamsburg and engage himself an acting job.

In truth, he kind of doubted the prospect of it. London, Bristol, Dublin, Paris, Vienna? Sure. Williamsburg? Really doubtful considering he'd never heard of the place. If he could find no creative outlet in this town, perhaps he'd just wander the Virginia countryside at his leisure and compose some music, set up one-fox plays in people's barns along the way, just keep to himself. Whatever he chose, it would be his choice. By tomorrow night, Sterling's task would be done and he would be a free fox. Free of commitment, free of chores, free of others. With this realization, Sterling suddenly sprinted across the large field he was traversing. He figured since he wasn't too far from his destination he probably had time to make the remainder of this chore a waterside adventure.

The Chesapeake Bay ran high and flowed ferociously on this day, slapping roughly up against the sharp rocks and countless oyster and clam shells that made up the natural jetty. Freak thunderstorms were pretty much a daily occurrence this time of year: every afternoon around four o'clock. Sterling wasn't sure if these had anything to do with the upbeat activity of the river right now, but logic and common sense told him if a big storm could churn up the sea, why couldn't a small storm churn up a river? All he knew as he strolled alongside the York was that he was glad he had no need to swim today. Trees and fields were his territory. Happy to be a land mammal, he was.

As Sterling wound his way through the mixture of leafy trees, cool grass and the rocky shoreline he thought of the song he'd written earlier. Now feeling relatively unburdened, knowing he was close to fulfilling his duty to the boy and soon approaching a new town, maybe a new home within his grasp, he strummed his mandolin and trilled his voice song with true gaiety and mirth. His scarves flowed round his neck and shoulders in dramatic time as he danced and sang alongside the river. He even added a few lines.

She's got a square face,
But I think she's lovely.
I'd go to her place,
But she's not too cuddly.
I'd love to dine before we say grace,
But she already ate all the bisquits and gravy.
I'd take her fishing
But she only eats chocolates.

Jennifer Susannah Devore

As his dancing turned to skipping, he picked up a scent. It was a heavy scent: the scent of blood, and lots of it. He stopped in his tracks and perked up his ears. He had wonderfully tall ears: erect, pointed and cupped perfectly to catch the slightest sounds from miles away.

As he sniffed, he now caught a sound, too. It was faint and very far away, maybe three or four miles. It was headed this way though, headed south. He listened more carefully, leaning into the wind to hear it better. Truth be told, this was now just an exercise in innate training. His ancestors' blood told him to listen very carefully; but, he already knew what it was. It was hounds. The authorities had found him, again. Sheesh, he hated hounds. Barking, baying, hounds of great nuisance. He had yet to meet one with even half a brain. To a dog, every one he had ever known was ruled by his nose and his stomach, never his mind or his heart. History told him these would be no different and it was now time to run.

In the past, he had tried to reason with hounds. Sterling's memories settled in as he ran down the shore. Countless times he remembered standing in trees, crouched in dens or backed into caves too small for the dogs to enter.

"For the thousandth time, you beasts, I am an actor! A balladeer, a musician, an artiste extraordinaire! I am Sterling Zanni diPadua! Zanni the Zany of Venice and London! Please, you beasts! I am known far and wide, across the Continent, up and down the duchies of Italy and throughout every hamlet city and burg of the British Isles. I am Zanni the Zany! I am not your run-of-the-mill fox, a hunting victim to be badgered and bullyragged by uncultured, obtuse-minded, foul-breathed mongrels such as yourselves! Away with thee!"

Each speech was essentially the same and would always include, after "Away with thee!", a deep bow and hat removal, all ending with a flick of his best scarf and a toss of his chin. Forever and ever though, Sterling's eloquent tirades (even once quoting the Greek tragedian Euripides, to no success) were to no avail. For the accompanying humans were just as dense, stupid and cruel as the hounds. They and their dogs were creatures of mob mentality, one no smarter than the other. While he liked humans in many situations, these types whom thought on killing, capture or chase as "sport" he found lacking in any sense, logically and morally. All running, jumping, baying, barking and trumpeting like idiots, like one mindless mass. No individualism, no creativity, no distinction. The barking grew stronger, still miles away, but fast-approaching. He had been dealing with these authorities since London. He knew the hounds of Virginia would be no different than the hounds of Maryland, Massachusetts, Pennsylvania, England or Ireland. Best to find cover. He could run as long as he needed to, but why waste his energy? A very tall tree would be the best place to wait out the situation. Actually, a tree sounded fun. Being an actor, Sterling had trained himself in acrobatics and a few hours of swinging and tumbling throughout the branches sounded like good fun and good practice. It had been a while since he'd had a good practice session. He'd gotten lazy since he'd been on the run. A little treetop fencing might help his footwork in addition to spinning and dangling in the branches. Excellent! Great fun!

Sterling ran faster down the shore keeping an eye out for the perfect tree. The problem was there weren't a lot of big trees along the bay, at least at this point. There were numerous small and scrawny trees, filled in with leaves but still too thin for secure cover. Sterling was a small fox, probably the size of a large raccoon. Still, he was fluffy and red, even if a bit thinned out and faded in these summer months. He needed something big and dense like an oak or a pine tree. Then, up ahead he saw a fencerow: ten, maybe fifteen trees clustered by the water and right in the middle of it, the tallest one shooting up from the pack, was a pine tree. With a destination in view, he held his mandolin and Samuel's satchel tight, pushed his feet snuggly into his red clogs and ran as if the hounds were right on his fluffy red tail. Within minutes he had safely leapt to the lowest branch of the pine. He had an amazing vertical leap. It was another of those innate actions he just knew from birth.

Annoyingly, he also leapt like this whenever birds were around. Five feet straight up in the air, no matter what he was doing at the time, and snapping at any low-flying birds. It appalled and embarrassed him every time. Though most foxes loved to dine on birds, not to mention a variety of mammals smaller than himself, Sterling did not. He preferred a diet of raspberries, apples, grapes, corn and crusty baguettes, preferably served with a soft, French cheese, an Irish cave cheese or New-York cheddar cheese when he could find them in the cities. He was a very adaptive animal and was known to even make do with a simple

Swiss cheese when that was all he could find. He had no need to eat his friends and felt just awful each time he scared a bird with his air bound leaps. The leaping was just something he did by nature, something he assumed all foxes did. Of course, being a loner he was not sure about the acrobatic habits of other foxes.

What he had been doing lately was training himself to speak instead of bite when he jumped. So, when he leapt at a startled robin or a frightened bluebird, he would yell, "Right then, so sorry about this, Mate!" as he darted up into the birds' personal space. It seemed to work. The birds were less scared and he was losing the instinct to snap and bite. Maybe one day he would lose the jumping instinct, too. For now though, it served as a brilliant invention of Mother Nature as he landed with no effort on the lowest branch of the pine, resting some ten feet off the ground. Looking up Sterling could see another forty feet of pine he could climb if necessary. For now, this would be fine.

The needles were bristly and a bit uncomfortable as they poked at his back, but they were full this time of year and combined with the pinecones made for excellent cover. He tucked all his brightly coloured scarves into his linen doublet and under his collar so as not to call any attention to the simple greenery of the pine. Relaxing a bit and surveying the land around him, he realized that blood scent he had caught earlier was overpowering him now. It was so strong in fact that it was now making him feel quite ill, as though he suddenly wanted to vomit. He braced himself with one paw against the tree trunk. His other paw mechanically went to his throat, he closed his eyes and his head leaned over and pointed at the ground, all the involuntary motions a body goes through before a violent purge. Just as Sterling was about to vomit, he opened his eyes and saw below him, on the ground and in a shaded clearing at the foot of the pine, the source of the blood scent. It was a man: a severely injured man who lay sleeping.

Sterling jumped down instantly, his pads landing silently on the carpet of fallen pine needles upon which the man slept. He was not dead. He was definitely sleeping, but sleeping hard. Sterling had to hold his snout the blood scent was so strong and vile. It would have not been so to a human, but Sterling had a considerable sense of smell, akin to his sense of hearing. He could tell the man was in bad shape. Infection was rampant in his body. Sterling looked at his face, his arms, his feet. Everything was torn and scratched. Every inch of exposed skin was covered in various degrees of cuts, scrapes, lacerations and slices and every stage of bleeding, from fresh bursts to solid clots. Perhaps these cuts and scratches alone may not have been so bad; but, it was clear by his wet clothing, this man had done the worst thing possible with this many open wounds. He had gone swimming and by the smell of the clothes, it smelled like pond water. Stagnant pond water was full of disease. This was not good. Sterling had to find a way to clean the man's wounds. Bay water probably wasn't much better, but it was something and a far cry cleaner than pond water; at least bay water was circulated and recycled regularly. He could fill his cracked mug with water and clean the cuts. He started toward the water's edge when his ears and nose perked up again. The hounds were much closer now.

Suddenly, Sterling realized what was happening. The hounds were not fox hunting, but man hunting. It hadn't occurred to Sterling when he first saw him, but as he looked closer at the man he saw he was black. His clothes were of poor quality and he wore no shoes. His hands and feet were badly calloused, even prior to his current state. He was clearly a slave and he was being hunted. He was a runaway slave. Oh, this was much worse than Sterling originally thought. Pond disease was nothing compared with what the men behind those hounds would do to this poor man when they caught him. Sterling pulled at his arms and tugged at his shirtsleeves trying to awaken him. Right on cue, there was a sharp, loud rumble in the sky, as though Mother Nature was also working to wake the man.

"Wake up, Mate! Wake up! They're coming now! Hurry up, Chappie!" Sterling pulled and pulled on feet, hands, trousers and sleeves but to no end.

The man was out like a snuffed candle. Sterling picked up one of the man's arms and tried to heft him over his shoulder. No dice. It was like a rabbit trying to lift a pig over his back. It was quite literally, physically impossible. The only thing Sterling could do was to cover him with more pine needles. He began digging violently with his front paws, churning up a large pile of pine needles, pinecones, dirt, twigs and even a tiny vole, who shook his fist at Sterling and ran under another pile of needles nearby. It was getting really humid and Sterling had to remove his doublet, leaving only a muslin blouse between himself and the coming dogs. They were getting closer. This was no use. They may be dense, but their noses were unreal and they'd find this man under the sea if need be. No, that's silly because dogs can't smell under water. Sterling chuckled a little. Then, his face lit up. He would dunk the man in the river! The dogs would lose the scent immediately! The water would wake the man, Sterling could tell him to duck under the water and Sterling would keep eye from above in the tree. He could then signal him by chucking a pinecone at his head to tell him when to come up for air. It was perfect, except for one thing: Sterling still could not move the man. Plus, it seemed to be getting dark awfully quickly. He looked to the sky and sighed. Great, just what he needed: a thunderstorm.

"Good Heavens, Mate! Wake up, I say! Wake up!" Sterling began throwing pinecones and debris at him and slowly, the man began to stir. "Excellent! Excellent, man! You've got to rise! They're coming for you! The dogs, the men, someone! They're just up the coast! We've got to get you into the water or they'll kill you, I'm sure of it!"

Remus slowly lifted his head and just stared. Tiny droplets of water began to prick his face as he focused on the trees around him. They were beginning to sway, but in an odd formation, not back and forth, but just in wide circles. Then, he saw a fox in a silk head-scarf and a gold earring screaming at him. He blinked and shook his head. It had to be the fever. The water dropped harder on his face and actually steamed off his body as it hit, he was so hot. He could hear nothing but the sky rumbling overhead and muted squeals from the creature in front of him. There was definitely a fox yelling at him. His arms were flailing all over the place as he yelled and while Remus wasn't quite sure, he thought he saw rings on his paws, a mandolin strapped to his back and funky, red shoes. He blinked thrice slowly. Yep, there was what appeared to be a musical, Italian fox in red clogs jumping and screaming at him here in the woods. Oh, if Remus wasn't close to his maker, he didn't know what to make of the scene before him. Soon, his hearing grew stronger though and he began to understand the odd fox.

"Dogs, man, dogs!"

It was too late. Remus finally understood but he could see the dogs through the trees. Not even a hundred yards away.

"Into the water with you! You've got to go now or they'll get you!" Sterling tried to lead him to the water.

Remus was just too weak, though. He couldn't even stand up straight. He just fell over with each try. Sterling was panicked but Remus seemed to have given up and said, "If they find me, they find me. I am ready to die."

"No way, Mate! Not with me you're not!" Sterling yelled back. "I can't handle two crises in one week! Lie down! Get flat!"

Sterling began to dig up more needles and leaves and covered Remus as long as he could safely do so. The rain had come down full-force now and it was making Sterling's job a lot harder. Every paw scoop was heavier and dirtier as the rain made mud of everything and Sterling was becoming rather upset that his blouse was becoming soiled beyond recognition.

Finally, Sterling had to protect himself, too, and leapt up into the tree, looking down at this latest crisis he'd come upon in these parts. He was beginning to think he should have stayed in Boston. Remus looked good, though. Sterling was built for digging and while he usually did so for berries in the snow and sunflower seeds under gardens, he was a master at it today and below the tree all he saw was a large mound of leaves and needles: average storm debris collected beneath an average tree. His only concern was this blasted storm. He looked at his pocket watch. Right on cue: four o'clock, summer thunderstorm.

The wind had really picked up and the rain was now blowing sideways. Sterling held on to the trunk with both paws. The thunder was wild and rumbling across the Chesapeake Bay in what sounded like thirty-second intervals. He could hear the river slap up against the rocks and the leaves brushed against each other with a cacophony that sounded like Mother Nature coming through Virginia with her giant broom, whisking away all the dry, summer dust. The lightning was not as bad as it could be sometimes, but Sterling counted at least three good cracks that were too close for comfort. He was soaked and his mandolin kept making plinky sounds as it the string-side bounced up and down on his back in the wind. Water was not good for an instrument, nor was it good for his fine scarves which were now, despite being tucked inside his shirt, drenched and sticking to his fur. Highly uncomfortable a sensation, it was. Oh well, the scarves would dry, the mandolin would now have its own unique sound and his blouse did need a good washing after all that digging. His clogs were good, though. He looked down at them and smiled. He loved his red clogs.

He looked down farther and regarded the pile of man and pine needles and it still looked good, too good. There was no movement and Sterling feared the worst. Of course, no one knows better than a runaway slave what can happen to a runaway slave when caught; so, maybe this man knew exactly how to keep still and not breathe for as long as his life depended on it. As Sterling pondered this, a clap of thunder resounded so violently and so loudly, right next to his head it seemed, that Sterling jumped involuntarily up to the next branch. Before he could catch his breath another clap came, followed by a strike of lightning that struck an upper-level branch of his own pine tree. Before flames could burn even one leaf, the torrential rain suffused the potential damage. The thunder just kept rumbling and shaking the earth. Sterling grew more and more concerned about Remus.

It didn't seem like it could rain any harder, but it did and as it continued to pour steady buckets minute by minute, Sterling was certain it would wash away the needle pile if it didn't stop soon. Between the wind and the rain, everything would be wiped out in moments, everything. If only those stupid dogs would just go away. But, they wouldn't. They'd just keep running and loping about like mindless clowns. "See," Sterling thought to himself, "they're not even smart enough to get out of the rain. Philistines."

Sterling shifted paws, placing his left above his right now. His shoulders were growing tired but this was one of the strongest storms he'd experienced, yet. Not quite as bad as the one up near Baltimore a couple days ago, but close. Taking his eyes off the pile for a minute, he was surveying the land again when all of a sudden it hit him. Where were the dogs? He couldn't see them anywhere. In fact, he realized as his ears shot up straight that the only sounds he heard were the plinks of his mandolin strings and the weather. No dogs. No barking, no baying, no trumpets, no chattering humans. Nothing.

He whipped his head around, hanging on with his other paw as he spun completely around on his branch, taking in a full three-hundred and sixty degree view. They were gone. He'd never even heard them recede. Thunderstorms can be noisy affairs, but he was amazed at his own lack of observance. That kind of carelessness can be dangerous. Still, this was great news! They were gone! The dogs and the man hunters were gone! Slowly, Sterling's eyes grew large as the explanation occurred to him. Of course! It was the water, the rain. He had been so concerned with getting the man into the water, Mother Nature simply brought the water to him. The thunderstorm was so forceful and deluging, it washed away enough of the scent to confuse the dogs. They relied so heavily on their sense of smell, it never occurred to them to use their brains and theorize where an injured man might take cover from a storm. Apparently the humans were no brighter. They just stopped cold and gave up. No scent, no action. Brilliant!

Taking one last listen and a quick spin around to view the area one more time, Sterling leapt down to the pile in one jump and began to dig out the debris he'd just placed there. With his tail straight up in the air and his nose and front paws deep the pile, he kicked back sheets and sheets of wet earth until the man was exposed. Lying on his side, Remus coughed and sputtered a mix of mud and rainwater. He then lifted an arm nearly destroyed with mud-packed cuts and gouges, and began digging muck and pebbles out of his left ear. After a minute of this, which merely pushed everything deeper into his ear, he leaned up on an elbow with great effort and looked around at his situation. There were no dogs, there was way too much rain and there was still that Italian-looking, fancy fox.

"Right then! Greetings, Mate! Sterling's the name, Zanni for short. How you feeling, Mate?"

Sterling was relieved to see the man alive and wearing a slight, if not befuddled, smile. That scent was still there, that very bad scent, but Sterling was a strong believer in positive thinking and wasn't about to greet this man with worry.

"Close call, all that. I really loathe the hounds. Hungry? I've got some berries and I found a bit of corn bread in my bag here. It's a bit soggy, Mate, but would you like some?"

Sterling offered up the piece of bread that completely disintegrated the instant it came out of the sack and into the rain.

Jennifer Susannah Devore

"Sorry about that, Chappie. Berries?"

He tossed the bread-paste over his shoulder and into the bay where a small bass found it quite delectable.

"You a fox, right? I mean, not like a chile dressed as a fox or a doll or somethin'. You a fox?" Remus struggled to sit up straight and stared at Sterling.

"Right, Chap! Like I said, Sterling's the name," The rain pelted his head as he bowed and removed his hat. "Zanni the Zany, actually."

"That's real funny. I like that name. Sounds like Granny. I liked my granny." Remus smiled at nothing, his eyes in a fog.

Sterling could tell this man was quite ill, fever most likely. His speech was a little slow and his manner was a little loopy. Plus, he could smell the heat and the mass infection. It was as though all those tiny scrapes and cuts mixed with all that mud and muck and caused a massive spread throughout his body. Sterling was no doctor, but he was a fox and blessed with superior senses. Best thing to do would be to stay put for a while, let the dogs put some mileage between them, then get this man to a real doctor in Williamsburg. Remus started laughing and coughing simultaneously and pat Sterling on the back lightly.

"Doan you worry, Honey. I gwin be fine, jest fine. I jest feel a little warm. I hate these thunderstorms, Honey. Make me feel like I'm cookin' bisquits in the oven and somebody done put me in with the bisquits!" Remus laughed at this image. "Kin you see me, a little, teeny, tiny Remus standin' over a big ol' pan o' bisquits on an oven rack? Now that's zany!"

"Remus? Is that your name?" Sterling dragged over a felled tree branch full of leaves and secured it the pine's lowest branches, giving the two refugees a little bit of cover. He then sat down cross-legged next to Remus.

"Yessir. Remus is the name my momma give me. It's Italian, you know. She tell me that," he straightened his back a bit, proud of this fact.

"I know, I know! I'm Italian myself!"

"Yes, Honey. I figured Zanni sound kinda Italian. You doan sound Italian, though. The missus o' the plantation gets lots o' her clothes from Italy. I hear the people who make her dresses when they come to the house sometime. Wines, too. Massa gets lots o' wines from Italy. You sound like a bottle o' wine, Zanni Honey!" Remus pat Sterling's head.

"That's funny, Chap. I do, don't I? You're famous, though! Legend says Remus was one of Rome's founders. My mum taught me about all the Roman myths."

"That's true, that's true, Zanni Honey. I doan know much more than that, though. My momma was gone when I was jest a chile."

Remus gazed out over the bay and started stirring the dirt with a small twig as he spoke.

"Story goes the massa took her from the kitchen one day, right in the middle of bakin' supper. He take her to the front porch an' another man, someone from South Carolina hand over an envelope of money and Massa give her to him. That wuz it. She didn' even get to get her clothes or say goodbye to my pappy, my brother or me. Jest carried off in a wagon, jest when I probably needed her mos'. My brother, too."

"Your brother? He was taken away, too?" Sterling leaned in closer.

"No, I got carried off my own self one day, got taken away from him at a bad time, too. Probably coulda been real nice to have a brother."

Sterling must have looked very sad at this, for Remus smiled softly.

"Doan you worry, Zanni Honey. That was a long time ago, maybe fifty years ago. I doan know. I doan even 'member what they look like. They jest ghosts to me."

"How old were you? I mean, when your mum was taken from you?"

Sterling was riveted. He left his family by choice, just for an adventure. He couldn't imagine being forcefully separated.

"Ohhh, I doan know, baby. I not even real sure how old I is today," Remus sighed and tossed a pinecone, underhand, into the frothy bay. "I know my momma was gone before I really knew her. So I was mos' likely still a baby. But walking, I know I was walking 'cause I recollect runnin' after her."

Sterling tried not to let a tear fall.

"As far as my age now," Remus continued. "I do recollect one time, when I first start to thinkin' girls wuz mo' pretty than scary, the massa take me to a big book in his office. I guess I been actin' up an' not pullin' enough cotton down to the barn. 'Posed to drag maybe seven hundred pounds of cotton the mile or so down to the barn. He tell me a young buck like me must be slackin' off if'n I drag only four-hundred pounds a day."

Sterling's eyes were wide. He'd never done much of a day's work as it was, let alone like that.

"So, he take me into his office an he open this big, leather book an' he tell me, 'Look, boy. I paid sixty pounds for you when you was jest eleven years old an' since then I doan think I'm gettin' my worth outta you, boy.' He then whip me, one time for each of my years an' it felt like maybe twelve times. Then, he get the overseer to take me back to my quarters where he take red pepper and salt an' rub it into my wounds, jest so I remember not to slack off. That was a real bad night, baby."

After that comment, the two runaways sat in silence for a while and watched the rain sprinkle the Chesapeake Bay. The storm was dying now. The thunder was more distant and far less ferocious. Only the occasional lightning strike could be seen over the water. Even the soothing sound of rain plinking the mandolin strings was ceasing. Ever so softly, birds whistled messages throughout the trees: "The storm is ending"; "Keep your eyes on the fox"; "The hurt man's okay".

Sterling thought about what this man's life must have been like. Fifty years. That's a long time to be a slave. Doing some quick problem-solving, Sterling assumed if the mother was sold off by the time Remus was about two, he'd probably been born into slavery and had known nothing but that life. He'd been a slave since the 1680's most likely. Sterling thought about his childhood and what a charm it had been: a home on the Grand Canal in Venice and a stone house in the countryside of Umbria. How could two lives be so unequal? Of course, Sterling's family didn't have two houses anymore. Sterling didn't have much of anything anymore. Never mind all that. This wasn't about him. This night was about Remus and keeping him warm, as dry as possible and cleaning those wounds somehow, at least enough to keep the infection from spreading overnight. Maybe Remus would know something about herbs. Sterling certainly knew nothing. His game was the theatre, music, costumes and wine. Not herbs and plants and such. He hated gardening almost as much as he hated hounds.

As the storm faded, the fireflies came out to play and, maybe sensing the melancholy friendship building between the two under the tree, hovered close by and lent a fairy atmosphere to the night of bayside camping.

"Doan you jest love the river, Honey?" Remus later asked Sterling as they mashed up some marsh mallow root to apply to his wounds: a delicate, pink flower Remus said would soothe irritation and hopefully calm surface infections.

"Oh, I do, Chappie. Spent a good deal of my life at riparian entertainments. Picnics, outdoor plays, pantomimes. Just love it," Sterling recalled as he scooped a small smear of the now pasty root and began rubbing it gently into the largest wound, a huge slice on the instep of Remus' foot.

Remus winced and coughed, then laughed at the same time. Laughing tended to make him feel better and he found himself laughing inappropriately more and more these days.

"Here, eat some of these," Sterling handed him a pawful of the unused marsh mallow petals. "They should help you stop coughing."

"True thing, Honey. Missus where I last worked, the lady there, she mix goat milk with mallow flowers for the children, mix with wine for the adults, to make a cough remedy. I do wish we had some wine, Zanni Honey." Remus lay back and chewed the chalky petals. "What kind of wine you like, Honey?"

"Anything Italian," Sterling quipped as he shooed away a June bug that was buzzing too loudly, too close to the ointment.

"Yessir! Anything Italian!" Remus laughed again and as always, coughed afterwards.

"So, what's a fancy, Italian fox like yo'self doin' on the Virginia-end of the Chesapeake Bay?" Remus asked. "'Sides, like I said, you doan sound Italian. The one what come to the house to bring the missus some fine dresses, he say they come all the way from Rome. You doan sound nothin' like him. Well, I hear him talking one day when he standin' 'round on the porch with Massa. I was sent to bring some extra fine cotton we grew to the Italian man. Guess he know cotton real well and maybe buy some from Massa to take back to Rome an' make some more dresses to bring right back to the house. Seems awfully silly to me. Dresses makin' more travel than ol' Remus ever get!" His eyes lit up a bit at the idea of such silliness and he laughed until he coughed.

"Oh, I'm Italian alright, Mate! *Vini vidi vici* and all that stuff," Sterling was determined to keep this man's spirits up until they got some help. "Thing is, I left Italy when I was still just a kit. Spent most of my life, up until a few months ago, in England, mostly London. Ireland for a little while."

"London, England. That sounds fine, jest fine. I see things 'round the big house that come from England. The missus always braggin' how many things come from across the ocean. London sounds real nice. Why you come here, Zanni Honey? Why you leave London?"

"Oh, it's a long story, Chum," Sterling topped off the marsh mallow root ointment with a layer of the flower petals to keep it all in place, not really ready to share his tale. "A bit of a vagabond's tale," he said with a wink. "And London's not that nice, Mate. Sure, we've got a right good bit of theatre and fashion and other arts, but it's a grimy town. Lots of crime, too. Disease, hunger. No, it's a great place in some ways, best in the world. But, with that distinction comes a lot of the negative, Mate. Yep, London and I've got a long history."

"I got nothin' but time, Honey."

Always the showman, always a ham, Sterling talked through the night. The crickets sang while the fireflies danced and Remus dreamed of what he thought London and Venice might be like. Streets made of water! That little fox had to be making that up! There's no such thing as streets of water! Sterling made up songs of summer in Venice and winter in London on his mandolin.

He began with life in Venice as a kit and all the glory that living in such a city could hold. He told of his parents and of their sadness when he suddenly felt the urge to leave Venice one day to study and improve his acting in London. He told of his early love of the theatre and the great names he met on the London stages. Then, he started his vagabond's tale and the horror that composed his involuntary immigration to America. Then stopped himself. Again, tonight was not about the negative and more so, not about himself. It was about keeping Remus positive and well and about what wonderful adventures they might share, because Sterling figured they'd certainly remain friends after all this and anyone whom could appreciate London without even having seen it was alright with him. Sterling changed the conversation abruptly, mid-course.

"So, Mate, what's the first thing you'll want to be doing as soon as we arrive in Williamsburg? Personally, I know nothing of this place except 'tis the capital town of this Virginia. Got to be something interesting there," Sterling checked some flower petals on Remus' knee as he asked.

"Oh, first thing ol' Remus know is he free! I finally free once I reach Williamsburg! I ain't known nothin' but work, baby. Hard work. All I know is I wake up, work, sleep, wake up an' work again. Sometimes, I think my back gon' break off it hurt so bad. But I ain't gots to do that no mo'. When I do get to Williamsburg, I got myself family there. A brother, a real successful brother," Remus smiled and winced as the beginnings of a new cough emerged.

"A brother? Excellent! Does he know you're coming? I mean, that you've, well, escaped? I assume you've escaped," Sterling's eyes met Remus' with embarrassment. He felt maybe he'd stepped over some line.

"No, I doan know he recollects nothin' 'bout me, Honey. We ain't seen each other since we was boys," his eyes began to well with tears. "One day, the massa say to me, 'Remus, you come down off that swing an' come wit me.' See, I wuz in charge of keepin' the flies off the food on the dinin' room table in the summer. They put me up in a swingin' chair over the table an' give me a big fan o' peacock feathers an' I use it to shoo away the flies. An' if I let them feathers touch any food, an' the massa sees it, oh I get a whippin' you woan believe, Zanni Honey."

Sterling listened intently, doing his best not to shed a single tear. He figured if Remus could talk about it and not cry, he could listen to it and not cry.

"Finally though, the massa, he say, 'You come wit me and Romulus', my brother, he look at me and nod, like it be okay. I go wit the massa and that's the last time Romulus an' Remus ever see each other. I got sold to another farm that day. I hear one day Romulus get sold to another down in Currituck, nice family, I guess. They let him work in the house an' read when he find time, even learn to write. I know, cuz he send me letters. They never given to me, until lately. The missus give them to me one day after the massa died. Said he been hidin' them from me all these years. She say she know I never could read them, but they make me happy jest to hold them," Remus took a drink of water from Sterling's leaky, cracked mug and returned to his story.

"One day, a new girl come to the farm. She been in a bad way back at her old farm, regular beatings by the young boys of the big house, hurtin' her for fun. Anyway, that massa say she trouble for stirrin' up the boys and sell her off to my missus, the widow Carleton. Turn out the slave girl can read and she read my letters to me. Finds out they all from Romulus an' he been free for years an' years now! Free! I doan believe it! She say that's why the massa doan want me to get the letters. Fill my head wit ideas. I think the missus never read them or she never give them to me neither," Remus pulled himself up straight and looked out at the river, the land, then straight into Sterling's eyes.

"Zanni Honey, she was right! After I find out I got a free brother, I think I can be free, too! I doan know freedom is an option for me. Lots o' free Africans in Williamsburg, I guess. Maybe half the people, Romulus say. Well, I decide I can't be a slave no mo'. I got to be free! If Romulus can be free, I can be free."

Remus patted Sterling's fuzzy head. He could tell the gentle fox wanted to cry and in all his pain, felt bad that he was making another creature feel so sad.

"Doan be sad, Honey. I run an' it's a good thing! Simple as that. Right now, I am free! Right this minute, I ain't picking cotton, I ain't fannin' flies, I ain't getting beat for eatin' a bisquit out the trash bucket. I doan even have to get up in the mornin' if I doan feel like it! I can sleep all I want, if I want."

Sterling smiled a strange, puckered smile, the kind that shows you're trying to smile and be upbeat, but really want to break down and sob.

"Listen, Zanni Homey, I figure my brother got money. His letters tell me he real wealthy. Got some shops or something. A real merchant. . . and free! He free! My big brother is free!" he stared out into the night and now he wept openly, releasing not only his salty reserves, but Sterling's as well, Remus' tears coating the cuts and stinging the scrapes on his cheeks, meandering to the corners of his mouth where the tears returned to the body from whence they came.

They both sat and cried, in sadness as well as relief and happiness. Sterling got up and walked to the river where he splashed his face, got control of himself and went back to Remus with a smile full of determination, no matter how difficult.

"Right then, Mate. What do you think he'll say when he sees you? You think he'll recall you?" Sterling still smiled, but with a struggle.

"Oh, he gwin recall me. We was like salt an' pepper, always together, before we got separated." Remus shifted positions to relieve the pain in his chest and wiped away his tears. "What I hope will happen is he an take me in. Let me work in one of his shops or something. I got excellent skills. I was a field slave, but I am real smart. I picked up lots of things 'bout wine and meats and dresses and such. I could do anything Romulus wants me to do. We both be free! Yessir, we can do anything we want."

"What about, well, you know, the escaping, Mate? He's going to have to hide you first. Those bloody hounds are right likely to keep on looking. Probably have a bit of postings around taverns, telling chaps what you look like and what not."

"The good thing is we all look alike to them," Remus laughed in all seriousness and coughed. "They woan know me from any other black man walking 'round town. Romulus say half the town is black men and women, children, too. Free children! How 'bout that? That's real fine, mighty fine!"

"I'm just frightened, Mate, what with all your injuries, someone could figure something out," Sterling fretted.

"I ain't worried, Zanni Honey. Plus, you know what?" Remus suddenly got extremely excited. "You could come live wit us! I mean, it seem like you got nobody here in America, an' I got nobody but my brother. Yessir, I think we could become jest like best friends. You could make up songs and little dances about our shops and then go sing them 'round town. You know, tellin' people all about our goods and bringin' them and they money to us! Oh, that sounds fine, just fine."

"That does sound nice," Sterling said thoughtfully.

He had planned to search for acting opportunities. He was "Zanni the Zany" after all. Of course, he was probably too well-trained to do something as lowly as local advertising. Nevertheless, he was all alone and thought it might be nice to stick around someplace with family-type people for a spell. Plus, how could he say 'No' right now?

"Right then, Chap. Sounds like a brilliant plan! What about the law, though. I'm still anxious. They'll certainly keep looking for you, Mate."

"Doan you worry, Zanni Honey. I got another plan. Romulus gwin buy

Remus back into his family! I figure if I cost 60 £ back when my back doan hurt an' my knees doan crick. I probably cosy only 'bout 40 £ by now. I know he got that much money. Maybe he could even trade me for some o' his store goods!"

Remus smiled broadly, as if proud that his price had dropped with age and without any realization of the inherent problem with being bought, sold or traded as a concept.

"Yessir, he could buy or trade me with the missus what lookin' for me right now. Heh-heh, she right. She shouldna give me my letters. I do love bein' free," he stretched one arm over his chest, trying to alleviate some soreness that was building in his shoulder. "Yessir, Romulus can buy me from her, plus a little extra for the trouble, and then I be an upright citizen. . .by the law."

Remus had been a slave for so long, born into it, watched his mother sold off, ripped from his brother's protective watch, probably never knew his father, watched friends sold off or maybe killed, but certainly punished. It was all so normal for him. He'd had the spirit and gumption to run in the first place, but his ultimate way out was to be purchased again, like a hog from a farm or a porcelain statue fresh off a ship from the Orient. Sterling wanted to slap him and tell him he was a human being and not for sale and even though that was the law, it wasn't right or humane and even though he had to deal with it somehow, he could never let it remain "normal" for him and even if he couldn't fight the literal chains they could someday place around his feet again, he could always fight them in his head and his heart, keeping his soul and his thoughts liberated for all time.

Remus looked exceptionally weak though, and Sterling thought now was not the time for a grand elocution on the rights of man. Tomorrow, however, Sterling would give him an earful on the ferry ride across the river to Williamsburg. Tonight though, Remus should rest and dream and think about his long lost brother. That was something that clearly gave him joy. Sterling was happy to even be remotely involved in such a reunion. He just hoped this Romulus was equally as excited to see Remus. Reunions aren't always mutually appreciated and one-way admiration is never pretty.

Remus continued to smile and cough as he closed his eyes. The fireflies dimmed, too, as if they had done their job and it was now time to fall asleep themselves. Remus shifted and rolled until he found a comfortable position, then covered his shoulders with his wet, filthy, linen vest. The rain had completely abated by now and the air was just sticky and warm, but not too uncomfortable. The sound of the river lapping the rocks and the crickets singing their nightly melodies helped Remus drift to sleep quickly and peacefully, all the while picturing himself in a crisp, clean apron, working as part-owner of a wine shop, working side by side with his brother. Romulus and Remus, together again. Tomorrow was going to be a great day.

As Remus drifted off, Sterling did a grounds check running up the limbs of the pine tree to survey the land. All was clear. No dogs, no humans, no lightning fires, no nothing. He climbed back down the tree, took off his own wet vest and cloak and lay them open over a branch, hoping they'd dry by morning. He removed the wet vest from Remus' shoulders, worried he'd catch influenza on top of whatever infection he could still smell growing within the man. Remus shivered a little, but Sterling thought the fresh air would be good for his wounds. As Remus coughed himself to sleep, Sterling pulled his mandolin down off a branch where he'd hung it upside-down to drain it of any rainwater.

Through his natural sense of rhythm and music, Sterling began to pluck a tune in perfect time with Remus' coughs and snores. A melody, slow and dark to match the night and the mood, came to him and he sang in whispers until Remus fell to a sleep, full of dreams of hope and bright futures.

Sleep by the bay, the fishes keep watch,
Under the moon, the fireflies flit,
The herons rest and the crabs relax,
Sleep in peace my new found friend,
Your family you'll soon see,
All together again.

Sterling ended on a soft *plink* and re-hung his mandolin on its limb, under a flush of pine needles to keep it dry in case of another storm in the night. He settled down right next to Remus, walked in a low, tight circle six or seven times, then planted his back legs and continued walking with his front legs until he completed a perfect circle, his snout nestled into his fluffy tail. He scuttled back just enough to make sure he and Remus were touching and he drifted off to

Jennifer Susannah Devore

sleep thinking about his new life in Williamsburg.

Sterling swatted sleepily at what he thought was a wasp. The hissing and buzzing grew louder and louder until it finally woke him completely. He swatted some more, but saw no wasps, no bees, no insects at all, short of the dozens of mosquitoes that were buzzing around the only two warm-blooded, tasty creatures sleeping under this particular tree. It wasn't mosquitoes, though. The sound was coming from Remus.

He was shivering so hard his teeth were seething and buzzing and rattling within his head. Sterling jumped up and leaned over Remus' head and set a paw on his forehead. He felt like boiling laundry lifted from a cauldron. He was burning up, as if he was cooking from the inside. As Sterling shook him, Remus coughed himself into a fit that just got progressively worse with each explosion, quickly making it harder and harder for him to catch his breath in between.

"Geez, Mate! Wake up! You're burning to a crisp! We've got to get you into the water! We'll cool you down then we'll head to Williamsburg tonight! Just get in the water, Mate! Come on, Chap!" Sterling tugged on his trousers with his strong teeth, but with no effect. "Come on! Get bleedin' up, Mate! Now! Into the water! We've not much time! I'm certain of it."

He then tried the gentle approach and leaned close to his face.

"Please, Mate. We've just got to get your fever down and we'll be fine. I'll drag you to Williamsburg if I have to. We'll find a cart or something. I don't know. But, let's just get you in the water. Please, Remus, old Chap."

Remus smiled and waved his hand at Sterling, telling him non-verbally to calm down. Sterling started to plead again and Remus repeated the action, then held up a hand, telling him to wait for a moment until his fit passed. It did.

"Listen, Zanni Honey, it's all okay, baby. Ol' Remus gwin be okay. You know what? I jest see Momma," Remus smiled so wide his mouth opened, but his eyes remained closed.

"You what?"

"I jest see my Momma. Ohhhh, she soooo beautiful, real peaceful, too. She sittin' on a swing under a big tree in front of a big house. She by a river an' I think she in London," he crinkled his brow a bit as he imagined this. "Yessir, it be Londontown. Momma's waitin' for me in London," he opened his eyes and looked right at Sterling, all four eyes welled deep with tears, two in utter joy, two in profound sadness. "Zanni Honey, Momma's waitin' for me an' I finally get to see London. London, baby. Maybe I see some people you know."

"Don't be silly," Sterling was irritated, strictly out of fear. "Right then, you're not going to London. You're going to Williamsburg, with me, right now. Remember, we're going to see Romulus? We're all going to run a shop together. I'm going to live with you and sing little ditties about our wine and candies and what-not. So, let's just get you in the water and we'll be off. Right?"

"Zanni Honey, hush," Remus grew serious now. "I bein' real honest here now. I gwin to see Momma. She wavin' at me as I lie here! They got swans where she is! Beautiful, white swans in a pond behind her! She not tired, she not scared, she real clean and peaceful, all dressed in royal purple, her favourite color."

"Please, Remus. Stop it. You're really frightening me," Sterling pleaded and began to cry.

"Please doan cry, Zanni Honey. I's sooo happy. Really, baby. I never been happier in my long, hard life. I so ready to go to Momma it hurts. I jest waitin' for you to listen to me. Listen to me, Zanni, so I can go. Okay?" Remus was serious and Sterling had to force himself to be quiet and listen. "I real tired of bein' tired. I jest want to see Momma and the swans, be clean and not sick and be dressed real fine, maybe in purple, maybe somethin' red. Oh, I like red. Please, Zanni Honey, listen to me."

Sterling was now crying so hard he could not speak. He sobbed so hard his chest burned as he took loud and great gulps of air with every sob. He lifted his head and looked Remus directly in the eyes, a very difficult task as he wanted more than anything to look away, run away in fact. He didn't even know this man but this was one of his saddest moments ever.

"Zanni Honey, I know this is hard for you. I know we jest met, but you's like a little brother to me, a funny little friend. The great Zanni the Zany from Italy. I do like your fancy scarves and your songs is real pretty to my ears." Sterling's sobs grew deeper, stronger and more silent. "Tonight's been the best day o' my life, little one. Ol' Remus promises you that. I ain't lyin'. The best day o' my life 'cause I met you an' I was free. Free, baby. One night of true freedom with a new friend and then off to Momma? That's worth all the pain an' struggle an' sadness I seen in my life. I am tired, baby. I'm gwin go to Momma now. She looks real rested an' I want to feel rested now. I jest need one thing from you. Hand me my vest."

Sterling got up and grabbed the soaking-wet vest off the limb where he'd hung it to dry. Remus pulled a packet of letters out of a pocket. They were drenched and stuck together, making a paper brick. Tied together with an old, red ribbon they were virtually unreadable they were so covered with mold and moisture from the years of being tucked away in a barn. He handed the stinky brick of words to Remus and sat back down, cross-legged, and waited. A small gathering of field mice, voles and a rabbit hid under some hedges along the watermark and watched the terrible scene unfold. The rabbit passed around a tiny handkerchief she kept with her at all times and they all shared it until it was as wet as if it had hung out in the storm.

"These are my letters from my brother. I know, they's a mess an' probably ruined now since I been running in the rain an' through creeks and rivers and what-not," he smiled. "I like that saying: 'What-not'. You say that a lot. 'What-not'. It's very London, I bet. I like the way you talk, little one. 'Chappie', 'Mate', 'what-not'. It's real nice. Well, I need you to do ol' Remus a big favour."

"Yes, of course, Mate. Anything."

"I need you to go to Williamsburg and find Romulus. Give him back his letters. Tell him I got them an' I loved them. I had that girl Ketty read them to me over an' over. She likely got real tired of me an' my brother! You find Romulus an' tell him that an' tell him I was on my way to see him an' help him wit his business. Tell him I love him, always has, and tell him Momma love him, too. She tell me jest now. She's holding a place for him in London, by the river. Real pretty there."

Sterling just nodded, unsure of the exact words uttered. Between blinking back tears and swallowing sobs, he just nodded incoherently. Remus handed over the letters and Sterling hugged them to his chest, tucking them under some scarves as if his own life depended upon their safety. He stared at

Remus and waited for more instructions.

"That's all, Zanni Honey. Okay then, I gwin close my eyes and go to Momma."

Sterling began to audibly sob again, shaking and trembling.

"It's okay, baby. Recollect, I am really and truly the happiest I ever been. Doan cry, honey. I can't be happy if I know you's sad. Okay? Smile for me. Let me see you smile," he pursed his lips and furrowed his brows in mock seriousness. Sterling obliged and nodded with the most haunting faux smile: all teeth, raised eyebrows and eyes red and swollen.

"That's better. Thank you, baby. Okay then. Momma sends her wishes and thanks you for lookin' after her baby. Good night, Zanni Honey. Ol' Remus loves you."

A noticeable wave of peace floated across Remus' face. Sterling could actually see it. It was like a piece of Irish lace dragging softly across his face and as it passed it removed any tension and anguish, leaving only softness and beauty. The field mice and the vole huddled around the rabbit and she covered them with her long ears, protecting them from sadness the best she could. They all cried as they watched Sterling pull through a red, silk scarf from under his collar and curl it solemnly around Remus' hands, which lay clasped on his chest. Then, Sterling dropped his head and let it all out with a deafening silence that drifted in invisible ripples across the salt marshes and grass meadows of Virginia's coastal plain.

CHAPTER NINE
New-York : December 1733

The morning was bitter but beautiful. It was only just after four o'clock. Dark, very dark. It was gorgeous out, though. The early morning sky was a cool navy blue, speckled with a few remaining stars on the city's west end. Snow sprinkled all through the night and left a velveteen carpet of pure white across the city. Only hoof prints and boot prints of the earliest shifts dotted the purity. A bracing breeze lilted across the harbour, dispatching glassy ripples over the black water to chip away at the silk-thin layers of ice that had formed around the perimeters of the harbour.

Linus's boots made a long stretch of prints as he walked the mile and a half from his house to Zenger's print shop. Linus loved the early hours of the morning. He had the streets to himself mostly; only the fishermen returning from their overnight expeditions and the florists setting up their stalls for the day with the fresh shipments from Holland and England shared this hour with him. Passing one of the smaller boats he waved at two men he'd become friendly with based purely on their sharing of this odd hour. They unloaded some long, sharp-nosed fish he assumed were pike. Taking both of them to hold one fish, they gave nods-up to Linus and yelled out, "*God morgon, Linus!*" Fellow Swedes, they were.

"*God morgon* to you, men! *Hur sta det till?* How are you?" Linus yelled back across the quiet morning.

"*Mycket val, tack sjalv!*" the elderly Swede shouted. "Very vell, tank you!" his apprentice, a Swedish boy about Linus's age added, always eager to practice his English, unlike his elder, whom equated learning English with disrespecting his heritage.

"*God dag!*" Linus ended the chilly morning ritual with a giant, half-moon, overhand wave. "Have a happy day!" he added for the young one.

The shop was extremely dark this time of morning, so Linus always made sure to leave his candles in the same spot every night before he went home. This way, when he opened the door, he could lean directly to his right, grab a candlestick already in its pewter holder, and light it with the long matches kept in a brass pitcher next to it. After that one was lit, he could carry it about the print shop, finding and lighting all necessary candles until his workspace was sufficiently bright.

Now that he could see, Linus hung his navy-blue, wool shortcoat, a gift from his *Mormor*, his grandmother back in Stockholm, on one of the many wooden pegs by the front door. He slung his messenger bag onto another peg and traded it for leather apron. Tying first the strings that went around the neck, he then grabbed the waist ties, crossed the leather strings in the back, brought them around and tied a bow in the front. As ritual, he walked to a shelf on the back wall and took down a tin coffee pot, a pewter mug and a canister of coffee grounds. Herr Zenger always kept a full canister. Linus had grown into the habit of taking coffee each morning soon after signing on as apprentice. Watching Herr Zenger enjoy the aroma and taste each day as if it was some sort of church ordination, he finally gave in, not able to fight the warm and inviting smell of the brew.

Linus scooped four large spoonfuls of a special Scandinavian blend of Yemeni beans. His mother loved to remind her New-York neighbors that Scandinavians drank more coffee than anyone in the world because of their long and cold winters. According to her, they drank even more than the Italians, the French and the Arabians. Linus and his father always thought this an odd impetus for pride, but they loved her and if it made her proud, so be it.

Laughing to himself about the uselessness of such a claim, Linus went back outside and lit a small fire in a pit about twenty yards away from the shop. He then took the coffee pot to the water pump, filled it after a few pumps to break the ice inside, then set the pot on the iron grate that rested over the fire pit. He then went back inside to check the ink station whilst he waited for the coffee water to boil. Holding his coat against his body to keep out the cold, he wished the shop could have a normal, indoor fireplace like everyone else. Before he finished the thought he knew that was just dumb. A fireplace? Flames? A business run entirely on paper products? *Mycket god, Linus*! Real smart idea! He kicked a stone and shuffled back into the shop.

Unfortunately, the ink supplies were low. He kind of knew they'd be, since he hadn't had to mix any for a couple of days now. Still, he supposed he wished fairies would come in during the night and mix the ink so he wouldn't have to. Ick! What a mess: smelly, dirty, sticky and worse than all that, it kept his hands constantly stained with ink, thus showing the world no matter where he went that he was a printer.

It wasn't that he thought printing was a low industry, on the contrary, he hoped to always be associated with it, but as a writer. The odd ink stains on his fingertips were one thing. One could always tell a writer by the ink stains on his fingertips. But the whole hand, the forearms. Those were the marks of a printer and an ink maker. It was okay, though. He was still youngish, fourteen, and one day soon he would be a writer. His Governor Cosby story had been very well received by Zenger and some of his colleagues. That being said, it was never printed because someone else, a real writer from London and hired by Cosby himself, had written a far more glamorous and Cosby-friendly account. This was the one printed by the *New-York Gazette*, the official printer for the colony. When Linus suggested they could run their own story about the arrival, Zenger said the moment had passed, people had read enough of the arrival and Linus' would just be a waste of paper. No offense, he liked his piece, but it just made no financial sense to print it. Linus learned very quickly that writing was not only about what you wrote, but how quickly you got it to the people. More importantly, it was also about whom you knew and if you could write to appeal to the correct people. Maybe it didn't even matter if the writing was accurate. That didn't seem right to Linus. It was a good lesson nevertheless.

Having been back outside to fetch his boiling water, he stirred it into the grounds and now enjoyed his morning coffee as he stared at the ink vats just waiting for him to commence his day's work. It was time. No more daydreaming about writing or savouring his coffee. Time to mix the ink.

Three wooden containers with lids stood waiting with wooden scoops attached to the undersides of lids. Linus hated the first container most of all. It was filled with lampblack. Lampblack was a fine dust, really fine. It was almost impossible to harvest, more so to actually scoop. Linus thought of all his nights as a child in Sweden, all his nights as a young boy here in New-York before he was an apprentice, all the nights he helped his mother light oil candles. He never dreamed that one day he'd be using the black soot that gathered within the lamp glass to make ink. Dipping his wooden scoop into the powder just released a black cloud of powder that got into his eyes, his nose and his throat. His face and blond hair were instantly covered with the soot: another telltale sign of a worker and not a writer. What a chore! He slammed the lid back down after gathering what he needed, releasing another puff of soot in a perfect circle which landed on the floor. Dumping the soot into a larger container, he closed the lid on it quickly to retain the sly substance and moved onto the containers of tree sap, linseed oil and a couple of other herbal concoctions that gave the ink longevity once placed on paper. Holding his nose, getting it all the dirtier in this very necessary process, he stirred the products together with the lampblack until it was thick and slimy. Until the nearly invisible lampblack completely folds in, Linus endures an endless sneezing fit. Finally, scooping a large lump of it into a thin tray, he takes a moment to enjoy another sip of his now cold, and even more sadly, lampblack-coated coffee.

"*Guten morgen*, Linus!" Zenger opened the front door, a pinky hue beginning to light up New-York just outside.

"*Guten morgen, Herr Zenger! Wie gehen Sie, Herr?*" Linus like the opportunity to speak German sometimes with Zenger.

Like the coffee, however, it was merely a morning ritual and that was it. Zenger was a child of war, Queen Anne's War, and was grateful to her and England for saving his family and thousands of other Germans from Louis XIV of France. He had been given the gift of safe passage to America out of war-torn Germany and Holland in the early 1700s, purely by her graces the way he saw it. He owed it to her, to England and to America to be as English and American as possible. Speaking English was the best way to honour her, even years after her death. So, he obliged Linus with a morning salutation in German, sometimes Swedish and that was it.

"*Es geht kalt, Linus. So kalt. Ein kaffee, bitte,*" he rubbed his arms to rid himself of the snow and cold and ordered a coffee from his apprentice.

Linus ran back outside to check on the fire pit. The snow had extinguished it and he lit it again and waited until the water boiled.

"Linus," Zenger asked as soon as Linus entered the shop with the coffee. "It smells like we've got plenty of ink. That's good. Are the ink beaters ready to go?"

"Yes, Mr. Zenger. I hung them out overnight. They are sitting by the tray of ink and ready to work," Linus pointed proudly to the inking area, all staged and ready for the day's actual printing to begin.

"Did you clean them last night?" Zenger asked as he closed his eyes and breathed in his coffee.

"Yes, Mr. Zenger," Linus made a face. He hated cleaning the ink beaters, really, really hated cleaning the ink beaters.

"Good job, Linus. I myself had to do it as an apprentice with Mr. Bradford. 'Tis a nasty chore, I agree."

Linus nodded enthusiastically. Cleaning the ink beaters was yet another sign of a worker bee. Why did he have to be fourteen? Why couldn't he be older, like twenty, and a notable writer? He didn't even need to be wealthy. He'd be just as happy being known as a writer and a scholar. Okay, maybe not as happy. He certainly wouldn't mind being successful. In all honesty though, especially when cleaning the ink beaters, he swore he would rather be a poor writer than a wealthy inker any day!

"What about the paper? Is it all moistened?" Zenger quizzed Linus as Zenger flipped through a journal on his desk holding all his appointments and duties for the day.

"No, sir. I hung all the pages last night before I went home," he pointed to the sheets and sheets of ecru pages hanging from every spare inch of rafters high above in the shop.

"I should like to have them moistened and ready to receive the ink by this afternoon. My journeymen are coming in soon to set all the type for the European reports," he continued to shuffle through more paperwork. "Then, this afternoon, I'm off to meet some gentlemen who are to provide me with some more common interest pieces that will make for great, uh, public enjoyment,"

Zenger smiled weirdly. "Pull down two sheets, spray them, then let's get a good start on the typesetting before Jack and Michael arrive. Two other gentlemen are bringing articles today at one o'clock. They are to be included in next week's issue, so I'd like to have the rest of this issue well underway, that way when we get their stories, they can be added with ease. Mr. Alexander is adamant about getting these issues out every Monday. "Tis called the *New-York Weekly Journal* for a reason, Linus. Business begins on Mondays and so do we.

For the next hour, Zenger and Linus worked side by side and spoke very little. Typesetting was a meticulous and tedious business. Each letter, space and punctuation mark had to be lined up with sticks into long, thin trays. Where Linus was still having difficulties was the mirror effect of printing. It was time-consuming enough to line up all the type pieces in order, but it all had to be set in the trays backwards! If he placed the pieces in to print "b-o-o-k" in just that order, the printed page would actually read "koob" and Herr Zenger reminded Linus over and over again that ink was not cheap and that mistakes like that could only be made very infrequently.

After cleaning the ink beaters and scooping the lampblack, trying to think backwards was the worst part of this job. Secretly though, Linus thought it would be hilarious to print an entire paper backwards. Only the wisest and the most riddle-minded folks would get the prank. His mother certainly would. She was probably the smartest person Linus had ever known, smarter than his father, that was for certain. Yes, a prank would indeed be fun. Punishment from Zenger and repayment of all materials would not be fun. Someday, he told himself, he would be able to write and print anything he wanted with no penalties whatsoever. Someday, he would be an adult and adults never got into trouble just for making pranks.

Later on, lunch was tasty and satisfying: steaming hot clam chowder and corn bread with fresh coffee. Linus loved lunchtime so much he ironically hated it, too. Especially in the winter, it was so comfy and warm and relaxing to sit and enjoy his soups and chowders, pretty standard fare at the local tavern in winter. Yet, as magnificent a feeling as it was, it was all the worse having to leave the warmth of the tavern and its huge fireplace and drudge back out into the snow and back to the shop. By the time he got back, he was always exhausted. He figured it was a combination of midday nap attacks and a full tummy. Like a well-fed puppy, a good lunch made him want to curl up by the fire and sleep. Today was going to be especially brutal, for Mr. James Alexander, Editor-in-Chief of the paper was coming by with Mr. Lewis Morris: both extremely important men about town.

Mr. Lewis Morris was a native New-Yorker, born to a family that owned swaths of land across New-York as well as New-Jersey. Besides being highly educated in the core disciplines of science, mathematics, languages, literature, history, art and so much more, he had also been the Chief Justice of the New-York Supreme Court. That was, of course, before Governor Cosby dismissed him for petty and personal reasons.

Amidst the cool breezes and blooming gardens during the spring of 1733, there came, finally, an outcome to the VanDam Salary Tryal of 1732: 2-3, in favour of Cosby. However, it needed to be 3-3, a unanimous vote of all three judges. Cosby thought by firing the two original judges he assumed would vote against him and replacing them with friends, he'd be free and clear to take VanDam's money. Simple as that. He never thought Lewis Morris, Esq., Chief Justice for over twenty years would vote against him. He did indeed vote against Governor Cosby and stated publicly in his decision that a royal governor should never use power and politics for personal gain. The other two judges, the replacements named Mr. James DeLancey, Esq. and Mr. Frederick Philipse, Esq. disagreed and remained on Cosby's good side.

Infuriated by Morris though, Cosby wrote him a letter in which he insulted and denounced Morris personally and professionally. He stated publicly that Morris was *unfitt to Judge in the King's causes*, that *his manners were impertinent* and that he could not depend on *his judgment nor integrity.* As it should have, this infuriated Morris. If there is one thing a gentleman and a businessman does not stand for, it is a false accusation. Not only did Morris write back a letter, but he gave it to Zenger to print and publish in a pamphlet along with Cosby's letter so that all of New-York could read it. After that, the game was on and it was to become ferocious.

That summer, Morris and his son, Lewis Morris, Jr., also a New-York politician of some influence, joined with Rip VanDam, Provincial Council member Cadwallader Colden, and an attorney for VanDam named William Smith, to found a new political party known as The Morrisites. Its goal? To send Governor William Cosby back to England. Of course, there was one other founding member of The Morrisites: a wealthy, educated, finely polished Scot named Mr. James Alexander, Esquire.

Mr. Alexander was also one of VanDam's attorney's in the now legendary *Cosby v. VanDam* salary tryal. Alexander was an aristocratic Scot whom had come to America back in 1715 after fleeing the wrath of King George I. Having been born with a strong sense of freedom, personal responsibility and basic logic, Alexander had led the Scottish opposition against British rule over Scotland and, all that having not gone very well, was forced to find a new home abroad or suffer very messy circumstances back home.

Not one to clean his wounds for long, having a strong educational background in law, philosophy and mathematics and having served in the British Royal Navy for a term before the Scottish uprising, he had no problem carving himself a new life in America and was today one of the most forceful, talented and successful lawyers in all of the New-York and New-Jersey colonies. All this and he was barely forty years old.

More importantly where Linus was concerned, he was the *Journal*'s Editor-in-Chief as well as head writer.

Sometimes, Linus thought about giving Mr. Alexander some of his short stories to read, but was always too nervous. Why would a man of that stature, accomplishment and wealth be interested in the musings and observations of a Swedish immigrant boy? In fact, Mr. Alexander was quite congenial and probably would have been happy to read some of Linus' work should he ever find the courage to approach him. For now, Linus just eavesdropped on conversations as he worked, sometimes slowing his movement in a task. Zenger would see this, have to stop his meeting and say, "Linus? Is everything alright over there?"

"Yes, Mr. Zenger. I. . .I. . .I guess I forgot something, or was. . .," he never could come up with a good fib and Zenger would just twist his mouth a little, raise an eyebrow and flick his hand in Linus' direction, telling him silently to get back to work and mind his own business.

Jennifer Susannah Devore

Then, he'd share a secret smile and quiet laugh with Mr. Alexander. They'd both been teenagers, too, and understood how very exciting the business meetings of adults could seem. If only they remained so interesting when one was actually an adult. What Linus wouldn't know for forty years would be that most businessmen would gladly trade their "important" lives for the carefree nature of a working youth.

"Linus? Do you have the coffee ready for Mr. Alexander and Mr. Morris?" Zenger asked, his polite way of telling Linus to shake off the lunchtime blues and get back to work.

Linus shook his head vigorously, forcing himself awake from his standing nap. "Yes, Herr Zenger. I am making it now."

"Linus, I have told you over and over that I am *Mister* Zenger. I am a New-Yorker, an American for over twenty years now. *Mister*, okay?" Zenger reprimanded as he carefully transferred the galley tray.

This was a shallow tray that would hold all the finished typesetting, all in correct, backwards order. The tray would then be carried to a large, marble slab where the typesetting could be ultimately blocked and wedged into place before going into the printing press and being inked.

"Yes, Mr. Zenger. I forget."

"That is because you are young and have known no hardship. You have not come from a wicked war in your lifetime or lived under the rule of cruel and absolute men. When you find a place such as New-York, such as America, you must thank the powers that be everyday that you are here, that you can call yourself a New-Yorker. Do you understand?"

Linus rolled his eyes a little and Zenger caught him.

"Go ahead and mock for now, lad. Just remember what I say. Someday, you will be happy to call yourself an American."

Linus thought Zenger was a nice man and admired him for being his own businessman and owning his own shop, but found all his New-York-this and America-that a little obsessive and weird. How different could life be for a fourteen-year old boy whether he was in Paris, Vienna, Stockholm, New-York or Dublin? Life had been good in Sweden and life was good here. People were people. Who cared where they came from? Linus snorted a little nose-laugh.

Adults. They were silly.

Suddenly, the front door burst open with a fury and a slam that made Linus jump. Mr. Lewis and Mr. Alexander came in together and had underestimated the wind's desire to hold the door as it opened. Linus ran to shut the door behind them, pushing against it with all his strength. Pulling the arm on the printing press had been helpful. He was getting stronger every week.

"Good morning, Mr. Morris. Good morning, Mr. Alexander," Linus greeted them from behind the door as he pushed.

"Good afternoon, Linus," Morris corrected him.

"Good afternoon, son," Alexander smiled at him.

"Yes. Good Afternoon, Sirs. I guess I am still a bit tired today. This weather mixed with a hearty lunch always makes. . ."

"Linus, if you could check the pages we printed this morning," Zenger interrupted Linus. "Make certain the printed half is completely dry so we can print the other side later tonight. Re-hang them on a higher rafter if need be. Then, collect all the loose type pieces and make sure they are all arranged correctly in their trays. We'll start typesetting these very special stories as soon as our meeting is finished. I don't wish to waste time looking for commas and b's and what-not. I'd like to finish all our printing before we go home tonight."

Zenger turned to his illustrious guests and began with basic chit-chat. Linus sighed quietly. He was already so tired, and not even because of the chowder and the cold. He'd been up since three this morning, working since four. He could tell he was going to be here well near midnight. With an obvious heave and rest of his shoulders, he walked to the type trays and began reorganizing the letters and punctuation marks. Everything was pretty much in order, but he always got his s's and f's mixed up, especially since even the type pieces were made backwards. Linus shuddered and rolled his neck. Just the thought of helping Mr. Zenger typeset an entire story backwards with backwards letters made him want to cry. Someday, he told himself. Someday he would write his own stories, forward, and give them to a printer and let someone else do all this work. Then, the world could read his work and he'd never have to have black hands again.

"Linus, please bring the coffeepot and two mugs for our guests,"

Zenger requested without looking up from a paper he was reading.

Zenger laughed and beamed as he took off his reading glasses, leaned back in his chair and looked at Morris and Alexander.

"Gentlemen, this is going to make headlines."

CHAPTER TEN
Philadelphia : December 1733

"Andrew!" Ben half-stood from his favourite chair at his favourtie corner table by the window in his favourite Philadelphia coffeehouse on Market Street: Monk's Nervosa Café. He gestured enthusiastically to his friend, Mr. Hamilton, who had just entered and was removing his tricorn from his head, shaking the cold, December rain off of it. "Come! Come! I've a goody! You must read this!"

Ben, dressed all in thick, drab, brown clothes, but with eyes that lit like sequins, rattled a news-paper high in his hand. "'Tis absolutely wild, my friend! Come, come!"

Ben had drawn some attention to himself and Mr. Hamilton. Some thirty years older and a silver-haired gentleman, Andrew Hamilton, Esquire was a sophisticate and highly placed in the professional as well as social communities. He smiled a quiet smile and nodded to those he passed on his way to the young Ben Franklin, an unspoken apology-for-all-the-ruckus delivered within each bow of the head.

"Good afternoon, Benjamin. What is the fluster, good friend?" Hamilton shook off his wet overcoat and hung it with his hat on a peg in the wall behind their table.

"This!" He thrust the large, two-sided news-paper at Hamilton by way of explanation, then pulled it back and prepared to read from it aloud. "It is the latest *New-York Weekly Journal* and it is all the talk in New-England!"

Ben leaned in toward Andrew, who silently ordered a coffee from Niles the tavernkeep and obliged Ben's excitement. Ben, looking around to check for eavesdroppers, commenced in a whisper, purely for dramatic effect.

"The *Weekly Journal*'s creative quarrel with Governor Cosby has given us another deliciously sly and fictive episode. Here, read! No, listen! No, read it!"

Ben thrust the large paper back and forth across the table, too excited to know whether to read it aloud or let Andrew read it himself.

"Why don't you read it to me? I cannot imagine deriving half the pleasure or the animation by doing so myself. Please," Andrew leaned back, crossed his burgundy velvet-clad legs, clasped his still-gloved hands on the top knee and bounced a chocolate-brown boot up and down as he awaited whatever it was that had his friend so amused.

"Okay, here it is. Hoo-hoo! It is really wild!" Ben could barely contain himself and Andrew nodded patiently, amused more so by Ben's excitement than anything. "Okay. I shan't read the whole thing, for it is quite long. I shall merely read you the first section.

> *A Monkey of the larger Sort, about four Foot high,*
> *has lately broke his Chain, and run into the Country.*

Ben's eyes left the page for a split-second to watch Andrew's response, then shot back to the paper.

> *There he has played many a Monkey Trick: Amongst*
> *the rest, he haveing by some Means or other got a Warr*
> *Saddle, Pistole and Sword, the Whimsical Creature fancied*
> *himself a General; and taking a Paper in his Paw he muttered*
> *over it, what the far greatest Part of the Company understood*
> *not: but others who thought themselves wiser pretended to*
> *understand him.*

Ben sat back in his chair, then leaned forward suddenly and bugged out his eyes at Andrew. "Well?! A monkey?! A monkey?! 'Tis too much!"

Andrew chuckled, though not nearly as entertained, but far more concerned than Ben.

"Do you not find this funny, my friend?" Ben was disappointed. "The monkey in question is clearly Governor Cosby!"

Ben then leaned in even closer, turning very private in his gossip, for he would never too loud in public; he was far too diplomatic and thinking for such obvious danger.

"Of late, he is known to have been heading to the country, play-dressing as a soldier and claiming land for himself and friends, those whom will only tolerate him so long as he buys them goodies and real estate. He brings gifts to the Iroquois Indians out there, too! All these gifts bought with money sent from London for the real soldiers' wages. He is the Monkey! Cosby the Monkey! The *Weekly Journal* is all but calling him a monkey outright. It pokes fun at his sycophantic followers, his awful, faux-friends whom just pretend to enjoy his company. 'Tis hilarious!"

"True, it is hilarious. Yet, I suppose I see it as more dangerous than humourous," Andrew thanked the tavernkeep as he dropped off a steaming cup of a Dutch-Senegal roast coffee. "Cosby is a wicked man and a vengeful one at that. What if he goes after the author of this article?"

"That is the beautiful element here. It is not an article. It is a 'paid advertisement' listed along with furniture ads and runaway slave reports. There is no author because it is an announcement. *A monkey has broke its chain and is loose*?! Genius, I tell you! Pure genius!"

Ben finally melted back into his chair and reached for his coffee, taking a long sniff, then a quick sip, then sat up quickly again.

"Besides, it is my inclination to believe that Cosby is too dense to understand the literary parallel."

"This may be true," Andrew conceded. "However, he is, ironically enough, smart enough to know he is a bit dense and, thus savvy enough, has put in place people around him who are indeed quick-witted enough to catch such a story's true meaning. Believe you me, someone will understand the literary parallel and as soon as they can they shall run to Cosby so he may also understand it."

Ben nodded gravely, then shook his head side to side with a laugh.

"Do you recall the 'Spaniel Story' last month?" Ben asked.

"I do. The *Weekly Journal* compared Francis Harison to a dog,"

Andrew removed his gloves and scarf, the fireplace's warmth finally thawing his chill.

"Ohhh, that was almost as funny!" Ben slapped the table, calling attention to himself again.

"If I recall, something akin to, '*A Five-Foot High Spaniel with a mouth full of Panegericks*' and how he '*dropt them in the New-York Gazette*'." Andrew laughed aloud at this one.

"Indeed! Excellent memory. Yes, yes. You know people whom know Harison. He is a Cosby supporter is he not?" Ben queried.

"We know some of the same men in law. He is an ardent supporter, very well-known for feeding Cosby-friendly stories to the *New-York Gazette*. Of course, being the official paper of the Crown in New-York, that does make sense."

"Still, if the *Gazette* can print stories in favour of Cosby, whether sanctioned by King George or not, certainly the *Journal* has the right to print fiction of its own," he winked on the word 'fiction'.

"The concept of a newspaper's 'right' is what worries me," Andrew confided in a hush. "You of all people should know what can come from tweaking the ire of colonial officials.

Ben shifted his lips to one side, inhaled loudly through his nose and nodded knowingly. Not only was Ben the owner, printer, publisher, main contributor and Editor-in-Chief of the *Pennsylvania Gazette*, his very own brother, James Franklin, was also a news-paper printer and had been arrested and gaoled a mere decade earlier for criticisms he wrote and published in his paper: *The New-England Courant*.

"How did we know it was *not* true?" Ben referenced the old article in question, taking the rare opportunity to back his older brother. "If you ask me, the Boston authorities *did* place too much interest and cost in their finery and garments. Perhaps, had they spent less time shopping and more time policing, the pyrate activity off our New-England coast might never have reached the levels of robbery and murder that it did."

"You may be correct. Probably are correct. However, it is the aftermath of that accusation that, as it pertains to the 'Monkey Story', matters. True or not, the Crown did not like your brother's theory and tossed him in gaol for it. I fear nothing has changed in the last ten years where such rights are concerned."

"True. Very true." A wicked smile crept across Ben's lips then. "I did have great fun running the *Courant* for that month back in '22, though."

Andrew snickered, then leaned his chair back and mimed a pouring motion to Niles and pointed to both his and Ben's mugs, thus ordering more Dutch-Senegal for the table.

"The point is," Andrew continued as his front chair legs made contact with the ground again, "if Harison is a dog and Cosby is a monkey, someone at the *New-York Weekly Journal* is bound to be caged sooner than later."

Andrew watched out the wide, paned windows as a new wave of rain pelted Philadelphia. Then, he looked Ben straight in the eyes and saw that the sequined glint had fueled from a genial flicker to an all-business flame that burned whenever a new idea was dawning.

CHAPTER ELEVEN

Ichabod was panting more heavily than usual. Of course, the weather was more disgusting than usual. Considering the deadly heat, Ichabod's latest grooming choice was worth the ridicule Dante had been throwing his way all day.

"You're barely half your normal size without all your fur! I'm like two of you!" Dante found Ichabod's new diminutive size quite funny. "I mean, you're not much larger than Savannah, really," he continued to laugh as he skipped backwards down Capitol Landing Road, addressing his two friends who walked with him out of town.

"Do vatch for that rock," Ichabod said quietly.

"What?" Dante asked as he tripped backwards over the rock in question in the middle of the road.

Savannah giggled. Dante just tipped back onto his tail and wasn't hurt. It served him right, though. He'd been needling Ichabod for days now and besides, what was wrong with being her size? Dante picked himself up, brushed the road dust off his linen knickers and could tell by the faces of his pals that the combination of the heat and his tired jokes was wearing on them. He tried to remedy it all with a weak, but appreciated attempt at a compliment.

"No, you do look nice, Ichabod. I mean, you look so clean-cut and your eyes really stand out without the mane," he smiled that smile he did with too many teeth showing when he was nervous.

"My dear Dante, I know I look nice. I alvays look nice. 'Tis not how vone vears vone's fur or vone's clothes, 'tis how vone carries voneself in vone's own body and I hafe alvays been fery comfortable in my own body: clean-cut or in full glory," Ichabod stopped in the road and posed for a moment as he caught his breath, his tongue hanging out, somehow even that was done with style.

"Why did we have to come down here? Why couldn't we just wait until Anthony brought your things to his store?" Dante implored as he watched a dragonfly buzz the group, his tail twitching instinctually at the prospect of a dragonfly snack.

"I know. I'm so sorry. I should never have dragged us out here today, but I was so excited yesterday when Anthony said his shipment was coming into port today," she watched the dragonfly with interest, then eyed Dante with a *Don't you dare!* -look. "It just sounded fun when we planned it last night. Breakfast followed by a walk to Queen Mary's Port? How did I know the temperature was going the shoot up like this overnight? It was lovely yesterday."

Dante let the dragonfly go along his way. "It's alright. At least we know autumn's not too far away. Just think about all those freezing, wintry days in February when we're wishing for the tiniest streak of sunshine to stretch out in. We'd give just about anything for a day like this."

All three stood there in the middle of the road for a minute. Savannah lowered her parasol and Dante and Ichabod took off their hats. They closed their eyes, turned their faces up toward the sun and let the warmth snuggle deep into their cheeks, all the while thinking about how good sunlight through a window pane felt in the chill of a winter's day. Then, it got really hot.

"Okay, zat is enough of zat," Ichabod replaced his hat and began the walk again. "If ve hurry, ve can get to ze port and back home before vone of those summer thunderstorms hit."

At the thought of that, all three continued down the road to meet Anthony. Ichabod looked at his pocket watch and noted they had made good time and should be at the main warehouse within ten minutes. By then, Anthony should have already picked up his shipments and be in the process of cataloging the products he would be storing at his Queen Mary's Port storage space until he had room for them in his shops.

It was a dear cost to store items, but he didn't believe in overstocking his shops. Too much stock behind the counters and stacked up against the walls and his customers might feel they were surplus shopping. Anthony had grown his merchant business from just one cart to two outdoor carts on Market

Jennifer Susannah Devore

Square and one real store on Duke of Gloucester Street because he had built not just shops, but a shopping experience for his guests. Silver tongs and ladles, attractive décor and window displays, fresh flowers on the counters, complimentary chocolates and always a bit of perfume spritzed inside the main store gave his customers a bit of luxury amidst a day of chores and errands. These subtleties had made Anthony's shops the first choice for many a shopper, even with somewhat higher prices.

This past year had been so successful in fact, he had hired three balladeers, one for each store. They were amiable and entertaining young men employed to strum their guitars and sing, softly of course, as his guests shopped. Anthony made it a habit to call his patrons "guests", never "customers". Balladeers were just the right touch, he thought. Music was a luxurious touch, but also relaxing. Anthony surmised that if his guests were more relaxed they might purchase more. That was the point of the chocolate, too. Of course, it was also to be kind; he really did like treating people well. Yet, he was also a businessman and what was wrong with giving guests the best experience possible while making a sale?

He had even heard of something intriguing about a store somewhere up north, a place owned by a Scandinavian family, a Nord-something: Nordstim? Nordskomme? Nordstross? He could never recall the exact name. Rumour had it though, they actually employed a harpsichordist to play for their guests. That, Anthony deemed, was high style. Someday, he would have a shop large enough to hire a harpsichordist to play indoors.

Anthony thought of his shops as extensions of his home and welcomed his guests, even if only to stop by and chat. Eventually, even the chatters would purchase something. Yes, Anthony was without a doubt a marvelous success story. From slave to wealthy merchant and still relatively young at that. Whilst there were still those whom reviled and loathed him for his skin colour, there were more who supported him and his businesses because they just liked him and his businesses. It was with those folks he concerned himself. The others could sail off to China for all he cared. He was simply Anthony and he was a gentleman merchant. No more, no less. He had healthy businesses and bank accounts and good friends. Life was good for him and he foresaw no change in any of the above. As Ichabod always said, "*Das ist das.*" That is that.

Ichabod tapped his walking stick on a warehouse door. Number seven. That was Anthony's storage unit. There was no answer.

"Maybe he's still unloading at the ship. You know they never keep exact schedules," Dante suggested.

Ichabod knocked once more, this time louder. Still no answer. Savannah tried the door latch, but it was locked.

"I think you're right. Let's go to the water," Savannah sighed at the thought of more walking.

The actual docks weren't far, just down the brick path. What it did mean though, was a walk back uphill to return to the warehouses.

Within fifteen minutes, they found Anthony who was loading a cart with barrels, crates and baskets full of everything from dried fruit, wooden cooking implements to tea and coffee. Plus, a small basket full of Savannah's whole reason for making the trek in the first place: art supplies.

"Oh, Anthony! How lovely! Look at these colours!"

Savannah marveled at her new collection of brushes, tubes of oil paint, boxes of pastel chalk and charcoal pencils. Best of all, it was all from Italy! Home to some of the planet's most talented artists ever: Botticelli, Canaletto, Carravaggio, Veronese, Bellotto, the list could on and on. It was a pricey little basket of goodies, but Savannah felt it was well worth the cost.

Savannah reached into her velvet, drawstring bag and pulled out a small pawful of coins and handed them to Anthony, who refused, looking around the docks.

"Let's wait and do this at the shop later. I don't trust some of the people around here," all three surveyed Queen Mary's Port.

Sure, there were plenty of people about and clearly money and products were changing hands everywhere. Nevertheless, it was better to be safe than sorry.

"Oh, I have one more thing for you, Miss Savannah," Anthony reached into a crate on his cart and procured a gold-trimmed, red leather box about the size of a child' violin case.

He kneeled down and set it on his knee for Savannah to get a closer look. She stretched up on her back legs and looked at it with her nose as well as her eyes which lit up as it dawned on her this was a gift.

"Is this a present? For me?!" she already knew the answer.

"Yes, dear. When I ordered your art supplies, the vendor told me you must absolutely have this in which to store it all," he opened the box slowly and exposed a royal blue, silk interior that melted over compartments of various size and length. "See, you can keep all your brushes here, your pastel box here, your tubes of oils here and whatever else you want to keep in here."

Savannah was stunned by Anthony's generosity. Well, maybe not stunned. People tended to give Savannah gifts and years of this brought her a certain sense of only the kindest and most humble expectation. Not that she ever really expected or demanded gifts; she truly, honestly appreciated the gestures. It was just that, in her head only and rarely voiced except to her closest friends, hoped for presents on many, non-traditional gift-giving occasions. This was one of them. A fancy shipment of art supplies from Italy? A great deal of money spent with Anthony? Maybe she did deserve a little something extra. Whatever the case, she was very touched and loved her new art box.

"Oh, Anthony! *Grazie tante*!! Thank you soooo much!! I shall organize it tonight. . .with a cup of my new jasmine green tea and pineapple cookies?" she asked expectantly if her other orders had arrived.

"Yes, Miss Savannah," he laughed as he brought out another, smaller basket filled with her comestibles and tea. "I hope you enjoy the tea. It's from a new supplier. A London company called Twinings."

"Are they new?" Ichabod titled his head, certain they were not, having enjoyed Twinings himself for years.

"New to me, Herr Ichabod," Anthony corrected himself. "They've actually been doing tea since I first came to Williamsburg. 1705, 1706? I have never been in the position to purchase their tea, though. They are a bit pricey and I was never sure if my guests would be willing to pay the higher costs."

Savannah smiled demurely as if she was somehow responsible for Anthony's success. "I always buy the expensive teas."

"I know you do and thank you. Because now, I am doing rather well. We shall see if the tea stays on the shelves or not," he looked back apprehensively at a very tall stack of crates marked in black, sprayed-on paint *Twining's - London.*

Savannah admired her treats, her art supplies and her gift. She then tucked them all tightly back into the two baskets. Dante and Anthony began setting them onto a wee, Dante-sized cart. Ichabod kind of helped by walking alongside them as they went to the cart, but not really ready to actually pick up anything. Ichabod kind of held his paws up as if ready to carry something, but nobody really expected to ask Ichabod to do any manual labor. He knew this, too, so felt pretty safe "offering". Savannah ran alongside, too, and stretched up on her toes to take three cookies out of one of the baskets before it was all tied down.

"Savannah, are you sure you won't just let me deliver this to your home? It is far too hot today to pull this," Anthony almost insisted.

"No, it shall be just fine. Amongst the three of us," then she looked at Ichabod who was blowing dust off his vest and paws, "well, between the two of us," she smiled at Dante, "it shall be no problem."

"I could have it at your door by tonight," Anthony tempted her again.

"No, that is the problem. I am far too excited and want to paint right away."

"Of course. Well, you go on and go slowly. Don't over tire yourselves," he admonished.

"Oh, ve shan't," Ichabod sighed. "Perhaps you could hafe me delivered to my door tonight?" he chuckled at his own joke.

Ichabod was hot and tired just standing there and was not looking forward to the walk back to Savannah's home, let alone the carriage ride back to his plantation home outside town.

"Stay at Mrs. Pritchen's tonight," Dante knew exactly what Ichabod was thinking.

"Excellent idea. Vhat are you serfing?"

"*I* am not serving anything. I do not know what Mrs. Pritchen is serving," Dante said with a slight quip.

"Of course. Vhat is *she* serfing?"

"I still do not know," Dante flicked his tail back and forth.

"Vell, it sounds lovely. Trafelling on a day like this is just torture," Ichabod glanced at the cart.

"Come. If we all pull it shan't take long at all," Savannah pleaded with her eyes for Ichabod to stop being so whiny.

"Yes, you are correct. If ve all vork together, ve shall be hafing Tvinings and treats in no time," Ichabod visualized himself lounging in Mrs. Pritchen's garden and snacking. "Alright, *das ist das*. That's that. *Kommen sie*. Ve go."

The three friends said goodbye to Anthony and worked diligently to get the cart going in the right direction. Anthony had already walked away, so they could not ask him for help. It was actually pretty comical. Ichabod and Savannah worked completely against each other: one pushing, one pulling, both their hearts into it. Dante stuck at the back trying to get the thing just facing the right way.

"Here. I'll do it," Dante moved up front, figuring they'd be there all day if these two dandies tried any harder.

"But, no, let us. . .," Savannah tried to insist, but Dante knew she was thrilled not to have to help.

Ichabod didn't insist at all. "Okay then," he said quickly and immediately began brushing off his paws and his sleeves.

Ichabod held Savannah's parasol for her whilst she donned her gloves; he tried to hold the parasol over Dante to shade him from the growing sunshine, but Dante shooed it away. He didn't need a parasol. Ichabod shrugged and held it over himself and Savannah as they walked.

As they started up the brick path, Dante readying himself by huffing and puffing in anticipation of a running burst up the small hill. Savannah and Ichabod heard it the puffing and it sounded like a bota bag being squeezed of its last bit of air. It sounded like wheezing.

"Dante, are you okay?" Savannah asked. "We're not even up the hill, yet."

"It's not me," he answered, still huffing and puffing.

"Well, what on earth. . .?" Savannah stopped in her tracks.

Right behind her someone stood wheezing, panting, barely able to speak and unable to even cough. It was Sterling Zanni diPadua.

His clothes were now shredded beyond recognition and his glorious red fur was wet, matted and dirty. His clogs, however, were still sturdy and dry, if not a really mucky red. His mouth was so dry it was flaked with white, dried mucus in the corners and on his lower lip. As soon as he caught their attention, he collapsed, a puff of dust exploding around him as he hit the ground.

"Goodness gracious!" Savannah squealed. "Help him! Dante! Go get Anthony! Ichabod! Help! He's not moving!"

Sterling laboriously raised a paw. "I. . .am okay," he struggled to emit each and every word. "Just. . . tired. Very. . .tired. Ran. . .from. . .Gloucester. . . to ferry. . .off ferry. . .to. . .here," his head dropped like a brick, then lifted again. "Water. . .please. . .water."

His head dropped again and Savannah motioned to Ichabod to give the fox his bota bag. Ichabod brought it to him and helped pour it into his mouth. Then, Savannah grabbed it and poured water all over Sterling's face, especially his lips.

"Thank you," Sterling's voice already sounded better, but he still lay face up on the ground. "Thank you. Please. . .may. . .I have. . .some. . .more?" he reached for the bag and this time drank of his own volition, no help.

Ichabod and Savannah just watched for a moment, unsure of what to do. He seemed okay, getting better with every drink, but they weren't sure. Maybe he was having a heat stroke or dying or something. Sterling coughed up most of what he just drank, but held up a paw right away. He could tell he'd really worried these three and wanted to reassure them he really was okay. What was with the poncy dog, though? He'd seen theatre flash before, but this guy was truly flash. He liked him right away.

"No, no. Really. I'm. . .okay now. Promise," he worked himself up into a sitting position, cross-legged in the middle of the road.

He threw his head back, coughed up a little more water, then shook his head vigorously, as if willing away all exhaustion. It didn't work and he slumped back down on the ground.

"Do you need us to fetch a physick?" Savannah worried.

"No, I just need rest, I think," Sterling said sleepily.

"I know just the place!" Savannah perked up just thinking about getting him settled into, where else but, Mrs. Prtichen's Tavern?

She smiled and looked up to see Anthony running down the path, pulling a full-size cart: much, much bigger than the tiny one he gave Dante and Savannah to use for her wee baskets. Dante was riding on the big cart, being thrashed around a bit with the few crates and baskets still left onboard. Anthony dropped the cart handles abruptly, toppling Dante on his back.

As Dante sat back up, then jumped off the cart, Anthony knelt down to look at the tired, little fox. Pulling a cool, linen hankie out of his pocket, Anthony dipped it in a pitcher he'd brought and wiped Sterling's face. He helped him sit up and gave him small amounts of water from the large pewter pitcher he grabbed from his stock, scooping it quickly through a water trough as he ran behind Dante. Anthony pet Sterling's head as he drank, then pet his back and tried to smooth out his vest and brush off the mud. A fine silk, Anthony noted to himself. Good Swedish clogs, he also noted. Savannah and Ichabod had noticed, too. His clothes were quality, but odd pieces and oddly put together. He certainly wasn't from Virginia. New-York, maybe? France? Italy? He looked very artsy, as if he came from a theatre district in some European capital. What was this funky fox doing running out of the woods of Williamsburg? Was something chasing him? All three friends must have had the same thought at the same time because they all looked back into the dark woods that bordered Queen Mary's Port. For as much activity and populace as the port held, the woods were a dark and different world just meters away. Anthony let Sterling sit up on his own and waited with everyone else for him to say something.

"Right then. Thanks, Mates," he still sat on the ground, too weak to move. "I'll be fine if I could just find a bed."

"Worry not," Savannah chirped. "We're going to take you right now to Mrs. Pritchen's. She's our friend and owns one of the finest taverns in Williamsburg. You'll be asleep in no time."

"Williamsburg? So the ferry pilot was wrong. He said I'd have another mile or two after the ferry drop. But I'm here? Brilliant, Mates, brilliant!" Sterling explained excitedly as he looked around and as Anthony lifted him off the ground. "Not a very big town, is it, Chap?" he asked Anthony.

Dante scurried to the cart Anthony had brought and began to shift around the baskets and crates.

"The pilot was right. The actual town is still a couple of miles that way," Anthony pointed up Capitol Landing Road.

Sterling slumped again, not happy. "Oh, Mate. That's right bad news."

"Put down that blue damask. He'll be more comfortable. Ooh, grab that red and gold pillow, too," Savannah pointed out some home décor amongst her new purchases for Dante to prepare. "Don't worry. We're going to take you the rest of the way."

Dante laid out the cloth and the pillows on the cart and Sterling smiled as Anthony picked him up and carried him. Sterling very much liked the makeshift bed Savannah had so quickly crafted. How lovely. It had been quite sometime since he'd slept on something so pleasant. It instantly reminded him of Venice. This little squirrel obviously had good taste. Anthony placed Sterling down gently on the cloth and pet his head again.

"You going to be okay, little one?" Anthony asked quietly, picking up his pitcher off the ground and offering Sterling another drink. He waved it away with a weak smile. Anthony insisted he keep it. "Don't you drink too much, too fast. You'll get ill."

"Thank you. Yes, I know," Sterling looked down at the ground with embarrassment at his little puke puddles of water. "I'm sure I'll be fine now, especially with these three. I'm quite certain."

Sterling had already begun to fall asleep and Ichabod, Savannah and Dante all positioned themselves so they could work together to pull the cart, all concepts of whining and worrying about dirty paws flew out the window when someone was in need.

"Oh, don't be ridiculous. You cannot even reach the ground," Anthony laughed as all three hung from the two handles, their tiny feet swinging in the air. "I shall pull the cart. You can't pull if you can't reach the ground. Hop on."

"No, it's okay. Betveen the three of us ve can," Ichabod insisted as his black shoes swung inches from the ground.

"Absolutely not," Anthony refused. "Dante, run back and tell my assistant Magda I'll be back in a bit."

Dante nodded and headed up the path. "I'll catch up with you!" he yelled back to the group as he left.

Anthony again told Ichabod and Savannah to hop on the cart and look after Sterling. Like two sparrows, they dropped from the handles, hit the ground, then hopped up on the cart in one jump. Anthony then went to the front of the cart, bent his knees, reached behind him, grabbed the wooden handles and pulled. The wheels began to crunch the bricks and oyster shells beneath them as Ichabod and Savannah held on so as not to be bumped off and onto the road. Savannah pet Sterling's head and he startled her as he awoke with a start.

"Oh, my satchel! I had a satchel! Where is it?! Oh no! Did I drop it along the way? Heavens no!" he struggled to sit up and stretched his neck to look for it.

"'Tis okay." Ichabod grabbed it. "A brown leather vone, yes?" he quizzed him.

"Yes, thank you," he dropped his head back down. "I've got to deliver it to the Raleigh Tavern."

"It vas under the cart. You must hafe dropped it as you fainted." Ichabod tossed it up into the cart.

"Oh! My goodness, I must find someone else here in Williamsburg!" Sterling screeched, too tired to speak or explain anything, but unable to leave his nagging concerns until after a cart nap. "I was sent to find someone here!"

"Calm down," Savannah said soothingly. "Calm down. We shall help you with that, too. Whatever you need. You just rest for now."

"No, I cannot! I promised a friend. I have to find a man named Romulus. His brother has sent me, a man named Remus. It is very personal and private, so that is all I can say until I find this Romulus person. I don't know his last name. Maybe you can help me? Do you know of anyone in town named Romulus? Anyone at all?"

Sterling's emotional and physical wreckage of late suddenly caught up with him and in the next instant he passed out with an airy *fouff* on Savannah's silk brocade pillow. Savannah's eyes all but bugged out at Sterling's words and she turned her head slowly, jaw slacked, and looked at Ichabod in amazement. Ichabod nodded slowly, then both turned to look at Anthony.

Anthony did not flinch, did not turn around, but continued his gaze on the horizon straight ahead. He did not blink and did not say a word the entire ride up Capitol Landing Road, to Duke of Gloucester Street, to Mrs. Pritchen's Tavern.

CHAPTER TWELVE

The tavern was completely silent. It was still early: too early for any of her guests to be up and even too early for Dante, who was usually up with the sun, like a chicken. No, it was still dark outside and Mrs. Pritchen's inner clock woke her just as it always had: up by four o'clock a.m., *ante-meridiem*. Now that she was getting older, in fact just plain elderly by most standards as she was now well into in her sixties, her clock was beginning to wake her well before four some mornings. This was one of those mornings. It was just after three a.m. and the silence was weirdly visible. Nothing moved, not shadows, not dust, not a vibration of any sort anywhere. It was the creepy, utter stillness that naturally, or preternaturally, comes with three in the morning.

Three o'clock in the morning was just a wrong time altogether. It was far past the late hours of those whom tumbled out of the pubs and down the roads to their homes; and it was well before the hours that belonged to even the earliest of the early birds, the ones who liked being the first on the road or first in the office. There was no remaining light from the previous day and hours to come before the light of the next. Some of the more superstitious folks believed three a.m. to be a witching hour: the exact opposite of three p.m. and somehow tied to a momentary opening of the spirit world's gates, thus allowing into our world as many ghosts and spirits as can squeeze in at that moment.

No, three a.m. was creepy and silent and for the most part, if you were up and on the street, not indoors, something was wrong. Who knew how many people there were like Mrs. Pritchen who enjoyed being up at three? Maybe lots. Still, none of them ever went anywhere. They just stayed inside, kept to themselves and listened to the silence they hoped wouldn't break.

This morning, the only sound was that of Mrs. Pritchen's considerable bum and all its cotton petticoats and overskirts shifting nervously on the long, wooden bench that stretched along one side of the long, pine table in her tavern kitchen. Each time she shifted, she'd place a different elbow on the table. Her eyes remained fixated on the worn, brown leather satchel sitting flat, and tied shut, on top of the table. It really was none of her business. She knew that. Really none of her business. She got up and portioned out some coffee grounds, Viennese and just enough to start brewing the small, personal pot she always made for herself when she woke. As long as she was up, she was up. Might as well be productive. She looked back at it, the satchel. It just sat there, mocking her, tempting her. It knew it was none of her business. It knew she knew, yet just sat there. Such a simple tie. It wasn't even a security system at all, just a simple string-leather bow. Actually, it looked kind of loose. She should probably go tie it tighter. That would be helpful of her. Sure. She'd be helping.

She placed the lid on the carafe, walked back to the table and confronted the bag. If it was really a secret, a bag full of secrets and privacy, it would have a lock of some kind, wouldn't it? Not just a tie. Oops. Darn it. That didn't tighten it. The bow sort of just slipped out altogether. Better get the bisquits ready.

She lifted the linen cloth that lay over a tray of bisquits which had been sitting out on a counter overnight, rising and now ready to place in the fireplace. The coals were hot enough by now and she moved the tray to an iron grate that sat high above the heat. Leaving the tray on the grate, she walked past the table again. Funny, it looked like some of the papers had fallen out, or were at least beginning to slide out. That table always did have a slight lean to it. The Raleigh Tavern. Big deal. Why should the Raleigh get to serve as an auxiliary post office and not her tavern? She could receive government items, too. That's what Ichabod had told her. These were "sensitive government papers and documents" that were eventually meant for Governor Gooch, just across Duke of Gloucester Street at the Governor's Palace. Why they had to go through the Raleigh first she was unsure. Obviously some sort of administrative task or brilliant record keeping feature of the local government. No wonder her taxes were so high. Officials were always making things far more difficult than necessary, adding superfluous steps just so lots of useless but titled people in redundant offices could feel better about their non-jobs: just give them a hefty salary, a lofty title and an unessential task and *Voila!* they were important. Besides, her tavern could serve just as well as the Raleigh as a postal stop. She might look into this a little more. She was a prominent businesswoman and should have more interaction with the town leaders. Maybe she could even get paid to do it.

She sat down again on the bench, sliding bit by bit toward the bag, her skirts and flounces rustling and filling the spooky stillness. The birds were still asleep out in the garden. Traditionally, the sudden silence of birds in the woods was an omen of something wicked, something evil headed that way. Mrs. Pritchen was a tough old gal, and generally enjoyed her quiet, pre-dawn, alone time; but, she wasn't sure how much she liked being this much quiet and aloneness in the pre-pre-dawn. Looking out a paned-glass window into the spooky, dark garden, she suddenly felt eyes upon her and, with a shudder that gave her goose bumps, she rushed to close the simple, linen curtain.

She then looked back at the leather bag and noticed there were a number of envelopes, but also various news-papers. Well, the envelopes were certain to be sealed; so, they would remain completely private. No matter what, she would be totally innocent of any prying into those. The news-papers, though. Those were different. News-papers weren't private. News-papers were for the people, right? News for the people by the people, or some such thing. She herself had advertised her tavern in news-papers all along the Eastern seaboard. The way she saw it, she had paid enough money to help support the news-paper industry, why shouldn't she be able to read these? With that justification, she quickly flipped open the bag's flap and pulled out a small stack of news-papers. She was right about the letters and other documents: all sealed with wax or tied with brown string. Oh well. There was still enough reading material to keep her mind off the witching hour.

She pulled from the stack a creamy-coloured, thick paper that was folded horizontally into thirds. She unfolded it to expose the front page. There were four, two-sided pages altogether: two actually, but they were creased down the middle and when opened like a book, made four pages. She set this paper aside, went to the counter and poured herself the first bit of brewed coffee. Without fail, she was always so anxious for that first sip of coffee that she would pour from the pot before there as even enough to fill her cup. It was extra strong and bitter at this stage and even though it was the same ritual every morning, she always acted surprised that the taste was so powerful. She then walked to the fireplace and grabbed two uncooked but warm bisquits, still stretchy and doughy, then slid onto the bench and shimmied those voluminous petticoats until she was comfy, as though shimming might burrow her bum a little nest in the wood. She set her blue, half-full, salt-glazed mug on the table and stuffed the entire, gooey bisquit in her mouth, holding it there as she snapped open the paper. The snap was louder than she imagined, as may well have been her conscience, as she whipped her head over her shoulder to look behind her, just a little aware that she was indeed technically snooping. She wasn't doing anything wrong. Right? Just to be safe, she stuffed the whole bisquit in her mouth and the pile of sealed letters and news-papers back into the satchel and closed the flap, keeping her chosen paper out, of course. She pushed the satchel way toward the other end of the table, establishing a clear physical separation between herself and the tempting vessel. Now then, back to her paper, her coffee and her bisquit. What, pray tell, what was going on in. . .where was this one from? She read the paper's nameplate:

The New-York Weekly JOURNAL
Containing the Freshest Advices, Foreign and Domestick
Munday May 6th, 1734.

"Hmm. 'Tis a few months old, but if I haven't read it, it's new to me. New-York City. Let us see what is happening with our friends up north," and Mrs. Pritchen pulled another barely cooked bisquit out of her apron pocket and ate most of it in one bite.

CHAPTER THIRTEEN

Although she was never happy to meet an animal in distress, Mrs. Pritchen was thrilled to have a new visitor, and a wee fox no less! Mrs. Pritchen had known a young fox friend named Bertram years and years ago in her Massachusetts days. Oh, she missed him terribly when he died near the turn of the Century. Though the pain was great when he left her, she had eventually found new friends.

When Dante, Savannah and Ichabod came into her life, she was more than happy to pull out all of Bertram's old dishes, utensils and furniture for them. But now, there was a new fox whom needed some help and there was a reason Mrs. Pritchen became a tavern owner and that was to help and host people and animals alike. When Savannah and the gang rolled that little fox into town, it was time for Mrs. Pritchen to step into action. She had made him up a room right away and the little fox fell asleep for the rest of the day and into the night. This morning, he would be greeted by a grand breakfast.

As the birds commenced their morning songs, Mrs. Pritchen went about prepping this breakfast. Of course, somehow all the bisquits she'd made earlier that morning were gone; so this morning she would serve bits of last night's baguettes. In fact, she thought that might actually make for a more Continental breakfast than plain, old bisquits. She could add a plate of cheese, maybe some nuts and seeds with yoghurt and honey. After all, he did look a little French or Italian or something. Being European, he would probably appreciate stale bread bits and seeds for breakfast.

She wasn't sure when, or even if, Sterling, that's what Ichabod and Savannah said his name was, would be coming down for breakfast. Nevertheless, Mrs. Pritchen set a lovely place at the table for him. Savannah and

Anthony were coming over for a late breakfast. Ichabod had stayed the night. Dante was out back gathering some fennel from the tavern's herb garden.

Mrs. Pritchen liked to sprinkle her potato dishes with fennel and she was preparing mushy peas n' potatoes for lunch, a recipe she'd learned from the wife of a visiting, London attorney one year. Mrs. Pritchen's DoG Street Tavern, as it was formally known, hosted some very impressive guests during Williamsburg's court times: General Court in April and October met at the Capitol and before 1710 was the only place to hear any type of case; by 1710 the Courts of Oyer and Terminer began meeting at the Capitol to hear felonious crimes and any other crimes punishable by loss of life or limb.

Mrs. Pritchen's name and reputation had been growing slowly, yet steadily since well before the days of Oyer and Terminer, in part due to simply having a fine establishment with fair prices, and in part due to advertising in any and all colonial news-papers: Virginia, Massachusetts Bay Colony, New-York, Delaware and beyond. She hosted some of the finest attorneys, politicians and royal visitors to come to the ever-distinguished and more and more fashionable Williamsburg. The more people who came to town, the more who stayed; the more people who stayed, the more money they spent. The more money they spent, the wealthier the town grew; the wealthier the town grew, the more influential it became and the more influential it became, the more people who came to town and so the cycle went on and on.

Some of Mrs. Pritchen's first guests were Ichabod, Savannah and William Byrd II of Westover. Mr. Byrd especially helped to give her establishment validation as a respectable and quality tavern; if he was okay staying there, who wouldn't be? Of course, Mrs. Pritchen did not only cater to the posh classes. She had given free room and board to her fair share of stragglers, waifs, destitute travellers and orphans.

A Miss Erin Tara O'Connor and her cousin, Master Connor Phillip O'Connor were certainly two of her favourites in memory. Though they were no waifs, she always believed their upbringing on the pyrated waters and ports of the Caribbean, being children of sea merchants, was a bit torrid. Still, she fell in love with both of them when they came to her, separately, after losing each other and their whole family in a great hurricane which left them stranded and orphaned in that autumn of 1718. They even had a friend with them she loved: a sea gull who called himself The Commodore. Funny bird he was. Loved crab meat in a crystal goblet and wore a red scarf with a French mariner's shirt.

Mrs. Pritchen wasn't sure, but she wondered if she had some sort of beacon over her tavern that silently summoned all the land's oddest, in the most likeable way to be sure, animals. However they came to her, she loved them all and this, in short, was why her tavern was so popular and so successful. She treated every guest, paying or not, wealthy or poor, noble or working-class, biped or quadruped, with equal dignity, respect and kindness. That was the mark of true breeding and etiquette, not like other trashy taverns who bowed and tripped over themselves to please the "important" guests and shoo away the "vagrants". After sixty long years, it was Mrs. Pritchen's experience that you could tell very little about someone by the way they looked. Be nice to everyone, she said. Besides, one never knew who was going to become somebody "important", regardless of their manner of dress or speech. Miss Erin Tara O'Connor and Master Connor Phillip O'Connor were a case in point.

They came to her in rags. Miss Tara was just fifteen years old and fresh off months of shipwreck and sea travel; Master Phillip was merely ten and himself straight off a pyrate ship and set to swing by the neck for the crimes of pyracy. Today, knowledge afforded by way of committed letter writing betwixt Miss Tara and Miss Savannah, Mrs. Pritchen knew them to be managing-owners of the successful O'Connor and Jameson Trading Enterprises of Dublin and London. They live respectable, non-pyrate lives, Mrs. Pritchen hoped non-pyrate, in Dublin with families of their own now. Miss Tara had even married a handsome seaman, a Captain Gareth Johnson Jameson of His Majesty's Royal Navy. Mrs. Pritchen heard that Tara had even attended Eton, disguised as a boy since girls were not allowed, before she agreed to marry Captain Jameson. She felt it was extremely important to earn an education before marriage. This was probably just a fabricated rumour, but Savannah swore the letters were true. She even had envelopes stamped with an Eton postmark to prove it. Mrs. Pritchen thought it all very silly. Dressing like a boy, not to mention getting away with it, for four years? Ridiculous. Then again, anyone who remembers Miss Erin Tara O'Connor could absolutely see this happening.

Much earlier, by five-thirty, most of the place had been up and moving. Her working guests had all eaten around six o'clock: two attorneys visiting from Baltimore; a young pewterer who was in town looking to open his own shop; a law clerk and final-year law student at the College who was also just starting an internship with an attorney in town; a physician's assistant trying to save enough money to attend medical school up at Harvard; and three first-year law students, boys from Delaware, getting ready to begin their first year of study at the College of William and Mary just down DoG Street.

Dante had eaten with the first group, then left to run some errands for Mrs. Pritchen. If she knew Dante, he'd also do a bit of fishing off his favourite bridge over Queen's Creek. He'd also most likely be back for the second round of breakfast and eat just as much as he did in the first. Fortuna only knew where that cat put all that food. He certainly was not a flabby tabby.

Ichabod was also sleeping late and Savannah and Anthony were expected to arrive for a late breakfast around nine. It was odd for Anthony to visit on a weekday morning, but Ichabod said Anthony told him he wanted to pay a personal visit to one of his best guests, just to see that Mrs. Pritchen was well and if her kitchen was in need of any supplies or stock. Personal attention to all his guests' accounts was just good business.

Around eight, she heard Ichabod and Sterling both moving about abovestairs. She heard the pitter-patter of their paws and nails on the floorboards above her, before they donned their shoes. She was very excited about chatting with this little fox. She planned to ask him all kinds of questions over breakfast and couldn't wait to surprise him with the special setting of Bertram's old dishes. Ichabod came down first, dressed in simple elegance and sophistication: lots of white lace and linen for a warm summer's day. He also sported a thinly crocheted shawl of sorts which he loved to flip over his shoulder.

"*Guten morgen, Frau Pritchen,*" he bowed slightly, then flipped the shawl over his left shoulder before taking his seat at the table.

"Good morrow to you, Ichabod. Did you sleep well? Are you happy you decided not to go all the way home last night?" she queried as she brought him a cup of the Viennese coffee.

"Indeed. Imagine how early I vould hafe had to vake in order to be back here this morning. *Nein, danke.* I need my beauty sleep. I do not function vell at all if I am shorted on my sleep," he took his first sip of coffee that day, closed his eyes as he swallowed it and a wee smile crept across his face. He gazed sideways at Mrs. Pritchen and quizzed, "This is Fiennese, *ja?*"

"Oh, yes, dear. Quite pricey, too," she boasted, her belly protruding as she lifted her chin and jutted her chest in pride.

"I can tell. It is vonderful. The Fiennese know their coffee. *Meine leibling kaffee,* my favourite," and he closed his opalescent black eyes and took another Nirvana-infused sip.

Ichabod and Mrs. Pritchen had about half an hour to chat before Savannah and Anthony arrived. It was nice to have a few moments alone with each other. Whilst they were certainly friends, they were sort of outskirt-friends: friends by way of other friends.

Sometimes, in most outskirt-relationships, it was awkward when the main friends, the ones that glued the whole group together, were absent and the outskirts were left to get along without any help, trying to fill those strained moments of silence. Of course, the more time outskirts could spend together, the less outskirt they remained. So even a half-hour could do wonders to help an already healthy friendship. That's what happened this morning.

Nothing big, no great secrets revealed, just good, comfortable chat with very little silence. They did talk about Governor Cosby and his troubles, the news she had read in the *New-York Weekly Journal* early that morning. Naturally, Ichabod knew well of all the unfolding events, the fights between Cosby and the news-paper. He also supremely enjoyed the recurring "Animal Stories" of the *Journal.* The one about the Spaniel he felt was particularly funny, and appropriate. He never did like Spaniels much. Big dogs. They were funny in a pathetic way.

Savannah and Anthony, both dressed impeccably in various pastel shades of linen and light silk, were eager to see Sterling this morning and everyone waited patiently by listening to Mrs. Prtichen read aloud the copy of the *Journal* she still had at the table.

"Listen to this," she said, snapping a wrinkle out of the paper. "It is an interview with a man calling himself a magician and able to foresee evil."

The letter 'C' has always proved unhappy, either to the government or governors themselves, or both.

Governor Coote, Governor Campbell, Governor Carteret of New-Jersey and Lord Cornbury of New-York.

All of whom were notoriously incompetent, corrupt or tyrannical.

Governor Cosby is a letter 'C' man. What has once been, may be again.

"Astonishing! Cosby must hafe vhipped somebody somevhere vhen that came out." Ichabod tossed back the last sips of his coffee and replaced the cup on the table for a refill.

"It is really unbelievable, what this Governor Cosby has done to his people. He has no respect for anything but the almighty pound and himself. He deserves such writing."

Savannah knew only a little about him, based mostly on what she'd heard from Ichabod and her old friend William Byrd, who happened to know quite a few business owners and men in the stock market up there, all Dutch friends from his days of business school in Amsterdam.

"The authors must be very brave. I could never write something so dangerous," she added as she sipped some green tea.

"I don't see a name on any of these stories," Mrs. Pritchen scanned the paper all over, looking for a name.

"Nobody knows who writes them," Ichabod said authoritatively. "They are purposely and alvays written anonymously, vith no name attributed. They know it is dangerous, plus, it keeps Cosby guessing and vithout the power to stop anybody from writing them."

"I have heard from Mr. Byrd that Cosby has become so enraged by the *Journal* that he has tried to have the printer arrested, twice! But it is not working, I guess. Maybe the New-York people are a far better lot than their governor. No one will admit the printer has done anything wrong, at least enough to go to gaol or tryal or something," Savannah relayed a bit of unsure information.

"It is called a jury indictment. They refuse to indict anyvone at the paper. A group of New-Yorkers, not gofernment officials, just citizens, are called together by Cosby to declare the printer should go to gaol for something specific," Ichabod explained as he nodded at his still-empty cup for Mrs. Pritchen to refill, whom smiled tightly, but set down her paper, got up and refilled it. "Tvice, this Governor Cosby has asked New-York citizens to indict the printer for printing material that makes him look bad. But nobody thinks there's enough efidence to prove the printer has done something wrong."

"'Tis ridiculous! Who cares if he looks bad or silly or stupid?!"

Dante burst into the kitchen through the back door, catching only this last comment, but always ready to argue any point against a royal governor.

"Who are you talking about?" he grabbed a baguette chunk from the counter and leapt into a chair as Mrs. Pritchen squinted at him.

"The governor of New-York. Governor Cosby," Savannah greeted him with a huge smile. "Good morning, Dante!"

"Morning, Savannah. Everyone. What about the governor? Who's making him look stupid? Who's getting indicted? What'd I miss?"

"Now, now, Dante," Mrs. Pritchen took the baguette from his paw and placed them on his plate. "We are just discussing something I read in a New-York news-paper. Nothing important at all. We are actually just waiting for young Sterling to come down stairs. We are not eating until everyone is at the table."

"Oh," Dante looked at the stairs. "Well, where is he? I am famished. I delivered all your pies to the other taverns. Mrs. Bettina asked if you could make more cherry next time. I guess her guests really liked it."

Mrs. Pritchen had started selling her pies over the last few years. She'd always gotten so many compliments on them from her own guests, she thought it might be a fun way to make extra money doing something she enjoyed doing anyway. As the season was going to change soon, she was already thinking about all the squash and pumpkins growing in her garden. They'd be ready to harvest soon and the town would be full of Mrs. Pritchen's famous pumpkin pies. Mmmm, pie sounded good to her right now. Maybe she'd make a pie today just for herself. Mmmm, pie.

Mrs. Pritchen served coffee and tea all around as everyone's thoughts left New-York and moved to various other topics as they waited for Sterling to descend. Savannah opted for a Japanese green tea that morning and asked sweetly for another cup. Feeling she'd had a little too much coffee lately, she'd switched to green tea for a while. It gave her a wee jump start, but never made her feel jittery like her espresso and she was sure today was going to be jittery enough on its own.

"Mr. Anthony, how did all your shipments come through from London? Did everything arrive as expected?" Mrs. Pritchen stirred a porcelain bowl of chilled, fruit and milk soup with a wooden spoon, breakfast's main dish for this second seating.

"It all came along fine, just fine. I had one crate of glass creamers from Naples drop, breaking every last piece; but, other than that everything arrived safe and sound and ready for sale," Anthony answered as he watched the stairs.

"Well, you take a look around and tell me if you think of anything I missed on that list I gave you. Hmm, maybe I shall just come into the store later today. It's been quite a while since I've taken myself shopping for fun. Certainly like to see all the new goodies from around the world. Maybe I'll ask Dante to take care of lunch and I'll make a day of it. I haven't been to the Peruke Maker's or Gadson's Garden Boutique in some time. Ooh, maybe I'll even pick up a new dress today at EthelLu's Dress Shop.

Maybe I'll even pay a visit to the Raleigh Tavern, say hello to my fellow tavernkeep and have a little lunch, a working lunch. Catch up on some tavern gossip, learn a little more about this post office business.

Yes, Dante, I shall ask you to watch the tavern today. It will be nice to get out and. . .," she prattled on and on for a while but nobody was really listening to her, just hearing her out-loud thoughts as background noise.

Dante grabbed the news-paper and read one of the "Animal Stories".

"Oh! That's hilarious! Spaniels *are* stupid!"

Ichabod pulled a small book out of his coat pocket and began reading as he savoured his coffee. Anthony and Savannah kept looking from each other to the stairs to the ceiling, listening to Sterling's clogs clunk up and down the hallways and in and out of his room.

Jennifer Susannah Devore

"Do you think Sterling will be down soon," Savannah whispered to Ichabod as Mrs. Pritchen continued talking to nobody and buzzing around the kitchen, now prepping lunch so Dante could take care of it.

Anthony just stared up the stairs. What did he mean he had to find a man named Romulus? Anthony slept horribly last night, wondering about this very question. What could this London fox know about someone named Romulus in Williamsburg? Anthony thought it all very suspicious and very worrisome. Oh, what was that fox doing up there? Come on already.

Clunk, chunk. Clunk, chunk. Clunk, chunk. Sterling's wooden-soled clogs on the wood steps announced his arrival well before the sight of him. Then, there he was. In all his soiled, rumpled yet clearly fine Italian garments. Mrs. Pritchen had done her best to brush the dust off everything and spot clean some of the mud patches; but without taking all his clothes and washing and mending them in an all day process, this was the best he was going to look. She had offered to do this for him and loan him some of Bertram's old pieces she kept around for sentimentalism, but he insisted on keeping his own clothes since he had so much to do today and figured the borrowed clothes would get dirty. He didn't know how long he'd be here or how he'd come across any money, so he didn't want to be responsible for someone else's precious things. His tail and his cheeks were brushed and washed clean and his teeth were as white as pearls. He looked good, he looked rested and everyone couldn't wait to talk with him.

"Good morning, young Sterling," Mrs. Pritchen approached him a little too energetically and Sterling backed up into the wall. "Would you like some chilled, strawberry and milk soup with a bit of baguette for breakfast?" her face was now directly in Sterling's. "I also have cheese and yoghurt if you like."

"Thank you, no. I haven't time," he slipped around her and grabbed his hat off the row of pegs by the front door. He then noticed, with grave disappointment, his satchel on the kitchen counter, open. Then, he saw Dante reading the paper, the news-paper with NEW-YORK in big letters across the front. His eyes went back and forth from the open satchel to the paper until he put it all together.

"Where did you get that paper? Do you subscribe to a New-York paper?" he demanded.

"What?" Dante looked over the paper in question.

"That news-paper you are reading. Where did you get it?"

"Right here on the table. Why?"

Dante's ears started to fold back. He did not like being accosted in his own home.

Sterling looked all around at every face in the room, but stopped on Mrs. Pritchen's. Hers was the guilty one. Silently, he bugged out his eyes at her, demanding an explanation.

"Oh, dear lad. I am sooooo sorry," she snatched the paper out of Dante's paws and began folding it up very nervously.

"Hey!" Dante whined. "I was right in the middle of a story."

"Sorry, dear. I'll give you some money later and you can run down to Mr. Parks and get a pamphlet or something later. I need this now."

She folded it as neatly as she could and stuffed it gently into the satchel, tied the leather ribbon and held it out in her hand, her arm extended and her teeth all showing in a very, very guilty grin.

"Again, I am sooo sorry, Sterling love."

He grabbed the satchel and threw it over his shoulder, shaking his head.

"'Tis just, I woke up extra early this morning and it was there and, well, I saw the paper sticking out a little and. . .,"

Sterling interrupted her.

"It was tied securely, a double-knot even," he parried.

"Uh, yes. Well, it must have slipped a little in all the commotion last night and, um, well, I. Well," she whined in a very high pitch. "It was a New-York paper and I just love knowing what's going on up there and, well, I didn't touch anything else. Promises!" She held up a hand in honour. "I didn't even hold a single piece of mail or wax-sealed parcels or anything. Just the paper. Promises!" she grinned wider and held her hand high and flat, hoping that would make her more believable.

The whole table now switched its attention to Sterling. His turn. Even though he'd really done nothing wrong, he could feel the disapproving glances of the table's patrons. His outburst was what the Venetians called *brutta figura*: bad form. She had hosted him in a desperate time of need, they all had. What did he do? He trounced down the stairs to a lovely breakfast and people politely waiting for him and first thing he snapped at and accused his host and hostess. *Molto brutta figura.* Sure he had cause, his nerves were raw and emotionally he was a total carriage wreck. But that was just wrong of him. All she did was read a news-paper. Poor lady. Stuck in Virginia, in this Williamsburg. Of course she wanted to know what was happening in New-York. Yelling at an old woman starving for culture? *Brutta, brutta figura*, Sterling.

"Oh, right then. Badly done. Do forgive me. Really. I do apologize," he bowed with great sincerity. "'Tis just that I've so much to tend to today, so very much. And this satchel. Well, you'd never believe what I've gone through to get this here. What I've gone through, period, in the last week. I've had just an awful journey. The satchel's made an awful journey, originally from New-York actually," he said tentatively as he quickly gathered all the evidence in his head about the New-York paper, where he found Samuel, how long Samuel had been riding, etcetera. "It holds vital documents for the royal governor here, I was told. Inter-colonial memos and such. Royal governor-to-royal governor type of things."

The table's glares had softened as they appreciated and understood the chaos surrounding such a small creature, except Anthony. Anthony wasn't exactly glaring, but he was so curious and anxious he could barely keep his queries to himself.

"Right then, first thing even, I've got to get this satchel to the Raleigh Tavern. I promise I shall be better company tonight. Well, I hope," he added.

His eyes glazed over as the magnitude of his tasks, especially the business of a dead Remus, came to the forefront of his mind.

"Right then, I am sorry. I know I've quite possibly made the worst first-impression in social history. But I've got to go. Really, very sorry. Dante?" he turned to Dante who still had a little attitude, but decided to let it go because, at heart, he was a good cat and realized Sterling was apparently all alone in this world, at least he was in Williamsburg; plus, he seemed kind of interesting and looked like he'd travelled a bit and Dante always liked meeting people who'd been outside of Williamsburg. "You told me the Raleigh is just down this main street here, yeah, Chap?"

"Yes. Straight down the road, Duke of Gloucester Street, or DoG Street as we call it. You'll see it on your left-hand side. It's a long building painted white. Black shutters, two chimneys," Dante reluctantly helped.

"Actually, there are three chimneys, if you include the kitchen," Savannah corrected Dante with a smile.

"Thank you, teacher," Dante smirked, then continued. "There hangs a large sign with a portrait of Sir Walter Raleigh on it. You cannot miss it."

"It sits just a few shops before Nicolson Store. If you see Nicolson's, you've passed the tavern," Savannah helped. "Would you like me to show you?"

"Yeah! I'll take you there! We'll both take you!" Dante could swap his attitude for kindness as quickly as he could swap Rome for Williamsburg: in a heartbeat.

"No. I mean, thank you, Mates. But, no. I cannot. I'll find it, yeah? I can be there in a dash. But, I will definitely need some help later," he quickly added in an attempt to mend this already fragile acquaintanceship. "It seems like a large town, not quite London, yeah? But I will need a tour guide. Later?" He smiled weakly, the gesture trying to be pleasant but consumed with concern.

"Yes, of course. You let us know when," Savannah felt sad, seeing through his weak smile. Poor little, stressed-out fox.

"There, there," Mrs. Pritchen could tell Sterling was concerned not only about his errands, but about being impolite. "You go do whatever it is you must do and I shall be here all day, waiting," she instantly cancelled her plans of a free day. "Whenever you return, I shall have a good meal and a soft bed ready for you. You will eat and nap and everything will be okay, " she kissed him on the forehead.

Sterling thought the gesture a little familiar, but very kind and already began thinking about that nap. He felt very bad about being so crusty toward her and refrained from apologizing again. After a while, too many apologies just sound fake. Right now, he was exhausted and he hadn't accomplished a single thing, yet. Hunger hadn't hit him at all. His stomach was so churned up with anxiety and sadness, he wondered when he'd ever be hungry again. Savannah could see all this in his black eyes and wanted to hug him. Anthony still looked disconcerted and Ichabod had that air about him that showed interest but the patience and confidence to wait until his involvement was necessary. Until then, this was all Sterling's business and he should be afforded the privacy he was clearly protecting. Dante just sat tall at the edge of his chair, ready to hop into action if anyone needed him.

"Right then, well done. I'm off," and with a final look at all the faces, he bolted out the front door, his red tail a mere streak on a mission shooting down DoG Street in the morning heat.

Savannah and Anthony exhaled loudly and then looked at Ichabod who just shrugged.

"He is a fery busy fox," Ichabod ate some baguette with uncustomary vigour, tilting his head to the right as he mashed it with his teeth. "Vhat? I am fery hungry and vaited qvite a vile to eat," he answered everyone's quizzical glances.

"Poor dear," Mrs. Pritchen began setting all the food down on the table, now that she knew there was no longer a reason to wait. "Well, he will be okay, I am sure of this. We just need to give him time to sort out everything."

"Do you know what?" Anthony suddenly interrupted. "I am so sorry, but I have to go to a, uh, a thing. Yes, it completely escaped my mind that I was supposed to go to a, uh, thing this morning. Over on, um, uh, Francis Street. Yes, Francis Street. Yes, I apologize, but I really must be going."

"But," Mrs. Pritchen stammered. "I have all this food. The soup, it's got milk in it. It will not keep much longer in this heat, I fear."

"Please, accept my apologies. We shall try this again next week. I must, I must go now," he bobbed up and down in his chair as if deciding whether or not to go, his face betrayed he really had no idea where he was going to go when he left.

"Very well. If you must. I understand business and business must always come first. I shall then sit and dine with Savannah and Ichabod to keep them company." She moved to sit in an empty seat.

"Um, actually," Savannah bit her bottom lip. "I forgot, I actually need to go with Anthony," she looked to Anthony with big eyes, to cover her story. "To the. . .thing. Right, Anthony?" She raised an eyebrow at him.

"Oh, me, too!" Dante added.

"Oh, yes. That is correct," Anthony covered. "The thing is supposed to involve Savannah and Dante heavily. Couldn't do the thing without them."

Ichabod just smirked and shook his head as he went back to his book. Mrs. Pritchen looked stunned.

"No, not you, Dante. I need you to run to Queen Mary's Port today."

"What?! All the way out there?! I was just there yesterday! Whyyyy?!"

"Stop whining. Because I ordered some herbal plants from a merchant in Spain and that just happens to be where they've docked."

Dante sighed, but decided to just get it out of the way and grabbed some more baguette as he darted out of the tavern, not looking forward to his big chore of the day.

"Dante! You don't have to go now!" she ran to the front door and yelled to Dante whom was already on the street. "Well, don't forget the cart then!" Mrs. Pritchen added.

Dante stopped in the street, heaved his shoulders with a visual sigh and ran back to the garden, taking the side path instead of back through the house. He emerged seconds later with a flat wheelbarrow of sorts and ran again, at a slower pace now, down DoG Street. He had thrown his fishing pole on the cart, too If he had to work, he'd be sure to play on the way back.

"All this food? What am I to do with all this food?" she complained to Anthony and Savannah as they jumbled into each other on the front porch, both donning hats and throwing bags over their shoulders.

"Let them go," Ichabod resolved from inside.

Mrs. Pritchen entered from the porch to listen, but still stood in the entryway, watching Savannah and Anthony.

"Ve shall enjoy a nice, qviet breakfast, " Ichabod continued. "Vhatever ve cannot eat and you cannot save, ve shall put out for the street animals," Ichabod said dismissively, without looking up from his book, of the larger, nude, unfashionable, cloven-hooved animals of Williamsburg.

It irritated him these animals had not learned the importance of walking as bipeds, up on two feet as opposed to down on all fours, or how to dress themselves. He had very little time for those whom chose not to better themselves, regardless of their situation. He certainly could be snippy when he chose.

"Oh fine. You two run along to your thing. And, Anthony? Will you come back for dinner later in the week?" Mrs. Pritchen pleaded.

"Absolutely. I promise," he yelled back toward the tavern.

"Sorry about all this," Savannah dashed back inside quickly to grab her parasol. "Need this! The sun is simply murderous out there today! *Ciao ciao*, Ichabod! *Ciao ciao*, Mrs. Pritchen!"

Savannah was out the door and running to catch up with Anthony as he darted down DoG Street after Sterling.

"*Ciao ciao*," Ichabod said to the air, again without looking up from his book.

Mrs. Pritchen set her hands on her very wide hips and looked around at the quiet room, finally resting her eyes on Ichabod.

"Well then, Master Ichabod. What has such a hold on your attention there? Shakespeare? Government minutes? Law books?" she inquired as she poured herself a fresh cup of coffee, then plopped her ample bottom onto the same bench where Ichabod sat, bouncing him up slightly.

He eyed her sideways in mild irritation at the bounce, his head still bent over his book.

"*Gullifer's Trafels*," he answered, still reading.

"*Gulliver's Travels*?" she was intrigued. "Isn't that a bit old?" she chuckled.

Ichabod regarded her sideways again, then turned his head toward her and set down his book, resigned to offer a retort to such a silly comment.

"Old does not eqval lacking in qvality or irrelefant. Moreofer, it is not yet a decade since first published and," he sighed a little, "if you must know, I am reading George Faulkner's new edition of *Gullifer's Trafels*, only released this year as Part III in a collection of all Jonathan Svift's vorks."

Mrs. Pritchen squinted and asked, "Why make a new version? What's wrong with the old one?"

"Because," he sighed again, "this vone is part of a collection and more interestingly, sheds some light, fia an introduction by Herr Faulkner, on changes made to the original 1726 fersion that Svift neither approfed nor supported:

politically astute changes made by his first publisher, Benjamin Motte, in order not to offend Qveen Anne and other powers-that-be. In fact," his tail wagged at this, "there is added to this fersion, a fictional letter Gullifer writes to cleferly expose his irritation at the censorship of his first release. It is *A Letter From Capt. Gullifer to His Cousin Sympson*. In a vord, Mrs. Pritchen, this fersion is newver." he nodded once and went back to his book.

Mrs. Pritchen shrugged and went back to the daily business of running her tavern. She took two pieces of the leftover baguette and shoved one completely in her mouth. She chewed it laboriously, swallowed with a difficult and audible *gulp* that made Ichabod wince, then pushed the other piece in her mouth and began the chewy process all over again.

She then pulled a blue dishcloth off a pewter bowl full of bread dough that had been rising overnight. She dumped the dough out of the bowl, onto a wooden board and began to pull and knead it into a state of elasticity. As she worked the dough, she turned her head back toward Ichabod and asked with a full mouth, "Who published this new one again? I forgot."

He winced again, this time at the pasty sound of her words bound by masticated, wet bread, took another sip of coffee, swallowed it, then turned a page and without turning his head answered her.

"George Faulkner, an Irishman."

"And who published the first one? The censored version?"

"Benjamin Motte."

"Good. Good. I think I'll go to Mr. Parks later today and get myself a copy of this new one. I'd like to read what an actual author thinks about censorship. Fascinating. Fascinating stuff."

She smacked moistly as she ate and spoke at the same time; Ichabod blocked it all out as he inserted himself deeper and deeper into the voyage to Lilliput of Captain Lemuel Gulliver.

Jennifer Susannah Devore

CHAPTER FOURTEEN

Savannah ran as fast as her wee, silk slippers would carry her. "Slipper" was actually the most apropos name for these particular shoes because her feet indeed kept slipping out of them. Pointy and tiny, the top part of the shoes were made of a rose, Shantung silk from China and just barely covered her toes. The rest of her foot was bare and supported by a small, pointy heel. The French called them mules; the British called them slippers. Whatever they were known as, Savannah called them a hindrance today as she did her best to keep up with Anthony. She'd never seen him run so fast; but, he was in turn doing his best to keep up with Sterling.

Sterling had fled Mrs. Pritchen's Tavern only moments before Savannah and Anthony, but was clearly a much faster runner. Being a fox, this made sense. Luckily, they knew exactly where he was headed and the Raleigh Tavern was not at all far down the road. Past a general store, a physick's office, three private homes and a silversmith they ran until they came to the Raleigh. It stood on the left-hand side of the road and beyond it, there in full-view at the end of DoG Street, stood the colony's Capitol Building.

The Raleigh Tavern stood majestically simple: a long, two-story, white clapboard building with black shutters and a black, front double-door. Leading to the door were four very plain stone steps. Above the door perched a simple, white, wooden pediment and on either side of this door hung two message boards: a public posting area for announcements, notes and advertisements of all kinds. On either side of these were three paned-glass windows. Atop it all rested a gray slate roof, inset with seven dormered windows and two red brick chimneys.

To the right side of the building was a small, white, picket fence. Its gate swung open inward to lead tavern workers down an oyster shell path. The path led ultimately to the Raleigh Tavern's kitchen. Unlike Mrs. Pritchen's tavern, the Raleigh kept its kitchen separate from the main building as fire prevention. Mrs. Pritchen knew this was smart; but, when she first started her tavern, it was just letting rooms in her private home. Even though she'd spent a great deal of money over the years upgrading and expanding her business, she never had built a whole new kitchen in the garden area as she should have. The bottom line was money. No matter how much she had, and in fact she had far more tucked away than anyone would ever imagine, the cost of constructing a whole new building was always just too much to swallow. Other business owners told her to "just use slave labour, Madam". This, she would never, ever do. A fair wage for a fair job. That was her belief and whilst slavery was a way of life for many in Williamsburg, in fact in all of the colonies from Massachusetts to Georgia to Spanish Florida, she did not believe in it and would not partake in it. Until she could bring herself to pay proper monies for a good outbuilding kitchen, she'd make do with an indoor kitchen and just be extremely careful.

Anthony and Savannah ran inside the Raleigh, slowing their pace and their breath as they entered the foyer. Immediately at the front door stretched a staircase that led to the abovestairs' rooms for rent. Savannah wriggled her nose. It smelled different from Mrs. Pritchen's Tavern. Her tavern smelled like roses and lavender and cinnamon. This place smelled like, well, men. It smelled of pipes, ale, burned meat and body odour. Of course, the Raleigh was far more populated than Mrs. Pritchen's and generally more successful. It was constantly filled to the brim with mostly male patrons. It was also a popular place for dining, even if one wasn't a guest. Mrs. Pritchen's kitchen tended to serve only guests. She also seemed to draw more women, families and young students whereas the Raleigh was a powerhouse meeting place for the biggest names in government, business and politics, even European royalty on occasion. Mrs. Pritchen had her share of VIPs and royalty, but not on a Raleigh scale. She was okay with this, mostly.

She ran a smaller, quieter, kinder, gentler, better-smelling tavern and she was well-known up and down the colonies. She had also owned and run her

Jennifer Susannah Devore

118

tavern herself since 1700, thereabout. The Raleigh didn't even come into play until 1717 and since then had already been through three owners and there were rumours it was about to change hands again.

No, aside from a desire to be a postal hub, she was proud of her standing in the community and felt very little competition with the Raliegh: just that perfect amount of healthy, business rivalry.

"Anthony, shall I see if he's abovestairs?" Savannah asked as she peered up the staircase, anxious to snoop.

"No. He should be right here. The mail slots are right here," he pointed to a built-in, pigeon-hole, wall cupboard, holding about twenty small holes and slots for various size packages and letters.

Savannah twisted her mouth a bit, disappointed she couldn't go up there and snoop without a good reason.

"You stay here. He's most likely in there, in the Apollo Room. I'll go check," he trailed off as he left the passageway and disappeared into a huge, blue-and-white room to the right.

Savannah peered around the corner into the room. It was much larger than Mrs. Pritchen's front room and chock full of gentlemen. Some were playing cards, one was playing the guitar and singing quietly, some were arguing rather vociferously. Probably about politics, she imagined. Her instinct was to hop inside and stay for a while. However, she was there on a mission and decided to stay put until Anthony returned. She watched him glide through the room and realized how very far Anthony had come in life.

From a slave, to a free-black, to a man with one wooden cart selling teas and coffees to a proper Williamsburg merchant and gentleman with three stores and more to come. It was rare a black man could stride freely through such a prestigious establishment. Naturally, Anthony received lots of resentment, from both sides. There were white gentlemen whom disliked him for his being black and there were blacks whom disliked him for being free and associating with the white, upper-classes. Long ago he learned to ignore all those whom gave him grief. As long as he had his freedom papers, well-worn from carrying them on his person for well over thirty years now, he held his head high in this town and associated only with those open-minded enough to choose character over skin-colour.

Savannah regarded Anthony with a combination of pride and melancholy as he wound through the crowd searching for Sterling. Then, she saw a flash of red. There was Sterling, standing on a wooden apple crate and talking to a man behind the tavern bar. He didn't look like the owner. Having spotted Sterling, Anthony stepped aside and took a seat at a small table by the window and waited.

"Oi! Where 'ave you been?! Do you know 'ow many peoples been buggin' me for their mail? Oi gots guvmint men comin' 'ere evry day askin' for mail! 'Oo are you anyway? Where's the usual boy?" the tavernkeep dragged the satchel over the bar.

"Right then, Chap. Terribly sorry. There was an awful accident. The boy who was carrying this, well, there was a thunderstorm one night, and, well, it seems his horse. . ." Sterling attempted to explain.

"Oi! Do you see 'ow many people oi've got to serve roight now?! Oi don't give a flip 'bout no bleedin' boy or 'is 'orse," he went back to pouring ale and coffee.

"Right. Okay then," Sterling was astounded that this man didn't care a whit about Samuel and Merlin. "You know, he said there are some vastly important documents in there. Governor papers. Something from New-York for the royal governor here. Gooch, I think his name is," Sterling helpfully added.

"Really? Is the royal guvnr named Gooch?" He laughed too hard and yelled to a tavern girl cleaning tables, "Oi! Girl! Stupid girl! 'Oo's the royal guvnr 'ere?"

She looked up blankly with a full tray of glass and earthenware vessels in one hand and a wet rag in the other, "Mmm," she thought for a second. "Gooch?"

"There! See, she knows 'oo 'e is and she's a bleedin' idiot. Now move along before Oi tell the fox 'unters there's a bleedin' fox in their midst."

Sterling looked hurt, really hurt. Why would this man say such a thing? Couldn't he tell by his clogs and his scarves he was a theatre fox? Couldn't he tell by his accent he was a fellow Londoner? Well, maybe not of the same caste, but definitely brothers-of-England. Wow. It seemed ignorance was rampant in all of His Majesty's domains. Hurt morphed very quickly and easily into confidence and pride.

"Are you havin' a laugh?! Is he havin' a laugh?" Sterling asked the crowd around the bar. "Right then, Chap. I need you to understand this. There are documents in that satchel headed directly from one governor to another. To your Governor Gooch. Sadly and astoundingly, it seems you are the official channel through which this correspondence must travel. Had I known this and had I not already handed over the satchel, I should have taken the documents to your governor myself."

The room was growing quiet as Sterling grew louder.

"Instead," he continued, "it is my intention to leave here and go directly to your governor's abode and notify his staff that there is a scoundrel of most offensive odours, not to mention grammar, holding vital papers from one of His Majesty's officials to another and that I highly suggest someone come here directly to procure this material before you soil it. Perhaps I shall recommend the governor himself come for it," Sterling bluffed, but with great believability. "Would you like a visit from the royal governor himself, good man. Hmm. Would you?"

The tavernkeep squirmed and spilled some ale on his foot, cursing aloud as he did so.

"I thought not. Now look me in the eye and repeat after me, using your best, King's English," Sterling stared deep into his eyes and bared all his teeth in a very scary smile. "Repeat: 'I will deliver the royal documents to the governor forthwith.' Let's go, Mate. Let me hear it."

"Oi, Oi," he stammered, "Oi will deliver the royal documents to the guvnr forfwif," he repeated mechanically.

"Close enough," Sterling hopped off the apple box and turned to his new audience. He loved an audience. "Right then, gentlemen. Back to your games. Back to your beer. Lovely town you've got here."

Sterling hitched up his breeches, lifted his pointy chin and clip-clopped out of the Apollo Room, in love with the sound his wooden clogs made on hardwood floors. He had been so sad when he started this morning and though he still had the worst part of the day to go, finding this Romulus person, his little confrontation actually brought back a bit of the old Sterling he hadn't felt in a while. He liked verbally embattling the mean and stupid of the world and, of course, he always loved an audience. He certainly didn't feel happy, but he did feel better. There was a buzzing murmur throughout the room as he strode out of the Apollo Room. He stopped abruptly as he approached the door, certain someone was following him. He whipped around so fast his tail enveloped his neck like a luxurious wrap as he did. There stood Anthony.

"Oh, hello!" Sterling shook his hand vigorously. "I forget the name. Sorry, but yesterday's a bit of a blur. I know the face well, though. I didn't get to thank you properly yet for bringing me to the nice lady's tavern yesterday. You were at breakfast this morning, yeah? Sorry about that, too. I wasn't much of a guest. I did mean to thank you later, though. It's Anthony, yeah? Yeah! Anthony! I knew I'd recall it!" Sterling started to walk out of the room, turning his head to talk as he did. "Nice place this, except the barkeep. What a wanker, yeah?"

"Um, yes, nice place. I wanted to talk with you for a moment," Anthony was so nervous and anxious he got right to business and dropped all formalities and niceties.

As they exited the Apollo Room Sterling turned to take another look at the place.

"My, what a busy place. Not quite like where we're staying? What is that?" he asked aloud, pointing to a phrase painted onto the wall over the doorway. "Wait, 'tis Latin. Oh, can I recall my Latin?" he asked himself. "*Hilaritas Sapientiae et Bonae Vitae Proles*" he spoke aloud. "Something, something, something. . .wisdom, something. . .the good life? Is that right? Anthony?" he looked back at Anthony.

"Actually, I believe it is something to the effect of 'Joy comes from wisdom and good living'. Something to that effect. You know, I really do think we need to chat," Anthony put a hand on Sterling's back to lead him out of the room and into the foyer.

"What? Right then. I really do have a busy day ahead of me. Oh! Greetings, fair lady!" he bowed deeply as he spied Savannah standing near the doorway. "So sorry about breakfast. I fear I was rather a boor this morning. I've got rather a bit on my mind these days."

Savannah curtsied a little, "Good morning again, Sterling. 'Tis alright. We know," she looked up at Anthony who was wringing his hands together.

"Could we maybe go outside to talk?" Anthony opened the door to expedite their exit.

"Yes, yes. Alright, Mr. Anthony."

They started out the door when Sterling stopped and said excitedly, "Oh, goodness. I meant to ask around in there. Seems like a good place to start."

"Ask around about what?" Savannah asked.

"I've got to find this Romulus Chap. An awful lot of people in there. Someone has got know him. Not your everyday name, yeah? Romulus? Italian, you know. Like me." he stated proudly.

"Actually, that is precisely what I wanted to chat with you about, Sterling," Anthony led him all the way outside and onto the front steps.

"Brilliant! You know of this man?"

Sterling was instantly excited, and sad. His chores could be over sooner than he thought, but the closer he came to this Romulus person, the sooner he'd have to relay the horrid news of his brothers death. Suddenly, the confidence he had felt only moments before was gone.

"Um, yes. I do know this man. Romulus." Anthony looked at Savannah, pleading silently for help, but what help he did not know. "I, I, well," Anthony looked self-conscious as two well-dressed men passed amongst the three of them and in through the front door. "Perhaps we should go elsewhere."

"Sure, Mate. Should we go back inside and get a table? Or, wait a minute, I want to find this governor Chap and tell him his documents are waiting here. Maybe we could walk and talk, yeah?"

"Of course. That would be fine, " Anthony conceded.

"You know, I know Governor Gooch personally," Savannah bragged just a touch, though not meaning to. "What I mean is I'd be more than happy to run over there and tell him about the satchel. He might prefer to send a courier to pick it up instead of waiting for its delivery. You two chat and I shall tend to this. Would that be okay, Sterling?"

"Thank you. Absolutely, dear," his smile dimmed a bit as his chore set in, but Savannah still saw all his teeth and it was just a little unnerving. "Again, so sorry about all that rubbish this morning. You'll be back for dinner, yeah?" he asked.

"I will. I shall see you later this evening then," she curtsied just a touch then turned to Anthony. "Anthony, why don't I meet you on the bridge behind Mr. Parks' Printing Shop in about an hour?"

"Yes, yes, of course," he answered absentmindedly, consumed with a silent barrage of questions in his head.

"Anthony? One hour? The printer's bridge? Is that enough time?" she confirmed.

"I think," he snapped out of his haze. "Yes, possibly. If I am not there, please do not wait. I shall find you later if need be. So, shall we walk?" he turned back to Sterling who was eyeing a bluebird.

To Savannah's horror, Sterling leapt at the bluebird, snapping those strong teeth, but intentionally away from the bird. "Right then, so sorry about that, Mate!" he cried as he came back to earth.

"Good heavens!" she shrieked.

"Sorry about that, dear. Bad habit I'm trying to break. Never caught one yet, though. Just the jumping is a problem. Not to worry," he smiled at her and shrugged at the bird who was flying off, shaking his wing in anger at Sterling.

"Sterling?" Anthony was done with the niceties and chit-chat. He needed to know what this fox knew about Romulus.

"Yes, let's away," Sterling bowed to Savannah and he and Anthony crossed in front of the Raleigh, then onto a small expanse of grass that grew in between the Raleigh and its neighbor, a private home.

They headed behind the Raleigh, toward Nicholson Street, a quieter, less-populated street that ran parallel to and behind DoG Street.

"Where are we headed?" Sterling inquired. "Are we going to this Romulus now?"

"Yes. But it must be done in private. We must have great privacy," Anthony replied in a monotonous tone as he led the way, speaking not a single word until they arrived at Anthony's destination.

Dragonflies, butterflies and bees buzzed all around them. Happily however, in the shade of the small, bamboo forest the day's heat was actually pleasant here.

"My goodness, it's so cool inside here," Sterling said, suddenly suspiciously eyeing the bamboo and Anthony. "Why exactly are we hiding in bamboo?"

"This is all very precious, very sensitive information we are speaking of," he explained.

"Is it, Mate?"

"Yes." Anthony sat on the ground, cross-legged and rested his hands in his head.

"Are you alright, Mate? This is about Romulus, yeah? You said you know of him, yeah? Is he, oh goodness. He's not. . ." Sterling assumed the worst.

"No. No, far from it. Romulus is not dead." Anthony looked up at the treetops and their silvery, long leaves. "Well, that's not completely true. He is dead, in a way."

Sterling's eyes transfixed on this Anthony fellow he'd only just met. Very odd, he was.

"What do you mean, 'in a way'?" Sterling squatted down, rested his elbows on his knees and awaited some remark. "What, Chap? What is it?"

Sterling couldn't take anymore bad news. All he had wanted to do a month ago was to escape his own predicament, find a nice place to settle, maybe find a new theatre troupe to join. Since then, he'd encountered way too much for a wee, London fox: he found a wounded boy and his horse in the Maryland woods; been entrusted with the journey of vital, inter-royal government correspondence; found a wounded, runaway slave by the river; befriended him then watched him die; been entrusted again with more letters and, this time, also with a secret; been accosted by a brusque and crude tavernkeep and now this, whatever this was.

"What? Please tell me. I cannot take anymore secrets. Please, just tell me. Where is Romulus? Is he dead, is he alive, what?"

Tears began to leak first from Anthony's right eye, then his left. He just stared at Sterling as his eyes wept.

"Romulus is alive. I. . .I am Romulus. How do you know of me?"

As Sterling told Anthony of Remus' tale, of his memories of their early childhood, of the last time he saw Anthony, of his joy over the recent receipt of Anthony's years of letters, Anthony just stared ahead. He had a sort of Zen thing going on as he watched a beetle crawl up and over mounds of fallen bamboo leaves. Up one side and down the other, silent crunches as his six legs wandered with purpose from the base of one chute to another.

Could this all be true? Why would anyone make this up? Of course it was true. It was remarkable. All this time, all these years. He never went to get his baby brother. Remus was only up in Maryland, he knew this.

The beetle found a small piece of something and gathered it up along his way and rolled it arduously with his front two legs.

Sterling told Anthony about Remus' vision of their mother and how she was waiting, holding places for them alongside a river in London. He told him about the purple his mother loved and the red that Remus loved. He told him about the red scarf he placed around Remus' hands and how very, very happy he was when he passed. He was free and so he was happy.

Over an hour later, Sterling was finished. He was wiping his snout and his face, tired and exhausted from crying. He was emotionally tortured from not only the recap, but from the sharp realization that Remus was indeed his friend and he was dead. He had been so engrossed with and dedicated to his journey that he'd barely allowed himself time to reflect upon the passing of this man whom had become his friend so briefly. Sterling had sobbed and sobbed but as he wiped his eyes with the end of a tattered, purple scarf he saw that Anthony, Romulus, had not reacted at all.

Strange. Maybe he didn't remember his brother well. Then, he remembered the letter packet. He'd been carrying them in a pocket in his breeches since Remus gave them to him. Tied with a simple string, maybe thirty thin envelopes were smashed into a block. Rain, blood, sweat, mud, time and natural oils from years of handling had compressed them into a musty, fragile hard-pressed brick of memories. Sterling handed them over to Anthony.

"He wanted you to have them back. He wanted you to know he was proud of you and that you were his inspiration. You were the reason he ran away, to be free, like you. He said if you were free, he could be free, too," he finished his tale.

Sterling was done. He was ready to pass out. Still exhausted from his journey, now exhausted from all this, all he could think about was Mrs. Pritchen's promise of a nap and a meal. He looked to Anthony and still saw nothing. No reaction, no sound, no nothing. What was wrong with him? Was he even listening? Was he that cold and unfeeling? What was going on?

"Mate? Antho. . .Romulus? You're understanding this, yeah? Did you hear me? You've got a long lost brother, and he's dead. He's gone. Do you get this, Chap?" Sterling grabbed Anthony's arm and shook him somewhat dramatically.

Anthony then dropped his head between his shoulders and wobbled it limply as Sterling shook him, as though he had no muscles in his neck. Almost imperceptibly, his body began to shake. His shoulders began to heave up and down, very slightly. Then, with a sudden and violent intake of breath he raised his shoulders, then his head toward the treetops and threw open his eyelids.

As his head came back down he looked deep into Sterling's eyes and Sterling saw Anthony's pupils expand and swim in their own juices. Nothing escaped his watertight corneas now. No drips, no tears, no leaks. It all just rested on the topside of his lower lids, billowing there like invisible pillows full of saltwater. He blinked not once but just poured his soul directly into Sterling's heart through his eyes. Then, with another sharp intake of thick summer air that gave him a brief choke and a cough, there amidst the beetles and the bamboo, Anthony wailed.

He wailed for Remus and he wailed for his mother. He wailed for her pain and the father he never knew. He wailed for the day he left Remus and for the years and lifetime of Remus' servitude. Mostly, he wailed for himself, for his own guilt. He could never re-read those letters. He didn't need to. He knew verbatim what they read. Every letter ended the same way.

Just hold on, baby brother. Romulus is coming to get you. Just a little more money in the bank and I can buy your freedom. Just a little longer. Someday soon, very soon, your big brother is coming to get you.

Someday had come and gone. Now, Remus had gone. Anthony dropped his head again, then lifted it again and wailed for *someday*. His chest was beginning to hurt, a lot. Exactly where his heart rested, he felt the first of what would be countless sharp pains. He knew nothing of the human body, had none of a physick's schooling, but he was certain his heart was physically breaking, actually cracking and tearing into bits. With each inward wheeze, he was sure he felt something snap, a muscle pull then break apart. The pain was nearly unbearable. He rolled over on his side and curled up in a ball, his body involuntarily using the fetal position to protect and cradle the body's most precious organ.

In his head, a montage of all the images he could muster of his mother and his brother came together. As he rocked back and forth, his wails turned silent and his heart shattered beneath his breastbone. Sterling just watched and waited, unsure of what to do. Should he go? Should he go get help? Should he find Savannah? Should he stay? He waited.

When Anthony's wails turned to sobs and he stopped rolling, when he finally lay still in the bamboo grove, Sterling approached Anthony carefully. He walked on all fours in a circle six times, an automatic and innate behaviour he never really understood, like jumping and snapping at birds. On the final circling he curled up next to Anthony's feet, planting his back paws and bringing his front paws around to complete the motion. He wrapped his huge, fluffy tail around his body, warm as the afternoon was, and slowly rested his pointy, black chin on Anthony's very fine, very expensive, Italian shoes.

CHAPTER SIXTEEN

The next morning, Savannah watched the early morning crowds meander down DoG Street. As quickly as a girl could switch her favourite dress, the weather changed in Williamsburg, not much, but there was a definite something going on in the air. It was still too warm for a coat of any kind and Savannah was sick to death of all her summer dresses; but, she had been able to start sneaking some fall colours into her wardrobe and tuck away her parasol, only to bring out her umbrella and keep it on the Japanese coat rack by her front door. As she watched the passers-by on their daily errands of shopping, meeting and working, she noticed they, too, had sought solace from the oppressive, summer heat in fall wardrobe tones.

She sat on the small, front porch of Anthony's shop, his third in town. At her side was an empty basket for whatever she may find to buy this morning. Chances were good she'd find something. Savannah loved having new purchases in her shopping basket, even if it was something as simple as a candle or a sheath of writing paper. She looked around at the building itself as she waited for Anthony, who seemed to be running late this morning. He was always open well before this many people were on the street.

Anthony had so much to be proud of these days. What a beautiful shop. It was a nice size: one large front room, a small storeroom and a smaller room which served as his office, just big enough for a secretary desk, a rather fine one made of mahogany and imported from England, a leather side chair and, on the floor next to the desk, a Canterbury, a slotted rack made of cherry wood that held folios, documents, files and other important papers that could be accessed easily.

The shop's exterior was clapboard and painted a lustrous chocolate brown, the shutters and second-floor dormer trim all a rich blue slate, almost grey. The windows were always impeccably shiny and clean, and his porch was eternally swept and capped off with a welcoming mat, a rather posh and, at one time expensive, Persian rug. It had become too thin and the colours too diffused to actually display in his home or his shop; but it looked great in front of his black, front door. He thought it just the right spin on a traditional welcome mat.

On this day, to Savannah's thrill she watched a golden leaf fall from somewhere above and flutter quietly and hopefully onto the rug. She marveled at how beautifully natural art could meld with man-made art. The gold shades of the leaf blended majestically with the muted reds, blues, browns and blacks of the worn rug. Plus, the fallen leaf brought the promise of the coming autumn and, better yet, Hallowe'en, All Hallow's Eve, her favourite holiday of the year!

She had, in fact, been thinking about hosting a small gathering, a masquerade ball for the Spirits' Eventide. Games, food, costumes. She still had well over a month to plan it. She would talk to Ichabod about it. Maybe he'd want to host it. His home was big enough, that was certain. Everybody could just spend the night there. Just as she started thinking on what kind of costume she might wear, she heard the crunch of oyster shells underfoot as Anthony approached his shop.

"Good Morning, Anthony! I'm so happy to see you! I've been waiting all morning to hear about your talk with Sterling yesterday. I waited at the bridge, but like you said, if after an hour you weren't there I should go. So I did. Actually, I waited just a little while and. . .," Savannah chirped non-stop as Anthony worked his key into the lock and entered the store, not acknowledging her at all.

She continued talking once they were inside and even hopped upon the counter as she jabbered on and on, seamlessly mingling questions about Sterling and ideas about her Hallowe'en party. Not once did Anthony respond, just carried a box into the storeroom, then walked into his office, Savannah still chirping away on the store's front counter. He grabbed a folio from the Canterbury and unlocked the desk flap of the secretary. He pulled the flap down and from the cabinet behind it pulled out a wooden, Spanish chest. He next unlocked the chest with a tiny key that was taped to the underside of a drawer in the secretary. He opened the chest, procured some coins and put them into a leather pouch which he tucked into the breast pocket of his purple velvet frock coat. Purple just felt right for today; he wasn't sure why, but something made him think purple. Savannah continued talking up front.

"So, when you didn't show, I figured perhaps Sterling and you had gone back to the Raleigh or. . ."

Anthony interrupted her. He walked into the front room, pulled a large shoulder bag out from under the counter, put the folio he'd taken from the office in it and set the bag on top of the counter. He looked Savannah straight in her eyes, his were bloodshot and puffed.

"He's dead, Miss Savannah. He's dead." He went back to putting some items, foodstuffs and root beer bottles, into his sack.

"What? Who? Sterling?! Oh no! Sterling's dead?!" she cried.

"No. Not Sterling. Remus, Miss Savannah. Remus is dead," he began packing faster.

"Your baby brother? The one up in Maryland?"

"Yes. They murdered him," he added a couple bags of dried oranges from a hanging basket.

"Who? Who murdered him, Anthony?" she scuttled up to him, her nose very close to his face as he stuffed the oranges in the bag.

"They did. His plantation. His master's overseers."

"I don't understand. Did they hang him? What?"

"Might as well have. They hunted him like a wild animal, Miss Savannah. Sterling found him exhausted and infected. They hunted him 'til he could run no more and he died of the fever."

"Sterling found him? Remus must have told him all about you, about Romulus, I mean. Goodness gracious. How horrible for, well, everyone," Savannah tried to give Anthony a tiny hug, but he stood up straight and closed his sack.

"I've got some business to tend to today, Miss Savannah. The shop shall remain closed until I get back. If you need anything, Magda can help you down at the docks."

"But, Anthony. Wait a minute! This is horrid. We must do something.

You must do something! We can go to Governor Gooch. Surely he can do something, arrest them or investigate or something! Ichabod has loads of connections! He can do something, I am certain of it! We can go to him right now!"

Anthony leaned down on the counter, eye-level with Savannah and spoke very slowly, very clearly. "Savannah, you are the only one who knows my history with Remus. You are the only one in the world besides Sterling now who knows I am Romulus. The *only* one in the world. This is beyond terrible for me and something I have to deal with. Alone."

Savannah opened her mouth to argue. Anthony shook his head.

"No, Miss Savannah. I implore you. Please, please, *please* do not make a public issue out of this. Do not make any issue out of this."

Again she tried to speak.

"No. I am serious, Savannah. Dead serious. I have worked too hard for too long to let this undo everything that I have done for the past forty years of my life. My silence does not speak to my love for my brother or my anguish, but it is mine and mine alone and there is nobody who can be punished for this except myself, and I shall see to that for the rest of my days. Remus was a slave, by the law, and ran away, against the law. There is nothing you or I or anyone can do about anything. Not Gooch, not even our dear Herr Ichabod."

Anthony drew a long, hollow breath, holding a burst of tears and sobs that were just waiting in his throat, but stifled it. Savannah looked deep into his eyes and saw his pleading, saw his immense pain. She saw his eyes were raw and red from, most likely, a full night of crying. She started to cry as well now and leaned into him for another attempted hug. Once more, he pulled back and slung his sack over his shoulder. He surveyed the shop to make sure the back door was locked and his office door closed.

"Now," he concluded as he ushered her toward the front door, very professional in his manner. "Today I am going across the York River, to Gloucester County. I am travelling with Sterling whom is gong to take me to the body of my dead brother. We are going to bury him and should be home by late tomorrow night. If there is an emergency with the store or the market stands, please inform Magda right away."

Savannah just stood on the porch and watched Anthony walk down the three steps and onto DoG Street.

"Are you sure you shall be okay?" she asked as she held back her tears, for if he wasn't going to cry, she wasn't going to either.

"Yes, Miss Savannah. I have always been okay," he replied with a curt bow and headed down the road, down to business. Another gold leaf tumbled to its end and landed next to Savannah as she watched her friend walk away.

As the morning wore on, Mother Nature must have felt Anthony's sorrow for the she was to be generous the entire day. The sky was still a bright blue, but the temperature had dropped a good twenty degrees from last week. Sterling and Anthony walked in silence as they approached Queen Mary's Port. Normally, Anthony would stop into his warehouse lot and check on business. Had anything new been delivered lately? Had all the proper deliveries been made? Was the area clean and rat-free? Not today, though. Today, he and Sterling were on a quest and they just kept right on walking.

"Mister An-tonny! Mister An-tonny!" Magda, a young woman of about twenty and of Dutch origin, yelled out to Anthony as they passed the area that housed his storage units.

Magda was in charge of all Anthony's warehouse activities. Generally, the docks were no place for a woman. Magda could care for herself very well, though. Of good Holland stock, she was very tall, nearly six feet. She was easily taller than Anthony, William Byrd, and most men she had met since her move to Williamsburg from Amsterdam last year. Besides the height, she was big. Not plump by any means, but big. Large shoulders framed a large body and long, strong legs. Chances were good she weighed as much as Mrs. Pritchen, but was taller by a foot and it was all muscle. Years of a life on the docks, first in Amsterdam, then some years down in Marseille, back to Amsterdam and now Williamsburg, had given her a steady weight and proportionate build.

In addition to all this, she carried very visibly on her belt an ivory-grip, Scottish pistol, her grandmother's. It could be assumed one didn't push Granny around much. Genetically speaking, only a fool would mess with Magda. She clearly channeled Granny. Her face and her smile always said *Welcome friend!*,

but the girth of her arms said *I could harm you, Sir!* On this morning, Anthony
kept walking, not hearing her.

"Mister An-tonny! Mister An-tonny!" she yelled once more.

Sterling heard her, but Anthony was in a daze. Sterling shook his sleeve
and motioned toward the girl.

"*Het hallo!* Mister An-tonny!" she ran over to him when she saw he
noticed her. "How are you today, Sir? Oh, *hallo!* I am Magda!" she cheerfully
thrust her hand and introduced herself to Sterling.

"Oh, hello, I am Sterling Zanni diPadua," he shook her hand, impressed
at what a strong handshake she had.

They both looked at Anthony who just sort of stared at the both of
them, then snapped out of it in an instant. Business was business.

"Yes, good morning, Magda. How is everything?"

"Excellent, Sir. I haf received for you dis morning a large shipment
of sugar from Barbados, some coffee from Kenya and some beautiful ceramics
from Japan. The sugar vas. . ."

Anthony interrupted her, "I trust you to take care of everything, Magda.
You are a good worker. I know you know what to do."

Magda looked a bit uncertain, but he was her boss and so she smiled
and said she would see to all the storage herself today.

"I am sorry to be abrupt, but Mr. Sterling and I have some business
today across the water and we must be getting to it. In fact, I see the ferry just
about ready to leave and we need to be on it. Sterling?" He motioned with an
open arm toward the road for Sterling to begin walking.

"Okay den, Mister An-tonny. I will take care of everyting while you are
away. *Tot ziens! Reis veilig!* Goodbye! Travel safely!"

Magda waved goodbye, but Anthony did not wave back, only took up a
sprint so they could catch the Queen's Creek-Gloucester Ferry. If they missed it,
it would be another four hours before the next one. Sterling waved as he ran.

"Right then! Lovely to meet you, dear!" he yelled back to the big,
Dutch girl with the sparkling green eyes and the friendly smile, her auburn hair
glistening in the bright sunshine.

Anthony and Sterling left the warehouse area of the port and headed directly to the docks. Their ferry would be about a quarter mile from the warehouses. To get to the ferry, they of course had to pass numbers of ships: some packing up and loading goods, like hogsheads of tobacco, tar and pitch, and casks of bad Virginia wine to send off to Europe and Great Britain; some recently landed and unloading cargo for sale here, everything from Chinese silks and Barbadian sugar to slaves. It was a Dutch slave ship, fresh off a slave-trading journey from the Congo that was unloading as Anthony and Sterling walked past. Sterling's eyes darted nervously from the ship to Anthony and back again. "Please," thought Sterling to himself, "let's just get past here, Mate. No troubles, yeah?"

Anthony's jaw had visibly tightened, his eyes had drawn shut to mere slivers and his steps had slowed. He slowly scanned the wretched scene before him. He saw crates and hogsheads of various commodities being stacked up on the docks at the same time the other cargo was set upon the docks: the slaves. In single file, a foreman led what looked like five-hundred men, women and children, some still infants in their mothers' arms, down a long gangplank to the docks. They all wore shackles around their ankles so they could move only in short shuffles. Attached to the shackles was a long chain that attached first to manacles, which bound the wrists together, then finally to a thick iron cuff around the neck. Their movements were restricted to nothing. The foreman and other ship's crew pulled the slaves by these chains and tossed them on the dock in the same manner as they tossed a crate of coffee. Except the coffee was treated a little better. Every once in a while, a crewman would yell out "Dead!" and a slave whom hadn't made the crossing alive, be it from the lake of diseased urine, vomit and fecal matter that festered down in the holds of the ship where they were kept, or from malnutrition over the three month journey, or from suicide and depression of the state of their new lives, would be tossed into a pile of others whom didn't make it, but hadn't yet been thrown overboard. The men, children, women, babies in this pile would be tossed overboard on the voyage back: no funeral, no last words, no dignity. Anthony thought of his baby brother and his jaw pulled tighter.

Sterling walked faster, trying to get them out of there before something bad happened. He saw Anthony's eyes lock on the foreman, whose eyes locked back on Anthony.

"Oi! There's a good one!" the foreman laughed to a fellow unloader and pointed at Anthony. "Mr. Blair would like 'im, don't you think?"

"No, 'e's too uppity. Mr. Blair don't like the uppity ones. Mr. Blair'd teach 'im a right lesson. Look at 'im, 'e thinks 'e's better than us!" They laughed together and some of the others joined in. "Nice coat, Fancy Boy! You think you're one of us?! Careful, you'll smudge black all over that frilly blouse a yers!"

They rolled and rolled in laughter at this slur and Anthony's hands instinctively clenched into tight fists. His teeth were beginning to hurt they were being ground so hard. Then, as had always served Anthony well in the past, logic conquered over emotion and his fists flattened out and they protectively covered his satchel with his most important papers. He unlocked eyes with the monster and continued down the docks to the ferry.

Sterling let out his breath, which he hadn't even realized he'd been holding through the entire engagement. It had been less than a minute, but seemed like hours. As he ran to catch up with Anthony whom had now really picked up his pace, Sterling looked back at a cluster of slaves whom had been instructed to sit and await further transport to auction, probably either up to the warehouses or into Williamsburg. He saw that many of them showed no emotion, not even fear. They merely clung to each other in a vast, group hug. Some children cried, some mothers wailed at the death of their children. Mostly though, they were stunned into silence and bullied into a fear that even the slightest movement could get them beaten or killed. Sterling dried his eyes with a scarf and felt a renewed sense of duty for what he and Anthony were off to do. He stopped feeling sorry for himself that his roamings had been interrupted by all these new tasks and chores. Remus deserved better than what all those poor souls would get. He would do this not just for Remus, but for all those he had just seen for all those he would never see, but would forever know suffered at the hands of slave traders and slave owners. He would do this for mankind.

They made the ferry and found two seats next to each other on the periauger's port side. The sailboat was small, but swift. Six other passengers joined the ride and for the next three hours, through the shallow, winding channels of Queen's Creek and a jerky crossing over the York River, most of the patrons sat in silence. Two men across from Sterling argued in a friendly manner about the Molasses Act.

"Please, my friend. It has been going on for two years now. No one is enforcing it. It's going to be repealed. It's got to!"

"Ridiculous! A tax on molasses? It's a gold mine for the Crown. No chance. If you ask me, they shall raise it from six pence a gallon to twelve in no time!"

"You're mad. It shall be gone by Christmas."

So the men bantered back and forth for most of the trip. Sterling tried to get Anthony involved, but Anthony just stared ahead, mesmerized by the motion of the water. The only sound Anthony heard that trip was the melancholy slapping of the York River up against the sturdy ferry.

Back in her plush home, surrounded by textiles and fabrics as richly hued as the coming autumn colours, Savannah sat at a secretary desk of her own. Doll-sized, but still of exquisite construct, it was one of the cherished pieces Mrs. Pritchen had given her years back, one of Bertram's pieces. Savannah sat on an arm chair, Irish pine with an upholstered, padded seat of English chintz: pink roses on a yellow and red background. The whole setup stood on a thick, wool rug of Tyrolean design: birds, wolves, cows, shepherds, mountains and pine trees woven into a winter's landscape.

In her paw, she held a feather quill of black. Outside, the leaves of her treehome on the campus of William and Mary were beginning their process of preparing for winter. The green colours were fading and the other colours, the reds, purples, browns and oranges were staring to take center-stage. An adventurous few had even taken the early plunge to the ground. They would not be around next spring to resume their greening. Some leaves passed her paned-glass window in the growing breeze of the afternoon. She didn't notice a single one. Oblivious to the world, she spewed words onto parchment, silently voicing her fury, her disbelief, her fear. The only sound to be heard that day in the usually fairy tale-atmosphere of Miss Savannah Prudence Squirrel's beautiful home was the frantic and unbroken scratching of her quill's nib on parchment.

A mere half-mile away, Mr. William Parks sat on a somewhat uncomfortable chair outside a sparsely decorated drawing room in the Governor's Palace. His hat in his hands, a brown tricorn, he waited with his elbows resting on his knees. Watching the goings-on that day, he could see it was a quiet day in the Palace. He saw only two servants pass by on the second-floor landing where he waited. Without acknowledgment, one passed him and headed down the large, wooden staircase to the first floor. She had been carrying what looked like bed linens; the other walked right past his chair and into the room behind him. He carried a single bottle of wine, then returned without it and closed the door tightly. He nodded at Parks and descended the staircase himself. In a moment, the thick double-doors opened inwards and there stood the Royal Lieutenant Governor William Gooch sporting a sincere smile and two outstretched hands.

"Good afternoon, Mr. Parks. Good afternoon," he shook Mr. Parks hand with both of his, very rare and intimate form for a gentleman of such station.

"Good afternoon, Governor. I trust I am not late?" Parks bowed as Gooch kept shaking his hand.

Parks now recalled why so many Virginians liked this governor. He was a remarkably fresh change from the likes of many a governor in the years past.

"Please, come inside. You are right on time. I only hope I did not keep you waiting, Mr. Parks," Gooch walked inside ahead of Parks.

A servant began to walk behind Parks, prepared to pour out tea and be on-hand for anything the governor might need. Gooch waved him off with a nod.

"We shall survive well enough on our own. Thank you, Cedric."

Cedric bowed and left the room.

Inside, Parks was surprised at the Spartan nature of the furnishings. It was his first time in this particular room. He had been summoned by governors before, he'd been in Williamsburg since 1726; but, it was usually belowstairs and once for a ball in the dining hall and ballroom. This room was pretty simple compared to those: an expansive Persian rug, probably expensive, too; a marble-topped serving table, full of mini cakes, fruit and a tea service; a Pembroke gaming table, slid closed to conceal a leather backgammon board; and, two arm chairs shaped in a retro, Greek style. That was it. Besides some wall sconces and a generous helping of luxurious, velvet draperies puddling with inches of excess fabric at the floor, that was it. Gooch sat in one of the Greek-inspired chairs and offered the other to Parks. The two Williams sat smiling awkwardly for a minute, then the governor-William leaned over and pulled a very worn, mud-stained, leather satchel from under his chair.

"Mr. Parks, I have recently received some very disturbing correspondence from a fellow royal-governor. New-York's Governor William Cosby. I should like to share it with you."

The weather may have been cooler, but half a day of walking and sailing brings on body heat nonetheless. Travelling overland now for a couple of hours, Anthony was too warm to wear his light coat and tied it around his waist as they walked. He neatly folded his vest and put that in his satchel, careful not to wrinkle the vital papers filed nicely in their portfolio. Sterling noticed the portfolio and his nosiness got the best of him.

"What's in the satchel, Mate?" Sterling lifted a brow, trying to be cheerful.

"Nothing," Anthony trudged straight ahead.

"Right. Sorry. Just wondering," Sterling kicked a rock and began to strum a quiet tune on his mandolin.

He had been unsure as to whether or not to bring it, but he figured music was always good company during travel. Music was also good company during times of great emotion. Happy times called for happy tunes, sad times for sad tunes. Something about the connection amongst the ears, the heart and the music magnified intense feelings. As this was to be an emotional day, the mandolin would ergo be necessary. Not that he wanted to magnify any sadness, it was just that music seemed to help people get through that sadness a little easier.

They walked along in silence for another ten minutes or so, then Anthony spoke.

"It's my papers."

"What?"

"My papers. My freedom papers."

"Freedom papers? You're a landowner, Mate, not some vagabond. You're an upright landowner, aren't you?"

Sterling looked at Anthony as they walked, uncertain of what else to say. So he said very little.

"That's awful, Mate. It's not right. Not right at all."

"I agree. Still, if I'm questioned by anyone whom chooses to harass me," he nodded in the general direction of the monster back at Queen Mary's Port, "and I don't have these," he patted his satchel, "I could very well end up on an auction block with those others."

"Surely your townsfolk would vouch for you."

"If they had the chance. But, a black man wandering around the woods of Gloucester? I might never make it back to Williamsburg. Authorities could have me up in Maryland or down in North Carolina by nightfall. That's why I don't leave town, ever."

"Never?" Sterling wondered.

"Very rarely. If I do, it's for business that requires me or my signature, something Magda can't do, and it's almost always by sea and never without these," he patted them again.

"It's inhuman, Mate. Man is a wicked beast sometimes. Running for your life is no way to live."

"You ever been on the run, Sterling?" Anthony was tired of talking about himself and was curious about Sterling's history.

Sterling said nothing, but picked up his step.

"We probably ought to get moving. Thunderstorms won't help our situation," he looked up at the sky which was turning its standard shade of four o'clock, summer grey.

"So, Romulus and Remus?" Sterling switched the subject. "Quite a legendary brotherhood, yeah? Are those your real names? Or, are they, well, slave names?"

Sterling knew it was common practice for owners to rename their slaves figures from literature and mythology. This demonstrated to dinner guests and visitors how well-read and -educated they were; if they could think of names like Caesar and Magnus, my, weren't they smart?

"They are not salves names," Anthony said curtly. "Our mother gave us our names," he held his chin proudly.

"Were you twins?" Sterling asked. "I mean, are you twins?"

"We are not. But, our mother liked the legend behind Remus and Romulus. She named me first, then him."

"Do you know the legend of Remus and Romulus?" Sterling wondered.

"I know a little. She told me when I was very young and I remember only bits and pieces. Remus and Romulus were brothers who founded the city of Rome. They were the grandsons of a king, and the sons of a god. They were tossed in a river at birth and found and raised by a wolf," Anthony recited the bare bones history with no enthusiasm and in a dead monotone, never looking anywhere except the dirt path ahead.

Sterling nodded, but said nothing. The basics were correct, mostly. Still, there were big chunks of the legend missing and being the thespian he was Sterling was having a hard time letting a great story just hang there with so many holes. He was also having a hard time not correcting Anthony, another bad habit of his. But, this wasn't the time for a Roman mythology lesson. Not the time at all. Still, it was a long walk and the silence was unbearable. He didn't blame Anthony, but Sterling was a lively soul and all this quiet was killing him. He couldn't stop himself.

"Actually, there's a bit more to the tale, yeah?" he smiled at Anthony, who just glanced at him out his peripheral vision.

"Really? Never very interested in the whole thing after mother died and I was ripped from my brother," he replied with a sting. "I only know what I was told as a child," Anthony slowed his pace and turned to Sterling.

None of this was Sterling's fault. In fact, Sterling had done far more than anyone would ever expect of a stranger. Anthony was being nasty to him and he knew it. If anything, he should be thanking him.

"I would like to know the real story, the whole legend, actually. Perhaps you can tell me on our way?" Anthony tried to repair his attitude.

"Right, Mate. I can do that!" Sterling's ears shot up, perhaps with too much enthusiasm considering what they were doing, but he was thrilled for the opportunity to have some interaction, something to break to uncomfortable tension.

They jumped a small creek and a series of felled trees as they left their path and began to trek through a dense forest. Anthony brought out the dried oranges as Sterling reënacted the legend of Rome's founding brothers.

"See, Mate, you've got the fundamentals down right brilliantly. Remus and Romulus were brothers, twins. And their grandfather was a king, King of Alba. Their father was a god, that's true, too. He was not just any god, though. He was Mars, god of war!" Sterling ran up ahead of Anthony and on 'god of war' jumped up and landed with his feet spread wide and his hands on his hips.

Anthony half-smiled, admitting to himself that was kind of funny.

"God of war, yeah? Very nice. Their mum was a priestess named Silvia and because of that, being a priestess and all, they weren't allowed to marry, yeah?"

Sterling walked alongside Anthony again, but scooting sideways like a crab to keep eye-contact with him.

"Right then, so since they couldn't marry, they certainly couldn't have children. So, as soon as they were born, they were put into a basket and set afloat down the River Tiber. Like skipping stones or something. Just dreadful, Mate. Little babies floating down a river."

Sterling picked up a rock and tossed it into a nearby stream.

"So then what happened," Anthony was finally interested.

"So then, Mate, they were discovered by a wolf, a she-wolf and being a mum, she took pity on them and brought them back to her den to raise them. She fed them her milk with the rest of her puppies, and a woodpecker friend of hers brought them food. It was a lovely existence, for a while."

"Why? What happened next?" Anthony started walking sideways, too.

"Well, one day whilst the wolf-mum was hunting, a shepherd found the twins and took them back to his house, where he and his wife raised them into adulthood."

"That doesn't sound so bad," Anthony said quizzically.

"Sure, unless you're the wolf-mum. They say during a full-moon in

Rome, you can still hear her howling, crying for her babies who were taken away from her."

"Oh, I suppose that is sad," Anthony turned straight ahead again.

"Well, after they were adults, they decided their first task as men was going to be to place their grandfather back on the throne of Alba."

"Had he been displaced at some point?" Anthony turned sideways again.

"Absolutely, Mate! I forgot that part? Sorry about that. Yeah, granddad got kicked off the throne by his own brother."

"Really?"

"Really. So the twins got revenge by killing their granddad's brother and putting granddad back as king. Granddad was so thankful, he told the boys they could establish their own town anywhere they wanted."

"Is that Rome?" Anthony tripped on a root as he walked like a crab, too.

"Hold on, Mate." Sterling re-slung his mandolin over his shoulder, annoyed it kept bouncing to the front. "So, they agreed to found a city on the Tiber where the wolf-mum's den had been, as an homage to her for saving them."

"That's nice, real nice."

"Yeah, plus there were vultures circling the area and I guess that's a good omen."

"Vultures are a good sign?"

"I suppose. Legend says Remus first saw six of them and said that was a good sign, then Romulus saw twelve, which is even better," Sterling shrugged. "I don't rightly see it, Mate. I hate vultures."

They both shuddered at the thought of vultures and their necessary, but nasty existence.

"Anyway," Sterling continued, "they were building the town one day and Romulus was building the city walls and Remus laughed at him, said they were too short and would never protect them, and. . ." Sterling suddenly stopped and scratched behind an ear.

"And? And what?"

"Uh, nothing, Mate. That's it. Remus laughed, Romulus laughed, everybody had a great time and the city was built and they took a cappuccino break. The end."

Sterling pulled his mandolin around front and began to play a lively tune. Anthony eyed him curiously.

"No, that's not the end. You're leaving something out. What? What's the real ending?"

"Really, Mate. No other ending, that's it. Espresso and a fantastic town for all, yeah? Great shoes there, have you been? You must go someday." Sterling continued to play.

"Sterling, I want to know. Finish the story or we're staying here until you do," Anthony planted his feet.

"Right then," Sterling sighed and threw the mandolin over his back. "See, it's not a very pretty ending."

"What story does have a happy ending?" Anthony held up the shovel he'd been carrying for seven hours.

"Right. Well, when Remus laughed, he also jumped over the wall to prove to Romulus they were badly built. Maybe Romulus had some insecurity issues or something, but when Remus jumped back over and laughed some more. . .uh. . ."

"Yes?"

"Well, Romulus killed Remus and then buried him there in the new city he called Roma, after himself. The end."

"I see," Anthony said plainly. "Hmm, not a pretty ending at all."

"No. Sorry about that, Mate. I guess I kind of got caught up in the legend and wasn't paying much attention to the, well, finale."

There really wasn't much to say after that. The brief fun of the afternoon ended very abruptly and Sterling felt awful about it. Why couldn't he ever just let things like that go? Why did he always have to prove to everyone how well-read he was? How cultured he was? Boy, what a mess. From then on out, the day was just as horrible as it had started. The next few hours only got worse.

Anthony stood dumbfounded. He was dazed from not just the past twenty-four hours, filled with enough information and emotion to flip his world upside-down, but also just from the journey getting here. An hour or more walk to the ferry, three hours of motion sickness on the York River to Gloucester and almost four more hours of trudging east along the banks of the York had rendered him physically worthless. Worst of all, he now stood over a mound of leaves which served as the temporary grave which embraced his baby brother. The sight was something for which he'd been preparing ever since Sterling first told him where the body lay.

The plan had been to retrieve the body and give him a proper burial in Williamsburg. In the end, after seeing the body and its state of decomposition, not unexpected in the moist and warm climate this time of year, Sterling and Anthony decided it better to give Remus a simple burial right where he lay. In Anthony's deepest and most selfish thoughts, barely audible even in his own head, he agreed with his inner voice that there would be no questions in Gloucester, unlike a Williamsburg burial. Oh, he would have buried him in Williamsburg of course, if necessary. Still, as with many times in his life, it was best for a man of Anthony's position and background to just keep quiet and not call much attention.

There was nothing to say as they dug. Sterling tried a couple of standard "At least he's free now." and "He seemed peaceful when he died." varieties of consolation, but Anthony never answered. Rather early on, Sterling gave up on the chit-chat attempts and the two just dug in painful and very tense silence. They decided to move Remus up from the river banks, fearful that storms could erode the banks over the years and his remains would end up in the river.

Instead, they covered Remus with oak tree branches, thankfully still flush with summer's greenery, and dragged him gingerly over a mile inland and rested him on a lovely spot beneath a huge magnolia tree. There was no discussion, just an understanding of what needed to be done. No specific spot was chosen for the grave. Anthony merely began digging and Sterling helped.

Anthony mindlessly dug one side of the grave with the small shovel he'd brought. Anthony wasn't a labourer. He never had been. Even as a slave he'd been a house slave. This task was difficult all the way around. But, each time he felt a rush of tears or a burst of memory come on, he threw that pain into his labour and buried it in the soil as he dug deeper and harder. He tried to forget he was digging his baby brothers grave; he tried to pretend he was just digging a hole. Every few moments, Sterling could hear Anthony breathe in a loud, angry and constricted breath through his nostrils. The whole incident broke Sterling's heart, but he knew if Anthony could keep it together, so must he.

Sterling dug out the other end, his front paws excavating the earth at a much faster pace than Anthony's shovel. Eventually, he nudged Anthony aside and finished the entire grave for him. Within an hour, it was done. There in front of them lay a hole in the ground: about six feet long, maybe three feet wide, hopefully about five feet deep. Overhead, black vultures, six of them, circled the field. Sterling and Anthony looked at each other in silence.

The vultures had been circling the body for days and, disturbingly, had attacked it already to some degree. Fortunately, Anthony and Sterling made it back when they did. Much longer and there may have been no body to bury. Anthony just glared up at the vultures and they seemed to feel the heat of his rage. They dispersed and flew off to investigate the smell of something much smaller and furrier that was about to die on the other side of the river.

Anthony stood and stared without a single blink for at least ten minutes. Sterling stood next to him, his head down a bit, but looking at Anthony every once in a while to garner what was going to happen next. Sterling was starting to worry about the time. It was becoming clear they'd be spending the night under the stars. He was kind of hoping to be back at Mrs. Pritchen's tonight. Truthfully, he knew they never could have made that good of time and he was feeling really guilty about being tired of this whole event; but he'd made promises now to both Remus and Romulus, or Anthony, he wasn't sure what to call him now. How had he ended up doing all this?

He had only recently shed most of his own drama, his own horrid dilemma. He had been heading south looking for a lovely climate and perhaps some quiet town with a theatre troupe. A little acting, a couple of new friends, some summer lounging in a pretty garden. Throwing off the authorities. Not this.

Within a month he'd met a boy and his horse and had no clue as to if they were alive or dead. He'd nevertheless ended up having to lug the boy's government satchel down the coast; he'd then met a runaway slave, liked him right away, then watched him die; then met a poncy dog, a frilly squirrel, a cat with an attitude, a snoopy old woman and a wealthy ex-slave with an alias and then had to tell this ex-slave that his brother was dead; now he'd had to bring the brother back to this Gloucester place and help him bury his little brother. It was really all too much for a wee fox from London.

Ahhh. . .London. He thought about how nice it would be to wander aimlessly along the Thames today, running into old mates and tipping his hat at the lovely ladies. But no, he was in Virginia. Of course, this squirrel and her friends all appeared to be good folk. Perhaps, after he got back to Mrs. Pritchen's and ate and slept for a few days, things would look better and he might actually enjoy their company. For now, everything and everyone just seemed like a chore. Now, the dirtiest chore of all was beginning. Amidst Sterling's selfish, inner rant, Anthony had begun dragging Remus' body closer to the grave. Sterling snapped out of his self-pity and grabbed Remus' ankles. The summer heat really had not helped this situation.

The smell was something awful and both of them choked back dry vomit as the only sounds to be heard were the scraping of the body over ground and the moisture of the leaves that had been the body's mattress for the last few days. The moving of the body was also the cause of great distress to countless insects.

Nearby, the same rabbit and mice who had watched Remus perish, and who had kept watch over the body as best they could until Sterling returned, now stood under the magnolia tree, watching sadly. As Sterling and Anthony dug, the rabbit and mice ran back to their homes quickly to change for the funeral. All were now dressed in shades of black and navy and all the girls had teensy, black hankies of which they were already making good use.

With one final push, Anthony and Sterling rolled the body into the grave where it landed with a profoundly melancholic *thud*. Anthony stood over the grave and peered into it for only a moment. The rolling and dragging and pushing of the body did not leave things very pretty and this was not how he chose to remember his brother. Without a word, he went back to the dirt they'd displaced and began to shovel it back into the hole with great madness and horror. Sterling watched him in fear for a second.

Anthony's eyes were a brilliant white and protruded unnaturally from his face as he shoveled. Sterling could see his jawbone grate back and forth as his teeth ground over each other; his eyebrows knitted tightly, leaving two deep creases between his brows. He looked like an actor Sterling once knew, well-known for his stage portrayals of the Devil. Sterling was frightened right into working, for he jumped on top of his pile of dirt and began kicking it through his back legs with his front paws, first covering the mottled body, not allowing himself to cry when he saw the red, silk scarf finally covered completely with one flick of soil. Eventually, the grave was filled.

Sterling grabbed Anthony's shovel. This was easy enough to do for now Anthony was essentially a zombie. The anger was purged as the hole was filled and now he just stood numb. With the back of the shovel, Sterling patted the mound of soil that topped off the grave. He packed it flat, whacking the dirt over and over until it was barely noticeable there was a grave at all. He gnawed some magnolia branches off with his very sharp teeth and lay them over the grave. He looked to Anthony and waited for him to say something, to do something. Nothing.

Sterling figured something should be done to finalize the whole event and so he pulled something from his person and lay it on top of the magnolia leaves: an Irish linen handkerchief. He tucked a corner into the fork of a branch, to be sure the wind didn't take it away. He bowed his head for a bit and thought some pleasant thoughts about Remus being in London right now, lounging on the Thames with his mother, both donning their glorious red and purple silks. It made him smile. Then, he looked up at Anthony. Or, rather, down at Anthony.

Anthony had collapsed and now lay as he had two mornings ago in the bamboo grove along Nicholson Street. He didn't rock, he didn't move, he just lay curled up and hugging his knees. He made no sound, but his mouth stretched wide open in a single, silent scream of heartache. It never closed. His eyes scrunched tightly shut, but his mouth never changed and never uttered even a squeak. Sterling lay down as well, once again doing the only thing he thought might help. He curled up next to Anthony and rested his chin on Anthony's very muddy boots. Under a giant, waxen, magnolia leaf stood the little rabbit and her

Jennifer Susannah Devore

mouse friends. Once again, she covered them with her ears and once again they cried.

CHAPTER SEVENTEEN

A

Public Response
to an Injustice
in the
Court of Humanity

A letter of public opinion concerning
cruelties against one African gentleman from Maryland
and written by
Miss Savannah Prudence Squirrel of Williamsburg,
previously of London

Addressed to Mr. William Parks,
official printer of Williamsburg

Gentlemen, Ladies and Others,

Most recently I am newly learned of a great tragedy and miscarriage of justice in the natural courts of humanity. There has been of late the death of a good and kind man known only to us by the name of Remus.

Remus was murdered as he died from the fever, brought on by his many wounds sustained as he was hunted in cold blood, like a fox by the hounds, pursued for capture by his wicked slave owner and master whom would see him mauled, maimed or dead altogether before giving him his freedom.

Unfortunately, not only does our fair colony have no laws against such man-slaughter, but it does offer laws and assistance to the slave owners, monsters, whom would catch and retain their "property": a runaway slave. Remus was property only in the heinous, legal sense of the word. He was not, however, in nature's eyes a possession of another human being. Humans must not own other humans.

The laws that led directly to the death of Remus are unfair, unjust, unkind and inhumane. I call upon all decent-minded lawmakers, Burgesses, Council Members, attorneys, royal notables and colonial individuals alike to rise up and help to affect change in all legislature regarding human ownership. Repeal the Black Codes! Make Amends to the Africans you Stole!

With Restrained Fury and Garnered Dignity,
Miss Savannah Prudence Squirrel
of Williamsburg, formerly of London

"Safannah! You cannot print this!" Ichabod set it down on her secretary desk.

Dante grabbed it off the desk and began reading, his eyes growing wider and wider as he did.

"Savannah! It is perfect! Speak out and change can happen!" Dante twitched his tail in excitement. "Do you not care about slaves, Ichabod?" Dante's ears stood up just a bit.

"But of course I do. Do you see any slafes at my estate? Efer since Monsieur LeVau vent back to Paris, he took his slaves vith him and vhat have I done?" Ichabod resented Dante's remark. "I hafe employed indentured serfants and full-paid labourers. I hafe stuck to efery agreement for the indentured servants, seven years work for their passage here from abroad, then they are free. My paid labour get fery fair vages and I go vell oferboard at the holidays vith bonuses, time off and presents. Please, do not qvestion my hatred of slafery."

Ichabod was seriously offended and walked to Savannah's window that overlooked the school.

"You are right. I am sorry, Ichabod," Dante offered a paw.

"It is okay. I know you did not mean this," Ichabod shook Dante's paw and took a seat again.

"It was your letter, Savannah! It got me so riled up! Really angry! That is good! You want readers to feel that way," Dante re-read the letter.

"No vone shall read it," Ichabod persisted.

Dante and Savannah both looked at him and awaited a continuation.

Ichabod sighed and said, "Look. Efer since Bacon's Rebellion back in the 1620s the local gofernments hafe been fery vorried about rebellion."

"Rebellion? I am not advocating rebellion, merely a closer look at the laws," Savannah whined.

"It is not vhat you mean," Ichabod said, "but vhat the authorities vill read into it. Look at Dante. In the eyes of the Crown, opposition will be viewed as sedition."

She did and he grinned; she rolled her eyes.

"He is exactly vhat they are afraid of. A refolution on the steps of efery gofernor's house up and down the American coastline."

"Oh please," Savannah laughed. "Dante is no ruffian. That is what they're worried about probably, ruffians and mountain people whom don't understand how to deal with government through the proper channels."

"First, Miss Safannah, mountain people have their own gofernment and are not automatically ruffians. . .I think.

Second, Bacon's Rebellion vas led by Firginia noblemen. *Sir* Francis Bacon? He efen burned down his own uncle's home as he led a rage of terror through Jamestown, burning it all to the ground. Vhat they are concerned about is vhat the late Royal Gofernor, Sir Villiam Berkeley said."

"What? What did he say? I've heard of him, but not much. I only know he was not exactly upstanding or fair," Dante sat up straight, always eager for a bit of knowledge about the officials.

"Vhat he said vas, and I am paraphrasing here, that he thanked God for no printing and no schools because they could only bring disobedience and heresy and libels against their rulers."

"Libels? As in writing unflattering, untrue stories about them in newspapers?" Savannah clarified.

"Exactly," Ichabod sipped his Chai tea.

"Oh, gracious, Ichabod," Savannah giggled and smacked Ichabod's shoulder with her hand fan, a wooden piece from Japan. "But our Governor Gooch is nothing like that. He may well be one of the only Virginia governors ever to actually care about us as people, not just property of the Crown. He would never think something so stupid. I know for a fact he has even asked his Council to pass laws that help with our trade and commerce, something that helps everybody's livelihood."

Savannah stood by the window and fanned herself. It was still pretty warm these days.

"As a matter of fact, I know that Anthony has even spoken to him at the Governor's Palace. He was *invited* there by Gooch to congratulate him on his third shop, being an ex-slave and a fine example to the community and such."

"I do not disagree," Ichabod stood. "I know Governor Gooch vell. He is a good man, a fery good man. But this goes much further than Gooch. He has people to answer to, *his* royal governor back in London. Gooch is merely lieutenant governor. Not only does he have to answer to Royal Governor VanKeppel, but he has to answer to King George, too."

Ichabod pushed in his chair, as did Dante and set his tea cup and saucer on the breakfast table. He walked to the front door and opened it, waiting like a gentleman for Savannah to exit first.

"No, it is too much," he continued. "I applaud your social conscience and if I could do something to help publish it, I vould. Yet, efen I cannot pull those strings. They are strings vhich vould efentually strangle us all."

Savannah took a plaid umbrella out of its rack, tucked her paper in a folio and tucked that under her arm. She then looked around to be sure she hadn't left any candles lighted. She pulled on some pink gingham, cotton gloves and waited for Dante whom was checking the angle of his hat in her foyer mirror.

"Are we all ready?" she asked his reflection.

"Yes. Off we go," he skipped through the door before Savannah and nodded a thank you at Ichabod, whom in turn offered a sarcastic "Of course."

"Well, we shall see if he will print this," Savannah nodded a thank you at Ichabod as she passed through the doorway. "We shall go to Mr. Parks right now. He is a man of the people, a protector of the written word. I think he will jump at the chance to print such a letter for circulation. You'll see," she smiled at Ichabod as she closed her front door and locked it with a tiny, iron key.

Down the tree the three friends scampered and onto the campus grounds. The weather was delightful and Savannah wondered if she should take her umbrella back to the house. Then, she thought if she did, she'd surely need it later. Ichabod sensed her dilemma and took the umbrella onto his arm for her. Off campus and down DoG Street they walked, each confident in his and her own opinion, and each determined to be proved right.

"What do you mean you shan't print it?!" Savannah tried to retain some politeness.

"I am sorry, Miss Savannah. I cannot. It is just, well, too much," Parks turned back to his workspace, setting individual type into a composing stick.

Savannah looked at Ichabod, upset he was right. He shrugged, not exactly happy about it.

"Mr. Parks, please. I have written nothing untrue. I have written no libels. I have written nothing which could hurt someone, only that which could help many. There is absolutely nothing dangerous in there."

"Ah, but there is danger in there, Miss Savannah, see?" Parks turned back to her, his speech as fast and precise as his typesetting skills.

Dante was listening, but sniffing the air and finding mostly putrid smells. He was also finding the whole printing process fascinating.

"The whole thing is dangerous, see?" Parks elucidated. "Undoubtedly you know of Bacon's Rebellion?"

Savannah squinted at Ichabod.

"Yes, I know of Bacon's Rebellion. Yet, I am not calling for 'Death to royals!' or 'Burn the Palace!' I am not fighting some tax injustice like Bacon did, advocating aggression against the Crown. That was what that was about, right?" she leaned over and whispered that last question to Ichabod, whom nodded in the affirmative. "Right. Something about the Navigation Acts," she looked to Ichabod for further explanation.

"I know all about the Navigation Acts, Miss Savannah," Parks searched for a *Q* in his type tray. "Crown ruled all colonial exports must go through England first, see? No going anywhere else in the world, not even the Caribbean, see? Even though it is clearly mad to sail all the way to England first. Where is a *Q*? Oh, here it is. No. That is an *O*. Darn it all. Why are these not in order? Oh, I shall never find a good apprentice. So anyway," he continued as he searched for more letters, "the Navigation Acts made no sense whatsoever. They were just a new way for the Crown to make money off American products, see?

My grandfather in London used to talk about it constantly. Found no problem with it. Wondered why anyone would work in America anyway. Personally, I think it would have been nearly impossible to run a business from here. Aha! The *Q*!"

He placed it delicately into the composition stick, then turned back to the rack and looked for a *U*.

"I still don't understand," Savannah pleaded. "I can rewrite it a little. I shall remove the exclamation points."

Ichabod and Dante had turned away from the conversation and were now busying themselves by snooping around the print shop. Ichabod was flipping through a box of leaflets and pamphlets, seeing if there was something interesting to buy. Dante was more interested in the inner workings of the shop.

Carefully, he walked around looking in trays, crates and barrels and stood on his tip-toes to read printed copies that were hanging and drying from wooden rods that circled the shop's ceiling. Something still smelled foul and he was pretty sure it was the ink itself. He'd heard it was made from disgusting materials that were mixed with soot. As he walked toward the back of the shop he saw some giant ink stamps hanging from the wall. These must be the things they actually use to put the ink on the paper. Wow, they really smelled awful. It was all fascinating, though. Words and ideas traveling from the brain to the hand to paper. Quite a concept. Throughout the shop, Savannah's high pitch could be heard. Dante and Ichabod knew when she had a bee in her bonnet, she would not surrender easily.

"I am sorry to be so difficult, Mr. Parks, but I still cannot understand for the life of me why my letter is so outrageous. I told you, I can alter it. A little. Not much though, or it will obscure my message."

"Exactly. Your message. What precisely is your message? In one sentence. Tell me now," Parks set down all his work, crossed his arms and gave Savannah his full attention.

"Uh, well. . ." she looked to Ichabod for help, but he was busy shopping. Dante would only want her to add more fight to her letter. "Well, I suppose my message is that humans are not property and the Crown is wrong to support such a theory in commerce."

"Excellently put," Parks responded and Savannah smiled. "But, do you know what I hear when I listen to that? As a British reader?" Savannah shook her head. "I hear 'the Crown is wrong', see? I just can't print that. If you can find a way to write this without calling anyone into blame, I'll print it. Otherwise, I like my neck and I would like to keep it.

By the way, do you know how much of my revenue comes from advertising pamphlets?" he asked her as he went back to work; she shook her head. "The lion's share of it. Do you know who some of my best advertisers are?" She shook her head again. "Slave owners, see? I am printing an ad as we speak." He read it aloud from a scribbled piece of paper to the right of his trays:

Missing and Runaway Slave

Last seen on Tuesday the 8th of August at Barrett's Landing dock. Answers to the name of Shaw and stands over six feet tall. A large buck of over two-hundred pounds and strong as an elephant. Approach with caution as property in question is wild and possibly mad. Would prefer live capture, dead will still bring reward. Reward of 2 pounds, 50 shillings alive, 2 pounds dead. Return property to Mr. Charles Daniel McCord of Willowbrook Plantation, Charles City County, Virginia

Savannah was horrified. Ichabod and Dante had stopped what they were doing to listen and felt sick to their stomachs as they listened. Mr. Parks was not an uncaring man. He had just gone into a business that, at times, helped the slave trade. Usually, he didn't think about it. Right now, he was reminded of how wretched a thing it was. His look softened and he walked to his front door, looked out to both sides of the road and closed it, locking it with a bolt from the inside. He took a seat on a tall stool that bordered an empty printing table and called over the three friends.

"Come. Sit."

Savannah leapt from the stool where she had been standing to the cleared table, Dante leapt to the same tabletop and Ichabod pulled up a stool and perched himself atop it.

"What I am going to tell you, you cannot repeat. I was never specifically forbidden to speak of it, but I received the information under strict secrecy myself, see? I received it directly from," he looked around to be sure no spies had entered the shop, "Governor Gooch himself."

Their eyes began to grow and they all leaned forward, Ichabod a tad more blasé than the others, but he was clearly interested.

"He passed along some information to me about some very serious goings-on up in New-York."

"Ohh, I would love to go to New-York!" Dante interjected.

"Dante," Savannah shushed him.

"Sorry."

"Apparently, see," Parks continued, his voice at a fast pace now that the conversation was about to heat up, "in New-York, there is a war of words, a battle of barbs, a conflict that is by all means not convivial. There on the island of Manhattan resides a printer, like myself, of some success: apprenticed as a printer, worked as a journeyman printer, eventually opened his own shops and published his own paper."

"You don't have your own paper though, do you?" Dante asked.

Parks shot him a look.

"Not here, but up in Maryland, see? I founded and still own the *Maryland Gazette.* That's the whole reason I am down here now. Williamsburg is my Virginia office for the Maryland paper. I can discover news here, collect advertisements, get story submissions and send them all to the *Maryland Gazette,* see?" he explained.

"Why do you not open a Virginia paper? Call it the Virginia Gazette." Savannah suggested.

"It is a possible plan, Miss Savannah. See, as with my Maryland paper, it is smart business thinking to build a sturdy foundation on good, plain printing jobs. Show the people I can produce quality work: pamphlets, letters, church and government documents, books. Then, I tell them I'm publishing a news-paper and right away I have a base subscription already sold, see?"

"Yes, yes. But what about the governor?" Dante was at the moment not at all interested in the business of printing, but the business of gossip.

"Ah, yes. Back to New-York. Apparently, their royal governor, see, Governor William Cosby is in the midst of a paper battle with one of New-York's two printers. John Peter Zenger is one, William Bradford is the other. His problem is with Mr. Zenger, see? It seems Mr. Zenger has been printing, for over a year now, all manner of insults to the Crown and Governor Cosby specifically. The thing is, is they are all actually very creative, very funny jabs in the form of stories, songs, poems and phony advertisements," he laughed aloud, then stopped and looked around as if laughing might get him in trouble.

"There is nobody here," Savannah said. "Besides, you can laugh at whatever you like. That is your right."

"Oh, you are very naive, little one. See, you cannot laugh at whatever you like, not where kings and queens are concerned. Not even royal governors, see? Not at all."

He stood up and went to a corner of the shop that held a wine decanter. He poured himself a glass, then held up the decanter, offering some to the group. All waved him off, it being a bit early in the day.

"So what kind of stories?" Dante asked.

"Animal stories. They are in fact quite humourous."

"Wait a minute!" Savannah cried. "Is Mr. Zenger's paper the *New-York Weekly Journal*?"

"Indeed. The very one."

"We have read some of these stories! Just the other day! A fox, a London fox named Sterling we found down at Queen Mary's Port had a copy of the *Journal* on him and we read it just the other morning over coffee. We read the animal stories! Something about a spaniel and a monkey. It was funny!" Savannah laughed.

"Those are the stories in question. Your Sterling must have had an old paper. Almost a year old, see? Printed back last Christmas," Parks advised. "Well, those were the early signs of war, see? Since then, the *Journal* has had so much fun printing articles and poking fun at Cosby, his Council, his Judges, his supporters, Cosby fears that public ridicule could go one step further and affect the outcome of upcoming elections. They may have already taken place. Sometime at the end of September, see?" he ended with a sip of wine and sat back down at his work table.

"Do you have any of these papers? I'd love to see the songs!" Dante loved any opportunity to laugh at the establishment.

"I do, actually. I can also always get some from the Maryland shop. We don't keep many around, paper being so expensive and all. It's best to recycle them, see? But for some reason I thought these funny enough to keep."

"I thought you said you learned all this from Governor Gooch. However, you clearly already know all about the stories and the paper war," Savannah wrinkled her nose.

"Oh, I had read them. In the news-paper business, we keep an eye on what our brethren printers are up to, see? Plus, Zenger has made a name for himself in the industry based on these publications. I just never thought a vague animal tale could cause much of a stir. I just kept them because I thought they were funny. Governor Gooch showed me the real danger they're bringing about up north, see?"

"What is the real danger?" Dante's tail twitched left and right with a quick flick each time it came fully extended before coming back to the other side.

"The danger, see, is Cosby is becoming so outraged and so embarrassed by the way he is being portrayed in the paper, as a buffoon and a clown, that he is trying to throw Mr. Zenger into the New-York Gaol."

"Outrageous!" Dante cried as he shot a paw up in the air.

"Dante, calm down," Ichabod blinked slowly. "Continue, please, Mr. Parks."

"That's about it. Cosby wants to gaol Zenger for making him look foolish. Even tried to get a jury of New-York citizens to indict him, find enough evidence to start a tryal, but they wouldn't do it. The people said he did nothing wrong, see?"

"But, he's just the printer. No offense intended," Savannah smiled.

"None taken," Parks replied.

"My point being, and not that anyone should be gaoled for writing funny stories, just stories, right? Because nobody made up lies or anything about Cosby, right?" she asked.

"Correct. No lies. Just stories and songs and some factual articles about the local government. All true, though."

"Okay, so back to my point. Even if somebody could be gaoled, even though they shouldn't be, why go after the printer? Why not the authors?"

"Everything written is anonymous. There is no author name printed. They are all a mystery, see? Precisely because of what is now happening. No one wants to be gaoled."

"Is there any idea who has written these items," Ichabod queried.

"There is speculation. In fact, some people say there is no question who wrote them. Multiple authors, all members of the Morrisite Party."

All three looked at Parks for more detail.

"Cosby's Court Party opponents? They all back Lewis Morris, see?"

More stares.

"The former New-York Supreme Court Judge who Cosby fired because he didn't like the way he ruled in a particular case. See, Cosby sued someone for a lot of money and Morris didn't agree. So, Cosby fired him and replaced him with a more Cosby-friendly judge."

"Ahh, *ja*. I know of this," Ichabod turned to Dante and Savannah. "I thought of it that morning ve read the animal stories. I thought it all sounded familiar and I thought this Morris person had something to do with the stories. He is the author himself, *ja*?" he turned back to Parks.

"Nobody knows, see? The stories could be coming in the mail from readers, personal enemies of Cosby, maybe even cabinet members inside Fort George or City Hall. Nobody knows. But, many people suspect it is someone within the Morrisite Party," Parks leaned back in his chair and watched a spider at work on the printing press arm.

"Maybe it is Zenger himself?" Savannah wondered.

"Not likely," Parks answered, watching the spider begin work on a web and feeling bad he would have to destroy it as soon as he used the press.

"Why?" Dante and Savannah asked simultaneously.

"Well, not to be mean, but the fact is Zenger is just not educated enough to write that well. He doesn't even have that good of a grasp on the English language, see? He is German and still struggles with some complexities of the language. Also, some of his printing has major mistakes. Why, he even printed the wrong date on the *Journal*'s début issue! He printed *October* 5, 1733 instead of *November* 5, 1733. Hoo!"

Parks slapped his knee, then looked around the shop again and leaned back into the conversation.

"No, the stories, songs, everything, they all come from a mind with a good grasp of politics, history, writing skills and a basic, natural talent for detail. No, not Mr. Zenger. He is the printer and the printer only."

Everyone sat quiet for a few minutes and ingested all this information. Then, Savannah remembered the whole reason she'd gone there today and she went instantly back to business.

"Okay, so what does any of this have to do with my letter? My letter that calls only for the closer inspection of the Black Codes and the way we treat a specific group of people. I have written no song that will affect an election. I have made no fun of our dear Governor Gooch. I would never do that. I love our governor. I love our King!"

She crossed her arms, raised her eyebrows, pursed her lips and waited for somebody to argue with that last statement. She was a loyal royalist and nobody could argue differently.

"I never said that, dear," Parks tried to calm her. "What I did say is that your letter is dangerous and the person in danger could be me," Parks claimed.

She stared at him, her arms still crossed, unbending.

"What Gooch told me, and this is the secret part, see, is that Cosby is going to try another Grand Jury indictment, you know, ask another jury to send Zenger to tryal and, eventually gaol. If that doesn't work, he's going to find a way to gaol him on his own, even if he has to do it by some illegal, royal privilege or some arbitrary act of his own. He is mad, see?" Parks leaned over his table and looked at each one in the eyes.

"I still don't understand. I am sorry to be so persistent, but that has nothing to do with you. Cosby cannot gaol you for my letter," Savannah persisted.

"No, but what he has done is send a memo to a few colonial governors, including our Gooch, warning them to 'watch your printers, watch your back' and telling them he has alerted the royal governors back in London about 'possible, mutinous tones in colony news-papers'," Parks' voice was growing stronger.

"I am not inciting mutiny!" Savannah stood up on her stool.

"I know that. My point is that, in the end, I have no power, see? Even Gooch does not. Now that Cosby had made this fuss, powers in London are going to be watching us, the printers, closely. Very closely, see? Gooch imparted this information to me not as a threat, but as a friendly warning. Figures abroad are going to be reading our news-papers and scrutinizing them with a fine-tooth comb, looking at every little word with a social microscope. If something is printed they perceive could threaten the royal establishment at any level, local or not, our Gooch may not have any say in the matter."

Savannah was still undeterred.

"Look," Parks sighed, "I must answer to Gooch. Gooch must answer to his superior, Royal Governor VanKeppel, VanKeppel must answer to the London Board of Trade and the Secretary of State, the Duke of Newcastle. Newcastle must answer to the King's Privy Council and they must all, everyone down the line, right to you and me, must ultimately answer to His Royal Highness King George II. End of story. I cannot print your letter because I cannot run a business from gaol, see? I am sorry, Miss Savannah. Very, very sorry."

Savannah slowly unfolded her arms. She finally understood, but she wasn't assuaged and she didn't feel any better about Parks' decision. She gathered up her purse, her letter, jumped off her stool and stood by the front door, her signal to Ichabod and Dante she was ready to go. Then, she turned to Parks.

"Mr. Parks, I thank you for your time. Whilst I do not agree with your decision, I suppose I do understand your situation. Clearly, I do not want you, or myself for that matter, going to gaol for merely writing a letter. Furthermore, the problem obviously lies not with us but with the higher powers-that-be in London. Perhaps I shall write *them* a letter," she raised an eyebrow, daring someone to comment. "Anyhoo, I now feel I have a whole new message to spread. The right to speak freely, to write freely. What if someone had told Shakespeare what to write?"

"Actually," Ichabod interjected, "Elizabethan writers vere under a great deal of scrutiny, vhat vith all the Catholic and Protestant conflicts."

Savannah blinked at him twice and continued, "What if Martin Luther had been curtailed?" Ichabod started to speak, but Savannah corrected herself, "Okay, yes, he put himself in great danger with the Church. But, even Martin Luther somehow got his ninety-five theses printed to tack all over Wittenberg!

Ninety-five letters scorning the Holy Roman Empire and I cannot get one stupid letter printed in Williamsburg!"

"*Der Freiheit des Christenmenschen*," Ichabod said as he walked to the door.

"What?" Savannah snapped.

"*Der Freiheit des Christenmenschen.* That vas the name behind Luther's main idea. *The Freedom of the Christians.*"

"Well, see? Even protestations of the Catholic Church got some inking. Icahbod, Dante, I would like to go now," she stood by the door and waited for Mr. Parks to open it for her.

"I am sorry, Miss Savannah. But, as they say, you can't fight City Hall, see?"

He opened the door for her and she and Ichabod went through it. Dante was still sniffing around the shop.

"Dante? Are you coming with us?"

"Um, yes. I was just looking around. Something really smells horrible back there, Mr. Parks," Dante ran to the front door to join his friends. "It's all very interesting, though. Fascinating operation, this business of putting ideas to paper."

"You know, Dante," Parks had a thought as he held the door, "I could use a little help around here. Not a full apprentice or anything, just some help with cleaning up, making ink sometimes, hanging paper, sweeping and such things. My current apprentice is an absolute disaster and I think I'm going to look for someone new. In the meantime, I'm going to need extra help. Temporary, see? A month at the most, maybe two. Interested? I shall pay you a fair wage, since you would actually be an employee and not an apprentice."

Dante sported a huge grin and was about to jump at the opportunity when Savannah put in, "Thank you, but, no. Dante does not want to work for you. He has to, uh. He has to, um. Oh! I know. Yes, he has plenty of work to do at Mrs. Pritchen's Tavern as Court Times are approaching in October. Isn't that right, Dante?"

Dante just stared at Savannah. He then turned to Mr. Parks and said, "I should like to think about it. May I come see you tomorrow?"

"You cannot work for him after all this!" she whispered to Dante who simply smiled at Parks.

"Yes, of course, Dante. Let me know of your decision. I think you would enjoy the learning experience."

Dante nodded, grabbed his tricorn off a wall peg and followed Savannah and Ichabod out onto DoG Street. The weather had definitely shifted. The air was breezy and there was a certain bite to it. Although not many, the more adventurous leaves were ahead of the crowd and beginning the earliest travels to the ground.

Savannah tried to reason with Dante, asking him not to support Parks. Ichabod told Savannah she was being naive and if nobody supported the press, that in itself could come to harm the public. As always, the arbiter of common sense, Ichabod suggested Dante take the job.

"I think you should take it, Dante. It is a temporary spot and a good learning experience for a cat of little training and education."

Ichabod then turned to Savannah; Dante made a face at him behind his back. "I saw that," Ichabod turned back to face Dante. "Don't be a baby. It is true. You are a clever cat, but you need some marketable skills. And you," Ichabod now turned again to Savannah, "I think that perhaps you could find another outlet for your frustration. In my experience, the theatre has always been, historically-speaking, a fabulous place to tell a good tale."

CHAPTER EIGHTEEN

Linus's face was frozen in a smile. It had been like this all afternoon. The last thing he had expected this morning was to be sent out on assignment, and to cover a party no less! The news came in just before noon and Zenger was anxious to get out a special edition paper by tomorrow morning. Linus had been tending his normal duties in the Broad Street printing shop this morning: mostly organizing type in its trays and mixing ink. Truthfully, he was bored out of his skull. He hated the drudgery and manual labour of the newspaper business. He was daydreaming about all the other options he had.

Maybe he'd go to school. Was it too late? Probably not. He'd done very well in school back in Sweden. He'd only stopped attending when he came to New-York. He could almost certainly get into a school of some sort; because this certainly didn't seem to be working. His talents were being wasted making ink paste and "rinsing out" ink beaters. How degrading. Just as he was pondering his legal options for backing out of his apprenticeship - none - Zenger burst into the front door.

"Linus!" he cried as he pushed open the thick, creaky, wooden door. "I've got work for you! Get your notebook and your quill; you're on assignment!"

"What? What assignment?" Linus had dropped his work without missing a beat and had already stuffed his journal and portable quill and ink set in his satchel whilst Zenger was still talking.

"It is the election, Linus! The New-York City Council elections! The results are posted at City Hall. I need you to go read them in-person. I was just at Vedder's Chelsea Coffeehouse and all of a sudden, out the front windows, the streets began to go wild, like a riot! People all running in one direction: uptown," Zenger tossed his jacket and hat on the wall pegs and began to tie on his apron as he continued his story.

"Then, this gentleman stuck his head inside the coffeehouse and yelled, 'Election results are posted! Election results are posted!' Everybody stormed out and ran left. I ran right and headed straight here to put my youngest reporter on the story. Whatever the results, 'tis clearly going to be a good article," he poured himself a cup of coffee, the last of it, and went right to his print trays.

"You mixed the ink this morning, correct?"

"Yes, Mr. Zenger! Of course!" Linus was beyond excited. "What do you want me to do exactly?"

"Get the story, boy! Find out who won what. Rumours on the street are Cosby's people lost! The Morrisites may have won!"

Zenger tightened the strings of his leather apron at his slender tummy.

"Now go! Get the story and get it back here by three. We've got a ton of work to do tonight, Linus," Zenger was already deep into his work, filling a composing stick with an all-purpose headline and date that would work no matter the outcome of the elections.

The New-York City Common Council Election Results
Wednesday September 29, 1734
. . .defeats. . .

Linus was out the door in a flash and headed to City Hall in a full sprint. It was warm for a late-September. It must have been eighty degrees, maybe closer to ninety. He was sweating already in the shop. Now that he was outside, the sun blazed on him and he wondered what happened to the tease of cooler weather they'd had last week. He'd actually been able to wear a coat in the mornings and he was downright chilly in bed at night. Not that he wanted to be cold, but he was tired of the immense, summer heat and like everybody else in town, he felt brighter and happier as a wash of cooler temperatures, light breezes and the first falling leaves took hold of the city. Never mind all that, though. He was on assignment!

Maybe this one would get printed. No, he was positive it would get printed! He wasn't covering this on speculation like he had Cosby's arrival or that shipwreck in the harbor back in May, or the wedding of Mistress Kaivan Pturm, daughter of New-York's most powerful, Russian landowner, Lando Pturm. All of those were stories he wrote hoping they'd get printed. This one though, this one was an actual assignment! Maybe all those other stories had an effect on Zenger. Well of course they did! He'd sent Linus to cover a very important election. He wasn't going to blow this chance, his first chance to get published? Linus picked up his speed and passed all the other excited New-Yorkers on their way to the marble pillars of New-York's City Hall.

The crowds grew ever more thick and boisterous as Linus approached Trinity Church which stood just a few blocks from City Hall. Women were jumping up and down; men were cheering and tossing their hats up into the air. The women, Linus thought to himself, seemed awfully happy considering the irony that they weren't even allowed to vote. The colonies seemed very backwards that way.

Whilst Sweden didn't hold elections anywhere, they had had a few female leaders: most notably Queen Christina in the 17thCentury. Of course, she was pretty wild, was raised by her father as a prince rather than a princess, dressed like a boy often and took her oath as a king. Her nickname was even The Girl King. Overall, she was a strong and powerful symbol for Swedish women everywhere.

When one considered the British women under Queen Elizabeth I, less than two centuries ago, the women under countless reigns of Egyptian queens and the wise females of many an ancient Celtic society, what had happened to women as a class along the way? What had happened to the enlightened views of the Elizabethan-era men? How had it all devolved so much in just two-hundred years? That was another story, one Linus would write later. For now, as he approached City Hall, totally breathless, he refocused on the task at hand. Who won?

He pushed his way through the crowds, being jostled, bumped and shuffled about like a walnut rolling around the back of a wagon cart. He finally made it to the steps of City Hall only to be pushed back by a very rude, plumpy, smelly woman in a frightful, purple hat. She grabbed him by his shoulder and actually yanked him back down a step in order to advance herself. Maybe his sympathetic views on women were wrong. Always the gentleman though, he said nothing and worked his way back up the steps, telling himself maybe she was just angry at being a woman in colonial Britain.

She stepped on the tail of a cat whom had gotten caught up in the melée. The cat shrieked and she yelled at it to get out her way and Linus decided he didn't care what her problem was. She was just nasty and nobody had a right to be like that. Linus watched the cat dart out from the crowded steps and then turned back to his chore: reaching the two posting boards that hung on either side of the grand entry doors of City Hall. He pushed and shoved as politely as he could, uttering timid and useless apologies as he went. "Pardon me." "Excuse me." "Sorry about that." Just as he reached the top step and was laying eyes on the announcements posted, he heard a scream. The rude, plumpy lady wailed as though her tail had been stepped on by the mob.

"Heavens, no! We've lost?! How could we have lost?!" she addressed the crowd in general. "You idiots! Do you have any idea who my husband is?! You've put my husband out of office! Morons! All of you!"

She stormed down the steps like a bull crashing its way through a fence, her elbows butting anyone and everything out of her way.

"Idiots! You'll be sorry! All of you!"

The majority of the crowd laughed at her as she passed and some even threw bits of crumpled paper or old fruit at her. Some agreed with her and left the scene nearly as angry as she. As Linus drew closer to the announcement boards, he read what everyone was beginning to chant:

Morrisite Party defeats Cosby's Court Party!
Landslide Victory!

Well, the postings didn't read that way exactly. It was, after all, City Hall. Cosby's domain, his offices. The postings were simple and factual and in a rather tiny print. Linus imagined Cosby fought to even keep them from being posted at all. In fact, Linus was amazed, considering what a toad Cosby had turned out to be, that the elections occurred and finished in a lawful manner at all. If he was a tavern gambler, Linus would have bet good money on Cosby rigging the elections in his favour and keeping his Court Party in power.

Nevertheless, no matter how tiny the print or how resentful the postings, the people knew the outcome and the crowds had created their own headline. Headline! It was perfect! Linus wrote in his pad.

Landslide Victory for Morrisites!

Naturally, he was bumped as he wrote it and he got ink from his quill all over his hand. Plus, even though he'd corked it well after dipping his quill, he was pretty sure his ink bottle had leaked in his bag. He could feel a warm moistness against his right hip. Either that or something, or someone, really disgusting was touching him. He hoped it was his ink.

He copied some more details from the postings: names, figures, titles. He then turned around and looked at the crowd. It looked like a sea of wigs and hats and he wondered how he'd ever descend the marble steps back to the main road. He hunched his shoulders inward, held his bag tight next to his hip (Ick, there was that warm feeling again.) and jumped right in, dispensing with any "Pardon me" or "Excuse me". Once he made it to the street, the crowds were thinning. The first throngs of people had gotten the news as it was fresh and were now spreading the word all over New-York.

As Linus looked at the inky mess of what he'd written, he decided it was good, basic and factual, but no doubt boring. It needed a personal touch. The City Hall bells pealed twice. He had one hour to write his story. He sat on a bench and watched some ships' masts sway above New-York Harbour. What did the story need? He tapped his quill to his bottom lip in thought, then spat as he realized he'd just gotten ink on his face. He cringed and licked his lips, making a bigger mess as he watched the crowds, dying out but still joyous and noisy. Then it hit him: the people! Naturally, the people! That's what this election was all about: the people of New-York sending a message to a tyrant. He would interview a few of them, talk about how they felt about the outcome and what they disliked about Cosby. It would be great! Then, he thought to himself that that wasn't very good reporting. Well, it was, but only halfway. Didn't a good story need opposing sides?

As much as he hated Cosby and as much as he understood that the *Journal* was essentially, well clearly, the anti-Cosby news-paper, he thought maybe he should include a couple of comments by Cosby supporters. He could certainly include a reporting of the rude, plumpy Cosby-woman. He began to scribble in his pad, writing in detail her obnoxious words as well as her appearance, her manner, her clothes. Who was her husband? That would have been fantastic to know! Oh, if he was a better reporter he would have asked her right then. Drat! Well, he'd be a great reporter right now. He gathered up his bag and his pad and headed into the street approaching anyone who looked as though they wanted to talk about the election. It turned out everyone except the Cosby supporters wanted to talk about it. It was clear which folks were Cosby supporters.

To a person, they all did the same exact thing when Linus approached them, pen and pad in-hand, asking "Pardon me, would you like to comment of the election's outcome for the *New-York Weekly Journal*?" Cosby supporters scowled, bared their teeth, hissed or spat at Linus, pushed him aside aggressively and stomped off into the New-York heat.

CHAPTER NINETEEN

The light from Ben's candle carried a murky shadow across his Philadelphia printing shop. It was late, or early, depending on how you looked at it. It was three o'clock in the morning. The candle lit the way as he walked quietly across the hardwood floors, his leather, Indian-crafted moccasins making no noise as he approached the back door.

Outside waited a man on a chocolate-brown horse. In the moonlight, however, the horse looked black as the ink that was dried on Ben's hands and apron. The horse snorted and the rider yanked the reins, then pet his mane to quiet him. He then stomped one hoof in protest. He was the last of his friends to go. Everyone else had gone hours ago and he was huffy and impatient.

"Let's ride already!" he snorted more loudly this time as he began to alternate stomping all four hooves.

He could sense they were almost ready to go. Any minute now he'd be galloping through the Pennsylvania woods, the wind in his mane and only the moonlight guiding him through the dense forests. He'd watched his friends set out and all three of them, all black horses chosen for camouflage in this nighttime mission, shot out of town like a handful of lightning bolts from the hand of Zeus. Before that, even though he'd still been in his stall across town, he'd sensed the activity. Others had gone, too. Horses on a mission earlier that night. Pounding the bricks with his hooves, he made it very clear he would wait no longer.

Ben, in his white nightcap oddly paired with his printer's apron and his moccasins, hefted up one last satchel thick with leaflets to the rider, a girl of about thirteen. So focused was he on this plan of his, Ben didn't even notice his nightshirt's linen sleeve had caught the flame of his candle as he lifted his arm

Jennifer Susannah Devore

to pass the satchel up to the girl. In a second, the ruffle and string tie at his cuff were ablaze. The girl screeched, breaking the night's silence. The orange glow grew upwards and began to fill in the alley's darkness. Before it reached his skin, however, he snuffed it out on his leather apron, leaving a slight discoloration on its front. The girl shook her head and sniffed a tiny laugh through her nose. Everything she'd heard about Mr. Franklin was right.

She was part of Ben's contingency "B" plan: a second team of riders sent on this task, just in case team "A" met with any danger or difficulties. She pulled a strap through the bag's handle and buckled the strap tightly and quietly, positioning it perfectly to balance the other three hanging off various buckles on the horse's tack. Ben said not a single word to the girl, just as he had said not a single word to the other three riders this night. She, too, said nothing but nodded with a smile and pulled her hood tightly over her head, exposing only her eyes. She leaned fully over onto her horse's neck as she grabbed a handful of his mane and wrapped it around her right hand. Whispering something into his twitching ear, she held on tight, kicked her heels into his sides and in an instant, Zeus let fly from his fist another bolt into the Philadelphia night.

Ben looked both ways down the back alley of his shop. He saw nothing, tucked his head back in the door and closed it, latching it from the inside. A small, yellow flicker glided like a phantom through the shop and up the stairs. Outside Benjamin Franklin's print shop, downtown Philadelphia was black and the world was silent and asleep. There was only that single, yellow flicker of Ben's candle visible in a second-floor, paned-glass window above the shop. Then, like a phantom summoned back to the dead, the yellow disappeared in a flash.

CHAPTER TWENTY

Linus danced against the backlight of an evening bonfire. New-York Harbour sparkled in the near background. The New-York nights had finally turned cold, not winter-cold, but the kind of cold one expects of New-England in October. The streets were alive with dancing, laughing and general festivity. In the weeks since the election and its monumental defeat of Governor Cosby's Court Party by the Morrisites the city had felt refreshed, light, fun. Linus danced for the Morrisites, but he also danced for himself. His article covering the election had been printed! He was a published writer now and because of it, tonight he was on his second, paid assignment. Paid! Zenger was paying him to do a social piece: the change of attitude in New-York, the air of freedom from a tyrant's spaniels.

Linus spent the evening talking with folks, interviewing them, listening to their happiness and relief.

"Cosby should know better than to try to squash a New-Yorker!"

"How dare he try to indict an innocent printer!"

"Long live Zenger!"

"Long live the *New-York Weekly Journal*!"

"Back to London with the lot of them! Bon voyage, Cosby and Harison!"

The people were delighted with the Morrisites' victory. In the afterglow of it all, something else had taken over the town. No one knew where they came from, but literally overnight, thousands of one-page sheets printed with hilarious songs filled the streets, the coffeehouses, the taverns and homes.

Tonight, Linus and his fellow New-Yorkers, native-born and immigrants, New-Yorkers and Americans by birth and by choice, danced and sang in the city built by the Dutch. The cheerful and silly ditties that had infiltrated the city, showing up one morning in the earliest of hours, stacks and stacks placed around town businesses and stuffed into postboxes and under doors, filled the air. Even the stables had copies hidden in the haylofts, stalls and troughs. The horses, the pigs, the cows and the farmers alike celebrated a turn of the screw, a turn that would eventually edge out the horrid and selfish Governor William Cosby.

Late that night, well past midnight, as Linus strolled home, his mother surely fretting his late hour, he hummed his favourite melody of all the songs. He could still hear revelers singing the lyrics aloud and proud. Their happy, and probably now drunk, voices carried over the cobblestones of town and into the evening clouds. As Linus hummed a little hum, he could sense a fresh, clean and brand-new day full of the unexpected headed straight for New-York.

> *Tho' pettyfogging knaves deny us Rights of*
> *Englishmen; We'll make the scoundrel rascals fly, and ne'er*
> *return again. Our judges they would chop and change for*
> *those that serve their turn, And will not surely think it strange*
> *if they for this should mourn!*

CHAPTER TWENTY-ONE

"What the. . .?!" Cosby bellowed throughout the halls of Fort George, violently shaking a small piece of parchment in his hand. "Phipps! Where the Devil are you?! Get yourself to my chamber now!"

Cosby's heels echoed throughout the cold, stone walls of his vast home on New-York's harbour. *Click clack, click clack, click clack!* In a very fast, one-two tempo, Cosby powered up and down the hallway in front of his bed chamber, his pointy high-heels sending sharp *pings* echoing through the hallway and off the walls.

"Phiiiiiipps! Where the bloody hell are you?!" Cosby screamed at the top of his lungs as he approached the intersection of his hallway with another and looked right, then left. *Click clack, click clack, click clack!* Back down the main hallway he stormed, reading then shaking the paper at the four guards who stood watch at all points of the hallway. They may have found his behaviour frightening, perhaps even amusing, but their rigid, military faces betrayed nothing, just stared ahead at the wall directly across their position.

"Phiiiiiipps! I said. . .oh, there you are," Cosby turned to find the wee Phipps shaking nervously at attention looking up at Cosby.

"Yes, Sir. What is it, Your Excellency?"

Phipps bowed by extending one leg forward, placing a palm on each knee and dipping his head all in one smooth motion. In reverse, just as fluidly, he stood back up and waited for Cosby to speak.

"Have you read this, Phipps?!" Cosby shook his paper at Phipps. "This, this, this song?! This, this chant?!"

Phipps had read it. In fact, Phipps had had the melody in his head all week long. He found it brilliant. He wished he'd had the courage, not to mention the creativity, to write such a thing.

"Yes, Sir. I believe so. Which one is it?" Phipps asked, instantly regretting the latter query.

"Which one?! Which one?! How many are there?!" Cosby roared.

"Um, well, I think, well, I have only heard one. . .in a cof. . fee. . .hou. . .se," Phipps' words slowed and his volume lowered as he watched Cosby stare him down, his eyes growing larger and his glare glowering stronger.

"In a coffeehouse? Are the peasants of New-York singing about me in coffeehouses?!" he stared at Phipps as if the wee man was personally organizing the events about town.

"No, Sir. Well, just the one time I . . .I mean. . .I don't know, Sir. I think. . .maybe," Phipps tried to be authoritative, but still looked remarkably meek.

Cosby paced up and down a short section of the hallway directly in front of his chamber door. He never went inside his bedroom but hovered around it in paralyzing anger. He looked at the paper again, then at Phipps.

"You're a smart man, Phipps. I assume," he rolled his eyes and calmed down as he placed his hand around the back of Phipps' neck, creating an unnerving, faux friendliness. "Now, what does that agile brain of yours tell you this part of the song means?" Cosby folded the paper to a line and shoved it in Phipps' face.

> *We'll make the scoundrel rascals fly,*
> *and ne'er return again.*

"Um, well, I think. . .perhaps that. . .," Phipps gulped hard. "I mean. . .that your friends and you should. . .," Cosby glared at him, as if daring him to finish his sentence. "ThatmaybeyoushouldallgobacktoLondon," Phipps finished in one long word and looked at the ground as he did so.

"Interesting," Cosby was growing more angry.

Now, Cosby was not very bright and it was true that he needed help comprehending the hidden meaning behind these songs, just as he had with the Animal Stories. But, as with the Animal Stories, he was savvy enough to know that they were about him and that they weren't good. He knew they were demeaning and they were harmful to his power, to his authority. The elections had proved this so. His face was getting hot and his neck sore from the general strain in his head. His hand tightened around the back of Phipps' neck.

"Phipps," he seethed with more faux friendliness, "one more thing. What, pray tell, do you find this line to mean."

> *Our judges they would chop and change*
> *for those that serve their turn*

Again he gulped, "That you would. . .most likely, Sir, you would. . .swap judges who think as you do. . .Sir."

Cosby let go of Phipps' neck and began to pace.

"Right then, Phipps. Off you go," he dismissed Phipps with a wave of his hand as he continued to read the song sheet.

He grew more and more furious the more and more he read it. The thing about the truly mean is that the less intelligent they are and the more obvious this fact is made to them, the more mean they become. For without the mental capacity to work and frame their anger in a creative and constructive manner, for example in song or word or picture, they are left with only the most basic and simple method for channeling that fury: physical aggression. Worse still, if the mean one in question happens to be in a position of power, all the worse for the weakest targets of that power. For when the raging power cannot find the right one to blame, the cleverest to blame, it will find, in the end as a last and desperate measure, the least resistant one. It will seek and land on top of the one least likely to fight back, or so it thinks.

CHAPTER TWENTY - TWO

"There," Savannah stood back, squinted one eye shut and scrutinized her canvas. "Is that better?"

Ichabod looked up from his wooden, letter writing box and extended his snout a little as he stretched his neck to look at Savannah's painting.

"*Ja*, it is much better. I can see your clouds hafe much more definition. Except," he paused.

"Except what? What?" Savannah was preparing for criticism.

"It is just that your clouds are so dark. Almost like rain. I thought you hafe been vorking all summer on getting your skies that perfect Italian blue," he tilted his head to one side. "Do not misunderstand, you hafe much improfed, but it looks like an ice storm is coming. More like vinter in Domodossola than summer on Portofino."

Ichabod went back to his letter writing and Savannah continued to squint. He was right. Without even realizing it, she had long ago dropped her focus on a classic, Italian, blue sky. Somehow, she had been incorporating more and more greys and blacks into her sky: more storm and tempest than serenity and tranquility. It just seemed to creep in there without her noticing it.

"You know, I think it's this past autumn. It has affected me. I still feel like myself, my happy self and I still derive great pleasure from the silly things in life, my outfits *par example*," she twirled for Ichabod who smiled with a little nod. "In fact," her eyes popped open in epiphany, "I probably have become more interested in the silly things lately, just as a way to deal with all this Anthony business, plus Parks not printing my letter. And Dante! How could he go work for Parks? After the way he turned away my writings."

Savannah looked at her sky again, then across the river and hunched her shoulders, protecting herself from the unexpected chill of the day. It was over eighty degrees yesterday and so she had brought no scarf or wrap with her this morning. Then, all of a sudden the temperature dropped to below sixty, and it was even colder on the water.

"I don't know, Ichabod. I suppose things will get better around here. It's certainly nice having Sterling around. I do like him ever so."

"Yes, he is a fine fox. Fery intelligent, vell-trafelled. I like that," Ichabod added as he looked at his pocket watch. "*Ach*, look at the time, Safannah. Ve probably should be going. The party is mere hours avay and I know how you like to fuss with your Hallove'en costumes. Vhat is it to be this year? A lady pyrate? A vitch? A Greek goddess? A mummy? Oh, that vould be funny. A sqvirrel mummy. Fery funny," he put away his quill and papers. "I hafe no idea vhat I am going to be, but you know me. I haf a trunk full of things. I can piece something together. Maybe Othello the Moor or Pierrot the sad clown. Maybe I just stick a few black feathers in a black hat and call myself a crow. I do like the sparkling things; maybe I am part crow."

Ichabod pushed the cork in tightly on his portable jar of ink and placed his gold nib carefully in its velvet compartment in the writing box. Under his boots, as he stood, newly fallen leaves shifted and floated. He looked up to see Savannah was not dissembling her easel or putting away any paints. She was kind of just staring into space. "Safannah, are ve going? There is not much time. Plus, ve still haf to go by Anthony's and haf a bottle of vine sent ahead to the party."

Savannah just watched the river, more whitecaps than usual today. She barely heard Ichabod speaking. He called her name once more, a bit more forcefully and she snapped to attention.

"Oh, sorry. You know, I'm not going," she tapped her canvas with her paintbrush.

"Vell, I must go. It vill take me longer to get home and, like I said, I still hafe no idea vhat to vear tonight," he stood up straight, his writing box in one hand, his walking stick in the other, a short nod to Savannah. "So, I shall see you first at Mrs. Pritchen's and ve can then valk to the party together? Or, vould you like to just meet at the party?"

"No. I mean I'm not going to the party," she kept painting as she spoke.

"Vhat do you mean? Not going? You lofe this holiday! Better than Christmas, I think. Besides, eferyfone vill be vaiting to see vhat your are vearing."

"I just can't, Ichabod. Everything is so horrible. In fact, I don't know how you can go," she turned and looked him in his black pearl eyes.

"Vhat exactly is horrible?" he asked softly, rarely seeing her like this.

"Everything. Anthony, Remus, Parks, slavery. All of it. The world is a mess and we're going to a Hallowe'en party? How irresponsible is that?!" She put her paintbrush in a glass of water on the ground and surveyed the river once again. "Look at it. It just flows on and on and it doesn't matter what happens here on the land. It just goes on and on. How can that be? Doesn't anything we do matter?"

Ichabod stood next to her and watched the river with her in silence for a moment. Then, he took her paws in his and looked her in the eye.

"It does matter. Eferything ve do matters. Good and bad. And you are good. Fery good. You haf helped more people and animals than you realize, changed so many lifes. But, you can't change Anthony's situvation. Vhen he is ready to no longer be sad, he vill no longer be sad. You can't bring Remus back from the dead. And, I know it is a tragic and efil blemish on the face of humankind, but you, efen you, Miss Safannah, cannot stop slafery," he stopped her as she started to speak.

"Parks is not being efil, he is protecting himself, and you I might add. Besides, efen if he did print your piece, it vould solve nothing. Maybe a few people vould feel bad for a few days. But then, it vould be back to business as usual. That is how people are. They are fickle in their emotions, especially vhere tragedy and news are concerned. Vone story that strikes their fancy today vill be, qvite literally, old news tomorrow. Do you think anyvone cares this month about the embarrassing affairs last veek of the Danish princess? No. It is ofer and they are looking for more news about another princess in another bad situvation somevhere else. Humans are foolish, mostly. But, I think they try to be good, mostly. Parks is not your enemy and neither is Dante." She looked at him with squinty eyes.

"Dante has been your friend for a fery, fery long time and you must not let his vorking at Parks' print shop affect that. It is a new experience for Dante. Good knowledge for a young cat vith no education and no family monies."

He let go of her paws and walked to the river bank. He picked up an empty oyster shell and brought it back to Savannah.

"See this? It is empty. It vonce had an animal in it. An oyster. Maybe it efen made a pearl at vone time. But now, it is gone. The pearl, the oyster. Carried off by the rifer." As he spoke Savannah began to cry. "It does go on and on and ve can't stop it, no matter how ve try. Ve can vork at it and ve can make ourselfes feel better day by day for the effort. But, until the vorld vorks together, you and I cannot stop the rifer. Ve can, howefer, keep our little portion of it tidy, clean, honest and respectful and hopefully your good nature, your kindness, your commitments vill influence others to do the same.

People vill not change because you order them to. In fact, they vill do just the opposite. You must be subtle, make them think change is their idea and it vill be a truer and more enduring change. Letting yourself get down and extracting yourself from society vhere you are no influence to anybody is not going to help. You must do something that helps your little portion of the rifer. Then, your grey skies vill turn to blue. You can hafe your summer on the Mediterranean and still be a good citizen. Okay?"

Savannah cried for about half an hour and it started to rain, turning her painting into a mess of indistinguishable swirls and blotches. Ichabod hugged her and let her cry and together they watched the river scurry past them in an endless stream. Eventually, she stopped crying and, ironically, was happy when she saw her painting was ruined.

"I'm tired of painting anyway. I didn't like what I'd made."

She put away all her brushes and paints into their special box and closed it quickly before the sudden rain could ruin the velvet interior. The canvas was ruined, so she covered it with a large piece of tarp she kept in the bottom of her tote bag so as not to get paint all over her dress.

"I think I shall try something new for a bit. Perhaps I will go back to painting later. For now though, I think some other creative outlet would be a good change. Maybe I shall write something!" She was instantly excited about the idea. "Yes! I could order a gorgeous new journal from Anthony. Actually, I think I saw some new tapestry-covered ones in his shop last week. Very fancy, from India."

"Vhat about a play?" Ichabod suggested again.

"What play? Ohhh, a play. Yeeeees. I had forgotten about your idea. Instead of my article, write a play," she stopped a thought with her head tilted up at an angle. "I like it!" she decided. "What could I write? A play about slavery maybe?! Yes, that would do something!"

"No, I think that vould not be good," Ichabod shook his head. "It is too preachy, and maybe dangerous. People do not like being told vhat to think. And the gofernment vill still be vatching vhat you write, efen on a stage. No, you must be a little sneaky, surreptitious."

"Hmm," she hefted her tote over one shoulder and held her canvas under one arm. With the other hand she carried her paint box. Ichabod took the canvas from her, carrying it in his free paw. "Well, what could I write?" They began their walk back to town, hiking up the riverbank to the main road.

"You vill think of something. Do not force it or it vill not be good," Ichabod advised. "So, should ve meet at Mrs. Pritchen's or at the party?"

"Oh, I'm still not going," she chirped, much happier about it this time.

"But, I thought. . ."

"No, no. 'Tis okay. I feel better. Really. But, I still don't feel like a party. I do feel like writing, however! I'm going to try to get to Anthony's before he closes and get one of those journals. I don't know what I shall write, but I feel it. Maybe a poem, maybe a short story, something. Maybe my play!"

Ichabod looked at her intensely, searching her eyes to see if she was really okay. She was. Better, at least.

"Vell, maybe I von't go either."

"No, you should go! Please, don't let me ruin your Hallowe'en!"

"It's okay. I don't mind actually. I vould hafe to go all the vay home, pick a costume, then come all the vay back. No, I did not plan this fery vell, did I? Besides, Dante is not efen going. He is helping Mr. Parks with some newspaper deadline. No, I think maybe I shall just go to Mrs. Pritchen's.

The place vill be fery qviet all night. I can read, hafe some brandy, vatch the Hallove'en refelers go by on DoG Street."

"What is Mrs. Pritchen going to do tonight?"

"Do you not know? She is going to the party, too! She is going to dress up!" his eyes lit up, the whites that encircled the black pearls were rarely seen but when they were revealed it usually meant he was very excited.

"Really?! What, or who, is she going to be?"

"Vell, I haf to say that she had no idea until I gafe her the perfect costume suggestion. It's so perfect a disguise that because of the secret legend surrounding it, no vone vill efen know who she is, efen vhen she tells them!" Savannah stopped in the road and waited to learn. "She is going as Mrs. Silence Dogood," his whites still showed as he delivered the name.

"Who's that?"

This was not the appropriate response.

"That is the secret! You hafe not heard of Mrs. Silence Dogood?"

"No," she jumped to avoid a puddle. "Should I have?"

"Absolutely not. Vell, you should not hafe. I should not hafe either. But I do," he grinned showing all his teeth.

"Tell me! Tell me!" Savannah's spirits had been turned around and she was ready for some of those silly things she loved so much in life.

"Vell, it all starts vone night in Philadelphia. I vas there vith Monsieur LeVau many years ago. I vas in a tafern near Rittenhouse Sqvare and ended up sitting there for nearly four hours this night, vaiting for LeVau. Vell, I don't haf to tell you that vone sees many a character come and go over four hours in a tafern. At vone point, fery late, this man comes and sits next to me. He orders a pint of ale, starts talking and nefer stopped. He talked for maybe two hours and the more he drank, the more he talked, spilling all kinds of precious and, according to him, fery secret information about an organization he used to belong to, a townsmen's society, a business group, a gentlemen's gathering called The Junto."

Savannah's steps slowed their pace. Ichabod was such a good storyteller that with the oncoming darkness, the chilly wind and the rustling leaves, it was almost as though he was telling a ghost story.

"Now, this Junto vas not really a secret society or efen a gentlemen's society because although they vere primarily successful, or at least strifing businessmen, many had started in the club as apprentices to farious craftsmen of Philadelphia and it vas originally known as the Leather Apron Club." Ichabod leaned into Savannah as if sharing another secret, "Please, you see how much he talked to me? Like I vould ask for such detail. Who needs this much information for a story at a tafern? It makes for good storytelling now, *ja*? *Ach*. Okay, I digress," he leaned back up straight.

"Vell, this man vas a former member, an apprentice himself at vone time, I think. Vone Friday night at vone of their meetings at some coffeehouse in Philadelphia, he tells me, that vone of their lead members shares this big secret vith eferyvone at their Junto table. Now, the Junto vas not, he tells me again, a secret society. But this lead member svears eferybody at the table to secrecy for a story he is going to share. Some months later, this other man runs into me at the Rittenhouse Sqvare tafern, drinks too much and tells me the whole thing."

"What was it? What was it? Tell meeeeee!" Savannah danced in place and clasped her hands and grinned, showing all her teeth.

"The tale, my dear, is that of the mysterious Mrs. Silence Dogood. . ."

Late that night, as Ichabod lounged in blissful solitude in the gaming room of Mrs. Pritchen's DoG Street Tavern with a snifter of brandy and a new copy of Lope De Vega's *The Dog in the Manger*, and as Dante worked across DoG Street, in ink up to his elbows well past midnight, including that disgusting task of cleaning the ink beaters, and as Mrs. Pritchen uncharacteristically caroused, drank wine and reveled at the John Custis Estate near the College, Savannah was in her tree home, scribbling and scratching ideas and thoughts into her beautiful, new, tapestry-bound journal. She made lists and crossed them out; she wrote musings and crumpled them up until her candle burned itself out. She then lay her head on her writing desk, just to rest her paw and her eyes for a moment, and she fell asleep.

Outside, on the All Hallows' Eve of October 31, 1734 the weather finally turned for good. Chilled winds were blowing down from the north and the leaves braced themselves for their final days. It was a new season in

Williamsburg and plenty of change was riding in on those winds.

CHAPTER TWENTY - THREE

"Alrighty then," Savannah stood at her writing desk and took an inventory of everything on it. "I've got my journal, my inkwell, my feather pen, extra nibs, extra stack of parchment paper, candles for when it gets dark, my dictionary, some Shakespeare booklets, just in case of research needs and," she wriggled her nose and looked all around the room, "well, I suppose that's it. It's time to get to work."

Savannah had been bitten by the writing bug and had decided to start working, full-time, on her play. Ichabod's tale of Mrs. Dogood was so stirring and hilarious that she had come home last night and played around with various ideas based on that tale. Finally, early this morning, it had come to her: *The Mysterious Silence Dogood*. After a few hours' nap in the late-morning she ran into town to stock up on materials such as the extra paper, nibs and ink. Her favourite ink was a dark red called "Dragon's Blood". She bought an extra bottle of it, but knew it was best to always print in black ink. It was far more professional and everyone could read it.

She then went home, cleaned her house very well because she found it impossible to create in a messy atmosphere, and dressed in a lovely auburn and rust dress. She tied the bodice loosely since she was staying indoors and wore her favourite rust, silk house slippers. She also took out for the first time since last year a lovely orange wrap made of a very light wool. She draped it carefully over the back of her spider-back chair, just in case a chill came through the tree later in the night. Now, sometime around two o'clock in the afternoon, she stood with paws on hips and realized it was time to write, time to work. If she was going to do this, now was the time. Yessiree. Now was the time. She slowly pulled out her chair and as she was going to sit, noticed some lint on her wrap.

"Oh my, that looks awful. I'd better brush that off. Now where is that silver coat brush?" She disappeared into her dressing area, opening and closing drawers until she found it. "There we are," she brushed the wrap as it lay over the chair, then leaned back and scrutinized the wrap. "Much better. One cannot have a linty wrap. Hmm, I better put this back where I found it."

Once again she disappeared into her dressing area where she found a different wrap altogether that she thought might be of a more suitable colour. She tucked away the orange one she'd just brushed, took out this new one, an eggplant colour, brushed it and now placed it over her chair.

"Now then, to writing," she touched the new, purple wrap lightly with her paws as she pulled the chair out and finally sat down.

She took her pen and dipped the nib into the inkwell, black ink, and opened her journal. As she opened the journal, she realized how lovely the leather accents were on it.

"Is this real gold leaf, I wonder?" she asked aloud to nobody. "Hmm. 'Tis very fine."

"Okay, back to the play," she reminded herself. "What to write first? Ah, the title page! Of course, one always begins with the title page."

She thrust out her arm, freeing her elbow from the snugness of a sleeve and brought her paw down on the paper and began to write the title of. . .

"Oh, you know what?" she asked herself. "You know who does great title pages? Shakespeare. I should look at a few of my booklets here."

She replaced her pen in its holder, put a pink ribbon bookmark in her journal and began leafing through the stack of booklets she'd set on her desk for this very reason. In fact, she had amassed quite the collection over the years. Not only did she have nearly every Shakespeare play in a hardbound edition, almost all of them gifts from her good friend William Byrd II, but she was now collecting the very fashionable *Walter & Tonson Shakespeare Booklets*.

Whatever the reason, a renewed interest in William Shakespeare, his mysterious life and his prolific body of work, sprouted some hundred-plus years after his death. It was a booming business for the printing industry and while Andrew Walker and Jacob Tonson were direct competitors, they were both doing remarkably brisk business around the globe. Based on the simple, business formula of volume-buying, they were able to get a great price for their paper which they turned around and handed down to the customer. The more customers purchased the inexpensive booklets, the more reason Walker and Tonson had to buy more paper. With greater volume, they got a better price and were able to give that price break right back to the paying customer.

Through this practice of free-enterprise, Shakespeare prices had gone down considerably over the years, bringing his art to the masses, as the man himself may have desired in the very beginning. Shakespeare and the theatre were for everyone, not just the noble and royal classes. Now, it was indeed accessible to all. Savannah's original volumes had cost upwards of a pound each in previous years: no issue at all for a man of William Byrd's worth. Yet now, the Walker & Tonson booklets were going for a mere pence a play: down even from four pence a year before. For Miss Savannah, this was a dream come true and she had collected every single one printed. Today, she opened a copy of *The Tragedie of Romeo and Juliet* and scanned its title page.

"Ah, now this is a title page," she looked at the page, then began reading Act I. "No. 'Tis not time to read," she turned back to the title page and set it on the desk. "Alright, I shall model mine after this one."

She picked up her quill, re-dipped it in ink and started the first word of the title:

The

"My, doesn't that look lovely?" she admired her handwriting. Re-dipping, she continued with the second word:

The Myst

"You know," she thought to herself as she removed her quill from the paper and dipped it once again in the inkwell, "I think a nice cup of tea would be perfect about now. I think it would really get my brain going, too. A lovely green tea, something with jasmine. Mmmm."

She left the quill in the inkwell and moved to her kitchen and put a kettle in the fireplace, hanging it over a small pile of firewood that was burning for warmth. Fire was a constant danger and though she always burned a small amount of wood, she kept a large bucket filled with water right next to it at all times.

She turned around and opened the glass door of her Norwegian *kas*, a cupboard given to her as a gift from Mrs. Pritchen, she pulled out a wooden tea caddy marked "Japanese Sencha Green Tea". She then pulled down a smaller caddy marked "Jasmine". Next, she brought down a china teapot, an English import with hand-painted peonies, and a matching cup and saucer. Into a third caddy, she poured a scoop of the green tea and a scoop of the jasmine tea, just some dried jasmine flowers. She ground it all together with a wooden pestle, then scooped some of that mixture into a sterling silver tea strainer and hung that into the teapot by its thin, silver chain. Returning the caddies to their shelves, she then pulled down a tin of lemon curd bisquits, took three out and placed them on her saucer. Putting the tin away, she closed the doors of the *kas* and turned to the fireplace. Seeing that the water was now hot, she grabbed the kettle with a mitt and poured the steaming water into the teapot, replaced the kettle over the fire, good for refills, and put the whole arrangement on a silver tray and carried it into her living room, setting it on her desk. She sat down, poured out into her cup, no cream or sugar, ever, and sat back to smell the aroma. She then dipped a lemon bisquit into the tea, took a nibble and smiled.

"Yum. Now, that shall give me the brain energy I need to write this play," she took one more sip, then set the cup down on the saucer and enjoyed the lovely *chink* that only comes from good china on good china echoing through the room.

Taking up her quill, she finished the second word of her title and even moved onto the third:

The Mysterious Mrs.

"Yesss, that looks marvelous," she appreciated her work. "Now, for the next word," she re-dipped, then thought of something. "Oh, I was supposed to do something today. What was it?" she asked herself slowly. "Perhaps I've made a note somewhere in my date book."

For the next four hours, Savannah wrote a little, ate a little, cleaned a little, wrote a little, organized a little, accessorized a little and wrote a little more. She did get through the title page, the cast of characters, and actually a very healthy portion of Act I. She realized though, at some point that while she had the whole play in her head, she needed an outline. She set aside Act I and started anew with a proper and well-structured plan of her idea: an outline. First thing, she'd need a new journal.

CHAPTER TWENTY - FOUR

"Can you imagine?" Ben leaned back in his chair, clicking his tongue in disgust as he read a tattered news-paper. "Mr. Hamilton, have you heard of all this nonsense going on in New-York?"

Monk's was busy that night. The Philadelphia rain was coming down steadily, falling at just the right rate for people to say, "This feels like coffee weather." So they went. Philadelphia's coffeehouses were bursting with jovial citizens who chose to spend their Friday evening in the convivial warmth of such establishments. Andrew Hamilton was one of those citizens and so he went to meet with friends he knew would also be thinking "This feels like coffee weather." Andrew arrived at their favourite table with a piping hot cider in one hand, a leather notebook in the other and a folded news-paper under one arm.

"Ah, indeed, Mr. Franklin. I have been reading of it this very night at the office," he set down his cider and removed the paper in question from his underarm, hoisting it knowingly in the air before setting it down on the table. "It is madness, I tell you. True and real madness. This Cosby fellow has no working parts in his brain, I am sure of it."

"Ha! Yes!" Ben liked that statement. "No working parts! Yes! 'Tis like a carriage wheel without an axle. Just loopy movements all over the place. A hoop going nowhere fast! Ha!"

"Really. How can he think this can hold? He has no right," Andrew re-read the paper as he sipped his hot brandy cider.

"No right?! No right, my friends?! Tragically, he does have the right! The supreme right! The right he shall take from whatever source he may! From whomever he may! Unfortunately, 'tis Mr. John Peter Zenger, 'tis the fine people of New-York who have no rights!" Covington, the limner, struck the table with his fist.

It was rare for the young portrait painter to ever raise his voice; limners weren't, by nature, a volatile creature. Covington rarely even put in at these Junto meetings, usually just listened and nodded happily. Yet, for him to project his voice like this, let alone to show force, this said quite a lot. He, like many an American who knew of these events, was angry, very angry at the most recent actions in New-York.

"I know, I know. 'Tis unfair, unjust," Andrew kept re-reading.

"What I do not understand," began Ben, "is exactly how Cosby got Zenger gaoled. I mean, I know he did it 'to maintain order'," Ben used air quotes, "but how, bureaucratically-speaking, did he finally get an indictment? The *Journal* here says he did not actually get an indictment; but that does not make sense. Cosby must have gotten one to get him behind bars. You're the attorney here, Mr. Hamilton. Enlighten us."

"He did try, a third time even, for a Grand Jury indictment. He ordered a burning of all news-papers, especially the Animal Stories and the songs, as you all know." Most at the table shook their heads in disgust; Ben hid a smile. "But, my sources in New-York tell me that the burning was kind of the final straw, for both sides."

"Meaning?" a young silversmith asked from the end of the long table.

"Meaning that when Cosby ordered his Provincial Council to order a public news-paper burning, they decided to pass that task along to administrative officials in City Hall, deeming that it was no business of the PC. In turn, City Hall officials thought it was no business of theirs either, and so they also refused to order the burning."

Some eyes grew wide around the table. Who defies the governor and the PC?

"From what I understand, Cosby threw an absolute hissy fit when this was reported to him," Hamilton continued. "Still, City Hall stood its ground."

"But based on what?" A law student at the table played Devil's advocate, taking the side of Cosby. "There must be reason and substance behind such defiance. As wrong as a burning may be and as wrong as an order to gaol

Zenger may be, it cannot just be met with a 'no'."

"Based on the fact that three times a New-York Grand Jury of Citizens voted not to indict Zenger and that on those and other occasions the Assembly of the Provinces of New-York and New-Jersey refused to meddle with the operations and business of the *Journal*," Hamilton took a drink of his cider then folded his hands on his crossed legs and looked around the tables, waiting for further discussion.

"So, in short," the law student summed up, "there was no precedent to interfere with Zenger or his paper. The act to imprison him would be purely arbitrary and groundless."

"Exactly," Hamilton blinked a long blink.

"Outrageous!" Covington cried out. "Then how on earth did Cosby finally get him in gaol?!"

"Simple. Cosby by-passed the entire legal system. He ordered the New-York City Sheriff to do his bidding. The Sheriff was sent to Zenger's shop and personally arrested him. No crime or reason. Just shackled him and led him out of his shop and down the street to the gaol. Rumour has it he was still in his printer's apron and preparing the next day's *Journal*. His young apprentice was left all alone. Scared to death, I imagine."

The group sat in silence for a moment, all thinking privately what such an act could mean to them, there in Philadelphia. Ben especially: owner, publisher, editor and writer for the *Pennsylvania Gazette*. He pictured himself being dragged off to gaol for his own spicy sense of humour and tendency to jab at the establishment: in the same manner as his own brother, in the same manner as Mr. Zenger. As he thought this, his jaw tightened and his eyes narrowed. Then, he spoke up, verbalizing what each and every single man there was pondering.

"If a New-York governor can do this, any governor can do this. . .about anything, in anyplace."

Each man shook his head again. Some sipped their drinks, some rose and left quietly in anger. Some just zoned out into the near distance, alone with their fears. Ben and Andrew looked straight at each other. In an unspoken instant, Andrew saw that flicker of fire alight in young Ben's eyes. Oh, this was not going to end here. Andrew just knew it.

CHAPTER TWENTY FIVE

"I don't know, Ichabod," Savannah scratched her chin and squinted one eye. "It is so small, too wee for a real production."

The day was cold, really cold. It was snowing even! Snow was one of Savannah's favourite things in life, along with new shoes, gentle rain that lasted for three days and pretty, little sweets in tiny, pink boxes tied with string. Winter had come on quickly this year and the sweltering days of summer that had stretched too far into autumn now seemed years in the past. Savannah wore a red, wool cape trimmed in white fur, as fluffy and soft as her own tail which was at its peak right now. Her tail loved the lack of humidity. Today, it glittered with thousands of tiny snow specks, light bouncing off them as the December sun tried, mostly with failure, to shine through the thick, white clouds. What pinpricks of light did get through, were magical. Ichabod, as usual, was donned all in black, except today he'd mixed in a little navy blue by way of his embroidered waistcoat and gloves. The French fashion experts said never to wear black and blue together; so, all the more reason for Ichabod to do it. In fact, it looked marvelous and luxurious, all trimmed in gold and spotless except for the snow flecks glittering about his suit and his equally fluffy tail.

"It is tiny, I concur. Nefertheless, it is here and it is vhat ve hafe," Ichabod stood on the stage and surveyed a non-existent audience, bowing to his left, right and center.

Savannah paced back and forth across the boards, right to left, left to right, giggling at Ichabod all the while. After a few minutes and a bit of inner dialogue, she turned to Ichabod and nodded. Behind the audience seating was a stubby lobby which quickly offered to the guest the front doors. Outside, perpendicular to the theatre's face, was the Palace Green running lengthwise from Governor's Palace all the way to DoG Street. The Green was busier today than Savannah and Ichabod had seen it in a very long time, maybe ever.

Court times had descended upon Williamsburg and with each session, four of them a year, more and more people came and afterward more and more people stayed. The town was almost unidentifiable from the small burg into which they both came to live some twenty years ago. Along the Green, strode every type of Williamsburg and visiting folk: lawyers, pages, housewives, children, craftsmen, labourers, gentlemen, farmers, royal connections, government officials, horses, sheep, dogs, cats, rabbits, rats, the odd cow and many a goat. Savannah also saw the slaves. Immediately, she wondered what she was doing standing on a stage and being thrilled about snow glitter on her tail. Ichabod saw that look and was not about to let her fall into that hole. Immediately, he went back to talking about the stage.

"'Tis no Globe Theatre, but I suppose efen Shakespeare vould hafe used any stage he could hafe, *ja*?" Ichabod broke her train of thought.

"I'm not so sure about that, but *we* must produce wherever we can," Savannah smirked.

In a moment of realization, as far from the torment of slavery as a thought could be, she twirled and twirled around the stage. Her winter-white, silk polonaise dress and red cape, both ballooned and spun like an ink-stained, white rose.

"A play, Ichabod! We are going to put on a play! How thrilling! I am so excited!"

"You are Villiamsburg's newest *artiste. Brava*, Madame!" Ichabod bowed to her dramatically.

"What would they call me?" she asked mid-twirl.

"Vhat vould who call you?"

"You know. People. When they see me here, working on my play. What would they call me? A writer? A playwright? A manager? What?" she started to slow her twirling, as spinning whilst watching her skirt billow was making her very dizzy.

"Vell, you are going to write the play, *ja*?"

"*Ja.*"

"*Und* you are going to produce the play, *ja*? Organizing it, managing it, selling the tickets, *ja*?"

Savannah blinked a few times. All laid out, that sounded like an awful lot of work. She had written the play, of course. In fact, she still had a bit of work to do, just polishing it a little. She had even envisioned herself in charge of a large group of people, making suggestions about their acting, telling set designers where to place flowers and furniture, helping actors and actresses with their costumes and just generally putting on a party of sorts. But, selling tickets? That was so, well, trade work. She didn't think she would actually have to go door-to-door and collect money.

"Do I really have to sell tickets?" she tilted her head and squinted one eye at Ichabod.

"If you vant people to see it you do," Ichabod knew exactly what she had been thinking. "Look, of course, you can get help. Ve can place adfertisements at the taferns and maybe get Parks to print some vone-page ads to post around town."

Savannah squinted a little more, still not happy about doing any business with Parks.

"You can hire people to do many things," Ichabod continued. "Scenery, costuming, efen help vith ticket sales if you like."

She started to speak but Ichabod stopped her.

"I vill be your producer, your financier, your impresario. Meaning I vill fund the entire enterprise."

Her eyes lit up and she clasped her paws as her face burst into a huge, silent smile.

"*Ja, ja.* It's okay. I hafe plenty of money. I shan't efen miss it. Ve vill go hafe a coffee and sit vith qvill and paper and make a list of vhat ve need to do and vhat ve need to buy. Howefer," he saw her start to speak again and held up a navy leather-gloved paw, "you must be fery clear in your understanding about making a play, Safannah. Yes, it is fun, fery fun. I lofe the theatre. Yet, to make a play is a lot of vork, fery hard vork. Yes, ve can hire many people. Ve vill pay fery good vages and they vill vork hard for us, do just vhat you like. But you are the writer, the manager. You must vork as hard as anyone you hire, harder. If this play does vell, eferyvone vill call it *a* triumph. If it fails, eferyvone vill call it *your* failure."

Ichabod straightened his greatcoat, a black velvet affair with gold buttons and a black lace trim on its high, standing collar. It matched the black-and-navy suit beautifully, but the collar was so high and so fashionable that it covered most of his face. All Savannah could see when he propped it up was his ears: two tiny, black triangles. He looked at Savannah and waited for her agreement. She thought about it all, digested everything he said and she agreed it would be hard work, but that she was up for it. Behind the glamour and fun of the theatre was a serious task. She had a message to get across to the general public and if she couldn't do it in print, she would do it in drama. . .and some comedy.

She and Ichabod shook paws right there. There, center stage of Levingston's Theater, the colonies' first commercial theatre, Miss Savannah Prudence Squirrel of London and Williamsburg, became Virginia's first female and the world's first squirrel playwright. She was now in the company of London's two greatest women, in her estimation: playwrights Katherine Philips and Aphra Behn. Of course, depending how this one-off went, she might like to join the sole company of Mrs. Aphra Behn and make a healthy living writing plays.

Ichabod held his paw out for her and led her off-stage into where, in just a few months' time, her audience would sit in judgment. As they walked down the stairs, they both got a creepy feeling. Their fur stood up on their backs and they stopped instantly, frozen in place with only their eyes shifting behind them.

Just behind the stage, they heard something rustle behind the curtain. They felt something watching them. They whipped about face, but saw nothing except a flash of blue fly from the wings and out the backstage door. Then, like candies from a jar, four cats spilled out from the wings and chased after the blue flash. They were not cats like Dante. These were rogue, outsider cats who were rarely seen in town. They were, to Ichabod's immense displeasure, nude. Never mind, for they and the blue flash were gone in a flash, leaving Savannah and Ichabod to just stare at one another. Had it been a ghost? A theatre spirit in blue and his naked, ghost cats? No, that would be weird. Savannah and Ichabod shook their heads and put it down to the weather and hunger. After all, it was lunchtime.

They walked quickly down the Palace Green toward DoG Street, checking behind themselves every once in a while. Down DoG and to the left waited Mrs. Pritchen's Tavern, fabulously busy right now. If they could find a seat, they would spend an afternoon of pre-production discussions over hot, cinnamon and honey cappuccinos on this cold December day.

As they walked, the delightful sound of snow crunching beneath their shoes, Savannah turned to Ichabod and asked once more, just for clarity.

"So, what would they call me? You know. People?"

As Ichabod and Savannah talked and drank at the Raleigh, Dante was hard at work with William Parks. It was also a busy time for the town printer: legal documents, official orders, court papers. He had still not found a new apprentice and so Dante had agreed to stay on until Parks did find someone new. Actually, Dante was quite enjoying himself. He knew he didn't have to do it forever so it was more of a fun, learning experience than daily drudgery. Not that it was a bad profession, but Dante just had no desire to remain in ink and foul-smelling soot for the rest of his days. As it was, his glorious tabby coat had already become stained blue in so many large patches he was beginning to look like a cow. Not to mention his paws! Forget it! They were permanently blue. He looked like he was wearing mittens at all times. Plus, he was missing out on an awful lot of fun having to work all the time and Mrs. Pritchen actually had to hire someone to temporarily replace Dante: a young, Indian boy studying religion at the William and Mary Brafferton School. Mrs. Pritchen wasn't happy about hiring someone new right now. Nobody knew the tavern like Dante. Still, she understood honouring a commitment and she would have been disappointed if Dante had left Mr. Parks in a mess after promising to stay.

As for missing fun, even today he had to decline the invitation from Ichabod and Savannah to join them at the theatre. It sounded fun, and serious, like there were big goings-on to discuss. But, no, he promised Parks he'd help him print two-hundred legal documents: yesterday's court proceedings.

"Dante," Parks called from across the shop, in front of the huge printing press, his hands busy kneading together two ink beaters, both moist with a fresh application. "I am ready for another sheet of paper." He then began rolling the beaters back and forth over two metal plates of type resting in the press. Alternately, he would knead the beaters and re-apply ink to the plates as he waited for Dante.

"Yes, right away. Just a moment," Dante called back over his shoulder.

Up on tip-toes and on top of a ladder, Dante stretched up and carefully hung a freshly-inked sheet next to dozens of others, all slung over a series of ropes strung across the ceiling. Making sure it was hung straight and exactly on the fold, he then ran to the back wall where he leaned against it the press peel: a wooden tool that looked like a flat, half-moon stuck on the end of a long-handle. The straight edge was used to transfer the wet pages to the ropes without touching the ink job or tearing the sheet. Dante then grabbed another sheet from a tray on the desk on the back wall. Dashing to the press, he very carefully lay it on the underside of what looked like the lid, except it had two cut-outs the exact shape of the metal plates underneath.

"Excellent!" exclaimed Parks. "Now, let us print!"

Checking the edges to insure a clean job and that no wrinkling would occur, Parks gently dropped the lid down on the press, the paper only being exposed to the metal plates within the two cut-outs. Then with great strength he pulled a giant lever toward him one time and pushed it back into place. Dante watched with amazement as all the tendons, veins and muscles in Park's arms tightened and pulsed during the seemingly simple action. Dante looked at his own arm, flexed it a little and frowned. He would ask Parks later if he could work the press once in a while.

After letting go of the handle, Parks lifted the lid and there on its underside was a printed piece of paper: two sections of printed words with a wide border and a separation down the middle. It never failed to amaze Dante. Just yesterday these were mere words and orders from the minds and mouths of court judges and lawyers. Now, they were actually printed on paper for others to read. Printed on paper! From the brain to a paper! Amazing!

"Dante, let's get this up on the ropes and bring me another sheet. We're making good time, but we've got many more to finish, see?" Parks began re-inking and kneading his beaters.

"Yes, sir!" Dante happily grabbed the peel and held it out as Parks gingerly placed the newest sheet over its flat edge.

The night wore on and finally, all two-hundred sheets, plus twenty extra, were finished. Dante's last job of the night was to put away the ink beaters.

"Dante, do not hang them on their pegs, yet. Forget not, you must clean them first, see?" Parks reminded him, watching him over his reading glasses as he stood at his desk calculating the court's running tally which would be due in one lump sum at the end of the month.

Dante groaned. What an awful process. The cleaning of the ink beaters was enough to cause him to quit right then and there. Why did he have to do *that* job? Couldn't Parks do it? It was his shop. Parks saw the look and decided he could indeed clean his own ink beaters tonight. After all, Dante was helping him out rather a lot.

"Oh, do not worry about it, Dante. You know, I really appreciate all your help, see?" Parks looked out the window at the cold, dark night. "I tell you what. I can do this on my own. 'Tis a frightful task, see, but it rather fazes me not after all these years. You go home. Get some sleep. 'Tis another court day tomorrow, so more court notes for us to print, see?" Parks went back to his accounting and hummed as he looked at the numbers. "Perhaps it is not too late to visit with your friends. I know you said they had something very important to discuss today."

"Thank you, Mr. Parks. How kind of you! I appreciate this. I do think Savannah and Ichabod might still be up. Savannah is planning something big," he made an excited face, all teeth showing.

"If Savannah is involved, I am sure it is indeed something big. She is what my granny would have called a Princess Hellcat, see? She's certainly full of fire, but with just enough propriety and elegance that no one sees it coming, see?" Parks laughed as he added some more figures.

Dante took his coat, scarf and hat off the pegs by the front door and pulled on his snow boots as he said goodbye.

"Thank you again for the early night."

"My pleasure, little cat. You work hard and it does not go unnoticed, see? When I find a new apprentice, I shall do something special for you, not to mention Mrs. Pritchen for loaning you out at such a busy time," he smiled at Dante who was pulling on his mittens, happy to be covering his blue paws.

"Well, I appreciate it, Mr. Parks. I shall let you know all the details of the big to-do tomorrow morning. Until then, *Ciao ciao!*" and he waved backwards in the style of the Italians and ran out the door, hoping it was not too late to visit with his friends.

CHAPTER TWENTY - SIX

"Have you read the latest offering from New-York, my dear friend?" Ben waggled the newest *New-York Weekly Journal* at Andrew as he took a seat at their table in their coffeehouse.

Philadelphia was beyond cold today and the coffeehouse was beyond packed. Were Andrew and Ben and his Junto not regulars they would have never gotten a table on a day like this. In fact though, there was always some member of this group there it seemed. It could be five in the morning, two in the afternoon or midnight. Someone from Ben's group was always there. A table was never an issue. Tonight, the snow fell hard whilst inside Monk's it was warm, stuffy actually, and smelled of cinnamon, tobacco, firewood and coffee, of course. The specialty tonight was an espresso and Viennese blend called a Pressed Vienna. It packed the equivalent of six cups of coffee into one large cup. It was a wallop of caffeine and the whole place was really buzzing from it. Ben included. He was all jittery and extra happy.

"Hey, Andrew? Did you hear me? Have you read this, yet?" he shook the paper more excitedly at Andrew who was now settling into his chair and taking his first sip of coffee.

"Ah, this explains your vigor!" Andrew laughed as he got his first taste of the strong blend. "Good coffee tonight. Wild, but good. And, no, before you ask me again," he good-naturedly warned as Ben held out the paper again, his eyes huge and his mouth wide open in a weird, whacked out smile, "I have not read any New-York papers in a few days. I have been preparing for a tryal and really should not even be here now. I am just so exhausted I need some extra energy to get through the night. So, you shall have to update me on whatever has you so riled up, friend, besides this coffee."

"It is the latest from Mr. John Peter Zenger!" Ben trilled.

"Mr. Zenger? How can that be? He is in gaol," Andrew crossed his right leg over his left and leaned comfortably back into his black, wooden chair.

"'Tis a ghost!" he winked. "Someone is getting his daily journals from gaol and printing them in the *Journal*!"

"Well, huzzah! The show must go on, I presume. Well done," Andrew held up his cup in salute to Zenger's ghost writer and all at the table followed suit.

"Huzzah, *Journal* ghost!" they all cheered three times and clinked their cups on the third.

Everyone around them cheered as well, mostly out of plain old coffee jitters. But Ben went back to his paper and re-read the latest, in truth nearly a month old but still good gossip from the New-York City Gaol.

CHAPTER TWENTY SEVEN

The

New-York Weekly JOURNAL

Containing the Freshest Advices, Foreign, and Domestick
MUNDAY November 25tth, 1734

To all my subscribers and Benefactors who take my weekly Journall.
Gentlemen, Ladies and Others,
*   As you last week were disappointed of my Journall, I think it Incumbent*
upon me to publish my Apoligy which is this, On the Lords Day, the Seventeenth
of this instant, I was Arrested; taken and Imprisoned in the common Gaol of this
City, by Virtue of a Warrant from the Governour, and the Honorable Franciss
Harison, Esq, and others in Councill of which (God willing) yo'l have a Coppy,
whereupon I was put under such Restraint that I had not the Liberty of Pen,
Ink, or Paper, or to see, or speak with People, till upon my Complaint to the
Honorable Chief Justice, at my appearing before him upon my Habias Corpus
on the Wednesday following. The Chief Justice discountenanced that Proceeding,
and therefore I have had since that Time, the Liberty of Speaking through the
Hole of the Door, to my Wife and Servants. I doubt not yo'l think me sufficiently
Excused for not sending my last weeks Journall, and I hope for the future by the
Liberty of Speaking to my Servants thro' the Hole of the Door of the Prison, to
entertain you with my weekly Journal as formerly.
*   And am your obliged Humble Servant,*
*   J. Peter Zenger.*

Jennifer Susannah Devore

The atmosphere inside the posh Custis Estate couldn't have been further from that of the estate grounds. Whereas the vast lawns were covered in a light dusting of snow, the trees barren and brittle, inside the estate was filled with warmth so comforting and welcoming it was actually visible as a yellow and orange glow. The russet-coloured walls and dark pine floors radiated like the Mediterranean sun as the candlelight of fifty porcelain wall sconces flickered and feathered throughout the hallways and main ballroom. Nowhere did the light dance more lusciously than upon the groaning boards that lined the ballroom's four long walls. Traditionally, they were called sideboards; colloquially, they were called groaning boards because the long serving counters, waist-high and usually marble-topped to withstand heated dishes, often held so much good food and drink that the furniture quite literally groaned under the weight of the owner's bounty.

In fact, it had become somewhat of a game over the years for children at any gathering to crawl under such groaning boards, the winner being he or she whom could stay under the longest without being scared as they counted the audible groans. Naturally, this was a game feared by most mothers. No mum wants her child smushed by a giant ham. So the game became more of a dare to whom could stay under the groaning boards the longest before one's mum found them. Tonight's children may have indeed been in danger of a good ham-smushing. It was Christmas Eve after all! On no other night in the year should a groaning board be more apt to collapse under its own weight of fruits, meats, sweets, wines, vegetables and Chesapeake Bay seafood than this night! Moreover, this was the John Custis Estate, town residence to one of the Virginia colony's wealthiest and most prominent gentlemen ever!

Spanning a good eight lots, the Custis Estate, more commonly called Custis Sqaure boasted numerous outbuildings and an already legendary group of ornamental gardens, flowerbeds and experimental planting arenas. Much of the gardens were part of an on-going trading project with a fellow naturalist back in England: Mr. Peter Collinson. Mr. Collinson and Colonel Custis would send and receive across the Atlantic different varieties and specimens native to America and England, each giving an exoticism to the other's grounds back home. Throughout the year they would write each other, comparing and contrasting how well each species did in its new foreign home. This time of year the gardens were not at their finest, but the grounds were nevertheless still expansive and impressive.

In addition to the fine land, outbuildings and gardens, there stood rows of slave quarters alongside the main house: a huge, brick affair built in the classic, stately, symmetrical Georgian style. As warm and festive as the main house was tonight, the slave quarters were just as cold and dismal. The only respite from the daily pain and drudgery of being a Custis slave was Christmas Eve and Christmas Morning.

Tonight, the slave village was alive with music, dancing, special feasts of chicken and ham sent down from the main house and the sheer relief of not having to work, unless of course one was a house slave. Many in the slave quarters wanted to sleep, but the thought of missing out on their one night of festivities in the year was too much temptation. Sleep or feast? Feast, of course. In fact, the village was filled with such merriment this night of the year it was hard to imagine the truly horrific existence they endured the rest of the year. Because of this, most chose to put that out of their minds for this one time and enjoy what they felt was surely a rare blessing and goodness handed down by their Master Custis. For by tomorrow night, things would be back to normal.

Back inside the main house the smells and sounds of Christmas were swirling around the ballroom. What seemed like miles and miles of marble groaning boards supported what seemed like the town supply of porcelain, silver and china bowls, tureens, platters and plates, plus glass, crystal and pottery drinking vessels of all shapes and varieties. The only thing more plentiful than food at a Christmas party was drink. More port, ale, wine, rum punch, apple cider, wassail, scotch, apple brandy, whiskey, coffee, tea and drinking chocolate stood ready for the taking than one could imagine even King George was enjoying back home this night.

The scents of steamed vegetable and cheese dishes, savoury meats, roasted oysters, mussels and clams still in their shells, toasty soups and hearty meat stews, poached and buttered seafood and fish of all types drifted over the groaning boards and filtered throughout the dance floor which was filled with guests holding hands and dancing in circles, twirling and swirling to the very popular Sir Roger de Coverley Dance, also known as the Virginia Reel.

Whilst Savannah loved to dance, she had decided to sit it out for a while after she unwisely accepted an offer to dance with Tobias-George Bluth, whom had spilled red wine on her tail twice before they even got to the dance floor. She hadn't spent nearly an hour brushing, fluffing, powdering and perfuming her tail to have it stained by some clumsy law student, sweet as he was. So for the moment, Savannah sat on a French-blue, satin divan from Switzerland, sipping her drinking chocolate and keeping her tail wrapped in a linen napkin of salt and soda water to ward off any permanent damage. Her chocolate was good though, and this took her mind off her tail. Always looking for a way to spice up a beverage, she did this very literally with her current drink.

It occurred to her that whilst the thick, hot drinking chocolate was very tasty on its own, it was a bit bland. As she had wandered earlier across one of the groaning boards, along a specially woven table runner put in place especially for the smaller animals whom would be attending the party, she noticed a small shaker full of a very exotic chili powder, apparently shipped in from Spain's territories in the southern colonies. She wasn't sure, but thought perhaps a pinch of chili powder might make a fantastic Spanish-style drink. She was right. It was fantastic! In fact, it was so good that not only was she on her third cup, which was making her teeth hurt a bit, but for some odd reason she was keeping it a secret. There was no reason to do so, but because it was so good she felt some strange compulsion to not tell a soul about it. Then, Ichabod came by and sat next to her.

"Qvite the party, *ja*?"

"Mmm, yes," Savannah swallowed the sip in her mouth quickly as if Ichabod was going to try to take it from her or something.

"Vhat is wrong vith you? You look funny," Ichabod observed.

"Nothing," Savannah had just ingested a clump of chili powder that had congealed in the chocolate and was now working its way up into her nose and through her sinuses. Her eyes reacted by watering heavily.

"Safannah! You are crying! Vhat is it? Vas it Tobias? Did he hurt your tail? Vhat a klutz. I tell you these Austrians are all alike, not a bit of grace in a hundred of them," Ichabod shook his head.

"No, it's not Tobias. It's," she sneezed four times in a row: teensy, tiny sneezes like those a fairy or an elf might make.

"*Ach*! Are you okay?"

"Aren't you supposed to say *Gesundheit* to me?" she sneezed about seven more times then wiped her eyes with her handkerchief.

"*Gesundheit*," Ichabod obliged flatly as he rolled his eyes. "That is so predictable. Vhat is wrong vith you anyvay?"

"It is. . .," she hesitated telling him, then realized how very strange the whole idea of a secret about chocolate was. "It's the chocolate. I put chili powder in it."

Ichabod laughed.

"I drank some too fast and I guess it got in my nose. It is very good, though! I just sprinkled a little in my cup and Mmmm! The spice and the sweet go so well together. Would you like some?"

"Thank you but no. It sounds vonderful, but efen the tiniest bit of spices make me sneeze efen vorse than you just did. A cup of that concoction vould probably kill me," he gestured at the cup with his eyes, accusing the drink silently as he glared at it.

"Well, don't tell anyone about it," she leaned in toward Ichabod and whispered.

"Vell that's an odd thing to say," he looked at her like she was crazy.

"I. . .I. . .," she stammered defensively, sitting back up straight and raising her eyebrows. "Just don't. It's my idea."

"Veird. But, okay. I shan't tell anybody about chocolate and chili powder," he said in a spooky voice while wiggling his fingers and showing the whites of his eyes that usually were never seen. "It shall be our little secret."

"What? What's your little secret? I want to know," Dante bounded up to them, his fur all wet and matted and out of breath from hours of non-stop dancing.

"Nothing," Ichabod said plainly and took a sip of his apple brandy.

"Tell me!" Dante insisted.

"Ugh," Savannah gave in. "It's my drink."

"Why? What's in it?" Dante was intrigued. "Is it illegal? Is it pyrate booty?!"

"No! It is not illegal and it is certainly not pyrate booty!" Savannah was offended and Dante was disappointed. "Why do they call it booty anyway?" she wondered for a moment, her head tilting up in thought.

"So, what is it?" Dante asked again, eyeing the dance floor and scanning the room for a new partner.

"It is drinking chocolate with a little bit of chili powder in it. It is very good," she hid her cup from Dante, physically still keeping it a secret.

"Chili and chocolate? Big deal. I've had that before."

"No you haven't," Savannah crossed her arms and started to pout.

"Yes, I have. Remember that artist, the painter, who stayed with Mrs. Pritchen last year? He made some one night for us. He said it was something he'd had in Madrid."

"Hmm" Savannah did not like being upstaged; as far as she was concerned, this was her drink, she had invented it and that was that.

"Where's Anthony? I went by his shop and it's all closed up. I assumed he'd be here," Dante looked around the room.

"I know. I thought so, too. He has been so busy lately with this new store. He is insistent upon opening number four by the spring. I told him he needs to rest and at least enjoy Christmas. But, I guess he didn't want to. I worry about him these days," Savannah sipped her chocolate.

"He vill be okay," Ichabod patted her back. "Antony has been through much this year. It vill take some time to heal. He is a big boy and knows how to care for himself. Do not vorry about Antony. Anyvone who can bargain wholesale prices the vay he does from those boorish, Portuguese vine merchants can take care of himself. Like I haf said many times before, when he is ready not to be sad, he vill not be sad," Ichabod tossed back the rest of his brandy and looked around for a server to bring him another.

"So, vhere haf you and Sterling been tonight? Talking with the Custis Players, I assume," Ichabod turned back to Dante and referenced a troupe of actors brought into town specifically for the Christmas season.

So as to avoid an incident like that which had brought Sterling to

America in the first place, (an incident which was still a secret to all but Sterling and the Maryland authorities) these actors were called the Custis Players, proving to any law enforcement officials that they were employed and sponsored and not just a band of rambling rabble rousers and indigent ne'er-do-wells.

"I think Sterling is still over there with the actors," Dante's blue paw reached out and took Savannah's cup. "Mmmm, that is good. Needs more chili powder, though."

"Hmph," Savannah left to get one more cup, even though she was feeling really full and sickly with chocolate.

On her way, she spotted Sterling and the Players and wondered if any of them would be right for her production. Still months away from anything close to rehearsals, her play was nevertheless still on track.

"Savannah, Love! Come over here! You must meet my new friends!" Sterling lifted a wine glass in invitation.

Savannah decided she'd had enough chocolate and was only having some to prove her point, whatever that was. So, she set down her cup and leaped to Sterling's group in one bound, landing upon the shoulder of young Master Daniel Parke Custis, son of Colonel John Custis.

Twenty-three, handsome and the only surviving son of the family, (Sadly, two had died within a year of their birth.) Daniel was quite the catch about town. Wealthy by birth, his father was a prominent member of Gooch's Governor's Council; his maternal grandfather, Mr. Daniel Parke, had not only served on the Governor's Council also, but was the royal governor to the Leeward Islands. Young Master Custis' wealth and good looks brought the girls to him like mud to boots. His generosity, kindness and charming character brought everyone else. If Daniel Parke Custis was at a party, that's where the fun was.

"Why, hello, Miss Savannah!" Daniel was surprised as she leapt upon his velvet-clad shoulder.

"*Buon Natale*, Daniel! Merry Christmas!" she chirped.

"Some party, yes?" he asked as he handed her a blue, marzipan seashell from his plate, her favourite treat of all.

"Indeed!" she gobbled up the marzipan, holding it with both lace-gloved paws.

"Savannah, this is Marcella, Lucius, Mary Jane, Ferguson and Lionel. They're the performers for tonight. I was helping them rehearse earlier. You'll love it! They're doing Edmund Spenser's *The Fairie Queene*!"

"Oh! I love *Fairie Queene*!" Savannah squealed, her mouth full of pasty, blue confection.

"Savannah is writing a play!" Sterling bragged to the group.

"Really? That's fabulous! What is it about? Is there a part for me?" the Italian girl Marcella straightened her posture as she asked.

"Mmm, well, it is not quite ready for casting. In fact, I may not be ready for a cast until well into the spring. However,. . ." Marcella immediately lost interest and was already turning her attention back to Daniel.

"Of course it is going to be a sell-out when it is finished, right, Savannah?!" Sterling added.

"Um, well, I hope so. Really 'tis more of a message than a commercial endeavour," she wiped marzipan from her face.

"Nonsense," piped in Lionel. "Everything is a commercial endeavour."

"Not art," argued Mary Jane, an attractive, English girl wearing very fine pink and red silk ribbons in her sable hair.

"Especially art," Linus retorted as he took a sip of wine.

"How so?" asked Sterling, offended that art could be cheapened. "I have never taken a shilling for my art."

"'Tis fabulous for you," Lionel snapped. "Clearly, you are fortunate enough to have no need for payment. A wealthy family, I presume," Sterling nodded slightly, a little embarrassed. "Really, 'tis good for you. However, there are legions of actors, musicians, jugglers, costumers and the like who do not have such luxury, but whom wish to retain a living in performance art. Until we can make acting a proper profession, a viable industry whereby respected businessmen can make money from our work, we will be seen forever as the bastard child of the ancient court jester. A joke and a waste of space."

The group became quiet for a moment. Obviously, Lionel had some issues about his life's work, but it brought everyone in the group to thinking about his or her own situation and wondering what he or she was doing with his or her life. Then, as if a silent agreement, all the actors lifted their heads and their wine glasses and cheered, "Skin off your nose!"

"Skin off your nose!" was an old, thespian toast which referred to a white, theatrical makeup so toxic that it actually pulled a thin layer of skin off one's nose when washed off after a performance.

"We are not vulgar, we are not ruffians, we are thespians! I thank Lady Fortuna for the likes of Mr. Levingston and Mr. Custis here," Daniel bowed his head and smiled as Mary Jane toasted their hosts.

"And Miss Savannah, too!" toasted Sterling, his glass aloft. "For someday we shall be the envy of every common man!"

"Someday, people shall call out our names and scramble to touch us as we walk the streets!" Lucius raised his wine glass.

"They shall plead with us to grace their stages and pay us wages greater than a king's!" Lionel lifted his glass to Sterling's and Lucius'. "We shall rule the earth someday and the average folk will name their children after us."

"We shall always be ahead of our time and proud to be out of touch!" Ferguson added and raised his glass, and though the others kind of wondered what he was talking about, he was one of them, so they didn't question it.

"They shall beg the gods that we may acknowledge them as our friends! They shall die to be us! They shall spend their inheritances to copy our fashion and hairstyles!" Marcella was the last to raise her glass to the others and squished in close to Daniel as she did so.

Together they cheered mightily, "Skin off your nose!", and suddenly felt sorry for anyone whom wasn't a thespian that night.

"Sheesh, 'tis only acting," Dante said under his breath as he walked past them, causing a glare or two from the actors and a quiet giggle from Savannah and Daniel.

Everyone loved an actor; nobody liked a pompous thespian.

As the night pressed on, Savannah learned more about the emotional needs of the fragile creature known as the actor. Was she going to have to deal with this in her production? She liked the look of Mary Jane and thought she might be right for a part in her play, but she seemed like an insecure mess. No matter what Savannah said to her that night, she took offense. When Savannah had commented how pretty blue ribbons would compliment her black hair, Mary Jane had said, "You do not like the pink and red? Do they look bad?" Savannah wasn't sure how much of that she could take. Luckily, the troupe had to go and make final preparations for their play.

It was rare, even unheard of, for actors to engage with actual guests in the main room of a party, but Daniel Parke Custis was a bit progressive and personally invited them into the fold, much to the chagrin of his father. Still, they were allowed to stay as long as they were prepared and timely for their performance. Colonel Custis had a great many important guests here tonight and even though the troupe was Daniel's idea, his father now embraced them for what they were: a status symbol to show up his friends.

Long after the sun had set, ushers came into the ballroom and held up a large, black swath of fabric to hide the light from the wall sconces near the entry door. Then, they lowered the fabric, re-lighting the room. Then, they lifted the fabric again, darkening the room, then lowered the fabric one last time, making the room light once more. This arduous flash of lights, off and on and off and on, was the silent, polite signal that the performance was about to begin. Once everyone was seated, the ushers came back with candlesnuffers to exterminate the wall sconce flames for good.

Savannah, Sterling, Ichabod and Dante had front row seats in the private Custis Theatre. As the footcandles were lit at the bottom of the stage and the red, velvet curtain was rolled up, Savannah realized how much she wanted to go home and write. This was all going to be for her soon! If she could just finish her play. Oh, why was the writing part so difficult? She had already planned what she'd wear opening night and what kind of wine she'd order from Anthony and the perfect basket she'd bring with her each performance night, for all the flowers the audience would throw her, of course. If she could just get the stupid thing written, she'd be the best playwright since Mrs. Aphra Behn! As the curtain rolled up, she saw two slaves running back toward the ballroom, their hands full of dirty dishes. She then felt two things very deep in her belly.

One, she would stay for the play out of politeness to the actors, but then she had to leave. What was she doing at a Christmas party run by slave labor? Hadn't she grown at all this year? How could she be so hypocritical? All night the slaves moved fluidly and silently around her bringing her precious chocolate and chili peppers and marzipan goodies and all she had done was to take no notice of them and enjoy herself like a vapid little imp. She fought the urge to fly out the front doors right now. Ichabod was watching her and knew exactly what she was thinking. He put a paw on hers and silently begged her to wait. He would escort her home the minute the curtain rolled down.

The second thing she felt in her belly? She needed to finish her play and hopefully, someday soon, put an end to all this horror. What an awful, awful Christmas.

Anthony sat cold and shivering with only a large groundhog named Beauregard, whom he didn't even know was there, keeping him company. Anthony pulled his brown, Italian wool scarf tighter around his neck and buttoned to the neck his expensive, London greatcoat: a brand-new Christmas present to himself. He also pulled his knees closer to his chest as he huddled undetected in a small grove of pine trees. For nearly three hours he'd been there, just watching. He'd shown up in time for the party, the finest bottle of port wine in his stock placed nicely in a basket and surrounded by other goodies for Mrs. Frances Custis. It was a big night for Anthony. For years and years he had been the go-to for party catering. Everyone in town knew his wines, chocolates, bisquits and teas were the finest in the Tidewater area. Yet tonight, tonight was a milestone. Tonight, Anthony was a guest.

He had never been invited to a fête such as this, certainly not one given by such a prominent member of society. It was almost as if his years of hard work, saving, studying his goods and providing fine quality had erased his skin colour. It was though he was finally seen as a man and a merchant, not a black man and a former slave.

Still, when he arrived he saw the smoke and glowing cresset fires of the slave village. Like small fire-globes, cressets were wrought-iron, hanging baskets filled with lightwood pine and set ablaze all over town when the sun went down and winter brought its chill. At the slave quarters he saw the working community alive in song and rhythm, jubilant in dance and merriment and he sneaked around to have a peek. That was over three hours ago. He hadn't moved except to sit down in the dirt and place his basket under a tree. Beauregard, the shy groundhog, couldn't help but smell the treats.

"Blueberry yummies!" he thought to himself as he sniffed the fresh, blueberry muffins. Although, he didn't dare take one. One never knew with humans which were nice and which were not. This one seemed nice, he could certainly smell that about him, however, he also seemed troubled and that was a dangerous time to get too near a human. Sometimes their emotions allowed them to act in strange and inexplicable ways. He'd probably do best just to sit back and watch this one.

As Beauregard watched him, Anthony watched the slaves. From afar, the Christmas Eve celebration seemed to grow happier and happier as the night went on. The happier they seemed, the sadder and more sick Anthony grew. For tomorrow or the next day, they would no longer be happy. Maybe they would be hungry, maybe they would be tired. Maybe they would be whipped and maybe they would have a limb cut off for something trivial like stealing a leftover, Christmas-ham bisquit. Maybe one would run away and be hunted like his brother and be shot dead in a field. . .if he was lucky. If he was not, maybe he'd be brought back to the estate and made an example to all the other would-be runaways.

No, Anthony had tried. He promised Savannah he would go to the party and he would be merry for the season, but he could not. How could he? How could he, with any conscience or character pass by these slaves and enter one of the grandest Christmas parties in Virginia? He could not. The only difference between these slaves and himself was luck and money, all of which could disappear tomorrow, a mere flick of fate's wrist. No, he could not celebrate his good fortune, not while these others were so unfortunate.

Anthony stood up, took one last glance at the glowing village and walked away, leaving his basket behind. Strangely, the farther he walked from the village, the louder and stronger the laughter and singing became. It grew so loud in his ears he thought he might go mad. Tearing off his scarf and his new coat, he tossed them to the ground and ran for home, not stopping until he was safe inside his very warm, very fine Williamsburg townehome.

Feeling a little bad for the odd human, but having the munchies nevertheless, Beauregard apprehensively approached the now abandoned basket, looking all around to make sure no one was coming back.

"Mmmm, I was right! Blueberry!"

He took a large blueberry and orange muffin out of the basket and dragged it back to his home under the pine tree. Moments later, he came back for two more, just in case. Then, he heard something in the trees, saw a flash of blue behind him and faster than groundhogs usually run, ran back into his hole. A few minutes later, he poked his nose back out when he thought it was safe. No more rustling, no more blue flash. He did, however, out of the corner of his eye, heading back into the trees behind his, catch some movement. Cats. Four nude cats. This, he thought, was very strange indeed.

"Merry Christmas, Mr. Zenger," Linus bundled up his collar and scarf in one hand as he held out a large turkey pie in the other hand. "Shall I slide it under the grate?"

Zenger looked up at the guard, as unhappy as any of the prisoners on this Christmas Eve.

"Is it alright, sir?" Linus asked up at the grizzled man, probably not much older than himself, just worn ragged until he looked a full generation older.

"Right then. 'S Christmas ain't it? Slide it under. But I wants me a bite. I ain't got nuffin to eat tonight but some sick ol' chicken. I think it ain't even good," he held his stomach. "Bad chicken, mess you up."

Linus took the wooden fork he'd brought for Zenger, after having it approved by the warden, and scooped out a small portion for the guard.

"More than that, wittle boy! What do I looks like? A mouse?" the guard demanded.

"Oi! I wants me some pie, too, Mate!"

"Over 'ere, boy! Gimme summa dat pie!"

"Look everybody! 'S li'l Father Christmas! 'Es brung us some Christmas pie!"

The other prisoners of the New-York City Gaol laughed aloud and harassed Linus. He had to get out of there and fast.

Linus scooped more and the guard grabbed it, shoving it into his mouth and swallowing it all in one motion. Linus figured the man never even tasted it. He handed back the fork and disgustingly left a mark of mouth slime around the tines. Linus had to hold back a dry hurl and wiped it on the back of his pants so as not to hand it over soiled to Mr. Zenger. Christmas in gaol was bad enough without someone else's mouth slime. He slid the wooden plate under the bars of Zenger's gaol door. There was about an inch of space where the door ended. The plate made a horrid scraping sound as Linus slid it to Zenger. He took the pie and smelled it. It smelled wonderful, like home, like ink, like his family.

"How is my wife? How is Catherine?" Zenger asked as he dug into the flaky, golden crust and then into the juicy, steamy turkey stew within.

"Honestly, sir?" Linus wrinkled his eyebrows in worry.

"Yes, honestly. How is she?"

"Crabby," Linus said firmly.

Zenger raised an eyebrow and tilted his head to one side as if to say, "Of course, that's Catherine."

"How about my children? The boys? How are the boys?" he clearly was less concerned about his daughters as he rarely asked about them.

"They are well and busy. They have been a great aid to your journeymen printers and myself. Do not worry, sir. With all our help, we are getting the *Journal* out on-time every Monday."

"Are you getting my diary pieces from here?"

"Yes. Mr. Alexander and Mr. Morris have been collecting them from a messenger, I guess. They bring us a new diary installment once a week and tell us to head up the front page with it."

"What else is going in the paper?" Zenger's mouth was full as he talked and making Linus a little queasy again.

"Well, Mr. Alexander, Mr. Morris and your journeymen meet once a week, when they bring the diary pieces, and they discuss what to put in there. Mostly, except for your dilemma and local advertisements, it seems to be the same kind of stories about Cosby. They're really sticking up for you!"

"Yes. It would seem," he said bitterly. "Of course, I have been sitting in here for over a month and all for the want of bail set at a mere £400," he took another bite without finishing the last one.

"'Tis a great amount of money, Mr. Zenger!"

"To you and me, yes. To the Morrisites? No. Why do they let me sit here? After everything I have done for them. It makes no sense. There must be a reason."

Zenger put down his fork and looked off thoughtfully into space, watching a spider build a web in the corner of his cell.

"Yes," he turned back to Linus, a smile in his eyes. "There must be a reason. Alexander, Morris and the others have been good to me, and I to them. No, they would not abandon me. There is something afoot. I am sure of it."

Zenger went back to his pie and Linus decided it was time for him to go. His mother had planned a traditional, Swedish, Christmas Eve celebration. He promised his mother he would not be long. She was holding all celebration until he returned.

"*Vafor kan icke hans son komma med honom mat?*" she had asked as Linus was putting on his coat to go to the gaol.

"English, *Moder*, I mean, Mother. You must practice your English. We are Americans now."

"Why cannot his own sons to bring him food to him?" she said with some effort.

"Maybe they are, Mother. But I feel so bad for him. Should he not have more than one visitor on *Julafton*? I mean, Christmas Eve?" Linus always mixed up Swedish with his English when talking to his family, especially his *moder*.

"*Du er en god pojke*," she kissed him on the nose. "You are good boy," she smiled and tried her English again. "But hurry," she added slowly. "Tradition say I must the candles light for *Julafton*. So, we. . .*vanta*?" she searched her brain for the correct English word. "*Vanta*? Wait? Yes! Wait! That is correct word, yes?" Linus smiled at her affirmatively. "We wait for you. We wait for you, Linus. Okay?"

"*Ja, Mor*. Yes, Mother."

Thinking about his mother as he ran home from the gaol, through the cold, downtown, New-York streets he imagined the feast awaiting him at home. Lucky for Linus, this was the second big celebration for their family Christmas.

They may be speaking more English and they may be living in America, but they were still Swedish at heart and it was very important to Linus' family to bring the Christmas traditions across the sea.

Almost two weeks ago, the first tradition had occurred in their home: the celebration of Saint Lucia, the Christian virgin martyred far back in the Fourth Century. As tradition dictated, Linus' youngest sister woke early that morning, December 13th and donned a long, white dress and a red sash. She then wore a wreath of evergreens on her head, set alight with candles inside the greens. (This part always made *Moder* worry.) As she walked to her parents' bedroom, she was joined by her brothers and sisters. The boys wore long, white shirts and pointy, black hats; the girls wore the same white dress and red sash as his baby sister, Hanna. In a procession through the house, all the children woke the parents and Hanna served them a breakfast-in-bed of *kaffee* and Lucia buns.

Tonight, the second celebration of *Julafton* would offer a great *smörgåsbord*, or buffet: *julskinka*, Christmas ham; *lutfisk*, dried codfish; apples and other fruits. The house would be decorated full of red-capped *tomtes*, or Christmas gnomes from back home and the straw-and-evergreen ornaments his *Moder* always strung about the house. Linus' favourite part of the night? The *pepparkakor* and *Julbok*!

Pepparkakor had been a yummy favourite since Linus was a baby: gingerbread cookies shaped like *Julbok*, the Christmas goat! The goat cookies were an ancient tradition meant to honour the goats that pulled the noble chariot of the Swedish god, Tor. Linus just liked the gingerbread and thought the goats were funny. His least favourite part of the night? The *Risgryngrot*.

Naturally, year after year, Linus' sisters loved this tradition; his parents liked it, too and always hoped for the best as the year went on. *Risgryngrot* was another Christmas Eve tradition: rice porridge in which is hidden one almond. Legend has it that whoever gets the almond will marry in the New Year! Linus had never gotten it and took the tiniest portions of *Risgryngrot* each year to lower his odds of ever getting the almond. Marriage? Ick! His sisters gobbled up spoonfuls upon spoonfuls of the rice dish in hopes of the matrimonial nut. Every year one of them got it and every year. . .no one ever married. His oldest sister was twenty and his parents had basically given up, resigned to having an old maid for a daughter. Still, there were four more girls and two boys. Maybe this year someone would marry.

As Linus broke into a sprint, his home now in view, he thanked Tor for his large and loving family. Then, he asked Tor to look after Herr Zenger and to please, please, please not give Linus the almond in the *Risgryngrot*.

Beauregard lay back in his den, very warm and very comfy. Except for one thing: he was still munchy. Oh, why hadn't he grabbed more of those muffins? Mmmm. He thought about how tasty they were as he rubbed his large, fuzzy belly. Maybe that basket was still out there. Such a thought gave the drowsy groundhog a sudden spark of energy and he sat up straight, grabbed his red, Christmas scarf off his bureau and headed for the front door.

As he poked his pudgy nose out into the winter air, he could smell that, yes, the basket and its coveted treats was indeed still there. He could also still hear the festivities of the slave village and, well, something else. He wasn't sure what it was, but he sensed something, someone. Whoever it was, he sensed niceness, but with an edge, like that man who'd left the basket in the first place. Maybe he was back. Beauregard frowned. Why hadn't he just dragged the whole basket into his den? He tried to be classy, tried to be gracious and just take a little and that was wrong. He should have taken more. Now, someone else was here and they were going to take his muffins. They were now, in Beauregard's mind, his muffins.

He poked his nose out farther to sniff it out, but nothing registered. Maybe it was those nude cats again. Put some clothes on, he thought. He saw no blue flash, though. The blue Christmas ghost in the trees, he laughed to himself. Then, he tucked his nose back in a little, just in case.

He did sense something, though. Instinctively, he pulled his nose in farther, but kept his eyes very alert in the darkness of Christmas Eve. He was about to go back into his hole completely when, out of the corner of his right eye, he saw it. The flash. The blue flash was there again, then it was gone. Beauregard thought maybe it was a bird, but it made too loud a ruckus as it crossed the dead, winter carpet of leaves. There it went again! It was much larger than a bird, much noisier, that was for sure! It was definitely human, but fast. Then, it flashed again, but this time much slower. Beauregard should have been frightened, but he was more intrigued. He stuck his nose all the way out of his front door and looked from side to side. No, this was no ghost. But what was it? He sniffed the air some more. Nothing, nothing except blueberry muffins. Well, whatever the flash was, it was gone. But the basket was surely not.

There it was, sitting on the cold, crunchy, yellow leaves that lay on the ground. *Crunch, crunch, crunch, crunch.* Beauregard made his way slowly out of his den and toward the basket. *Sniff, sniff, sniff.* Oh, he could smell the blueberry goodness. Almost there. . .almost there. . .eek!

Suddenly, out of nowhere, a tattered and ratty, woolen-gloved hand latched down on the handle of Beauregard's basket.

"Hey! That's mine!" Unafraid, Beauregard couldn't stop himself and snapped at the hand, but then felt bad for such horrid manners. "Please. I mean, if you don't mind."

It was the blue flash. The blue flash just stood there. Of course, it wasn't a flash anymore. It was a man. A tall, thin man with dark curls that landed on his shoulders and a dark, Dutch-style beard, fashionably known as a VanDyk beard. Of course, there was nothing fashionable about this man. His beard probably just grew that way due to a lack of exact grooming and his clothes were an odd mixture of ancient finery and modern cheapness.

The blue flash Beauregard had seen was a long, velvet frock coat made of a robin's egg-blue and rows of gold buttons. By now though, many of the buttons, obviously solid gold, had either fallen off or been pried off and sold. The rows were now just haphazard sprinklings of gold, like stars tossed onto a blue, summer evening sky. His trousers looked like a bad linen that couldn't keep a firefly warm, and his boots had twine wrapped around the toes keeping the soles attached to the rest of the boot. They were also soaking wet with the sleet that had been falling for the last few days. This guy's feet had to be freezing. Over all of this was a fine, leather greatcoat and a woolen, Italian scarf. Beauregard knew because he had the same exact scarf. As he looked down at his own scarf, admiring the quality, it hit him. This man's leather coat and scarf were the same items that other man was wearing! This guy must have stolen them! He must have attacked, maybe killed that other man!

"What did you do?" Beauregard screamed and ejected himself out of his den. "Where did you get those clothes?! I knew that man! He left me muffins!" Beauregard leaped for the tatty boots, his great teeth bared and ready to battle.

"Whoa, little fellow," the blue flash stepped back, but totally without fear or excitement. He was very mellow, very blasé. "I didn't do a thing to anybody."

"Then where did you get that coat, and that scarf?" Beauregard still showed his teeth, just in case.

"I found them, little fellow. Right back there," he pointed to the dense woods behind him, the front side of the Custis property.

"Found? But, I saw a man wearing them tonight. He left my, I mean, this basket here," Beauregard pointed to the basket with his nose.

"Well, he left this coat and scarf back there, just threw them away," the blue flash pointed with his nose.

"Hmmm," Beauregard thought for a moment and the blue flash waited patiently, arms crossed and sporting a huge smile. He liked this little groundhog.

"I promise. I saw him do it myself. He went running through the trees and just started tearing off his coat and scarf. Looked fairly upset while he did it. I waited for a while to see if he was coming back, but he didn't." He held open his arms, showing off his new find. "It's Christmas, it's cold, I'd have been a fool to let something so fine and warm just sit in the trees. Merry Christmas to me," he said without a note of guilt.

The blue flash sat down cross-legged and began to rummage through the basket. Beauregard felt a little offended, but then again, it wasn't really his own basket, was it? This man was finding it the same way Beauregard did earlier.

"These the muffins you said he gave you?" the blue flash held one out in his hand.

"Um, well, yes. Not really gave. But, well he left them here for me," Beauregard rationalized.

"Well, here you go. Have them all. I'm stuffed. I found some potatoes and cake they threw out tonight" he gestured toward the main house. "Wasteful,

Jennifer Susannah Devore

224

silly, pompous people. A whole cake they threw out because it was a little smushed. Big deal. Tasted good to me. They also threw out some squash and some kind of a rice dish. Truthfully," he leaned in toward Beauregard, "it was nasty. I can see why they tossed that stuff. Still, I'm full now and that's a good thing."

Beauregard listened to the blue flash and ate a blueberry muffin hastily, just in case this guy changed his mind. Then, he heard some crunching leaves behind him. Without thinking, Beauregard backed into his den just in time to see the four nude cats come out of the woods. He'd been in fights with cats before and, as a rule, he didn't like them, except that fancy one in town. He always seemed to be carrying a sword and looked like he was really good friends with that frilly squirrel and that poncy dog. Beauregard would watch them sometimes and wish that he could be friends with them. Of course, he'd never have the courage to approach them. He was just a lone groundhog with a limited wardrobe. They would probably never be friends with him anyway.

The four cats in his presence currently though, were now prowling around his basket and rubbing up against the blue flash. They were his. He was going to give them his basket. The blue flash reached into Beauregard's basket and grabbed a sealed jar, opened it and popped some of the tiny, green contents into his mouth.

"What are you doing?" Beauregard had wanted those.

"Eatin' olives."

"Ever hear of asking?"

"Sorry, little fellow. Did you want these? Here. You can have them. They're a little salty for me anyway. By the way, the name's Bruce, Phillip the Bruce," he held out a hand to shake after he poured the olives out of the jar and onto the ground in front of Beauregard. Some rolled under the dead leaves, but most rested right under his nose.

Two of the cats leaped for the olives, frightening Beauregard backwards.

"Figaro! Buddha! Leave those alone. Those are his olives," the blue flash scolded his cats who backed off and licked their paws, then their faces to show how little they cared about it all.

"No, that's okay," Beauregard held out a paw shook the blue flash's hand. "That's Scottish. Bruce. You don't sound Scottish."

"Only half. My father was a Scot. My mother was a Norsewoman. Both from the hills and lived off the land. Very intelligent folk. That's pretty much all I know. I've been an orphan since the age of six."

"Six?!"

"Absolutely, little fellow. I've travelled all over the world. Mostly, it's been a good life. I never knew my parents long enough to miss them. I'm all I know and I like me. I enjoy the pleasure of my own company immensely," he popped a piece of cherry candy in his mouth and closed his eyes to savour it.

Beauregard and Phillip the Bruce had quite a bit in common, they found. Both were orphans for as far back as they could recall and both were alone and both liked their own company. Now, they were enjoying each other's. They decided to equally split whatever was left in the basket amongst themselves and the four cats. They were called Figaro, or Figs for short, Buddha, Little Man and Boomer. Figs was clearly the leader, a gorgeous and fat calico with an uppity attitude and a really strange *meow* that sounded more like a cross between a duck's *quack* and a bird call. It was more like a *chirp* than anything.

The other cats were quiet but intense and had the habit of simply staring at Beauregard for long stretches of time, making him very nervous. Even more than that, they didn't talk. They were nude and they didn't speak English, or any other language as far as Beauregard could tell. They, however, had no problem communicating with their leader, the blue flash. Right away, Beauregard's favourite was Buddha. He kind of looked like a vampire cat. He was silky black and had two gleaming front teeth that thrust down in very fine points. Beauregard noticed that if Buddha stood too close to a tree or the blue flash's leg his vampire tooth would drag across the surface as he turned his head. Beauregard found this very, very funny. Mostly, because Buddha didn't appear to know this about himself.

The six of them sat and enjoyed the contents of the basket for nearly an hour as Beauregard learned more about Phillip the Bruce.

"What do you mean exactly when you say 'domestic hermit'?" Beauregard leaned back against a tree trunk and sipped his glass of wine.

Luckily, Anthony had been thoughtful enough to include two wine glasses in the basket that never made it to the Custis party.

"Well, in a way, I am technically a 'pet' of the Custis Estate, although I loathe that term. I am, in fact, paid a small stipend to enliven and entertain their bourgeois and dour existence as 'ladies and gentlemen'," he rolled his eyes at the phrase 'ladies and gentlemen'. "Are we not all 'ladies and gentlemen'? We're all male and female, one or the other, that's about it. The rest of this social labeling and polite titling is just verbal garbage meant to make the spiritually and mentally weak but wealthy feel better about themselves. It's all sub-mental social trash."

He threw back his fourth glass of red wine and laughed, then pulled a flute out of his rucksack and played an impromptu tune to which his cats all instantly stood up on two legs and began to dance and meow; except Figaro who chirped. Beauregard laughed and danced, too. Then, as soon as the song was over, he took the opportunity to question Phil the Bruce further about this 'domestic hermit' business.

"Now, how does one become a domestic hermit, Phillip the Bruce?"

Beauregard poured himself a little more wine, all prepped to hear the tale, then sat back and brushed the last of the muffin crumbs off his MacPherson-tartan kilt. He was Scottish, too.

"Little fellow, this is usually something I do only in the summer," he began.

"It is a seasonal job?"

"Strictly speaking, yes. See, I answered an advertisement posted outside the Raleigh Tavern in town."

"People post advertisements?! For a hermit?!" Beauregard knew humans were weird, but this was really odd.

"Too much money, too little sense, I guess. But, it works for me. They, in this case the Randall Family over this past summer, posted an ad for someone to live on their property, in a shack in the hills."

"Why?"

"Well, from what I guess, they think it's romantic to have a wandering intellectual, a genius bum on their grounds. 'Tis something to tell their friends about and then they have dinner parties, invite me in and show me off, like some kind of pet," he sat back and laughed. "My dear guests," Phil mimicked the silly host, "watch! He can discuss Plutarch at length. Hermit, discuss Plutarch at length for our guests."

"Eww, he's so deliciously grimy! How could he know who Plutarch is?" he then mimicked a vapid female guest.

Beauregard rolled back on his spine and laughed and laughed, "That's ridiculous! As if one's garments could betray an education!"

"As I said, too much money, too little sense," he continued. "The whole idea is that in the summer, students and tutors are usually out of work and this is the time we travel. It is also the time we have no money and thus, the arrangement is actually beneficial to all: free housing for the hermit, entertainment for the host."

"So, 'tis winter now. Why are you still here?" Beauregard bundled his scarf around his non-neck tighter.

"I was supposed to leave the Randall Family over in Surry County in September, which I did. I was then supposed head back to school up at Harvard, but I just couldn't bring myself to do it. I couldn't take one more moment of arrogant, incorrect professors so certain their worldview was the only one when, in fact, all they were, were sheltered men with no exposure to anything but their school. Most had never left school or Boston, never traveled anywhere, never met anyone other than other professors. What could they teach me about Rome and Syria if they'd never been there themselves?"

"Have you been to Rome?" Beauregard found him fascinating and leaned in for a better listen.

"Of course. Athens, too. Paris, Dublin, Salzburg, Vienna, Munich, London, Lucerne, Brussels, Amsterdam, Budapest, Bern. All the major cities of Europe. They should make me a professor. Maybe I shall apply at this William and Mary College," he stuck a thumb out in the general direction of the school.

He stood up to stretch his legs and all four cats excitedly circled in and out of them.

"You're not going, are you?" Beauregard was suddenly disappointed, very worried his new friend might head for Boston this very moment.

"No, little fellow. This is where I'm living at the moment," he spanned his arms open wide to show the entire Custis Estate.

"The Custis Family hired you as their decorative hermit?" he was thrilled!

"No. Actually, I've had to keep a pretty low profile. They don't know I'm here. That makes it a little tougher to get food when it's winter and the family doesn't know you're here."

Now Beauregard felt bad about the muffins and the olives. That was really nice of Phil to give him those. He must be starving. Now that Beauregard looked more closely, he was awfully thin and pale.

"Maybe we could get you some leftover turkey or ham from the party or the slave village?" Beauregard suggested.

"That was my thinking when I came over here. Well, except the turkey and ham part. I'm a vegetarian: no meat, only breads, fruits, vegetables, nuts, tubers and the like. I do not eat animals."

"Me, too! I'm a vegetarian, too!" Beauregard bounced up and down he was so happy to have something else in common with this man. "Only, I didn't know that's what I was called. But I only eat veggies and such, too! You know what sounds delicious? A hot, corn soup and some corn bread pudding. And gingerbread cakes! For dessert! Mmmm. . .gin-ger-bread-caaa-kes."

Beauregard stared into space for a moment as he pictured the warm and chewy treats. Then, he snapped to and stared at this Phillip the Bruce. He couldn't believe how much he had in common with his new pal. Oh, he hoped he wouldn't leave. Beauregard would help him find food and clothes and keep him company. Surely then, he'd not go back to Harvard, all the way up in Boston. Maybe he would stay here and become a William and Mary professor! Then, they'd be best friends forever! Because friends don't ever move away from friends, do they? No, they stay in the same town forever and ever! Oh, this was the happiest Beauregard had ever been!

"Shall we try to round up a Christmas Eve, vegetarian feast, Phillip the Bruce?" Beauregard asked as he stood up on his hind legs, straightened his kilt and sporran and pulled down his cream-coloured, Irish, cable-knit sweater over his belly, which instantly popped right back out. The turtleneck of the sweater stuck up almost to his nose, for he had no neck to speak of; but, he secured his scarf around his non-neck and pulled on his mittens which matched his sweater.

Phillip the Bruce buttoned his new greatcoat, tightened his new scarf and pulled on his old, ratty gloves which were full of holes. Beauregard made a mental note of this and would do what he could to find him some proper gloves. Maybe as a Christmas present!

The two, nay, six new friends began the crunchy and bitterly cold walk over the packed snow of Virginia's winter. Figaro took his usual position directly behind their master, leading all the other cats. However, this time, Buddha was not second in line. Tonight, Buddha walked to the side, running round and round Beauregard, his new friend. Beauregard walked next to his new friend and stared up at him once in a while in utter and complete fascination and happiness. So much so that Beauregard, on more than one occasion, walked nearly straight into a tree.

"Careful there, little fellow," Phillip the Bruce laughed. "And you know what, Phillip the Bruce is kind of long and tedious to say, not to mention pretentious. Why don't you just call me Bruce."

With that, the stars grew more sparkly, the air sharper and Beauregard's heart grew more full; and, although he would probably never admit it, so did the heart of Bruce, resident hermit, cynic, intellectual and all-around nice guy.

Jennifer Susannah Devore

CHAPTER TWENTY - EIGHT

The
New-York Weekly JOURNAL

Containing the Freshest Advices, Foreign, and Domestick

AN INFORMATION IS HANDED DOWN!
MUNDAY January 25th, 1735

To all my subscribers and Benefactors who take my weekly Journall.
Gentlemen, Ladies and Others,

As you have of late followed my imprisonment in the New-York City Gaol and read my weekly diaries from my cell, you will know of the cold and discomfort I endure as Old Man Winter blows his fury up through the cement and iron home I must currently call mine. Great thanks are sent to my children, my wife, my journeymen, my apprentice and all the City's Morrisites for helping the Journall to stay alive during my unjust imprisonment. Together, they are actively dashing the hopes of Governor Cosby: to keep me in gaol until my Journall is shut down. Never! The written word shall survive!

As an aside to my readers, whilst I have the greatest faith and gratitude for New-York's best lawyers taking my representation, James Alexander, Esq. and William Smith, Esq., my spirit is beginning to wane and I wonder how much longer my printing business, my Journall and I can last as I sit in this gaol cell. Further, I

Savannah of Williamsburg   Ben Franklin, Freedom & Freedom of the Press

231

worry on the state of my family. How will they eat? Where will they live if I am set free someday soon? This, I fear, may never happen. For, of recent, I have learn'd that I am not to be set free as Messrs. Alexander and Smith had hoped.

Though three Grand Juries, at the request of New-York's attorney general, found me innocent of any wrongdoing-found no good reason for me to stand tryal or remain in gaol and stated I was to be free, alas, Governor Cosby would not have this. He is mad with power! Insane with rage against me!

Having failed, A THIRD TIME, to force a grand jury indictment, Governor William Cosby ordered Attorney General Richard Bradley, Esq. to force upon me an INFORMATION! This is the legal equivalent of an indictment, but with one great difference: NO GRAND JURY IS NECESSARY! ONLY THE ATTORNEY GENERAL NEED FIND EVIDENCE AGAINST ME! I AM TO STAY IN GAOL ! BRADLEY AND COSBY ALONE HAVE SENT ME TO TRYAL AND QUITE POSSIBLY MY DEATH!!

To keep my faithfull readers informed of my official charges, I shall apprise you here: **I am accused of printing and publishing "false, malicious, seditious and scandalous libel" in two issues of the New-York Weekly Journall.**

The reader is reminded of articles in which Cosby's bad behaviour was cited:

1) Allowing French ships into New-York Harbour and dangering colonial security;

2) Cosby's lawsuit against and demands for payment from Rip VanDam;

3) The firing of legendary New-York Supreme Court Justice Lewis Morris.

In short, my Journall printed the truths about Cosby and this angered him so much he is Hell-bent on destroying my life, single-handedly if necessary.

Fair journalism must present both sides of this story. Since no member of Governor Cosby's followers would allow for direct comment, the Journall offers the reader the Attorney General's official complaint against me:

Paper attacks on the local government were designed, written, printed and published with the intent to cause public unrest and rebellion. Printed and

published weaknesses of the government make it difficult for those in power to govern effectively,

I ask you, my fellow citizens and readers, if Governor Cosby and his lemmings can gaol me and destroy my life for no valid reason, are you next?

Thro' the Hole of the Door of the Prison, to entertain you with my weekly Journall,

I am your obliged Humble Servant,

J. Peter Zenger

CHAPTER TWENTY - NINE

Winter came and went. Finally, the snows had melted completely and the cold days were becoming fewer and fewer. Savannah had commenced, maybe a touch early, with one of her favourite springtime rituals: tucking away all her boots and thick, tapestry mules. It was time for light, silk mules, gladiator sandals, open-toed shoes and, when the mood struck her, bare paws on the cool grass of the Palace Green. In spring and summer Savannah could run for hours and hours up and down the Palace Green. Yes, winter was over and she couldn't be happier.

Of course, winter had been good to her in some ways. With all her outdoor activities off-limits, she had been forced to work earnestly on her play. With Sterling's help, she had learned many of the subtle nuances of the theatre and, more importantly, how to write a play that actors would actually want to perform. Not knowing much if anything about directing or writing for the stage, she quickly learned one very clear point. Never outright tell an actor how to act. Apparently, 'tis quite the faux-pas to write emotion into a line of dialogue. Exclamation points and the like can be very insulting to your average thespian. They don't need to be told when to raise their voice or inflect upon a word or pause or sigh. Try to tell them and watch them become verrrry difficult indeed.

Most of winter's lessons went like that. Sterling taught and Savannah, much to Sterling's bemused irritation, questioned everything that came out of his mouth. In the end, she believed she a had a real feel for the odd but wonderful world of theatre folk and over the chilly months she made quite a bit of headway on her oeuvre. Ichabod even helped for part of the time, while he was in town. Most winters, though, he spent at least a month in Spanish Florida. He loathed the snow and loved the sun, his black fur growing warmer and warmer as he stretched out in the Florida rays. This year was no different and he ended up staying for nearly two months.

Dante worked hard for Mrs. Pritchen, who had spent the winter trying hard to diet, but growing only bigger and grouchier with each day cooped up inside. Dante still chipped in some time with Parks at the print shop when needed. Anthony worked quietly and feverishly getting his next store ready to open and through the whole season, said not a word to any of his old friends, only gave simple nods on those awkward occasions he bumped into them on the street. Never a stop-and-chat, always a walk-and-nod. Savannah had pretty much given up on their friendship, not totally, though. If he wanted to be friends again, she would love that. But, she certainly wasn't going to beg. She did have some dignity. All in all, winter in Williamsburg was quiet, peaceful and a little boring. Yes, winter came and went, and really, that was all it did.

CHAPTER THIRTY

The

New-York Weekly JOURNAL

Containing the Freshest Advices, Foreign, and Domestick

DISBARRED!

MUNDAY April 25th, 1735

To all my subscribers and Benefactors who take my weekly Journall.
Gentlemen, Ladies and Others,

As you continue to follow my imprisonment in the third-floor of the New-York City Gaol and read my weekly diaries, delivered from my cell, you will know the warming days of Spring bring some comfort in this, my sixth month of imprisonment. Thanks be to God for the kindness and generosity of friends and supporters. My family endures as I await my tryal. The Journall still thrives even under this, the latest ill news from my cell.

*Messrs. James Alexander, Esq. and William Smith, Esq. have been removed from my Case and **disbarred**! They are prohibited from practicing law in the Supreme Courts of New-York and New-Jersey for speaking out against the firing of Lewis Morris, Esq. from the same New-York Supreme Court months ago, for daring to question the very authority of Judges James DeLancey and Frederick Philipse, for questioning the very legitimacy of this tryal and for calling **the actions of Governor Cosby in these matters illegal**,*

"Consider the consequences of what you offered." *was the warning to*

Jennifer Susannah Devore

236

my attorneys by DeLancey before bringing down his ill-gotten gavel.

*"**I stake my life!**" cried the response of my attorney William Smith!*
*"**Very sure!**" came from my attorney James Alexander!*

"You have brought it to that point that either we must go from the bench, or you from the bar.", was the sentence brought down.

Unjust! Unfair! Unkind!

I now ask of you, the reader, what is a poor, German immigrant printer to do? The colony's best legal minds disbarred from my tryal and I am left alone still in this gaol cell. Worse still, my friends, I have been given a replacement attorney. A Defense Attorney called John Chambers, Esq. and well known to the folk of this town as Recorder of the City: a post gifted to him by his friend and political ally. . .Governor William Cosby!

Dear reader, what is John Peter Zenger to do?

Thro' the Hole of the Door of the Prison, to entertain you with my weekly Journall,

I am your obliged Humble Servant,

J. Peter Zenger

CHAPTER THIRTY - ONE

A little stressed but keeping it together, Savannah spoke with her three main actors before showtime, in the green room of Levingston's Theatre.

"Okay, what's your first line?" she asked Stephen, the lead and an enthusiastic, friendly fellow of about twenty and owner of a fluffy head overflowing with dishwater-blond locks.

"*An indentured servant! Me?!*" he recited in-character, well-steeped in the personality of his role, on and off stage.

"Excellent. And you, Jason?" she turned her head toward another actor, a tall, dark and handsome-type from New-York and waited for his recitation.

"*Ben! Ben Franklin! Get down here this instant!*" he dutifully recited with a bit less flair than his stage mate, saving his performance for the stage.

"Rebecca, your first line?" she asked the only female of the cast, a passionate and animated blonde of mid-thirties imported directly from London by Ichabod for the part.

"*Dear Sir, it may not be improper to inform your readers that I intend, once a fortnight, to present them with a short story which I presume will add somewhat to their entertainment,*" she recited with sheer perfection in her inflection. This girl understood acting at its core.

"Sterling, what's your first line as narrator?" Savannah was happy to have finally found a role for him and the play did need some explanation here and there.

"*It was a dark and stormy night in a candle-lit room. Boston. 1722.*" He recited spookily.

"Brilliant! Everybody sounds fabulous, everybody looks fabulous. We can do this. Stephen, fix your collar. Jason, check your apron, it's askew. Center it. Where's wardrobe? Sterling? Have you seen Thyra? I think Rebecca's got a loose string on her hem."

"I just saw her with Ichabod. I'll get her," Sterling put down his scone and coffee and ran off to find the wardrobe supervisor. Savannah patted her actors on their backs, jumped off her little stand and leaped directly onto the catered services table on other side of the Green Room and, without a thought, grabbed a flute of champagne. Then, she set it down. That could be bad luck.

'Twould be a little like celebrating ahead of time. No mission accomplished, yet. She would hate to look the fool. Better to save the champagne for after the curtain rolls down. Have some tea for now. Yes, tea would be good. A nice calming, herbal tea. Chamomile maybe. Her inner dialogue was rambling.

Opening night should be more fun than this; but, Savannah's tiny stomach was one huge knot. Her head hurt, her teeth ached from grinding them in her sleep last night and she was exhausted from countless nights of restlessness. She had been so nervous last night that even the extra large cup of warm milk she drank and the dried, lavender blooms she stuffed in her pillow case didn't work, and the lavender and milk regimen always worked in the past. This was much worse, though. This was her theatre début.

By her choice, she decided to write something, to create something personal and stick it out there on stage for the whole of Virginia to see, inviting criticism from every Tommy, Ralph and Donna in the colony. Oh, why hadn't she just kept her opinions to herself? She knew her mouth would get her into trouble someday and this was it. She'd be laughed straight out of town; moreover, she'd get herself into trouble. Maybe she could catch a ship back to London right now! Sure. There was probably one waiting at Queen Mary's Port right this minute. If she ran, she could probably catch it. Yes, London is lovely this time of year.

Wandering aimlessly backstage, Savannah could hear the growing mutterings, giggles, stirrings and general rowdiness of the audience on the other side of the red curtain. The small orchestra, four instruments, was tuning up and the audience sounded impatient. She walked up to the curtain and lay down flat on the floorboards. She then poked her tiny nose under the curtain dowel which rested on the ground, its curtain unfurled fully. She then lifted a tiny bit of red velvet so she could see the audience. There they were.

My goodness they were a wild bunch: a solid mixture of every walk of life in Williamsburg. There were the wealthy men of town and their wives, all dressed to the nines. There were the ruffians, gypsies, musicians and artists who rarely came out of the woodwork except for such occasions. There were the William and Mary students, tattered but clean. . .sort of. There were the merchants and tavernkeeps, excited about the prospect of all these folk looking for food, drink and merchandise before and after the play. Savannah noticed the merchants and tavernkeeps chose aisle seats so they could leave early and prepare for the après-theatre crowds. There were also the animals: cows, horses, pigs, sheep and large dogs stood outside and watched through the windows. Savannah had wanted to invite them in somehow, but Ichabod just about had a heart attack at the idea of cattle and pigs inside the theatre.

The smaller animals, the well-dressed mammals and birds, took front row seats and waited patiently as they munched on tiny snacks brought from home, except the robins. The robins ran up and down the front aisle, stopping at the end of each row and craning their necks, looking for the best seats possible. They never really sat, just ran and craned, then did it again. Savannah was exhausted just watching them. They totally stressed her out. She would have to ask Dante to usher them to seats and make them stay there.

In a front row seat, right next the largest seat in the house, a red tapestry and gold-leafed chair known commonly as the King's Box, named so for obvious reasons, Savannah noticed a very strange gentleman. He sat next to a smaller man and spoke only to him, but in what looked like mean whispers. He neither smiled nor laughed, but took notes, mental and on paper, then turned to the little man next to him and whispered things with a nasty, cringing face. He looked angry and irritated about everything; his eyebrows were in a permanently deep "V". More importantly, because of where he sat, he must have been someone of great importance. The King's Box was empty tonight because, well, Savannah wasn't really sure. She had hoped Governor Gooch would attend. Perhaps he was awaiting a private, command performance. "Oh my goodness!" her inner dialogue screamed. "Have I forgotten to offer him a special invitation?!"

She had actually sent him a personal invitation by messenger; but, was she supposed to plan a special showing just for him? A command performance? Oh gracious! Savannah knew she'd mess up something and this was huge! The angry man was probably there taking notes on Savannah's theatre and business etiquette! He was probably going to report back to Gooch about her and have the play shut down because of some oversight of government protocol! Savannah threw her tiny face into her tiny paws and shook her head back and forth muttering insults at herself. She then peeked through her paws at him to see if she recognized him.

Savannah tried to place him, but just couldn't. Maybe he wasn't with the governor's staff. Maybe he was just a common man from town, maybe visiting from Richmond or London. A new theatre production was a big deal. It wasn't unheard of for the very wealthy to travel, even across the Atlantic, for a new play. Of course, he didn't look particularly wealthy. Of course, one never can tell by clothing alone. Of course, though she would never say it aloud to anyone but Ichabod, she didn't completely believe that; sometimes you could tell, a little. She scrutinized him more closely from under the curtain roll.

Savannah thought he remarkably resembled a snake: a long, sharp face; a waxy, pointy nose upon which thin glasses rested; and, an unnaturally shiny, bald, oblong head. She couldn't be certain because he was sitting, but she guessed he was quite tall and his limbs were clearly lanky. His shoulders looked like a wooden hanger holding a suit coat and his neck was long and willowy. It was just like a snake's, well, snakes didn't really have necks, did they? But, that section just below a snake's head? That first wiggly part? That's what this man's neck looked like. He gave Savannah the willies. She shivered and decided it best to quit looking at him. He was already going to give her nightmares. She turned to the rest of the audience and took in the group as a whole.

All in all it appeared a boisterous, eager and amiable crowd. It didn't matter what their socioeconomic strata were; you put a bunch of theatergoers in one area and they turn into a happy crew. Just as she pulled her nose back under the curtain dowel she saw a finely-attired youth lob a ham bisquit at a friend deep in the groundling pit, near the orchestra. The ham and bread separated into three pieces and nailed three different people. Boys were dopey.

"Savannah, Love? Everybody's ready. Wardrobe is all set," Sterling got down on the floorboards and looked Savannah in the eyes.

She jumped up and brushed off her skirt, looking down at Sterling as if he was insane for being on the floor.

"What are you doing down there?"

Sterling jumped up and said, "Right then, it's time for the opening act. Are you ready, Love?"

"Yes, " she said without blinking. "Ready. Well done. Brilliant. Wonderful. No worries. All ready."

Sterling then pulled five oranges from his shoulder bag and tossed them in air, juggled them and began to sing something peppy, an original composition, but in Italian for the special occasion: *The Square Face Song.*

> *Ha una faccia quadrata, ma penso che sia bella.*
> *Andrei al suo posto, ma non è troppo cuddly.*
> *Amo pranzare prima che diciamo la tolleranza,*
> *ma già ha mangiato tutti i biscotti e sugo.*

"That. . .is. . .so. . .funny! I like the *biscotti e sugo* part," her head wiggled side to side as she sang the last line in her head.

She'd heard Sterling practice this piece for months, but in English only. Who knew *The Square Face Song* could be so entertaining in Italian? She had promised Sterling he could be the Opening Act since he only got the role of narrator. In truth, he had been a very good sport about it, considering he had initially assumed he'd get the lead role. If not ego-bruised, he accepted his part with grace and now it was time for him to quell the crowd and ready them for Savannah's theatrical debut.

"You are marvelous, Sterling. Thank you so much for all your help. Truly. By the way, your red turban and matching scarves are a marvel unto themselves," she admired his gypsy ensemble.

He was covered head to toe in flashy silks and countless gold pieces, all topped off with a beautiful and sincere smile that bespoke a confidence and peace that was sadly absent when she first met him last summer. She very much liked this odd, flashy, little fox from Venice or Maryland or London or, well, she never was really sure.

"Right then, Love. Skin off your nose!" Sterling bowed deeply and dramatically, his turban falling off his head in the process.

Savannah smiled and knew he'd be perfect to prep the audience.

"Then, off you go, dear," and Savannah tossed a length of scarf over his tail that was trailing on the floor.

She watched him take his place center stage behind the curtain. He then turned to her, where she'd scurried off into the wings, stage left, his right, and winked at her. She winked back and gave a head nod to a very serious and ready Beauregard who was so happy and nervous to be part of Miss Savannah's play that he was very likely to wet himself.

It had taken him a while, but slowly and surely through the year, Beauregard, despite Bruce's solitary leanings, had infused himself into Williamsburg society little by little and now, months later, could actually call himself a friend of the very popular Savannah and her crew. He tried his best to bring Bruce into the fold, but Phillip the Bruce was, and always would be, a loner.

One thing Beauregard had learned was Savannah's devotion to fine fashion. Tonight, Beauregard had dressed in his finest, summer-weight kilt, short jacket, white blouse and Tam O'Shanter hat, complete with the little red pom-pom on top; and, although he had failed in bringing Bruce to many a previous gathering, Beauregard was successful in talking him into attending Opening Night.

As soon as Savannah gave Beauregard the nod, he effortlessly tugged the rope-and-pulley system that would raise the curtain dowel. So it went. The red curtain rolled up and the crowd quieted, until they saw Sterling. Then they cheered, laughed and howled as his feats of juggling, comedy and musical talents wowed them all.

Savannah hid in the wings. What would they think of the play? Ohhh, why hadn't she just gone to London? She could probably still make that ship if she ran.

CHAPTER THIRTY - TWO

THE MYSTERIOUS SILENCE DOGOOD

A Play
By
Savannah Prudence Squirrel

An Ichabod Den Vries Production

ACT I. Scene I.

INT. BEN'S BEDROOM - NIGHT

A small writing desk sits in the corner of a mostly
bare room. Only a BED, a DESK and a NIGHTSTAND
decorate the room. CURTAINS BILLOW from a light WIND
coming through an open WINDOW. Occasionally, a FLASH
of lightning strikes.

OFFSTAGE we hear YELLING.

NARRATOR ENTERS STAGE RIGHT TO CENTER STAGE

> NARRATOR
> It was a dark and stormy night.
> Boston, 1722. Downstairs is the
> industrious print shop and newspaper
> office of one James Franklin and
> his publication The New-England
> Courant. Also, a young boy of fifteen
> works here. His younger brother, Ben
> Franklin. Ben lives here, in this
> very room above the print shop. Ben
> is a bright boy, a feisty boy. He is
> a funny boy and...

STAGE LEFT, FOOTSTEPS pound the stairs,
approaching. Young BEN FRANKLIN bursts through
the door. He lights a CANDLE and paces to cool
his obvious anger.

Narrator EXITS STAGE RIGHT.

                         BEN
         An indentured <u>servant</u>? <u>Me</u>. Benjamin
         Franklin. I should be at Harvard.
         What justice is it that a young
         man - a very gifted young man -
         wastes first in his father's candle
         shop and now this? A slave to his
         own brother for seven years as a
         printer's apprentice. No, Sir. 'Tis
         <u>not</u> justice -

Ben STOPS, MOVES DOWNSTAGE CENTER and ADDRESSES
audience.

                         BEN (CONTINUING)
         …More the insult, my own brother
         James treats me worse than any
         servant has ever been, both by hours
         at labour and by his own fist. It
         wouldn't be so terrible if he would
         at least consider my writings for
         his New-England Courant. But, no -

Ben resumes pacing

                         BEN (CONTINUES)
         …he dismisses me out of hand. No
         consideration given to my skill,
         my creativity, my ability to
         contribute, my desire to matter.

Ben lights another CANDLE on his desk and moves it to
his NIGHTSTAND, he opens a BOOK and READS into the
night.

Curtain DOWN

Curtain UP

ACT I. SCENE II.

INT. NEW-ENGLAND COURANT PRINT SHOP - DAWN

The print shop has a PRINTING PRESS centered in the
room. A variety of printer's TOOLS hang on the walls,
a few TABLES and WORKBENCHES surround the perimeter of
the room. A series of ROPES for drying are strung from
one end of the room to the other like a collection of
clothes lines. Through the front door enters 28 year-
old JAMES FRANKLIN. Removing his COAT, HAT AND SCARF,
he looks around and instantly becomes furious.

                    JAMES
          Ben. Ben Franklin, get down here
          right this minute.

Ben charges downstairs, enters the shop and grabs an
ink-stained, LEATHER APRON off a peg near the front
DOOR.

                    BEN
          Good morning, brother. You're early.

                    JAMES
          Early? Early? I am right on time. It
          is half-past five. You are clearly
          almost two hours late.

Ben senses his brother's frustration but ignores it.

                    BEN
          Goodness. Almost two hours? That is
          late. I must have read Mr. Cotton
          Mather too late into the night.
          Fascinating read, brother. Fascinat
          -

                    JAMES (INTERRUPTS, COY)
          Oh, you were reading Cotton Mather,
          were you? How pleasant that must
          have been. Was it good?

                    BEN
          Oh, yes. Quite.

Savannah of Williamsburg   *Ben Franklin, Freedom & Freedom of the Press*

                    JAMES
        Would you mind if I had a look, Ben?

Ben runs upstairs to retrieves the BOOK, Cotton
Mather's "Essays to Do Good"

Narrator ENTERS STAGE RIGHT to CENTER STAGE.

                    NARRATOR
        Ben is pretty excited. A shared
        interest? There is nothing Ben would
        love more than to find some common
        ground with his brother. They are
        so unalike. It is as though they
        are from different families. As you
        can see, though, James does not
        share Ben's interest. He huffs and
        puffs in anger as he paces the shop,
        biding his temper and stoking the
        embers of a fire Ben forgot to put
        out last night. This carelessness
        disgusts James even more. Embers
        burning overnight in a print shop?
        Oh, here comes Ben and, oh my, I do
        not trust this smile on James' face.

Narrator EXITS

Ben returns and presents James with a proud smile and
Cotton Mather's book. James reaches for it, disguising
his true fury.

                    JAMES
        Is this it? May I?

                    BEN
        Yes, it's just wonderf -

James tosses the book into the FIREPLACE and jabs it
into the embers with an iron POKER.

                    BEN (CONTINUES)
        ...what are you doing? What is the
        matter with you?

He leans the poker against the fireplace and suddenly
lunges for Ben, throwing him to the ground and pinning
him down by pressing his forearm onto Ben's throat.

Jennifer Susannah Devore

                         JAMES
          What is the matter, is you, brother.
          It is that you are nothing more than
          a worker, a servant, my servant.

James presses his arm harder on Ben's throat as Ben
struggles and coughs.

                         JAMES (CONTINUING)
          Your high-minded folly is not
          appreciated. You are not smarter
          than me, you are not better than me
          and you are not, I repeat, not at
          Harvard. You are a lowly apprentice.
          Your job is to reset the type each
          night, to clean the ink beaters each
          night, to mix the ink each morning
          by four a.m. and most importantly…

James pulls Ben up by his collar and drags him to the
fireplace, shoving his face dangerously close to the
embers.

                         JAMES (CONTINUING)
          …to extinguish any and all embers
          before retiring. Is this all clear,
          Harvard Boy?

James leans close into Ben's face and stares him dead
in the eyes. Ben nods silently.

                         JAMES (SINISTER)
          Moreover, my apprentice does not
          consume the scribbling lunacies of
          any writer with the name Mather. Not
          Cotton Mather, not Justice Mather.
          God help you if I find anymore Mather
          Family writings in this building. Is
          that clear, little brother?

Ben SQUEAKS meekly.

                         JAMES
          What? I cannot understand you.

                         BEN
          That is because you are on my
          throat, Master.

James gets up, leaves Ben on the floor.

                    JAMES
          Am I clear, boy?

                    BEN
          Oh, yes, Master. Great, mighty
          Master.

                    JAMES
          I am glad we understand each other.

                    BEN
          May I show you something, Master,
          please?

                    JAMES
          Show me what?

Ben helps himself off the floor and leads James to a
TABLE which is covered by a BLANKET. Ben motions for
James to remove the blanket, which he does. James sees
a CASE of perfectly set type, a pair of clean, but
smelly ink beaters and next to the table is a vat of
freshly mixed ink.

                    BEN
          Master, it occurred to me I could be
          twice as useful with another set of
          tools. I - I acquired these -

Ben gestures toward the case.

                    BEN (CONTINUING)
          …yesterday afternoon. Now, there
          will always be a set of type ready,
          even when the other is in use. I am
          so happy to surprise you with this.
          Master. I even woke up around two
          this morning, just to mix the ink
          and clean the beaters, since I fell
          asleep reading last night. When you
          came in, I was just waking from a
          little nap I took around four this
          morning.

Ben smiles tightly at James, then goes about resetting
the OTHER CASE of type on another TABLE. James starts
to say something nasty, but is interrupted by a

Jennifer Susannah Devore

250

visitor to the Courant. The SHERIFF ENTERS. James
motions for Ben to keep working. He is a large man
dressed in knickers, knee socks, suspenders and a
flowing, white, ruffled, shirt. His clothes are too
small for his large frame and he clearly is bothered
by the ruffles.

                    SHERIFF
          Morning, Mr. Franklin.

                    JAMES
          Good morning, Sheriff. To what do I
          owe the pleasure? Can my apprentice
          get you a cup of coffee?

In the background, Ben mimics his brother's false
kindness and hospitality, mouthing each word with
mocking gestures.

                    SHERIFF
          No coffee, James. I am here on
          official business. Justice Mather has
          requested I pay you a visit.

                    JAMES
          Justice Mather? Really? We were just
          talking about Justice Mather.

James looks back at Ben and laughs. Ben offers a fake
laugh and goes back to his work.

                    SHERIFF
          It is regarding an editorial you
          wrote in yesterday's Courant. It
          would appear Justice Mather is
          contemplating charges against the
          writer and publisher of the piece.
          He deems the content libelous.

                    JAMES
          Libelous? Ridiculous. I take umbrage
          with such assertions. As a newspaper
          of the people, I believe we are
          within our rights of expressing
          opinion of our government.

                              SHERIFF
          Mr. Franklin, that is not for me *or*
          you to decide. The authorities have
          merely instructed me to give you
          fair warning, Sir. You jeopardize
          your freedom, should you continue to
          publish such opinions. Good day to
          you Mr. Franklin.

The sheriff EXITS.

James is left standing, worried. Ben keeps working,
and avoids any eye contact.

Curtain DOWN.

Curtain UP.

                    ACT I. SCENE III.

INT.   NEW-ENGLAND COURANT PRINT SHOP - LATER

Like clothes on a clothesline, large, wet, printed
sheets of PAPER hang on the drying ropes. James hangs
the last of them with the help of a HANGING STICK.

                              JAMES
          Well, now aren't I the productive
          printer? You see, Ben? I don not
          waste my time on frivolity. Nose
          to the grindstone. That is James
          Franklin. Now go check those first
          pages I hung for ink smudges.

James prepares to leave for the day.

                              JAMES
          And, Ben? I want both sets type and
          all tools ready by morning.

Ben ignores him and checks the print on the earliest, dried pages. He glances at the opinion piece printed there.

                              BEN
              Uh, James, I mean, Master?

                             JAMES
              Stop calling me Master. What is it?

                              BEN
              Sir, this editorial seems to
              directly defy the Sheriff's warnings
              of today.

                             JAMES
              Ha. Young Ben, here is where you
              observe the difference betwixt a man
              and a boy…
                       (gestures)
              …besides, I am short on subjects
              this week. Not to mention,
              everything there is true. They
              cannot arrest me if it is the truth,
              can they now?

James goes back to preparing to depart. Ben begins reading the editorial piece thoroughly. James shuffles through some other PAPERS.

Narrator ENTERS STAGE RIGHT.

                           NARRATOR
              Ben thinks this is bad news for
              James. He may loathe his brother,
              but as you can see by the worry on
              Ben's face, what James has written
              may indeed affect them both. It may
              indeed affect the entire New-England
              Courant.

Narrator EXITS.

Ben finished reading the paper and sets it carefully on a table.

                              BEN
            Yes, it is all true, every word of
            it. Nevertheless, this cannot be
            healthy to send off to the citizens
            of Boston, Sir.

James laughs, dons his coat, hat and scarf and EXITS.

Curtain DOWN

Curtain UP

                    ACT II. SCENE I.

INT.   BEN'S BEDROOM - NIGHT

Ben alternates between writing feverishly and pacing
the floorboards. The curtains in the window are again
dancing from the light wind.

Narrator ENTERS STAGE RIGHT

                           NARRATOR
            My goodness. What a day. Ben has not
            forgotten James' violent outburst
            nor shall he ever forget. After his
            duties were finished downstairs, Ben
            found himself restless and irate. It
            is late. Maybe three in the morning.
            James will not be happy if Ben
            oversleeps again. But, as you can
            see, Ben is not worried about James.
            No, Ben has something up his sleeve.
            Aha, do you see that twisted smile?
            Ah, he rises again to pace. Excuse
            me.

Ben rises from his desk and paces with a wide and
devious smile.

Narrator EXITS

Jennifer Susannah Devore

                    BEN
     The difference 'twixt a man and
     a boy? I shall show you the
     difference, dear brother.

He sits and writes, his feather QUILL scratching
loudly on the PARCHMENT.

                    BEN (MUMBLING)
     Let us see if a mere boy could do
     this.

He stops, chews on the end of his quill, then realizes
he is chewing on a goose feather. He GAZES at the
billowing curtains.

MOONLIGHT shines through the window onto the curtain
and a ghostly, PRETTY WOMAN, of about thirty, dressed
in ANGELIC WHITE appears from behind the curtain. Ben
GAZES at the beautiful creature, it is creation of
his imagination. He smiles wickedly and returns to
writing.

                    BEN
     Yes, let us see a *boy* take on all of
     Boston.

As if the billowing curtain spits her out, the ghost-
woman moves DOWN STAGE CENTER and recites what Ben is
furiously writing.

                    GHOST-WOMAN
     To the author of *The New-England
     Courant*. Sir, it may not be proper
     in the first place to inform your
     readers that I intend, once a
     fortnight, to present them, by the
     help of this paper, with a short
     story which I assume will add
     somewhat to their entertainment.

Ben pauses and contemplates. She awaits his action
in order to continue. He resumes writing and she
continues speaking.

                    GHOST-WOMAN
         In the meantime, desiring your
         readers to exercise their patience
         and bear with my humours now and
         then… but I would not willingly
         displease any, and for those who
         will take offense - to my stories
         - where none is intended, they are
         beneath the notice of your humble
         servant…

Ben GAZES off again. She waits. Suddenly enthusiasm
washes over Ben and he strikes his quill into the air
in victory. Again he writes and she speaks.

                    GHOST-WOMAN
         …Mrs. Silence Dogood.

Ben rests the quill in the ink well. She bows to the
audience, a CRACK of thunder sucks her, gracefully
back behind the curtain. The curtains calm, the
MOONLIGHT FADES. Only the main candle lights Ben's
desk. He rests his head and falls off to sleep.

Curtain DOWN.

Curtain UP.

                  ACT II. SCENE II.

INT.   NEW-ENGLAND COURANT PRINT SHOP - NEXT DAY/DAWN

It is early when James arrives and before Ben has come
downstairs. James is instantly irritated, even though
Ben is not due for work for another hour. Without
noticing, James steps over an ENVELOPE that has been
slipped under the door
.
Narrator ENTERS STAGE RIGHT.

                    NARRATOR
         It is early. Not really even dawn.
         Still a few stars in the morning
         black.

Jennifer Susannah Devore

Narrator gestures to window and pre-dawn light

                    NARRATOR
          James is ready to drag Ben out of
          bed, undoubtedly by the hair - but
          it is lucky for Ben something has
          distracted his brother.

James bends over to pick up the envelope.

                    NARRATOR
          Shall we see what has caught the
          attention of Mr. James Franklin?
          Let's.

Narrator EXITS.

                    JAMES (MUTTERING)
          What's this then? "Editor: New-
          England Courant" Well, that's me.

James opens the envelope reads a bit and LAUGHS aloud.

                    JAMES
          Well, then. Very nice. This should
          be an excellent addition. Just when
          I needed some new material, too.
          What a fortunate new subject to
          print.

He walks to the back of the shop and gathers his
coffee preparations.

                    JAMES
          With all of Mather's supporters
          boycotting me, maybe the humourous
          tales of Mrs. Silence Dogood
          will bring entertain my readers
          and perhaps bring a few new
          subscriptions.

He finishes up the coffee and reads, chuckling and then and idea hits.

> JAMES
> Yes, <u>indeed</u>. Not quite a hard-
> hitting news scandal, but fun
> indeed. We will increase production
> and distribute your letters to the
> <u>whole</u> <u>of</u> <u>Boston</u> -

Excitedly, James calls for Ben.

> JAMES (CONTINUING)
> Ben - where are you, boy? Ben get
> down here.

Curtain DOWN

Curtain UP

ACT II. SCENE III.

INT. NEW-ENGLAND COURANT PRINT SHOP - LATER

The shop is bustling busy with not only Ben and James, but four of James' other WORKERS and a JOURNEYMAN. Two are operating the PRESS, as one pulls the lever to smash the ink down onto the paper, leaving a PRINTED PAGE, the other lifts it, hands it to Ben and replaces it with BLANK page. Ben is all smiles as he uses a drying stick to hang each freshly printed page on one of the drying lines.

Narrator ENTERS STAGE RIGHT

NARRATOR
It is Saturday and a busy day at the
shop. Another edition is coming out
soon and there is plenty of work
to be done. Every Monday all of
Boston awaits the latest New-England
Courant. And with the addition
of Mrs. Silence Dogood, James is
certain it will be a good week - a
very good week indeed. As you can
see, Ben seems to be quite pleased
with the hard work - I wonder if…

Suddenly, the front door flies open. TWO RED COAT
GUARDS burst into the shop. They are followed by the
Sheriff and he appears to be angry.

NARRATOR (CONTINUING)
…Pardon me. I'll just be off now.

Narrator EXITS.

SHERIFF
On behalf of the Massachusetts
General Court, I hereby request
the person of Mr. James Franklin,
contributor, editor and owner of *The
New-England Courant*.

Startled, the workers stop their activity. Ben makes
eye contact with the Sheriff and gives a slight head
nod to the side, gesturing at James with his eyes.
The guards lunge toward James, his workers muster the
courage to shield their boss. James steps forward. He
is inky, filthy and brave. He wipes his hands on his
apron.

The sheriff nods at James, James nods back. The
sheriff unrolls a SCROLL and reads aloud.

SHERIFF
Mr. James Franklin, I hereby place
you under arrest and charge you with
sedition and libel.

James, oddly, seems pleased.

                    JAMES
        Sedition and libel? Based on what,
        may I ask? My articles refuting
        Mather's blatherings on small pox
        inoculations? It figures. I expected
        this... government quieting the
        citizenry, eh?

James' pleasure turns to ire. He begins to raise his
voice. He gets louder with each word and thrusts a fist
into the air.

                    JAMES (CONTINUING)
        ...Speaking the truth gets one tossed
        in the gaol? Keep the little people
        silent? I *think* not. No *paper*, no
        peace. No *paper*, no **peace**.

The staff, including Ben starts to quietly chant this
until the sheriff stops them with gesture of his hand.
He turns back to James and continues to read the
charges.

                    SHERIFF
        No, Mr. Franklin. You are charged
        with libelous and seditious writings
        as it regards your latest article
        criticizing the wardrobe of the
        Massachusetts General Court -

                    JAMES(INTERRUPTS)
        Their *wardrobe*? Are you insane?
        That's what got their goat? Of all
        the things I have written about
        those overbearing, fat, lazy, posh,
        mindless idiots and they take
        issue with an article about their
        wardrobe? Ridiculous. Besides,
        it's true. Do you realize it is
        well-known they spent over one-
        hundred and fifty shillings on their
        wardrobes this past season?

                              SHERIFF (CONTINUES)
                    ...your insinuations that the General
                    Court has allowed piracy to flourish
                    in Boston Harbour and along the
                    New-England coast due to their lax
                    attention to security and in lieu
                    of their great regard for their
                    clothing purchases has enraged the
                    Court.

The sheriff rolls up his parchment and looks James,
somewhat sympathetically, in the eye.

                              SHERIFF
                    It appears to be the straw that
                    broke the camel's back, James - I -
                    have no choice.

                              JAMES (CHUCKLES)
                    That's ludicrous. I've written far
                    worse.

The sheriff pulls out another paper and reads it
aloud.

                              SHERIFF
                    They have instructed me to direct
                    your attention to this that you've
                    published... and I quote, "The pride
                    of apparel will appear the more
                    foolish if we consider those airy
                    mortals who have no other way of
                    making themselves considerable but
                    by gorgeous apparel. They draw after
                    them crowds of imitators who destroy
                    by example and envy, one another's
                    destruction.

James smiles and looks around at everyone.

                              JAMES (INTERRUPTS)
                    That is good.

                    SHERIFF
You also wrote, "'Tis thought they
will sail sometime this month,"
as it regards the Navy's intent
to patrol the coast, to fight the
pirates, if wind and weather
permit." Thereby, Sir you are
questioning the Court *and* its Navy.

                    JAMES (INTERRUPTS)
Well, *they* didn't sail until weather
permitted and the *pirates* had no
problem sailing in storms. The Navy
are a lazy bunch. 'Tis a Lazy Navy.

James liked that rhyme and bobbed his head a bit as he
said it, bringing a quiet chuckle from his staff.

                    SHERIFF
Right then. Enough of this. James
Franklin, you are under arrest and
may be released from the gaol upon
issuing a proper, public apology to
the Massachusetts General Court in
your newspaper.

The guards grab James by the arms and lead him out the
front door. James yells back to Ben.

                    JAMES
Ben, you are in charge. Keep the
Courant running until I am released.
Every Monday a new issue. Do not,
I repeat, do not print an apology.
Wait for my communication from gaol.
Tell my story, though. Tell of the
Lazy Navy and the slobs of the
Massachusetts Court.

James makes a scene, fighting to keep them from hauling
him through the door. The staff look alarmed, Ben does
his best to keep his wide smile hidden. With one final
thrust, James disappears through the door.

JAMES (OFF STAGE)
                  JAMES (OFF STAGE)
         Ben, one more thing. Print any
         Silence Dogood letters that come in.

Ben rushes to the door, his feigned concern is
betrayed by his smile.

                       BEN
         Don't worry Master, I will. I will
         publish every letter from Mrs.
         Dogood. I'll publish every last
         word.

Curtain DOWN

Curtain UP

                ACT III. SCENE I.

EXT. BOSTON/BUSY DOWNTOWN STREET - DAY

The street is buzzing. In THREE separate sections,
various people are reading Silence Dogood letters in
the COURANT. DOWN STAGE RIGHT a MAN and WOMAN have an
animated discussion. UP STAGE LEFT three GENTLEMEN
are doing the same. UP STAGE RIGHT a DRUNK MAN from
the tavern reads and entertains himself. All are
laughing and having great fun.

Narrator ENTERS STAGE RIGHT.

                    NARRATOR
         Indeed, Ben did not print a public
         apology. Truth be known, he was
         having the time of his life with
         James behind bars. He did, however,
         continue to write and publish the
         mysterious Silence Dogood stories.
         In fact, the public loved them and
         sales increased heartily.

Narrator EXITS walking through the scene and greeting
each person as he departs.

One reader with the gentlemen draws attention to them.
He reads and they all laugh.

>   GENTLEMAN #1
>   Listen to this… Mrs. Dogood speaks
>   here on how to write the perfect
>   eulogy for a funeral. "Having chose
>   the person in question, take all his
>   virtues and excellencies, etcetera.
>   If he have not enough, you may
>   borrow some to make up a sufficient
>   quantity."

All three laugh. The reader continues.

>   GENTLEMAN #1 (CONTINUING)
>   "To these," she says, "add his last
>   words, dying expressions, etcetera.
>   Mix all these together and be sure
>   you strain them well."

As their laughter explodes, the drunk man attracts
attention.

>   TAVERN MAN
>   And (hiccup), and (hiccup)… she
>   continues to say, "Then, season
>   all with a handful of melancholy
>   expressions such as '*dreadful*',
>   '*cruel cold death*' (hiccup),
>   '*unhappy fate*', etcetera…

He laughs until he is interrupted by another hiccup.

>   TAVERN MAN (CONTINUES)
>   Oh, oh, listen to this. "Having
>   mixed these ingredients well, put
>   them into,"

He laughs uncontrollably, then tries to gather his
composure and almost yells the final instruction he's

Jennifer Susannah Devore

still laughing so hard.

TAVERN MAN (CONTINUING)
"put them into the empty skull of
some Harvard Boy."

He laughs uncontrollably and thrusts his mug of ale
into the air, spilling some which causes him to laugh
some more and then a hiccup.

The MAN standing with the WOMAN attracts the attention
now.

MAN (LAUGHING ALL THE WHILE)
Perk up your ears. The saucy wench
quips, "There, let this all ferment
for the space of a fortnight. By
that time, it will all incorporate
into a body. Then, having prepared a
sufficient quantity of double rhymes
such as...

The WOMAN begins to read.

WOMAN (LAUGHING, INTERRUPTS)
May I? "...power, flower. Quiver,
shiver. Grieve us, leave us. Tell
you, excel you. Expeditions,
physicians. Fatigue him, intrigue
him, etcetera."

They're all laughing. The MAN interjects.

MAN
Okay, okay. Here is how to finish the
most proper funeral eulogy. "You
must spread this all on paper and if
you can procure a scrap of Latin to
put at the end, it will garnish it
mightily."

Back to the three GENTLEMEN. ALL are LAUGHING louder
and louder.

                         GENTLEMAN #2
                    Rydensis puella, quae edit
                    malun immaturum, decedit.
                    In ventrae turgescit; defleta
                    spumescit nec vinum divinum impedit.

The stage rages with laughter.

Curtain DOWN.

Curtain UP

.

ACT III. SCENE II.

INT.   NEW-ENGLAND COURANT PRINT SHOP - DAY

Ben and staff are busy at work. It is another day of
full production.

Narrator ENTERS STAGE RIGHT.

                         NARRATOR
                    It has been nearly two weeks now
                    that James was taken to gaol. He
                    sits there still and in his absence,
                    The New-England Courant is doing a
                    brisk business. The Silence Dogood
                    letters, which have arrived on a
                    regular interval are helping sales
                    immensely. Today, the men are hard
                    at work to create the next issue
                    of the Courant, including a latest
                    Silence Dogood letter and an article
                    written by James from behind the
                    iron bars.

Narrator EXITS.

Jennifer Susannah Devore

                         PRESS OPERATOR
          Ben, are you sure we should print
          this article from James? He's likely
          to get himself into even more
          trouble. We haven't even printed his
          apology, yet.

                              BEN
          Nor will we. No, we will print his
          latest work from gaol. We shan't let
          four good hours of typesetting go by
          the wayside.

The PAPER SETTER lifts the freshly printed PAGE and
reads.

                         PAPER PLACER
          But, listen to this. "I wonder
          on the stupidity of many of my
          countrymen."

He glances under his glasses at everyone whom has
stopped working to hear and pauses until he knows all
are listening.

                    PAPER PLACER (CONTINUING)
          "… who know little or nothing
          of the happy contribution of an
          English government, and who are as
          unconcerned to know the liberties we
          enjoy thereby, as if it were a thing
          indifferent with them."

Again, he looks around for reactions and stops on Ben,
whom is smiling. The PAPER PLACER sighs, the PAPER
HANGER interjects.

                    HANGER
Ben, he has requested here that
we fill the rest of the issue with
selections of the Magna Carta. The
Magna Carta, Ben? It's madness. Do
you realize how, well, *magna*, the
beast is? It's huge. That's why they
named it the Magna Carta. The "great
charter"? And not great because it's
fabulous-great, but because it's
huge-great. He's really pushing his
luck, Ben.

                     BEN
Absolutely. Yes, we shall print
bits of the Magna Carta. Tiny
bits, obviously. We shall show the
Massachusetts General Court that
that is how the citizens of the
Massachusetts Bay Colony are to
be treated. Yes, show them that
if even a wretch like King John
could understand, though not always
accommodate, the rights of man some
seven-hundred years ago, surely some
fat cats in Boston can do the same
today.

Ben EXITS and runs upstairs.

                  PRESS OPERATOR
Where are you going? Clearly, we've
got a load of work to do, Ben -

                  BEN (OFF SCREEN)
To find my copy of the Magna Carta.

Curtain DOWN

Curtain UP.

Jennifer Susannah Devore

ACT III. SCENE II.

INT.   NEW-ENGLAND COURANT PRINT SHOP - DAY

Ben and the men are working on a new issue. Ben's
supervision has the synchronization and production of
the team more efficient than ever.

Narrator ENTERS STAGE RIGHT

> NARRATOR
> Under Ben's supervision, the print
> shop was operating flawlessly. Three
> weeks have passed. The scandalous
> issue was printed and distributed.
> And, yes, the Massachusetts General
> Court were indeed not so stupid as
> to miss James' message to them. In
> exchange, they *arranged* for James to
> stay in gaol for some time longer.
> Meanwhile, Silence Dogood's letters
> continued to run alongside James'
> rants and the usual, months-old news
> from Europe and advertisements from
> local businesses. Until one day…

Narrator EXITS

Suddenly, front door bursts open. James ENTERS.

> JAMES
> I'm back, Boys. Ben, let's get back
> to work.

> BEN
> Actually, we've all *been* at work.
> Pretty much non-stop since your
> arrest. They let you out… Welcome
> back.

They all move to shake his hand, but he wants none of
it. He pushes past them and looks for his apron. He
notices it on Ben and gestures for it. Ben hands it
over.

JAMES
I promised to print an apology in
the next issue. But I won't. I also
provided the Court with a note from
my physician telling them gaol was
most likely killing me. It's horrid
in there. Disease everywhere.

Ben SNIFFS around, catching the scent of something
foul.

BEN
It smells like it.

Ben moves a few steps away from James.

BEN
Perhaps you'd like a bath before you
get back to work?

JAMES
No time. There's already talk I've
frustrated the clergy with one of
the pieces I wrote in gaol.

BEN
The one in which you said, the
clergy "exhibited the highest
pitch of malice toward you and the
Courant?"

JAMES
And they do. Look at them. Already
wishing to toss me back in gaol
for criticizing them. All Cotton
Mather's friends, they are. *All*
rats.

James moves into the position of the Press Operator
and goes to work.

                              JAMES
          Nevertheless, I think it's best to
          name *you* the new editor-in-chief and
          printer-owner. Put your name on the
          masthead, just for a bit. Just in
          case.

Ben liked this idea, but looked oddly at James.

                              BEN
          Just in case of what? In case of
          legal action? So that I go to gaol
          in your stead?

                              JAMES
          Oh, you won't go to gaol.

James jerks the lever and slowly the operation gets
back under way. Ben instinctively picks up a broom
and starts to sweep. He mimics James behind his back.
James disgusts him.

                              JAMES
          Now, anymore Silence Dogood?

                           PRINTER #1
          We're working on one now. Just
          received it under the door this
          morning. It is even funnier than the
          last one.

                             HANGER
          I think she's an impostor.

                          PAPER PLACER
          What?

                             HANGER
          Sure. An impostor. Not even a woman,
          I'd bet.

                              BEN
          Really? An impostor, you say? A man,
          even?

The Hanger reads from a freshly printed page.

> HANGER
> Sure. Listen to this week's letter.
> "Whereby every single woman, upon
> full proof given of her continuing
> a virgin for the space of eighteen
> years, dating from the age of
> twelve, should be entitled to five-
> hundred pounds in ready cash."

All the men laugh loudly and brusquely.

> BEN
> That's wild.

> HANGER
> Indeed. What self-respecting woman
> would write such a thing?

> PRESS OPERATOR
> A woman of vile upbringing, I'd say.

> BEN
> A trollop. A real tart...

Ben sweeps DOWN STAGE RIGHT, his back is to the crew
so as to conceal his joy at what he is hearing.

> BEN (CONTINUING)
> ...So, you think she's not who she
> says she is? You don't believe
> her to be a simple, middle-aged
> goodewife?

> PRESS OPERATOR
> I think agree with him - I -

Shaking a thumb at the Hanger

> PRESS OPERATOR (CONTINUES)
> ...I think she's a man.

Jennifer Susannah Devore

                    BEN
Why a man? Why such general
agreement, gentlemen?

                  HANGER
She is, first of all, clearly well-
read. She is too intelligent to be a
woman.

                   JAMES
I am in agreement. Hear, hear. She
is much too smart not to be a man.
Besides, Silence Dogood? Is that not
a made-up name? Is that not what
the perfect woman should be? Silent
and doing good? Only a man knows
that is God's truest perfection of
womanhood.

They all congratulate each other on being men as
Ben sweeps up stage, doing all he can to stifle his
laughter.

Curtain DOWN

ACT III. SCENE III.

Narrator ENTERS STAGE RIGHT in front of the CURTAIN

                    NARRATOR
          As men, they were inclined to argue
          for the better part of an hour. It
          was decided that Silence Dogood was
          too bright, well-travelled, well-
          read, quick-witted, sharp-minded
          and all-around too brilliant to be
          anything other than a male, and,
          probably a wealthy, well educated,
          land owning, white gentleman.
          Naturally, Ben found it harder and
          harder to hide his secret until
          he could finally no longer contain
          himself. It looks as though he is
          about to spill the beans. Excuse me.

Narrator EXITS

Curtain UP.

INT.   NEW-ENGLAND COURANT PRINT SHOP - MINUTES LATER

                    BEN
          'Tis me.

The whole place stops talking.

                    JAMES
          What? What's you? That odor of
          urine, I thought it was the ink-
          beater cleaning fluid.

                    BEN
          No, that smell is definitely you. No,
          Silence Dogood. *I* am she. She *is* me.

                    JAMES
          What is this nonsense? "I am she.
          She is me." What are you babbling
          about?

                              BEN
          I am Silence Dogood, brother. I
          write the letters and slip them
          under the door. You found my very
          first one, right before you went to
          gaol.

Ben smiles proudly, his chest rises and his shoulder
fall back. The other men begin to laugh and offer
various congratulatory terms, slaps on the back and
handshakes. It is all a good and merry laugh for all.
All except James. He moves over to the type setting
case and stands alone.

Narrator ENTERS STAGE RIGHT.

                           NARRATOR
          What a good time. A goodly laugh is
          necessary in the workplace. Don't
          you agree? It keeps morale high.
          But not, it appears, for James. He
          is *angry* - unable to speak. Notice
          his jaw is clenched tight, that
          his face is reddening and that his
          breathing is becoming louder and
          more laboured, heavier and through
          his nose. Contrast him to with the
          others. In fact, oh goodness. Pardon
          me, but I think it's best if I
          leave.

Narrator quickly EXITS through the front door of the
print shop and leaves it open.

James suddenly lunges at Ben and tackles him to the
ground, beating him mercilessly and shouting wildly.
The staff attempts to get him off. They can't - he is
wild with rage. He has Ben by the neck, shaking him.

                            JAMES
          How dare you make a fool of me. Get
          out of here. All of you. If you
          ever want to work in this town again
          - **get** **out**.

The staff flees through the open door.
Ben is coughing, choking and barely able to speak.

Savannah of Williamsburg   *Ben Franklin, Freedom & Freedom of the Press*

                              BEN
                    It was a joke. An amusement. It
                    doubled your sales.

James pummels and pummels and Ben tries to fight back,
but just isn't strong enough.

                              JAMES
                    You'll pay for this you little imp.
                    Make a fool out of James Franklin?
                    You'll pay with your life.

Curtain DOWN.

Curtain UP.

                        EPILOGUE

INT.   BEN'S BEDROOM - LATER THAT NIGHT

Ben is packing a rucksack. His face is noticeably
BRUISED and SCRATCHED. He is moving slowly,
deliberately and he has a limp. He opens his window
and the curtains begin to BILLOW with MOONLIGHT
streaming through.

Narrator ENTERS through the door and moves DOWN STAGE
CENTER

                              NARRATOR
                    Needless to say, Ben moved into
                    action that night. James beat him
                    severely and Ben knew he could not
                    be owned any longer.

Narrator moves UP STAGE LEFT and WATCHES Ben.

Ben moves DOWN STAGE CENTER

Jennifer Susannah Devore

                            BEN
          Yes, I am packing. Clearly, it is
          time for me to go. Sadly, I must
          leave my books. I've saved some
          money, but what I need now is
          courage more than anything -

He wipes tears from his BRUISED EYE.

                       BEN (CONTINUES)
          ...courage to stand against that which
          I know in my heart to be wrong. For
          one man to behave as though he owns
          another is - is - evil and I must
          resist this evil with all my being -

Ben chuckles a bit and turns away from the audience to
hide his tears. He tosses a couple of books into his
rucksack.

                       BEN (CONTINUING)
          ...kept a few good ones to read on my
          passage to New York. Cotton Mather
          for certain.

Back to the audience.

                            BEN
          I *have* to leave, you know?
          Considering the legal scrapes with
          the Court in the affairs of James
          and the very physical scrapes in
          the affairs of my brother's fists,
          Boston is no longer safe for me.
          I am but a young man. I have no
          recommendations, not a reference, no
          knowledge of a person, place or safe
          harbour in all of New York and have
          very little money. Still...

Ben cinches his sack, pulls on a coat, hat and gloves
and goes to the window. He stops and addresses the
audience, finally.

                    BEN (CONTINUING)
...anyplace is better than Boston.
Anyone is better than one whom
thinks they can own another human. I
will not live in captivity, even if
it means death en route to freedom.
That is where I will find the courage
to run and with any luck I may,
someday, matter.

Ben wraps his scarf around his neck twice, tips his
hat, tosses his rucksack out and EXITS through the
window, the curtains go still.

Narrator moves DOWN STAGE CENTER

                    NARRATOR
Days after Ben sailed for New York,
James took out an advertisement
in his own newspaper. It read,
"James Franklin, Printer in Queen
Street, wants a likely lad for an
apprentice." As for Ben, only time
will tell if he is to ever, indeed,
matter.

Curtain DOWN

The End

CHAPTER THIRTY - THREE

Savannah's cheeks were beginning to hurt. She couldn't stop smiling. She couldn't stop crying. They wouldn't stop yelling. They wouldn't stop clapping. They loved it! They loved her play! They loved *The Mysterious Silence Dogood*! Everyone from the groundling, penny-seat ruffians to the wealthy, box-seat fops to the stuffy and august, grey-haired professionals of Williamsburg were all standing and cheering her and her cast.

Herself in the middle, they all linked hands and took multiple bows. A standing ovation! She'd never hoped for this! It must have been going on four minutes by now. She kept trying to give Beauregard the nod to lower the curtain, but every time he lowered it, he had to raise it again for the clapping never ceased. His stubby arms were getting a workout. Theatre protocol said the curtain must stay up until the crowd gives the signal by quieting down. Thus far, there was no quieting anywhere. Only one person seemed displeased: the snake-man at front row-center.

Savannah spied him as soon as the play finished. He'd closed his notebook, looked at his pocket watch and his little companion seated next to him and motioned to him they were leaving. The little one shook his head fearfully and gestured to Gooch with his dark, round eyes. The snake-man followed his gaze until it landed on Gooch, at which point the snake-man's eyebrows dipped deeper toward his nose and he turned back toward the stage, realizing they could go nowhere until Gooch left. Thankfully, Gooch had finally shown up for the play, much to Savannah's great relief. He showed just before the curtain rose and, whilst it was only a coincidence, Savannah was glad she hadn't made the huge social gaffe of starting before the highest-ranking patron arrived. Now, nobody could leave the theatre until Gooch left.

The audiences watched Gooch for their cues and while Savannah could tell their cheers and applause were genuine, she could also tell they wouldn't stop until Gooch did. The snake-man reluctantly resumed his faux-clapping and watched Gooch out of his peripheral vision. Even as the snake-man shot his little friend bitter and bored looks through his squinty snake eyes, the little friend stood and clapped eagerly and honestly.

The little one was a short, Mediterranean-featured fellow with a wide face, an eternal tan, a kind nose, a thick head of black hair and an even thicker black moustache. He seemed pleasant, but Savannah surmised he was emotionally weak by the way he kept shooting nervous smiles and raised eyebrows at the snake-man. Clearly, he was under some control by him.

Now, seven minutes of attention and praise was certainly gratifying, but the cast was getting a bit tired of bowing and smiling. Fortunately, Gooch was done. He stopped clapping, bowed to Miss Savannah and left the theatre. Instantly, the crowd stopped clapping and like Gooch gestured to Savannah with waves, bows and Huzzahs! As the crowd exited the theatre she bowed and curtsied as much as she thought appropriate, then looked into the wings and gave Beauregard the final nod to bring down the curtain for good: a sharp, fast, downward nod and a fast slash of her paw across her throat. Beauregard was ready and thrilled to oblige. He was pretty sure his role was pivotal to the play. As he pulled paw over paw, unrolling the curtain dowel, he scanned the audience for Bruce. He finally saw the familiar flash of blue from the back row. It was clear Bruce stuck around to give proper applause and ovation; he wasn't raised in a cave after all, just lived in one from time to time. Of course, he bolted as soon as the man next to him turned to make small talk. Bruce was generally aggravated by the average human and found it best to rarely engage in deep conversation. Good thing he chose to work in academia and live as a hermit. Beauregard smiled to himself, proud and happy that Bruce had actually chosen him as a friend. Of all the creatures on the planet, Beauregard was good enough to be a friend of Phillip the Bruce and his cats. Very nice, very nice.

The Raleigh Tavern was crowded and abuzz with the après-theatre crowd. Mr. Levingston owned a small tavern and café adjoining his theatre. It even offered indoor bowling for additional entertainment. However, it was small and could hold only so many people. Naturally, overflow spilled into the many other taverns about town; and, with the excitement and success generated by an opening night, the après crowds were larger than usual and stayed up much later than usual. Mrs. Pritchen expected her gaming room and dining room to be lively into the wee morning hours and across the road, the Market Square Tavern boasted the largest crab cakes in town. They would all be crazy busy until the sun came up. Yet, no one could come close to the popularity, quality and sheer social status of the Raleigh Tavern. It was generally standing room only on a normal night; but, when court sessions were open, or if something big was happening like a visiting dignitary or an opening night at Levingston's Theatre, the standing-room-only crowds flowed onto the front porch and into DoG Street.

Inside the Raleigh was dark in lighting terms, but full of life and spirit. The lanterns and candles were plenty, but the mass of bodies crushed together, creating the effect of an indoor forest at night with only flecks and flickers of moonlight sneaking through the window panes and candlelight peeking in and out amongst the silhouettes of the tightly packed populace. In a dark corner, darker than the rest, sat three figures hunkered over a table. They were smoking, drinking, whispering and plotting. Their silhouettes were distinct, even in the smoky shadows of the late night throng. Two of the figures displayed body language that clearly argued for control of the situation.

"I like your plan, Carvile. I will make some contacts around town and we shall move into action by week's end," the third one of the group, a powerful slave trader named James Blair sat back, crossed his legs and sipped a glass of port wine, displaying all the signs of confidence and superiority gained in the conversation.

"No," Carvile, otherwise known as the snake-man, said plainly. His accent sharp and high-pitched, a country accent like that which a swamp-dwelling, Southern, snapping turtle might have.

Nearly the entire top-half of his gangly body still hunched over the table; he held a pewter cup of ale in his right hand. He took a swig, looked around, then rocked back and forth, still over the table and now looking directly at Mr. Blair.

"You mak all the contacts you laak," he snapped quickly, "but you mak 'em tonaat. Tomorrow naaght, we go."

Now, he leaned back, crossed his legs and enjoyed his ale. In reply, Mr. Blair looked around nervously and clenched his fists on the table, under his chest as he leaned in close to whisper his response.

"I cannot make all my contacts tonight," Blair pleaded, clearly having lost any claim to supremacy. "If we can go tomorrow night. . ."

"Lower your voice," Carvile hissed a quick interruption.

"If we go tomorrow night," Blair succumbed in a low whisper, "we shall have not even half the numbers we could have by Saturday. Why the rush?"

"Because aa said so!" Carvile pounded a fist on the table, calling some attention which quickly faded as he lowered his own voice and leaned his pointy nose directly into the other's nose. "Aa am not interested in waitin' til Saturday. Aa want this done and aa want it done now! The numbers'll grow even as we march on the thee-a-ter."

He leaned back a little and smiled at his moustached friend who smiled back, just happy to not be in trouble about something.

"Well, I will see what I can do, but. . .", Blair furrowed his brow, irritated at how quickly he'd been relegated to second-in-command.

"You know what? Aa do not care what you can do! Aa came to you out of a courtesy to you, Mr. Blair. Aa saw this play! You did not!" Carvile drooled just a little, then wiped his mouth with his tongue. "Aa am here temporarily. Aa can withstand the aftermath of that drivel. You are the slave trader, the slave owner. That'd be one Hell of a revolt if tales of this play get into the wrong ears! Ha!" he was almost amused by the idea of a revolt.

"No, Mr. James Blair, maa concern is for the Virginia Gentleman at large, for *maa* Governor, the *real* governor back in London, and our King George; for the English way of laafe and the stability of this and all our England's colonies," his voice grew a little too loud and Daniel Ray, his moustached follower, gave a toothy grin and raised eyebrows to gently inform him of watching eyes.

Carvile lowered his voice again and pulled Mr. Blair's eyes into lock with his own.

"In the end, aa will be okay no matter what. Aa will go back to London soon and rid myself of this, this wilderness you call a taany corner of England. Aa may have been born and raised in the South Carolaana swamps, but aa was smart enough to get maaself out of this God forsaken wasteland you call America. You, however, your poor sap, will suffer the consequences of this play if it is allowed to continue one more naaght. Moreover, so will suffer King George's precious, colonial jewel of Virginia. Whaa he even wants it aa have no aadea," he looked around and sneered at the tavern folk.

"In short," Carvile summed up, his pitch higher, quicker, snappier and more vicious, "on behalf of His Majesty King George II and Virginia's Royal Governor Willem Anne VanKeppel, 2nd Earl of Albemarle, aa will put a stop to this seditious and dangerous play and that offensive and ridiculous Miss Savannah Squirrel."

Carvile sat back and took a long drag off his red clay pipe, all the rage in London since the red clay was an expensive import available only from the colonies, whilst white clay was a commonly available, domestic product. With his fashionable red pipe he blew smoke directly into Mr. Blair's face.

"Perhaps we might try a more legal or traditional channel? We could approach Governor Gooch. He may be able to close the theatre without a fuss," Blair meekly suggested.

"Legal?" he snapped and hissed again, spittle flying across the table. "This play is not legal, maa friend!" His voice now cooled to a chilly venom. "Traditional? This play is not traditional either, unless one speaks of the tradition of revolt, revolution and rebellion, maa friend. No, we shall not, aa shall not go to *Lieutenant* Governor Gooch for any aid, and do you know whaa, maa friend?" Blair shook his head, seeing a shimmer of evil emanating now from the snake-man.

"Aa shall not go to the *quasi*-governor because he sat laak a maandless fool, laak a giggling little girl in the King's Box for tonaaght's debut performance of *The Mysterious Silence Dogood*!" his voice began to rise again. "He laakd the play! He applauded the play! He is friends with the insipid and insufferable little squirrel," he now lowered his voice again. "So, no, Mr. Blair.

Aa shall not be seeking legal and traditional channels to save the Virginia colony from revolt, no matter how revolting," he laughed at this wordplay. "Aa actually faand your patch of dank and dismal forest here even more disgusting than the King's newest acquisition of dank and dismal New World: Georgia. Whaa he keeps scoopin' up and charterin' new colonies here is beyond me. Nevertheless, along with Georgia, Maryland, wherever else he so chooses to colonize, Virginia is part of King George's Dominion and safe and sound it shall stay," his final words were spoken as one, barely audible, long word. His eyes, on the other hand, screamed madness.

"Right," Blair was ready to leave, a little frightened of this man and knew his words mattered not. He knew Carvile's plan would go on with or without him. "So we go tomorrow. Good," he relented. "When? What time?"

"You'll learn," Carvile glugged more ale. "Later. Keep two candles burning in your bedroom window all naaght tonaaght. Laaght no other candles after three in the morning. That'll be the signal for all who join our cause. You'll be notified of the exact time and place." He leaned into the table one final time. "Remember, you may tell whomever you wish, but you be certain they are believers in our cause and not hers. The force is strong in that squirrel and if you bring to laaght our plan to any of her friends, we shall lose completely the element of surprise, and if we lose that, aa shall blame you, Mr. Blair, and, remember, there is none closer to the governor, the *real* governor VanKeppel than maaself," he finished his ale with a giant gulp, then with a broad laugh added, "and maybe his waafe."

Before Blair could stand, Carvile and Daniel were gone. All that was left was the smell of his pipe and the odd scent of barbeque that seemed to follow Daniel everywhere. Blair, now alone, reclaimed for himself an air of superiority and rudely demanded another port from a barmaid, proving his importance to at least her. Seeing a couple of his "contacts" he summoned them to his table without getting up. There, into the earliest hour of the morning, Blair advised a select few about the plan to bring down Miss Savannah and *The Mysterious Silence Dogood.*

That morning, as Beauregard and Bruce strolled home from a very late night of poetry reading and red wine behind Mrs. Pritchen's Tavern they noticed an unusually high quantity of candles still lit so late into the morning.

"Look," Beauregard pointed out a window of a particularly large, brick home on DoG Street, "there are two candles burning," he walked backwards for a few steps, looking back down the road. "I think they all have had two candles burning in those houses," he turned forward again and looked at Bruce. "That is strange, yes?"

"Quite. Perhaps it is a coincidence. Probably not, though. Maybe 'tis a signal," he offered.

"A signal about what?" Beauregard walked backwards again to keep an eye on the flickers whilst speculating with his pal.

"I don't know. Maybe a party?" he replied with utter boredom, the idea of bourgeois parties sounding just painful to Bruce. "A secret party? An exclusive, snooty, typically wealthy, white, landowner-type of party. Keeping other folks out to make themselves feel superior," he said with a somewhat inappropriate level of anger as he drank the last bit from his pewter mug and then, turning it upside-down and shaking it as though it had offended him, he drained it of any major residue and tied it to a leather string attached to his belt.

"A party? How fun! I wonder if we could go?" Beauregard turned back to face forward and now skipped at the idea of a secret party, his kilt flowing in the summer breeze and having completely missed Bruce's vehement opposition to such a party.

"Maybe we can, Beau. Maybe we can," he snorted, suddenly having ideas of his own on inserting himself as an uninvited guest to a party which disgusted him in concept, but perturbed him at being excluded.

CHAPTER THIRTY - FOUR

"Alright, people," Savannah stood atop the craft services table in the Green Room. "We had an excellent opening night. However, I think we can all agree a few mistakes were made and in tonight's performance we can correct those."

The cast and crew muttered to themselves, nodding and agreeing quietly, except Sterling, who couldn't imagine there was a thing he could change. His *lazzi*, or jokes, were perfectly timed and his Shakespeare was spot on; he never missed a line as narrator. In a display of full irony, very common for Sterling, his comedic portrayals of Shakespeare's most tragic characters brought the house to its feet. Nothing pleases folks more than watching the all too serious come up for a bit of air now and again. Humans know tragedy exists; finding humour in it is what helps them move on each day. Yes, last night Sterling Zanni diPadua, Zanni the Zany of Venice and London certainly demonstrated to Williamsburg the true meaning of the word, and the name, *Zanni*!

"Hellooo? Anyone in there?" Savannah knocked on his head as he replayed last night's performance in his thoughts.

"Yes, of course, Love. What is it?"

"What is it? What is it? It's nearly an hour to curtain up! There's so much to do! Do me a favour, check the crowd. Do we have a full house?" she threw her little arms up in the air in frustration and walked toward a pitcher of iced, caramel coffee.

"Savannah Love, we've got two hours to go actually, and nobody's out there. They're all next door at the Kitchen. You know. A little pre-theatre

Jennifer Susannah Devore

286

ale, wine, nibblies. Right then, they'll show up good and happy in a bit, yeah?" Sterling patted her on the shoulder and walked away to practice his juggling.

"Here, allow me," Dante came out of a throng of crew to calm down his friend. "You know," he began as he helped pour her coffee into a small, pottery mug, "you've really got to calm down. Everybody knows what they're doing. We had a great opening night."

Savannah squinted her eyes at him, then looking around realized she'd lost control of her group. They were all wandering off to various areas backstage to run lines, stretch, meditate or eat the free food of the Green Room, courtesy of Mrs. Pritchen. She may not have gotten her tavern on the official, royal mail route, but she had gotten to be the official sponsor of Savannah's theatrical debut. Mrs. Pritchen found some solace in that the Raleigh Tavern didn't get that designation.

Savannah knew she was over-the-top with her worrying and fretting, but this was the theatre and one could never let one's guard down.

"I know we had a fabulous night last night," she took the cup from Dante whilst scanning the backstage activity. "It's just that if I find I am satisfied, if any of us find we are satisfied, really satisfied, we shall lose our edge and inevitably, very possibly flop."

She gulped the contents of her cup and handed it back to Dante whose paws had finally lost their blue hue months after finishing his printing stint with Mr. Parks.

"See, we must never relax. We could lose our edge. At least not until final curtain," she bared all her teeth and sucked inward as the first wave of coffee jitters rushed through her veins.

Dante just stared at Savannah. Her eyes were completely bugged out and her tail was standing straight up and twitching.

"All right then, no more coffee for you," he took her cup and set it on the table, then took her arm and began to lead her back to her desk in the wings. "Look. Look all around you. Your cast and crew are professionals. Nobody is going to ruin a thing. Everything is fine."

Dante then turned back to the food table and whistled Sterling's "Square Face" tune as he looked for something good to munch.

"What? What is it?" he then asked as he turned slowly toward Savannah; he'd felt her staring at him and it made him very uneasy.

"Dante. . .you. . .whistled," she whispered in sheer and barely controlled panic.

"Yes? So?"

She said nothing, just stared.

"Aaaand?"

"Oh, Heavens!" she threw her arms up in the air and called for Sterling. "Sterliiiiiing! Quick! Ohhhh. This isn't good. This is not good," she began to pace as she awaited Sterling's arrival. "Ster. . .oh, there you are. Dante. . .just. . .whistled," she crossed her arms and looked from Sterling to Dante as she pursed her lips tightly and nodded her head very quickly, over and over.

Sterling looked at Savannah with alarm, to which she motioned silently toward Dante with another head nod. "Oh no, Chappie," Sterling set a paw on his shoulder. "Tell me you did not whistle, here, now, in the theatre, in the Green Room even."

"Yes. I whistled. So arrest me. What is the big deal?" Dante was oblivious.

By now, a small group of cast and crew was watching, murmuring to each other about Dante's faux-pas.

"Right then, Mate. Maybe no harm done. We've got to just fix it," Sterling took control.

"Fix what? I whistled. What is to fix?"

"Not in the theatre, Mate. Not in the Green Room. Don't you know 'tis very bad luck to whistle in a theatre?" Sterling asked.

"Bad luck? That's ridiculous," Dante laughed it off.

"Listen, Mate. 'Tis very, very bad luck," Sterling responded.

"Why?"

"Because, first of all, it just is. The theatre is a very illogical place," Sterling said matter of factly as Dante rolled his eyes. Sterling continued, "However, if you need a somewhat rational explanation, here it is.

In the very earliest days of the theatre, 1500s and what-not, sailors were actually employed to run the ropes and rigging up in the rafters. You know?

Curtains, lowering papier mâché planets, angels, clouds, suns, whatever on to the stage. Things that need to come from above need to be lowered with ropes. Sailors know how to tie the best knots. Being sailors, they used a system of whistles to communicate with each other across the theatre. Same kind of system they still use on ships."

"Alright," Dante shrugged. "So how is this bad luck?"

"'Tis bad luck because the system has stuck with the theatre. Not here, but still in London. This theatre's not quite big enough to need the whistle system," he gestured apologetically to the locals in the cast and crew. "Sorry, Mates. But it's true. Anyway, Dante," he continued and turned back to him, "if you whistle, it could be mistaken for a signal and someone could end up with a sandbag or a papier mâché moon on their head."

"Yet," Dante's eyes scanned the theatre, "we have no sailors on crew here, I believe. So there's no problem."

"It is still bad luck. Tradition says so. However, you can fix it by a simple action," Sterling concluded. There would be no more discussion.

"An action? I must do something, a physical action to change the fact that I whistled?" Dante laughed.

"I know, it sounds silly to an outsider," Sterling began to explain and Dante's smile froze at the word 'outsider'. He was no outsider. "To a theatre outsider," Sterling caught his look. "The theatre is a very superstitious entity."

The small crowd behind them nodded and mumbled in agreement. Dante laughed as he looked around, amazed at what he was hearing.

"I am sorry, but I am afraid the show cannot go on until you fix this, Mate."

"Oh, lovely!" Savannah threw up her hands again and paced up and down the Green Room. "Dante! Did you hear that? The show. . .cannot. . .go. . .on."

"Fine then. I shall fix my grave error," Dante said sarcastically and with spooky fingers, but could tell Savannah did not need this extra stress, so put his hands down and agreed to do whatever necessary. "Fine. What must I do?"

"Simple. You must turn around three times, leave the Green Room for one full minute, knock on the door, then reënter."

"Are you kidding me?" Dante was aghast at this silliness.

"As the Germans say, *Das ist das*. It is what it is. The show will stand dark until you do this," Sterling finished.

Sterling and the whole of the theatre's employ now stood with crossed arms and waited for Dante to do this. Savannah looked at him, her eyes morphing from irritation to pleading. Ichabod entered the Green Room just then, having spent the last few hours at the Kitchen visiting friends for a little pre-performance libation.

"Vhat is going on here? Vhy is eferybody standing around? Ve haf a show to put on, people," he said politely but sternly like a true impresario. "Lefingston's Kitchen is fery busy. Ve are going to haf a full house tonight."

"Mate, Dante whistled," Sterling brought Ichabod up to speed.

"Oh. Vell. Has he spun around and come back in?" Ichabod seemed to know all about this superstition.

"Not yet," Savannah kept staring at Dante.

"Vell then. Come on. Spin, leaf, come back and let the show go on, please," Ichabod summed up the issue very concisely.

Dante tilted his head once, his jaw a little dropped, he did a long blink and a deep sigh and very reluctantly spun three times and felt like a fool the whole time. One minute later, he was back in the Green Room and the theatre had regained its general buzz and hum.

Miss Rebecca Lane, the play's lead actress slid up to Dante, her blonde locks bouncing as she approached. Miss Lane was, in fact, an indentured servant brought to Williamsburg by William Levingston. In exchange for her passage across the Atlantic and a place to live and daily meals, she was to work as talent in his theatre for seven years, for free. Most of the actors in Mr. Levingston's were indentured servants. This was a fairly common practice in colonial theatre and it was often a good way for those not quite making a mark in the big cities of Europe to become known in a smaller venue, then return to Paris or Vienna or London with a bit more experience and clout.

They were enslaved, in a way, but weren't nearly in the same position as the African slaves brought to the colonies. The actors had a choice to enter an indentured servitude agreement. They were also, usually, treated like human beings. Levingston never beat or threatened his cast with bodily injury or death. In truth, what good was a roughed-up actress or a dead, male lead? If they ran off before their seven years with Levingston were up, legal action could be taken to recoup his monies. If a slave ran off before his lifetime was up, mutilation and death would be used to recoup the monies, anger and embarrassment by the slave owner.

Savannah and Ichabod felt the *Silence Dogood* cast should be paid for their work. Since it was Levingston's theatre they were leasing, they could have paid Levingston to "rent" them and not have to pay anything else to the actors. Instead, not only did Ichabod and Savannah pay Levingston to lease the theatre and the actors, they also paid a generous wage to all the cast and crew, indentured or not. Fair pay for fair work. Miss Rebecca Lane was one actress worth her weight in Spanish gold.

"I, for one, do not buy into these superstitions," Rebecca threw an arm around Dante's shoulders in solidarity. He got a goofy smile on his face and his whiskers twitched a little. "For instance," she continued, "I am not afraid to say *Macbeth* right here, right now." In an instant, the cast and crew hushed. "Oh, calm down. 'Tis not that bad," she addressed her fellow actors gathered behind her with just a twist of her head and a flick of her wrist. "Oh, for goodness sake, Dears. *Macbeth, Macbeth, Macbeth*," she repeated with defiance.

Many of the cast and crew performed various individual prayers, hand movements, turns and odd gestures to ward off the irrevocable damage Miss Lane may have just inflicted on the company and the building itself. Savannah nearly fainted.

"Right then. There is no cure for that!" Sterling shook his head.

"What is wrong with saying *Macbeth*?" Dante was glad he was not show business folk.

"It is a fery old superstition," Ichabod addressed Dante. "Some people beliefe in it, some do not. I, for one, do not. Miss Lane, it appears, does not. Howefer, it seems to be making eferybody here nerfous, so, Miss Lane, if you could please just say *That Scottish Play* three, no four times, to cover your previous outbursts, ve can get on vith this play?" Ichabod seemed a little miffed.

"But, why?" Dante asked again. "What is wrong with saying

Macbeth?"

"Oh, dear," someone whined in the background.

"Vell, efer since the fery first performance of *The Scottish Play* in 1606, as it must be called by the superstitious, the boy who played Lady *You Know Who* died on stage," Ichabod began a short lecture, the type he loved so much to give, but was interrupted by Dante.

"Who?"

"Vhat?"

"Who? Lady *You Know Who*. Who is she?"

"*Macbeth*. Lady *Macbeth*. This is ridiculous," Miss Lane rolled her head in irritation as all this nonsense was beginning to interfere with her performance preparation.

"That makes six, Miss Lane," Ichabod said. "Anyvay, since that first performance in 1606 vhen that actor died on stage, there has been a string of bad luck associated vith efery production of *That Scottish Play*. Not to mention, if you are somevone with a lot of time on his hands, you vill see that the vord *dark* is spoken more times in *That Scottish Play* than in any other Shakespeare play, and the vord *love* is spoken less than in any other. Add in the three vitches, The Veird Sisters, as they are called, and the gruesome death scenes, *That Scottish Play* is chock full of bad omens. So, ve don't say the name."

Dante was stunned by such thinking. He did not believe at all in superstition. What would happen, would happen based on the circumstances of current reality and not some vague curse or unspoken fears of the ignorant. Ludicrous. Regardless, Miss Lane obliged the fears of most and chanted *That Scottish Play* six times, spinning all the while just to tweak the spirits. Within moments, the theatre was back in business and everyone went back to their preparation routines.

Though no one would utter it, two cursed events had happened tonight. Whistling and The Utterance. Would it affect the performance? No one could say. Yet, Savannah downed more and more coffee until the cup verily shook in her paw. An hour to curtain up and she stood in the right wing, keeping one eye on her lead actor who read a book whilst pacing backstage, already well in character. Her other eye was on Beauregard, sitting dutifully on the floor next to the ropes and pulley wheel he would use to roll up the red, velvet curtain when the time came. Her eyes darted around the seating area of the theatre and she was beginning to wonder where the early birds were. There were always a few people who arrived an hour early, just to read a paper and enjoy the big, empty, quiet theatre to themselves for a while. Tonight, it was totally empty. That was a little weird.

The *avant*-theatre crowd, the pre-theatre folk, must have been busy drinking and carousing extra at Levingston's Kitchen tonight. The Kitchen was a small café and pub, but it also had bowling: inside and out. Being right next door to the theatre, it was the place to gather and revel before and after a production. Generally, there were two types of theatregoers who made a whole night of the two-hour event: the *avant*-, or *before*-theatre crowd; and, the *après*-, or *after*-theatre crowd.

The *avant* folk were, as a rule, older, quieter and a little more reserved and genteel. The *après* folk were, as a rule, younger, wilder and had a tendency to verge on the rowdy as carousing after a play meant the night didn't even start until after 9:00. The *avant*s would be in bed by the time the *après*s ordered their first pint of stout.

As Savannah looked for any signs of early birds, she heard the faint noises of a ruckus outside. She heard what sounded like yelling or arguing, but it was still early in the evening. The sun had only just gone down in the last half-hour. Williamsburg didn't get noisy until well into the night, if ever really. In fact, Savannah thought this sounded exactly like a tavern close to midnight. This sounded like the rowdiness of an *après*-crowd; but it was clearly too early. It was time for the *avant* people. What was going on out there? It was definitely getting louder and louder. Great. That was all she needed. Hooligans. But, the more she listened, and as she noticed others in the theatre begin to take notice, she realized it all sounded too noisy, too organized and cohesive for hooligans. These were not the hoots and howls of a theatre audience, not even an Italian audience. This was an extra boisterous crew. They sounded very drunk and very obnoxious. Had the town attorneys all assembled in one place? Then, someone screamed and Savannah smelled smoke. She bolted out of the backstage area, bounded onto the main stage and without effort leapt across the rows of box seats and open chairs and benches that filled the theatre. She ran to the main doors, which were cracked open, darted through the front garden and jumped onto a fencepost to get the best view. Her nose twitched and her tail twittered and there she saw it. There it was.

Behind her, on a table and bench, stood Ichabod, Sterling and Dante. Miss Lane and the entire cast and crew were all showing up quickly in the front garden. Having seen Savannah bolt from the theatre, they followed suit and were gathering on the grassy patches that bordered the theatre's white picket fences. As they approached in small groups, chattering and wondering aloud, they were stunned into silence as they saw what Savannah saw. The curses held true. Tonight, *The Mysterious Silence Dogood* made history and was beset by bad luck after a careless whistle and a deliberate vexing of the fates. Dante and Miss Lane looked at each other and waited for the worst. Ichabod looked to Savannah, whose tail went straight as a stick. Her lips puckered, her eyes narrowed and all her fur stood up on end. Her tail, stiff as a broadsword, began to twitch, shifting side to side like a metronome on its fastest tempo. She was so angry she slipped into a fury zone.

Her flower choker, strung especially for tonight and crafted of twenty pink rosebuds, was falling to pieces on the gravel walkway below, her neck muscles were so tense. She sat on that fencepost and absentmindedly fiddled with and tore at the roses, focusing all her emotion and energy on the scene in the very near distance. This was a mob. An actual mob was heading up the Palace Green. This wasn't Paris. People didn't form mobs and march in protest at the drop of a sandwich. This was Williamsburg; people were reserved and dignified, mostly. A little boring, but at least they didn't carry pitchforks and torches and march down the main street. Of course, they were today. Savannah could hear them chanting something, but, what? She couldn't quite make it out.

"Ichabod, what are they saying?" she leaned back to ask him. " 'Stop the world, I want to play'? 'Stop for Earl, Lops in May'? Why on earth are they coming this way?! Don't they know it's almost curtains up?" Savannah was very irritated by all this. "Good Heavens, I do not have time for this."

"My dear, I fear they are not saying 'Stop the vorld' or 'Stop for Earl'. They are saying 'Stop the sqvirrel! Stop the play!'."

He looked at Savannah, then to Dante, Miss Lane and Sterling. Ichabod had great, persuasive powers and a great many strings he could pull, but he had no idea about this. This, he could not stop. It had too much momentum.

"Stop the squirrel! Stop the play! What?! Me? Are they talking about me?" she was stunned, but also furious and not at all scared. "How dare they! Who are they? I don't know people like this!"

"You know pyrates," Dante said innocently. Savannah was not in the mood for this and ignored the remark.

"If they don't like my play they don't have to attend my play. They can stay home and clean out their belly buttons for all I care, but how dare they come down here and get in the way of *my* art and *my* audience!"

Ichabod had Rebecca set him up on the fence next to Savannah where he sat and spent the next few minutes successfully talking Savannah out of marching out onto the Palace Green to meet the growing mob.

"Unfortunately, I think they vill be here in no time, Safannah. You cannot take on a whole mob. You can talk to them here, vith all of us behind you. But, ve need help, real help. Sterling, go to the Palace. Get Gooch."

"Gooch? The governor? You mean, go *inside* the palace?" Sterling wasn't thrilled about actually setting foot inside the Palace. He wasn't exactly excited about voluntarily entering a government building.

"Please, Sterling. Go. Now. Safannah needs you."

That was about as stern as Ichabod got, but Sterling sensed this and ran out the theatre gates, his front legs stretching easily ahead in great strides across the walkway and up the Green toward the Palace gates; emergencies called for running on all fours. Moreover, this wasn't about him or his legal issues. Someday, he'd have time to discuss it with someone. It just never seemed the right time; it always seemed selfish to burden others with his problem, just to make himself feel better. Still, he was getting tired of carrying the secret all alone.

"I'll teach 'em all a lesson! C'mon, everybody!" Dante unsheathed the sword he always kept at his side, just in case of emergencies such as this, and thrust it high in the air and screeched like somebody stepped on his tail.

"Dante, stop it," Ichabod put an end to that right away. "Do not be ridiculous. You cannot take on that mob any better than Safannah can. You are still just a cat."

Dante grumbled and mimicked Ichabod as he reluctantly brought his sword down from up high. He knew Ichabod was right, but he wasn't about to give up lightly.

"They're just a bunch of farmers and merchants. Philistines! They don't care about art or theatre. We can take them, I know it."

"Dante, please. Vhat you can do is find Anthony. Find Mr. Lefingston, find young Mr. Custis, Daniel Parke. Find his father, find anybody large and preferably human. Unless you can engage some cattle or horses qvickly, but they are alvays so slow to get moving. *Ach*, it is like they nap all day long," he reflected for a moment on the tiresome ways of the hooved animals. "Anyvay," he snapped out of it, "find anyvone whom can form a barrier. It looks as though they vish to crash the gates. Ve can reason vith the mob later, but for now ve haf to stop them from getting into the theatre. Go to Lefingston's Kitchen. That is vhere all the men are tonight, at least the older vones right now. Just go find somevone." Dante still seemed hesitant. "Dante, they haf fire torches! Go!"

"Fire torches? What other kind of torches are there?"

"*Ach, mein Gott*! Damn it, Dante! Go!"

He'd never heard Ichabod curse before. "I'll do what I can, Ichabod. I haven't seen Anthony for ages, though. I don't even think he was here for Opening Night."

"Fine then. *Entschuldigung*. I am sorry. But, you must go now. Get somebody, anybody. Gather all the men you can find, maybe efen some of the bigger girls. Just get a big group forming. Ve need our own mob, I fear."

He was right. Dante watched the Green and saw that not only was the mob growing closer, but it was also much bigger than they'd all thought initially and moreover it was glowing. They did have torches, lots of them. They actually carried torches and, were those tools? Did they actually have garden tools? Pitchforks and shovels and rakes and hos? Oh, for goodness sake. How cliché! Nobody does that. Only people in plays and books do that. Have some originality, people.

Original or not, they were a deadly and dangerous lot headed right for

Levingston's Theatre. That much was clear. Dante sprang off the bench and over the picket fence. Down he ran to the left, away from the Palace and toward the Kitchen, just yards away. Might as well begin recruiting there. Naturally, they could see what was happening through the windows and all the strong and spirited men, though many were elderly at this hour, began filtering out of the Kitchen to watch the mob.

Dante spread the word to form a human fence outside the theatre gates. An eager group formed quickly and surprisingly methodically considering the level of revelry already reached. Whilst the Kitchen looked as though it was indeed hosting the standard, older, *avant*-crowd, there were loads of students tonight and in the great tradition of the young, male student they were always ready for a good fight. Youth and spirits often led to excess energy and passion which often led to solidarity and fraternity. This group was certainly ready to band together for some cause, or at least some adventure.

Savannah sat motionless on her fencepost, her choker nothing more now than a bare, green stem; pink, rose petal confetti sprinkled across her dress and the ground below. From her perch she had a totally unobstructed view of the impending conflict. As the protesters' silhouettes grew larger and the orange glow of their torches grew brighter, as the smoke grew thicker and the chants grew louder, she could clearly see tonight's conflict was no longer something of fiction or stage, but very real and headed straight for her stage nonetheless. It was clearly curtains for somebody tonight.

CHAPTER THIRTY - FIVE

"Stop the squirrel! Stop the play! Stop the squirrel! Stop the play!" They chanted over and over again.

"Snuff the fires! Go away! Snuff the fires! Go away!" Savannah's supporters retorted.

The two sides yelled back and forth at each other. Face to face, they screamed insults and obscenities at each other. The protesters thrust their pitchforks and torches dangerously close to the theatre supporters whilst the theatre crowd, strangely ready for a rumble, waggled and clattered their fancy foils and sabres right back at the mob. Only an invisible barrier of human decency and an actual, gravel path kept the two sides from seriously hurting each other. The protesters stood on the Palace Green and the theatergoers stood on the theatre property. The pathway was wide enough for carriages and mysteriously kept everybody that exact distance from each other. It was a strangely unspoken agreement to keep the pathway clear. Human nature obviously has some innate rules of preservation. Even so, everybody was wildly angry and caught up in rash emotion; but, they also had deeper, human instincts that kept their actions, and that distance, in check. They knew differences of opinion, especially about the theatre, were not valid reasons for bodily harm or worse. Instead, they hurled slurs and threats at each other.

"Back to your farms! Back to your shops!"

"Go home, artless Philistines!"

"I'm not a Philistine! I'm a Catholic!"

"Back to London with you, theatre rats!"

"What's a Philistine?!"

"Open a book! Close your mouth!"

"Plays are for sissies!"

"Pitchforks are cliché, Sir!"

"Who's on my foot?!"

"Something sticky is touching me!"

In truth, many of the participants, on both sides, had no idea what the main argument was. As is also human nature, mob mentality is a very contagious thing and once you get groups of people arguing and fighting for what may seem a righteous cause in the beginning, turns quickly to an excuse for bad behaviour. This situation was quickly degenerating into just that.

"Ichabod, what do we do?" Savannah was severely miffed, but at a loss for action. "Where is Dante? I thought he went for help."

"He did. He ran straight to the Kitchen. You see the support ve hafe now. So many law students. Our mob is almost as big as theirs."

"Well, where is he now?"

"I think he must haf gone to find other help, bigger help. Like a soldier or Mr. Lefingston or maybe efen Anthony if he can find him."

At the mention of Anthony's name Savannah grew sad. She had not seen him in months, at least not for any substantial period. Every time she did see him on the street or went by his shop he was too busy to talk. He never smiled anymore and Mrs. Prtichen said he quit hand-delivering any of her items. He had hired three new assistants and they were giving all the face time to his guests. He was in the midst of opening a fourth store, a real brick shop on DoG Street right next to the Capitol building. Savannah was so proud of him. Everybody was. It was clear to anyone and everyone in Williamsburg that he was becoming very successful and very wealthy. His clothes were becoming finer and finer, but his appearance more and more ragged. His forehead had permanent worry lines between his eyebrows and his mouth seemed to have grown into a cemented frown. He was also awfully thin, even more apparent in his light, summer linens. Yes, he was a busy and successful man, but he was not happy.

Ever since the death of his brother, his secret brother and secret pain, he had withdrawn from his life and his friends and focused only on business. Even Magda, his manager down at Queen Mary's Port, rarely saw him. Assistants handled all port business, too. He never even worked his Market Square stands anymore. Assistants for those, too. No, Anthony split his time between his main shop where he also lived and his new shop by the Capitol. Savannah doubted if he even knew she was producing a play, let alone if he even attended Opening Night. She had eventually quit going by his shops and stopping him on the street when it became clear he would not be returning the visits and would never make time to stop and chat. She loved Anthony dearly and appreciated his pain, but if he didn't want to entrust his friends to help him through his toughest times and he chose to cut them out of his life, she wasn't going to force herself upon him. Friends are support systems, but if one of them chooses to be an island, you have to let them be, but with no hard feelings. One never knows, they might just come around again, someday.

Savannah and Ichabod watched the melée from their newest, safer perch: atop an old mare named Juicy. Juicy was a dapple-grey horse, a swayback and a member of the *avant*-crowd. She had been grazing in the Kitchen's soup garden out back when the ruckus began. Slowly but surely, she *clip-clopped* over to the theatre and made her way to the front of the crowd. After some complaints by those whom couldn't see what was going on due to Juicy's ample bum, it was agreed that Juicy, who never wanted to cause a problem and was only curious, should move to the side of the theatre gates, but that Ichabod and Savannah should sit on her back to better survey the situation and have a safe position, like a general surveying his troops in battle. Ichabod did not do well in crowds and was very uneasy where great numbers of feet were involved. Constantly on the move, skittering this way and that, he would tuck his tail between his legs and zig-zag every which way to keep from being stepped upon. The whole thing made him nervous and anxious and eventually very grouchy if left to deal with feet for too long. High atop the fray was exactly where Ichabod felt he belonged: physically and socially.

Juicy was certainly safe, except her swayback was so pronounced that Ichabod and Savannah kind of kept rolling in toward each other, like sitting in a tea cup. The height was also making Ichabod dizzy. Still, it was better than all those feet below. He hoped Sterling would return with Governor Gooch soon.

"Ichabod, we cannot stay up here forever," Savannah rolled toward

Ichabod, stopping herself with a gloved paw on his shoulder. "They are calling for me, for some reason. I must address their concern before I can deal with this effectively."

She was not used to just sitting around while events unfolded, certainly not while they were centered on her.

"Not until Sterling comes back with Governor Gooch or the York County Sheriff or somebody. It is just too dangerous for you. You could be sqvished or efen killed. No vone vill notice a petite sqvirrel amidst all that chaos. Not even the sqvirrel in question."

"I am wearing a rather bright pink. I received lots and lots of compliments on my dress this afternoon. Surely, people will notice me."

Ichabod shot her a look that said, *Don't be silly.*

They sat quietly for another ten minutes or so. Ichabod found his dizziness was lessened if he looked out at the horizon and if he didn't talk. Savannah was getting antsy though, and kept running up Juicy's mane. Savannah would hold on to Juicy's ears as she looked at the Green, then would run back down her mane and into her swayback and plop down again, rolling into Ichabod. All this movement was making Ichabod nervous and focused on the patch of Palace Green that stretched diagonally from the Governor's Palace to the theatre, keeping an eye out for Sterling and Gooch. Where were they? How long could it possibly take to run over there, grab Gooch and come back?

"Son! Son! What is all that racket out there? I did not come to dinner to have my meal disturbed by the young hooligans of this town! What in Hades is going on out there?!" a very elderly, very grouchy man of about eighty waggled his cane in the air at no one in particular and yelled at a young worker whom was cleaning up dishes in the main dining room of Levingston's Kitchen.

"Don't know, Sir," he answered as he peered out the paned-glass windows and stacked dishes on a tray, his eyes never leaving the window. "Looks like some kind of mob, Sir."

"A mob? What in Hades would a mob want with Williamsburg?" he seemed instantly angered by this.

"Don't know, Sir. Lots of 'em stopping at the theatre next door. More seem to be coming up the Green," his blue eyes were alight with the fire of the torches.

Being a country boy, a real country boy from the woods of interior Virginia and country enough that he found Williamsburg to be the Big City, a mob headed toward the theatre was pretty darn exciting.

"They all have pitchforks and shovels like my Pa uses."

"Aw, dang it!" the old man slammed his fist on the table, shaking his tankard of ale. "All these new people in town. Why, I remember when there was nobody in this town. It was quiet and people knew their places. Then they opened that dang school. Brought in all kinds of youngins. Causing problems, drinking in taverns, bringing down property values. They even brought in those dang Indian boys at that Grammar School at William and Mary. Indians! That's probably where they got those torches out there. Can you imagine teaching natives to read?! Dang nabbit!"

The old man was off on a tangent and no one was listening but he was sure everything he was saying was vital and important to society. Even the underexposed country boy knew these views were ancient and ignorant.

"My granddaddy was right. He knew Sir William Berkeley, Governor Berkeley back in the good old days a hundred years ago. Grandaddy said Berkeley was a genius when he said 'I thank God there are no schools. Learning brings disobedience and heresy.' Well, look out the window! There's what learning brings you: Indian mobs with torches and squirrels producing plays! A squirrel! Everybody aware a squirrel's making that play next door?! A squirrel, dang it!"

He spun around in his chair with raised eyebrows and looked for support but he was making everybody really uncomfortable so no one would make eye contact even if they agreed.

The boy kept looking out the window and reported to no one specific, "Looks like somebody important is heading for the theatre. He's cutting through the mob like he's the leader. Has himself a little feller following him. A bushy moustached type."

"A little bushy feller?! Sounds like a Mediterranean to me. Well, keep your hand on your wallet, son. Lettin' in Mediterraneans?! Dang it! First the

French come and take our land over New-York, the Spaniards trying to keep all that swampland down in Florida, they don't know what to do with it! Now the Mediterraneans are coming to Williamsburg! Why, I remember when it was all good and British. Only reason we let the Germans in was they were good at making shoes and blowing glass! Dang nabbit! A mob of Mediterraneans! What next? The Chinese? They'll steal from you worse than the Mediterraneans!"

He ranted on and on much to the displeasure of many around him and eventually he even wore out himself, dozing off in his chair as his coffee went cold and the Kitchen emptied of nearly everybody as the mob situation had grown too large and too volatile to ignore. Only the manager and the boy stayed behind and eventually the boy just had to go, too.

"Can I go see the hubbub, Mr. Hopkins? I promise when I come back I'll clean up real good after the mob is done and gone."

He had already pulled the white serving cap off his chestnut hair and was untying his apron. It was a good thing he was pretty because his grammar was awful.

"Sure, but be careful. Close the doors on your way out. I don't want the mob coming in for snacks while I'm prepping for the *après*-crowd."

He threw down his towel ran out the doors, then came back, closed the doors, and ran at full speed up the gravel pathway to the theatre. The air was so thick with smoke from the torches he could only make out silhouettes ahead. They were angry silhouettes, though. Lots of arms, swords, tools, canes, hats and fists flinging about. This was going to be good. Back inside the Kitchen, Mr. Hopkins was ready for his last early bird diner to leave.

"Okay then, Mr. Barnes. You all done? Let's go ahead and get your hat and coat and get you to the theatre," he spoke to him as if he was getting a child ready for church after breakfast. "Looks like a big crowd tonight. Maybe you'll meet a nice lady."

"A lady?! A lady?!" Mr. Barnes woke up from his soup nap and began to angrily don his coat and hat, soup now dried on his bushy, white moustache. "There are no ladies anymore! Why, I remember when a lady would listen to what a man told her, make him dinner and shut up while he ate it! Now there are girls out there trying to go to school, getting sassy about it, too. Squirrel girls writing and producing plays! And actresses! Why, there's a little blonde actress in this play here and I've seen her around town, prancing and shopping like there's nothing wrong with what she does! Why, in my day, actresses stayed in the shadows. You went to the theatre, you watched them, you went home and you sure as Hades didn't bump into them while you were buying salt! Dang nabbit! Governor Berkeley was right. 'God, keep us from both.' "

"Both of what?" Mr. Hopkins asked as he pulled a ring of keys out of his apron pocket.

"What?! What?! I don't know. Probably actresses and squirrels!"

"Yes, of course, Mr. Barnes. Actresses and squirrels were certainly a lot different back then," he humoured him. "Now run along, Sir. You'll miss curtain up."

He ushered him through the front door and closed and locked it behind him, then leaned back against the door in exhaustion. Mob or no mob, he was happy to get his Kitchen cleared out early. Mr. Hopkins liked the *avant*-crowds, but they had weird habits and rarely ordered something different. They always ordered their same dishes each day. They complained about everything under the sun but tipped generously and knew a lot about wine, something the younger diners didn't fully understand. It was the *après*-crowd where he made his money in volume; it was the *avant*-crowd where he made his money in quality guests. By the looks of the crowds gathering outside, tonight should be a doozy.

Jennifer Susannah Devore

CHAPTER THIRTY - SIX

Sterling sat impatiently at the top of the stairs. The chair was comfortable enough: a thick, orange, wool-upholstered side chair of what appeared to be pine, at least to Sterling's eye. This was no time to admire American furniture, though. He needed Gooch and he needed him now. He'd dropped enough names and put on an urgent enough show belowstairs to get past the guards and up here. But, now he was required to sit up here and wait for the governor. Apparently, nobody knew exactly where the governor was, or at least that was the standard response for unannounced visitors.

"He has retired early for the evening," one guard had said.

"He is dining with friends," another said with utter surety.

"The governor is in his salon reading and has requested no interruptions," was the official statement from Gooch's personal secretary, delivered with all the royal and administrative conciseness and attitude one could imagine.

In the end, it was determined that, yes, Gooch was reading and, yes, he had turned in early for the night and, yes, he had requested no interruptions. Sterling, however, made a persuasive impression on the haughty secretary. He told Sterling to wait here at the door and he would see what he could do about engaging the governor. After all, the secretary surmised, Governor Gooch probably did not want, nor could he sleep through, a mob protest just across his Green. Sitting and waiting gave him time to think and he began thinking about his performance the night before.

Sterling hadn't even once received a standing ovation at Covent Garden for even his greatest role: Arlecchino, the famous masked, patchwork-clothed clown. But, last night? He was good and he knew it. Sterling also passed the time by reciting Shakespearean lines backwards in his head. He'd always found this a good exercise both for acting as well as the brain.

".nothing signifying fury and sound of full, idiot an by told tale a is it, more no heard is then and, stage the upon hour his frets and struts that player poor a, shadow walking a but Life's"

For some reason Macbeth was stuck in his head.

"Master diPadua?" the white-wigged secretary jerked open the door next to Sterling's chair, causing him to jump straight out of it.

"Yes? Yes, will Governor Gooch be able to see me?" he pleaded, his ears flat on his head and his whiskers all twitchy.

"Yes, please enter," he pulled the door wide open from the inside, allowed Sterling to step inside, then closed the door and followed the nervous fox inside.

Inside, was one of the most private and personal domains in all the colony: the governor's bedchamber. It was normally unheard of for a visitor to enter the bedchamber. This space was reserved for family, personal servants and, on some occasions, attorneys or advisors whom might wish to discuss more delicate and even secret business.

The chamber was actually far less ornate and plush than Sterling had been imagining as he waited outside. After all, he had been raised in Venice and London. Venice especially had set his taste very early and when he entered the home of a highly placed member of society, he expected to be bowled over by so much luxury that it should hurt. Looking around, he saw finery, of course, but it was all just a little subdued for someone whom was, in all essence, the symbol of royalty.

There was a gorgeous bed with a high canopy and beautiful red toile linens. There was a large, Pennsylvania-loomed rug next to the bed. There were a couple of side chairs with silk upholstered seats, a writing desk, a chest of drawers and that was about it. The centerpiece was a fireplace near the bed and adorned with a tile fireplace surround of blue and white Dutch tiles. A brass screen and implements finished the look. All very nice, all very expensive, to be sure. Yet, Sterling was disappointed.

He recalled that, back in Venice, as a young kit, the neighborhood baker's apartment, set directly above a tiny bakery on the Grand Canal, was more luxurious than this. Smaller, yes, but far more richly designed. This place had almost nothing on the walls. In Venetian *pallazzi*, in London country homes, in Parisian apartments, one could barely tell the colour of the walls every space was so stuffed with paintings and drawings and etchings of every kind. Sometimes, even solitary frames, pure art themselves, hung with nothing inside them but the rare glimpse of bare wall.

No, the Virginians, Americans and Colonials in general it seemed, had taste and money, but were afraid to go too far in design. They were afraid of something, maybe looking foolish, maybe just too scared to take chances with colour and textures. Nevertheless, the room was comfortable and spoke of vast power in its strong simplicity. Sterling then looked up at Gooch.

There he stood. He was tall and lean, not skinny, but firm and muscular in tone. His smile was wide and strong and he had a pretty good head of hair for a man of forty-something. At least what stuck out underneath his cap. The cap. The cap threw all of Sterling's confidence in him out the window. Being nighttime, Gooch was in his night clothes. Fair enough, if not a little early, Sterling thought; but there he was dressed and ready for bed. His cap was a long, pointy number which flopped over Gooch's head and hung almost to his rib cage. At its tip was a bright purple pom-pom. Plus, he was barefoot. Not very gubernatorial. His nightgown was simple, cotton and knee-length. Sterling wasn't comfortable seeing the governor's toes *and* knees. It just seemed un-royal. Thankfully, over all of it he donned a banyan: a floor-length, brocaded, silk-lined robe that buttoned in the front. Clearly, it wasn't buttoned past the knees. Still, Savannah had said Gooch was indeed one the "nicest governors you'd ever meet".

"*Buona sera, Signore diPadua. Come sta?*" Gooch greeted Sterling with genuine vigor and offered his hand.

"Eh, I actually come from London, the West End, Sir. But, right then, *buona sera*, Governor Gooch, Sir, Your Highness, eh, Mate?" Sterling half-bowed, half-extended his hand, totally unsure of the protocol here. Gooch seemed very unorthodox, almost as casual as his interior design.

"Please, have a seat, *Signore*, I mean, Mister diPadua," Gooch gestured to the secretary whom pulled out a chair from the wall, placing it in front of Gooch's writing table.

"Please, call me Sterling."

"Yes. Of course. Sterling. Like the silver?" Gooch asked.

Sterling laughed a little, but was still very nervous. He was sure the governor knew Sterling's history and this whole "nice act" was just to keep him in the Palace until the proper authorities arrived. His heart was beginning to *thump* so loudly he looked around, suddenly sure the governor and his secretary could hear it. Yet, he was there to help a friend and that was all he could focus on for now. Now, Gooch and the secretary were just staring at him.

Why were they staring at him? Say something. Say something! Oh, wait a moment. He did say something. Something about furniture. A question? No. A statement? No, it was definitely a question. The governor had asked him a question about furniture. No. Dishes? Nooooo. Oh, his name. Silver! Yes, that was it.

"Sterling, like the silver?" Gooch asked again.

"Right then. Yes. Sterling, like the silver," he laughed again, with a higher pitch and even more nervous now.

"Excellent," Gooch eyed Sterling suspiciously. Being a parent, he had developed a sixth sense that told him when something was afoot. This little fox was nervous about something and Gooch did what any good parent would do in the situation: pretend he already knew. "Sterling, do you have something to tell me? I already know, but I'd like to hear your side of the story before we deal with the consequences."

Sterling sighed, surprisingly more out of relief than anything. In fact, he was almost happy to turn himself in. He had been on the run too long and it was exhausting. Worried there was a sheriff around every corner, scared to death of every dog bark he heard, wondering if he'd be captured in his sleep and carted away. No, this was good. It was time to tell his Vagabond Tale.

"Right then, your Honour. It was just over a year ago, closer to two maybe," Sterling licked his lips as they instantly grew dry from anxiety. "I was happily strolling along and singing a song, plucking a merry tune on my mandolin, when I was approached by the Sheriff of Highgate. 'What are you doing, son?' he asked me. To which I replied, 'Singing a song, Mate. What are you doing?' And I promptly made up a song about a wandering sheriff."

Gooch tried to hide a smile; only Beddoes caught it and smirked a bit himself. "Go on," Gooch said with false sternness.

"An hour later I found myself in gaol, trying to explain through the iron bars what I was doing out there," he shrugged his shoulders and loosened a scarf that felt like it was strangling him of its own accord.

"You were without a sponsor, were you not?" Gooch surmised correctly.

"I am guilty of that, Your Honour, but nothing more," Sterling began to wring his paws.

"You sang at the sheriff. Generally speaking, they do not have a very refined sense of humour," Gooch added.

"Yes, Sir. I made two mistakes. I had no sponsor and I got cocksure and funny with a sheriff." Sterling lowered his head and waited for Gooch to say something; Beddoes stood still as a statue and awaited the same thing.

"You do understand the need for a sponsor, lad, do you not?" Gooch asked gently of Sterling.

"I admit I was singing and wandering alone without any sponsor. I also admit, most respectfully, that I was unaware of the need for a sponsor. I still am unsure of my exact crime and the need for a sponsor. Governor Gooch," Sterling's eyes grew moist as he pleaded for nothing more than an explanation. "all I wanted to do was sing and make folks laugh. I never harmed anyone and now, now I am homeless and on the run and in fear for my life everyday."

Gooch knelt down to Sterling's chair and picked up a paw. He knew Sterling was guilty of nothing real; but, ignorance of the law has never been a viable excuse. The least Gooch could do was to explain the law to him.

"A sponsor," Gooch began as he pet Sterling's paw, "is someone of wealth who believes so much in your talent that he wished you never to worry about boring things like work. It is also, in truth, a status symbol. Like having a talented and fancy pet. They get to tell their friends they are sponsoring this actor or that musician, etcetera, etcetera. They pay you to simply perfect your art and perform it at their whim. You had no sponsor."

"That is lovely and wonderful for all involved, I assume," Sterling was now crying and sniffling. "but I still do not understand. Why was I arrested because I hadn't the luxury of a sponsor?"

"It is a sad fact that the English are distrustful of someone whom does not work hard. I suppose they think if one can make a living, or at least just be happy, with something like art or dance or song, there must be something wrong with one or perhaps even mischievous, you know, up to no good, Mate." Gooch winked as he called him Mate and Beddoes turned his head; Gooch was never that casual with visitors.

"I wasn't being mischievous! I promise!" Sterling was beginning to panic.

"I know you weren't," Gooch stood back up. "Still, the law is the law. What did the sheriff do after he gaoled you?" He needed more information.

"Thing is, the sheriff asked me 'Do you have a proper sponsor' to which I said, 'I sponsor myself, Chap.' Again, being pithy, which is frowned upon. So, he smirks and tells me I'm no Shakespeare and how Shakespeare had proper sponsors, to which I say, 'Mate, I know all about Shakespeare. I don't need you to tell me about the Bard.' He didn't like that," Sterling sniffled as he laughed a little.

"Pithy is never good with a sheriff, lad." Gooch admonished.

"Well, after the sheriff determined I was indeed unsponsored, he took me before the Justice of the Peace whom then began to read me lengthy and boring segments of something called The Vagabond Act of 1604. 1604!"

"I didn't even know this existed. It's ancient! But, they sentenced me based on it. What is it exactly? Besides not being aloud to stroll and sing alone?" Sterling was beginning to breathe heavily.

"The Vagabond Act," Gooch, being a highly intelligent governor with a knowledge of all English law, ancient and contemporary, and possessing an excellent memory for anything he had read, paraphrased the Vagabond Act as if it there were notes on it posted right in front of him, "deems it illegal for any performer, including but not limited to dancers, jugglers, actors, singers, minstrels, palmists, fortune-tellers, begging sailors, begging scholars, intellectual hermits without a proper estate to live upon and plenty of other smart and creative folks, to do any of the above without a sponsor."

"And?" Sterling thought he might pass out he was getting so hot.

"And, that if found guilty, the performer in question must suffer one of three punishments at the Justice's discretion."

"Ohhh," Sterling groaned, "I recall something about the punishments, but I think I fainted."

"A public whipping," Gooch began.

Sterling groaned again and slumped over in his chair, certain these punishments were headed his way, if only for running away in the first place.

"The second option is gaol for quite a long time, mostly to keep performers off the roads, and finally, my favourite," he said sarcastically, for he had never been a supporter of the silly law, "being sent away to, and I quote, 'do the work one was born to do'," he finished by clasping his hands behind his back and began to pace, thinking about the situation at hand.

"So, the Justice told you he thought you were born to fox hunt. Is that correct?" Gooch turned on his heel and asked Sterling whom was wiping his eyes with one of his many scarves.

"Yes, Sir. He sentenced me to come to America, to Maryland where apparently those used to fox hunting in England miss it terribly and need some good, English foxes exported to the colonies so they can hunt just like at home. He tells me I'm to be shipped off to Maryland, in a cage no less and without my clothes and scarves, I was nude, your Honour, nude all the way across the sea, just so I can be torn to shreds by some idiotic hounds and their ignorant owners." Sterling broke down and began to sob. Beddoes walked to the tea table to prepare a cup of peppermint tea for Sterling. "Next thing I knew I was stripped and caged on the sea. That's how I got here. That's my secret."

Sterling slumped all the way forward, his head between his knees, his shoulders heaving.

"May I ask, how did you escape?" Gooch asked quietly and sincerely, completely unsure of what to do; this was unlike anything he'd yet encountered.

Did he uphold the law without question, or did he set Sterling free, simply because he liked him?

"The minute they carted me to my destination and opened my cage to move me to another holding pen on the plantation, I ran like the Devil. They could never catch me, the hounds weren't organized at that point and it was a fond farewell to thee!" he laughed nervously at the idea of outsmarting the hunters and hounds.

Sterling, Gooch and Beddoes as remained silent for a bit. Only the sound of Sterling's occasional sniffle or sip of tea and Gooch's sharp heels clicking on the floorboards could be heard. Finally, Gooch stopped and Sterling and Beddoes looked up, awaiting a declaration.

"Now, Beddoes, tells me you've got some sort of emergency involving our mutual friend Miss Savannah Squirrel. I think, considering your situation, this emergency must be truly dire or you would not have come here. That is a good friend, I must say," he smiled and winked at Sterling. "Tell me, what has she done now? Has she upset one of the old biddies at the market?" he laughed at the idea of Savannah's free spirit.

Sterling said nothing for a minute. He didn't know what to make of this abrupt change of subject. Was he free? Was Gooch going to deal with him later? He looked to Beddoes for some sort of visual signal, but Gooch's secretary just stood still as stone. Gooch looked at Sterling and raised his eyebrows, silently asking again about Savannah. Sterling decided it best to follow suit.

"Yes, Sir. Actually, it's quite bad," Sterling began. "Quite dangerous actually. She has. . .," he stopped as Gooch stood up and went to the window, seemingly ignoring Sterling.

"Beddoes, what is all that down there?" he pointed out the window towards the Palace Green. Beddoes walked up to look. "Is that fire? I thought I heard something. I just thought the theatre crowd was a little wild tonight. Lots of Italians, eh?" he turned and laughed to Sterling. "No offense, *Signore?*"

"Actually, Governor, that is what *Signore* diPadua was. . .," Beddoes tried to inform Gooch.

"Why all the torches? Are there not enough torches and candles within the theatre? They are awfully loud, don't you think, Beddoes? Are they hooligans?"

"Indeed, Sir. They are rather an aggressive crowd tonight, Sir. *Signore* diPadua does have some information. . .," Beddoes tried to make Gooch listen.

"It's another performance of *The Mysterious Silence Dogood*, is it not? That's right. I have officially granted it a three-month run. She doesn't know yet, Miss Savannah. Beddoes was just drawing up the official decree for her tonight, were you not, Beddoes?" Beddoes bowed once. "I am sending it to her, officially, tomorrow morning." It seemed Gooch like the word *officially*. "Good for her. I like that squirrel. Verrry smart, that one. Fashionable, too. And spunky! I knew her play would be a success when I sat in on rehearsals. Enjoyed it immensely opening night. Funny. That Ben Franklin boy? Hilarious! But why such the uproar tonight?"

"Your Honour, if you would please have a seat. *Signore* diPadua has grave news for you regarding Miss Savannah Squirrel and her play," Beddoes, with placid and stoic servitude, insisted Gooch come away from the window and take his seat.

Moments later, Gooch shot down the Palace staircase, Sterling following closely. Still barefoot and with his long, nightcap flowing behind him, his banyan billowed majestically as he bounded down the stairs two at a time. Sterling kept pace, his own array of silk scarves and fabrics streaking behind him in a perfect dance with his tail. Beddoes had been dispatched to gather a small contingency of Palace guards. This was a good job for Beddoes as he wasn't really a runner, really more of an organizer.

"Ten! Twenty! Bring them directly to Levingston's Theatre! I don't want blood, but we must be prepared. If they want blood, we shall have to oblige them. Tell my guards to arm themselves fully. Make a good show of it. Get Bennigan, my horse!"

"But, Sir. Would it not be quicker to just run across the Green? It shall take longer to saddle your horse than it should to run over there," Beddoes wondered respectfully.

"Forget the saddle!" Gooch said gallantly, Beddoes cringed at the thought of bareback in a nightgown. "But get Bennigan! This calls for a bit of a power play. I've dealt with Carvile before and nothing says power more than a man on a horse looking down on a man without a horse. And, I'm certainly not going to gain much respect in bare feet and my little hat, am I, Beddoes?"

"Very good, Sir. You might wish to remove the hat, Sir, Beddoes suggested and Gooch did so, handing it to Beddoes as he fled. "Would you like me to bring you some slippers, Sir?" he called after Gooch.

"If you can have them on my feet by the time I'm on Bennigan, yes. Now go, Beddoes! Go!"

"Very good, Sir."

CHAPTER THIRTY - SEVEN

The coffeehouse was nearly empty tonight. It was August in Philadelphia and only one word could best described it: miserable. August also meant longer days. With the longer days came more productivity and play.

This was the season for early harvest preparations, autumn and winter storage planning and, for those whom were fortunate enough to have some free time, the best time of year to cool off in Philadelphia's Delaware and Schuykill Rivers. Swimming was a favourite pastime and exercise option for young Ben Franklin. This time of year was also a busy time for the pubs, taverns, garden bistros, parks and waterways. This was not, however, a busy time for the coffeehouses.

The coffeehouses did not let rooms in the same fashion or volume the taverns did, if at all. Instead, they relied primarily on an income from food, spirits, coffee and tea. In August, nobody wanted coffee, at least not at two in the afternoon. That was a morning beverage and a late afternoon pick-me-up. For now, Monk's Nervosa Café was quiet, slow and well lit as the sun sprayed in through the paned glass windows of the front wall. In a corner, at their favourite table, sat Ben and Andrew.

Andrew was writing in a leather journal with a quill pen, dipping it into a brass inkwell every fourth word or so. Ben appeared to be dictating to Andrew, but a little too actively. As Andrew wrote, Ben kept talking and was nearly lying on top of the table he was leaning over so far to peer into the journal. Craning his neck in order to read upside down, Ben tucked his arms and elbows underneath his chest as he hovered well into Andrew's personal space. Always the gentlemen, Andrew said nothing directly, just cleared his throat and pretended a need to stretch.

"Ahem," Andrew uttered, "my goodness one gets stiff writing so much."

He attempted to stretch out his arms, but Ben just smiled and nodded eagerly, hunching ever more tightly over the table like a little boy watching his mother make Christmas candies.

"Yes! I agree! We certainly have been at this a while. It is so exciting! Don't you think?" Ben's eyes and smile were both wide and whacked out from way too much coffee.

"Yes, 'tis very exciting, Ben. You know, perhaps you should get us something cool and refreshing to drink. Perhaps a couple of shrub glasses piled high with lemon ice," he offered this as an adult would to a child and Ben responded as such.

"How splendid! Lemon ices! Yes, I shall return in a moment," he leaped to his feet and headed toward the nearest waitress, then, jumped back to the table, leaning right into Andrew's face. "Do not forget the part which reads, 'every man who prefers liberty to a life of slavery'. I love that part! You did not forget that part, did you?"

"I did not forget. It is right here," Andrew tapped an area at the top of the page with his quill. "I agree, it is brilliant."

"Brilliant. It is, isn't it?" Ben smiled as he wandered off to find a waitress, saw two and proceeded to select the prettier of the two.

Ben returned a good twenty minutes later. As easily as he could become engaged in one thing, he could be swayed and drawn to another: the ladies were always a distraction. Upon return, the ices had melted into goopy, yellow syrup. Far too sweet to drink without the benefit of shaved ice coolness. Never mind, Ben and Andrew were too enthralled by what they were doing. Within moments, Ben was back hovering over Andrew's journal.

"Does anybody know?" Ben leaned in extra close and looked around the coffeehouse.

"Only a very few and very trustworthy," Andrew answered without looking up from writing, his quill scratching the parchment energetically like a chicken in a pen.

"Shall it happen in time? Will there be any delays?" Ben's mischievous smile changed to a concerned frown.

"Not if I leave tonight. That, Ben," he looked up from his journal, placed his quill in its holder next to the inkwell and looked Ben straight in the eyes, "is why we must, I must, finish this forthwith. We must make haste if I am to ride tonight." Andrew scanned the room for any eavesdroppers, then continued. "Time is against us as the days are longer right now. That puts us at least at nine o'clock before I can depart. I must ride hard if I am to reach. . .," he hesitated in case anyone was listening, "my destination by Monday." He wisely avoided speaking aloud the name of the destination. "Now, let us focus on our task at hand. First," he held up a finger to stop Ben from speaking, "perhaps we can have a couple of new lemon ices?"

Ben enjoyed the opportunity to talk to the pretty waitress again and Andrew gave him a knowing nod at his pocket watch, silently reminding him to return this time before the ice melted.

"Oh!" Ben turned back to Andrew before chasing down his chosen waitress. "Did you write the part that reads, 'wise men use our utmost care to support liberty'? I love that part, too!"

"Yes, Ben. It is right here." Andrew tapped a portion of the journal's paper and couldn't help but laugh inside at Ben's enthusiasm and eagerness.

Yes, Andrew thought to himself, someday Ben Franklin would achieve far more than celebrity as a businessman and printer. He would certainly do many a great things. People would speak the name Benjamin Franklin for many a year to come, probably that of his children and grandchildren, too, Andrew surmised. That level of intelligence and drive had to be passed on, didn't it?

CHAPTER THIRTY - EIGHT

"Stop the Play! Stop the squirrel! Stop the play! Stop the squirrel!" the mob chanted over and over again.

They had marched their way to the final destination: the gates of Levingston's Theatre. The front portion of the mob, its leaders, held firmly in place on the gravel semi-circle which led up to the theatre's entrance. The back portions, the bulk of it and perhaps two-hundred-plus angry men, flowed out of the semi-circle and onto a vast portion of the Palace Green. On one side, this group flowed almost to the Governor's Palace; on the other, it flowed down the Green and spilled into the lawn outside Levingston's Kitchen.

Being summer, the Virginia sky remained a jeweled blue until well past eight o'clock and Savannah had loved the idea of evening shows, even if the extra candles were a fire hazard. To solve this problem, she had simply hired firewatchers: men and women whose task was to watch each and every candle, oil lamp, sconce, torch, chandelier and candle loop with extreme scrutiny. They were not allowed to watch the play, only the flames. If something began to burn out of control, they were ready with a snuff: a standard length handle for the footlight candles; extended length to reach the chandeliers and hanging loops that swung over the crowd. What Savannah had not counted on was hundreds of torches carried by angry farmers and merchants. What she had also not counted on was this total and complete obliteration of her theatrical vision by a group of men, and some women, she had never met. What was their problem? Was this because she was a squirrel? Were they squirrelists?

The theatregoers stood their ground as the mob continued to grow. Naturally, as town members came to see what the commotion was, the majority arrived via the Palace Green. Many of those just stuck to the back of the mob like a wet leaf to a shoe for no reason other than excitement: that far back, no one really knew what was going on. A game of "Mess Up the Message" had commenced near the front of the mob and by the time information was passed through toward the back, through fifty or more people, the message was a complete, well, mess.

"What is the ruckus, friend?" one man asked as he arrived at the back of the mob.

"I'm unsure. But, I am trying to find out," another who had been there for a while answered.

A few moments passed as messages were passed up and down the mob. Over the next half-hour or so, the following morphs of the original message flowed through like so:

"We are fighting the squirrel! The play must stop!"

"We are fighting the squirrel! The play must flop!"

"We are biting the squirrel! They say to stop!"

"We are riding the world! They say it shall pop!"

"We are lighting Earl! We start at the top!"

By the time this final message got to the back of the mob, besides other deviations and degenerations of the original declaration, most of the newcomers figured they had joined some just cause helping the world or a squirrel or someone named Earl and decided if they were going to join the fight, to join it with energy and vigor; and so the mob grew. At the very back marched Phillip the Bruce. Not one to ever join a group, a protest was a different story altogether.

When he saw the torches, pitchforks and agitated faces headed toward the Palace Green, Bruce knew something true and righteous was going down and he needed to be part of it. If this group of ramshackle and dirty farmers was headed toward the Palace Green, they were most likely headed for the Palace itself. What better figure to protest than King George and his sad, puppet minions? There were, of course, in the mob some very finely dressed folk he assumed to be merchant-types or at least minor nobility. He hated minor nobility.

Minor nobility were always the second- or third-born into a family that had started out poor. The father or grandfather had built the fortune through hard work or luck or some means and the children and grandchildren felt they were born just to spend it and waste it and, in Phil's experience, lose it. He knew these people, had spent time at various universities with them and didn't like them a bit. Why they were here, joining forces with the salt-of-the-earth folk, he had no idea. But, he figured maybe they were the guilty nobles. The guilty noble was one whom believed vehemently in *noblesse oblige*, a moral and social obligation of the wealthy to the poor; however, the wealthiest and truest of the guilty nobles, while they would march on palaces and throw alms to the poor, they would never actually so much as invite the poor into their homes or allow their children to socialize with the poor children. They were grand at throwing them money and royal balls for their benefit, but never real love and compassion.

Nope, give Bruce a disheveled, unshaven farmer or waterman any day of the week. They were true to the core and honest as the sea is deep. Tonight, there was a whole group of the labouring class headed toward the symbol of decadence and entitlement to take it all down a notch. Minor nobles or not, he was joining that group.

"We are lighting Earl! We start at the top! "We are lighting Earl! We start at the top!"

Bruce chanted this over and over. He didn't know who Earl was, but he assumed he was in the King's service, ergo evil and they were about to burn him at the stake. Maybe Earl *was* an Earl: a British nobleman just above a Viscount, but below a Marquis. Burning at the stake was pretty radical, a little 15th Century for his taste, but if that's what this group of good, basic, down-to-earth, non-materialistic folk called for, Earl must have done something to deserve it. Still, he was glad Beauregard wasn't here to witness it. A stake burning was not for the gentle souls of this world.

"We are lighting Earl! We start at the top! "We are lighting Earl! We start at the top!"

Some people, however, filtered through the mob and worked their way around to the theatre side after hearing, accurately, that the squirrel was in trouble. Others arrived to the clash by coming up the back streets that led west from the gaol and the Capitol, running behind DoG Street on the northernmost parts of town. These folks ended up right at the center of the feud, where the two sides met yelling and cursing on Palace Street. The theatre supporters were gaining in population, but the odds were still easily five to one in favour of the original mob.

Savannah was becoming so nervous she actually threw up over Juicy's side. Ichabod hugged her, but she was more embarrassed than anything. How dare she let herself be so weak, especially in public? This just made her even more determined to mete this out and stood up to fight, but fell again into Juicy's swayback. She decided to stay put until she could think of a better way to meet this mob face to face.

What she could see from her lofty if unstable perch was her supporters were full of vigor and determination for her. They thrust their fancy foils in the air, they whipped their lacy cuffs and sabres at the space still separating the fighting sides. All in very showy, very theatrical displays of protection they made it clear should they need to defend their squirrel and their art with violence, they would. Some had taken to the garden tables and benches and hurled taunts and threats from some relative height.

The entire north half of the Green was alive with yelling, cursing and the edgy stages of a full-on, town brawl. The mob stomped their feet on the grass and pounded their farm tools, sword tips and canes in time, all making an eerie, muted, thunderous sound that gave the very creepy feeling under one's feet that the earth might soon come alive with protesters of its own. The theatre crowd danced and fenced back at them, making their own ominous sensation as their sharp heels and silver-tipped walking sticks beat the gravel and tables in perfect, musical time.

Finally, Savannah could wait no longer. Where could Sterling and Gooch be? She had never waited for someone else to pull her out of a jam and she wasn't going to start now. She wouldn't wait and she wouldn't throw up anymore. Against Ichabod's advice she jumped off Juicy's back and onto a bench, then down to the ground.

"Safannah! Please! You vill get sqvashed!" Ichabod stood up to run after her, looked down, grew very dizzy and tumbled into Juicy's back. He grabbed onto her mane and steadied himself before calling after Savannah again. "Safannah! I am serious! Please stop! *Halten Sie!*"

"Come with me, then!" she yelled back as she ran.

"Absolutely not! No, thank you. Efen at this height I am safer than down there vith all those 'feet'," he said the word 'feet' with utter disdain as he hung onto Juicy's mane. "Ve must vait for Gofernor Gooch. He vill be here any moment. I know this!"

He let go of Juicy's mane, slid down into her sway, crossed his legs and nestled himself between Juicy's withers and her back, grabbing onto her mane again as soon as he was seated and comfy.

Savannah waved him off and Ichabod realized she was going to do what she wanted. She was just that kind of squirrel. She scampered across the garden, out the main gates and through her crowd, dodging feet and sticks and swords with the agility of a natural acrobat. Along the way, she took note of some of the shoes and thought it was a pity more people didn't wear better shoes, especially theatre folk. They should know better. She passed one pair of particularly attractive slippers with gorgeous leather heels, but wondered why someone would have gone to the trouble to make such a fine shoe, then cover it in a plain, brown cloth. "They certainly should be silk," she thought to herself and couldn't help but glance up at the girl wearing them. "She's awfully pretty. You think she'd know better, too." If only more people had her innate sense of fashion, there probably wouldn't be mobs like this.

She eventually made it through her crowd to the gravel road of Palace Street: the geographical nexus of this conflict. Of course, no one noticed her and she found herself wishing she had waited for Gooch if for nothing other than some height. Fortunately, there was never a shortage of trees in Williamsburg. There on the side of the road stood a great elm whose branches reached far over the road. In particular, one had plenty of offshoot branches which hung exactly over where the two mobs met. It would give her the perfect position of influence, power and most of all, safety from all these feet and dangerous tools.

Back she ran through the crowd and up the thick trunk of the elm. In an instant she stood on a branch that indeed hung straight over the quarrel. She yelled for quiet and that did not work. She waved her wee arms and that did not work. She jumped up and down, ran back and forth across the branch while yelling and waving her wee arms and that did not work. Frustrated, she thought

Jennifer Susannah Devore

for a second, then knew just what to do.

"What is that?" a protester knitted his brow and looked to the sky.

"Did you just hit me?" another accused someone next to him.

"Who threw that? Who did that?" a theatergoer whined.

"Are they throwing things now? Can we throw things?! Are we throwing things?" an excited oyster fisherman asked.

"No, it's coming from up there," a fancy merchant in the mob looked above. "In the trees."

Everyone began to look above their heads.

"'Tis the squirrel!" one of the protesters, a farmer, screamed. "Get her!"

"Get her?" a fellow protester, a merchant, questioned him. "We are not curs. We're here to stop the play, not kill a squirrel in a frock."

Savannah was glad to hear that. She threw down more sticks and pulled off small pieces of the bark and chucked it all below. Suddenly they were all staring up at her. Both protesters and supporters stopped mid-fight and looked up at the poncy, frilly, pink-fashioned squirrel with eyes of fury and tiny fists of tree bark.

"It's the squirrel! It's the squirrel!" one of the protesters yelled. "Stop the squirrel! Stop the. . ."

"Oh stop it! Just stop it!" Savannah cut him off and flicked a chunk of bark right into his forehead.

"Okay, okay, we see you! Stop throwing stuff!" his friend shook a fist up at the tree.

Slowly though, everyone in the mob began thinking the same thing: There she was, a pretty, intelligent, determined, and talking, which was kind of weird for some of the people, squirrel dressed all in pink, wearing a bare flower stem around her neck for some reason, and standing no more than ten inches high. *She* was the cause of all this turmoil? Some of the protesters began to feel stupid. Stop the squirrel? Her? Some even slowly lowered their tools and swords, and their eyes. They knew the play was destructive. They had been rallied together and told how bad it was and they knew there was a squirrel involved, but. . .her? They all began to re-think their positions and a quiet murmur began to grow. Then, the mob began to part straight down the middle.

Like a sickle through wheat, three figures cut through the crowd and stopped at its head, right at the gravel road.

The first to slither out was the Snake-man. Savannah jumped up onto a higher branch. She knew he wasn't actually a snake, but he resembled one so closely that her natural fear of reptiles made her fur stand on end and her self-preservation instincts kicked into high gear. Frightened by his sinister features, she froze and began a series of *click*s and *cluck*s with her tongue as her tail twitched. She didn't usually speak squirrel, but it kicked in without thought during squirrel emergencies. She knew when she saw him Opening Night she didn't like him. Sometimes you can judge a book by its cover.

"Miss Savannah," he spat her name out quickly and sharply, offering a deep, mock bow as he did so. "So pleased to finally have a formal introduction, Miss Squirrel," he laughed as he watched her fear.

"You!" She instantly replaced her fear with distaste and jumped back down to the lower branch, speaking English once again. "What are you up to? Are you behind all this?"

"Yes, Ma'am," he fake bowed again, his shiny, bald head glinting with the glow of the surrounding torches. "Aa fear you may have not been," he cleared his throat and looked with an evil smile at his fellow mobsters, "properly notifaad of our issue with this production."

"What issue? 'Tis a story about Benjamin Franklin, 'tis all," she leaned out to the very edge of the branch, causing a slight bounce.

"'Tis not all," he hissed up at her viciously, then regained his best, fake politeness. "We think, Miss Savannah, the play is about more than that. *We* believe that *you* believe it is a, oh, how do you call it in lit-er-ture? Ah, yes, a metaphor."

"Very accurate, Lord Carvile," a well-dressed man next to him nodded. "This play is indeed a metaphor, meant to shred the very structure and economy that sustains this colony!"

Carvile held up a hand as he closed his eyes, nodded and sported a small smile. Silently, he told this man to wait, that he would get to the main issue in good time. No hurry necessary.

"Carvile? Is that your name?" Savannah tilted her head at the Snake-

Man.

This was why he wanted his fellow mobster to wait. Carvile's smile grew, though his lips remained closed. He tilted his head now and waited patiently as he watched her think, searching her brain for his name.

"Carvile, Carvile, Carvile. Hmm. Carv. . .," she stopped mid-name and stared at him, recalling with dread who he was.

"That's raaght, Miss Savannah. Aa see you found it up there," he tapped his head with a finger. "You are a smart one," he spit a little with each 'S' he spoke. "Lord Charles Coulter Carvile, 9th Earl of the Smoking Loon, personal advaasor to Willem Anne VanKeppel, 2nd Earl of Albemarle, *the* Royal Governor, *in* London," he added for effect.

"Earl? Did someone say Earl? Is he *an* Earl? Or he someone *named* Earl?"

Bruce had worked his way up near head of the mob, but still wasn't sure what was going on and could see very little now that night had fallen fully. What could be seen was mostly through an orange-yellow haze of firelight and smoke.

Savannah's nose wriggled and she said nothing. Instinctually, she looked out at the dark horizon for help. Gooch? Anthony? Ichabod? Dante? Anyone? Dante had watched it all from below and was halfway up the tree before Savannah could even call his name. He arrived in a flash and buddied up next to her, his paw on his sword hilt, aware that this was bigger than anybody had guessed. Ichabod watched from Juicy's back and decided he had to get himself down, then somehow up that tree. She needed him now. He had worried long ago last winter that she would go too far with that play. She knew exactly what her metaphor was and so did this man. Ichabod had major pull in noble and royal circles; maybe he could say something to Carvile. Carefully, Ichabod turned over on his belly and started to slide off Juicy, then realized it was a very far drop down. He scrambled back up and pulled right on Juicy's mane, asking her to move right. She did just that and stopped next to a garden table. Easily, Ichabod jumped onto the table and thanked Juicy for all her help.

"Thank you fery kindly for your assistance and allowing us to sit upon you," he thanked the old horse.

"Thank you! You two are much easier to carry than the big guy I usually have to lug around," she laughed and whinnied and scratched a hoof on the ground.

Ichabod's sword clanked on the table as he climbed down to the bench and onto the ground, where suddenly surrounded by boots, feet and swords he remembered why he was up on Juicy in the first place.

"Back up, Juicy! Back up!" he yelled to Juicy who leaned down so Ichabod could grab her mane and she pulled him back up to the table where he jumped right back on top of her withers. "She vill be okay. Dante is there vith her," Ichabod assuaged his guilt and panted hard as he watched all the feet shuffling on the ground far below.

"Now, what is all this?! What on earth is your problem with my play? With me?" Savannah felt a bit stronger with Dante at her side. Having spied Ichabod's attempt to help her, she felt she had his spirit next to her if not his actual self. "Well? Speak up then, Lord Carvile. Your people have been prattling on all evening and frankly I'm sick of it! If you've an issue with me or my actors or my play, be men and say so because this is costing me a *lot* of money!"

She glanced down with some irritation at the stagehands' foreman whom had come out to watch the goings-on. He leaned against a tree in the theatre garden, his arms crossed and his eyebrows raised. He smiled with a closed mouth and nodded up at her, silently confirming that, yes, he and his men would continue to be paid by the hour whether the play ran or not. Savannah looked back to Carvile, placed her hands on her hips, thrust her nose out, opened her eyes wide, pursed her lips tight and extended her tail straight up and twitched it back and forth.

"I am waiting," she stared down the motley group of protesters, some of whom hadn't even the real courage to look her in the eyes.

"So, we know who you are. Big deal," Dante couldn't stop himself.

Carvile was saying nothing, just toying with Savannah and enjoying every minute of it. This was infuriating Dante. Nobody treated his friend like that.

"What business is it of yours, her play of the young Ben Franklin?"

"Aa do not take issue with the play itself. Aa take issue with her sub-text," Carvile finally spoke, his speech getting a little faster as his emotion rose.

"What did he say?" someone in the crowd asked someone else in the crowd.

"He said sub-text. The play has sub-text. I think that's bad," someone surmised.

"Excellent! That's awful! We hate sub-text! Sub-text, sub-text, down with sub-text!" another one chanted.

"You don't even know what sub-text is," Bruce sneered.

He was getting closer to the front of this scuffle, but still wasn't totally up to speed. He pushed his way past these men, certain that standing near such idiots wasn't going to get him any good information about the lighting of this Earl person, or *the* Earl if that was the case. Lighting *an* Earl would certainly be better than setting fire to just some guy named Earl, he was pretty sure. Yet, the closer he got, he heard comments about a play and, well, obviously, the playhouse was nearby. He had attended *The Mysterious Silence Dogood* last night, mostly as a favour to Beauregard whom was proudly working the curtains. As a rule, Bruce did not attend the theatre. This was all very odd, though. Was Earl getting lit? Was it part of the play? Was this a marketing scheme? Had he been snookered into going to see the same play twice? That would make him very irritated, for he was certainly too smart for any marketing ploy. He had to get to the front.

Back at the front, Savannah and Lord Carvile had finally gotten to the meat of this dispute and the crowds were offering cheers and jeers as needed. By now, Miss Rebecca Lane had moved directly under the tree. This way, she presented full and moral support for her producer. In fact, the whole cast had followed her and as the crowd grew, as more people arrived from the north, the conflict's focal point shifted to the spot directly under Savannah's branch. In a way, she had brought Carvile to her position and that gave her some psychological upsmanship.

"So you claim there is sub-text in *The Mysterious Silence Dogood*. I say you have seen a different play than the rest of us here," Savannah looked to her crowd and they nodded and cheered. Being artists, they knew there was always something beneath a script's dialogue.

"Do you think aa am a fool?" Carvile snapped.

"I do not know. Are you a fool?" Her crowd laughed and cheered.

"Your play is a metaphor," Carvile stated definitively and briskly.

"No it's not," Savannah retorted.

"Then it's a simile," he tried.

"Nope."

"Irony?"

"No."

"Wolfstein?"

"That's not a word. You just made it up. You have no idea what this play means, Lord Carvile."

"Your play has hidden meaning and aa know exactly what it is!" he looked to his crowd for enthusiastic support and they did cheer, kind of.

None of them actually had seen the play though, so they took his word for it.

"Alright, if there is hidden meaning, tell us. What is my secret message?"

"It is very clear what your secret message is. It is all about slavery!" he thrust a fist up in the air, drawing out the last word with relish and calling for the support of the mob; they obliged and yelled, lifting their tools and weapons into the air.

"Slavery? That is very interesting," Savannah said innocently. "However, my little play has only a woman, a boy and his brother. No slaves."

"Do not mock me, Miss Savannah. Your play attacks the very notion of slavery and indentured servitude. Whaa, the very relationship between Ben Franklin and his brother James is exactly that of mastah and slave."

Again, the mob yelled and rattled their tools.

"Slave? Master? Slavemaster? Who's a slavemaster? Are we hanging a slavemaster? Excellent!" Phil the Bruce was getting closer and quite okay with the hanging of a slave owner. In truth, he thought the idea of an Earl burning was a little extreme.

"I do not mock you, Lord Carvile. I merely wonder what it is you see in the play that I do not. I mean, what else? Besides questioning the legal right to own another human being?" she baited him.

"Exactly! It absolutely is legal to own another human being! Whaate or black, indentured or for laafe, it is our raaght as tax-paying landowners, British subjects, merchants and planters to support our businesses as financially efficient as possible. It is the law and it is how all of us," he swung his arm around to engulf the mob, "survaave and how this colony grows. Your own Capitol and College, church and plantation homes were all built with slave labor, with indentured labour!" This drew cheers from the mob and nothing from Savannah's side.

"So you are saying that even our fair Williamsburg was built on the bare backs of men, women and children forced into hard labor, with no choice in the matter?"

"Yes! Aa mean, they've had choices. Had they been left behind in Africa, they might not have come to know the beauty of God and the Holy Church of England. They would still be practicing their voodoo witchcraft. Because of us they are now working hard in this life to be rewarded in the next, in God's Heaven!" his words were beginning to run together he was now speaking so fast and spitting so much.

Dante and Rebecca rolled their eyes at each other.

"So it is from my play that you find the concept of slavery abusive and detrimental to the everyday lives of its victims."

"That is not what aa said. What aa said is that they will be rewarded with a Heavenly afterlaafe and whaale on earth, enjoy a far better laafe here in Virginia than on their blasted Dark Continent. Slavery is good for everybody!" he wiped his mouth and looked at his supporters.

They half-cheered at this; even they knew it wasn't really "good", it was just a fact of life. The whole crowd went a little limp. Most of them, including the theatergoers, indeed owned slaves or at least functioned daily on a system that used slavery. Everyone was beginning to think. Slavery was one of those evils, like cheap, provenance-free art or a thick, blood pudding: everyone knew it existed, but no one wanted to talk about it in detail.

"This is a matter of opinion, Lord Carvile. Who are we to say which is better, Virginia or Africa? I imagine Africa is sublimely beautiful and peaceful to the senses. I rather think I shall travel there someday, of my own accord and not captured with a net and shackled and manacled on a filth ship against my every desire! Nevertheless," she checked her rising emotion. She wasn't going to make any point if she was tearful and out of control; she had to be smarter than Carvile whom was indeed growing emotional. "My play neither makes a comment on slavery nor calls for any action on it, does it? After all, Ben Franklin is an indentured servant to his brother and that is not at all the same as a slave-for-life servant." She waited for him to finish her message.

"Indeed it does make such a comment! It is subtle and sneaky, aa shall grant you that. An indentured servant is a relatively voluntary position, so no one would think to link it to slavery. However, the flaaght in the naaght of your young Ben from Boston is a call to all to set free their slaves, for slaves and servants to run away. Ben was an asset to his brother. James could not have run such an effective, popular and successful news-paper were it not for Ben. We cannot run an effective and successful colony without the asset that is our slave population. Our legal and accepted slave trade!" he wiped his mouth again and walked closer to Savannah's branch.

"Whaa, aa imagine you had some sugar in your tea this morning. Think, Miss Savannah. Where did that sugar ultimately come from?" He stood on his tip-toes leaned in as close to her face as possible and whispered to her, "It came to you after a looong waaay around the slavery-deep Trade Triangle, maa dear. Europe's goods sold for African slaves, slaves sold to the Caribbean for sugar and spaaces, and those all come to your tea table in exchange for tobacco and cotton and raace," he stood up straight and addressed the theatregoers. "Slave tea. That's what all you dandies drink when you spoon your precious, expensive sugar into your fancy, expensive teas. Now, Miss Savannah, do you still find yourself innocent of slavery?"

"Sadly, I have never considered myself free of the slave trade. I know full well it touches everyone here. That is why one must do whatever one can to fix the problem that is too big to fix. Attention to the matter is something we can try."

"Aha! Then you admit you are drawing attention to the influence of slavery through your play! The more people who see it, the more people will think about slavery and the more people will raase up against it like Ben Franklin!"

"Those are your words, Lord Carvile. Not mine. Sounds effective, though. I don't think my little play could ever do something like that," she tightened her entire face so as not to roll over laughing with Dante, whom was doing the same thing, except his whiskers were twitching.

"Aa see what you are up to. We," he outstretched his arms, "all see what you are up to, dear, and do not laak it. More importantly, most importantly, Governor VanKeppel will not laak this stimulation of thought you are stirring up in his colonial jewel when he gets word of it."

Savannah laughed, "Do not be ridiculous! Governor VanKeppel cannot possibly believe that I, a wee squirrel, am going to do anything to influence the transatlantic slave trade. You have in your mob, on your side, Mr. James Blair, one of Virginia's most prolific, industrious and wealthiest slave traders! Not just an owner, but a trader, a purveyor in that all important Trade Triangle. I am correct, Mr. Blair, am I not? Many of those slave ships that sail into our Queen Mary's Port belong to you, yes?"

Mr. Blair said nothing, but stared at her. He was not about to engage in conversation with a squirrel about business, a squirrel *girl* at that.

"The fact is, Miss Savannah Squirrel, aa am officially, hereby canceling your play. Effective immediately, *The Mysterious Silence Dogood* and Levingston's Theatre are both officially dark.

"What did I do?" Levingston whimpered from somewhere in the crowd. "I knew I should have never let a squirrel and a dog lease my theatre." He wandered back to the theatre, rubbing his eyes with his palms and shaking his half-bald head as he slumped back to his office.

By now, Bruce had moved to the very front of the mob and, after hearing Carvile's blatherings about the soul-saving benevolence of slavery, the financial needs of the Crown and his general egotism, he wondered how he had gotten himself suckered into such a deplorable cause. He stood at the edge of the mob next to, ironically, a black merchant holding a pitchfork and looked across the open space at the theatergoers and saw none other than Beauregard, his furry mouth agape and staring incredulously back at Phil.

The two exchanged some hand signals, mouthed energetic explanations at each other and made lots of shoulder shrugs, upward palm gestures and eye bulges at each other. Eventually, Phil stood straight and proud and with great drama took two long steps and positioned himself with the correct side of this debate. Noiselessly, his four cats, Figaro in the lead, slithered through legs and around tool handles to cross the line and sidled up to their Phil and his pal Beauregard.

Back on the other side, the merchant whom had been standing next to Phil now looked at the empty spot next to himself. He looked across at Phil, whom just shrugged his shoulders and grinned. He then tightened his jaw in seriousness and waited for the finale of this real-life theatre to play out.

"In addition," Carvile commanded aloud to all within earshot, "aa hereby make it a royal craame for any individual to cross into Levingston's Theatre! Punishable by imprisonment of not less than one year!"

The mob went nuts and cheered like crazy.

"Oh, dear," Levingston mumbled and turned back around and headed toward the group, his palms now furiously rubbing his eyes red. "This is not going to be good for business, not good for business at all."

"You cannot do this!" Savannah was seething. "'Tis absolutely unfair! I have a right to say whatever I want in a play, even if it is a commentary on slavery!" she owned up finally to the true point of her play.

"Ah-ha! Aa was correct," Carvile glowed with righteousness. "My dear, you, in fact, do not have the raaght to say whatever you want. . .anywhere. You have the luxury of King George allowing you to wraate a play and show a play. You do not have the raaght to offend the Crown and its dominions, financial or otherwise."

Dante placed a paw on her back. She was beginning to fume and was ready to jump off her branch on onto Carvile's head.

"Now, my dear. It seems to me you have just admitted, in front of most of the town of Williamsburg that you have indeed written a play meant to stir up controversy against the system. That is known in legal circles as 'seditious libel' and may be punishable by long-term imprisonment, maybe even death."

The crowd gasped. Even the mob. They wanted the play stopped, they wanted no interference with their businesses, ships and farms, but they never called for the death of this little squirrel. She was wearing baby-pink, for goodness sake. Nobody wearing baby-pink deserved to die. Slaves maybe, but not creatures in baby-pink. Savannah began to tremble and lost her balance. She plummeted toward the ground and in her stunned state had no natural physical reactions to save herself. In a minute, she would either *splat* on the ground or be carted off to the gaol where she would eventually be put to death. Then she hit.

Thud. Not a *splat*, but a *thud.* There she lay in a taut, opened apron of what smelled like good, Italian leather. She also smelled coffee, not the drink, but the presence of beans, like the apron was in perennial contact with coffee beans. She sniffed and opened her eyes. Above her, holding the apron wide was Anthony. A tear was beginning to form in one eye. In those seconds of silence, he apologized to Savannah for his months of shunning her and she accepted. He had come around finally and, dramatically it seemed, at just the right moment.

She scrambled up his shoulder at stood up with her hands on her hips and bored her eyes into Carvile's. She said nothing, but stared. Carvile was a little unnerved by Anthony, but was not going to let it show.

"Miss Savannah," he pulled from his frock coat a rolled piece of parchment, unrolled it and read aloud, his harsh, nasal, country accent more pronounced as he yelled over the crowds:

> *It is ordered that the Sheriff for the County of*
> *York, do forthwith take and apprehend you, Miss Savannah*
> *Prudence Squirrel, for writing and enacting a play of seditious*
> *libel through your production of The Mysterious Silence*
> *Dogood. For your tendency to raise factions and tumults*
> *among the people of this province and inflaming their minds*
> *with contempt of His Majesty's government and fiscal systems,*
> *and generally disrupting the peace thereof, you are hereby*
> *committed to the common gaol of said County of York and City*
> *of Williamsburg, Virginia.*

Savannah fell back over in a new fainting spell and Anthony caught her again with his apron.

"Anyone attempting to stop the Sheriff shall be equally charged and additionally charged with obstruction of justice. Sheriff," he turned to a large man whom had emerged from the crowd.

The sheriff's eyes said he was sorry, but he was under orders from the Crown. He moved toward Anthony to take Savannah but Anthony moved the apron away, carrying Savannah out of his reach. The Sheriff gave Anthony a weak look, but reached again for Savannah. It was at that moment a series of shrieks were heard: one by Dante and several by Carvile.

"*Dies improbi capilli, Cara*?!" Dante screeched as he catapulted off the branch and landed directly on Carvile's invitingly bald head, the claws of all four paws dug deep into his scalp.

"What did he say? What does that mean?" Beauregard tugged on Phil's knickers.

"It's Latin. It means something like *Bad hair day, Dear*?" he translated with a hearty chuckle and fingered his own, luxurious, natural, spiral curls. Phil the Bruce had very pretty hair for a hermit.

Carvile flung his arms all about, trying to pluck Dante off his noggin, but then felt another piercing pain far below. On the ground, Ichabod used his sharp, tiny teeth, the strongest in the colony, to bite right through Carvile's stockings and into his ankle. Carvile shook his leg vigorously to pry Ichabod loose but Ichabod held tight, his teeth well into muscle. The crowd began to roar with laughter, both sides, as Carvile danced in a frantic circle trying to shake a poncy dog and a cavalier cat from his body, screaming all the while. Round and round he spun like a man on fire, arms flailing, legs kicking, Dante and Ichabod attached firmly and securely.

Anthony quickly tucked Savannah into his linen, vest pocket to protect her, but she regained consciousness and poked her pink-hatted head out to watch the excitement. She was amazed that Ichabod was fighting. Ichabod never even ran or talked loudly, let alone actually get into a brawl! The sheriff attempted to remove Ichabod and Dante, but backed off after several of these attempts. There, in the middle of the mobs was a tiny cyclone, all fur, claws, arms and legs. It was like a dervish of leaves in an autumn wind, but it was made of animals. The sheriff was, to be blunt, scared to death. They were like wild beasts. No longer were any of them the posh and well-heeled sophisticates most people regarded them as. Carvile had misjudged Savannah's moral support system and had also misjudged his mob. They still supported slavery as much as they supported breathing, but they weren't convinced this little squirrel was their downfall, nor were they convinced this play about Ben Franklin, whom many of them knew and liked very much from earlier days in Philadelphia and London, was going to topple their individual businesses, farms and plantations. In short, nobody came forward to help him, not even his moustached friend. Daniel Ray just stood back and looked up at Mr. Blair.

"Should we help?" Blair asked Daniel.

"No, you don't want to get involved in that," Daniel replied flatly.

As Carvile realized he had lost total control of the situation, he screamed about the pain as much as his frustration. Eventually, Anthony, never a believer in violence, pulled off Dante and Ichabod. Still, he did take his time. Dante was ready to go again and Ichabod was a little shocked at himself, but proud he had braved the sea of feet to help Savannah. Carvile nodded a breathless, begrudging 'Thank you' to Anthony, then stood as straight and proud as he could and brushed off his frock coat, now covered with orange cat hair. He dabbed at his bleeding scalp with a lace hanky and bent down to rub his bleeding ankle. Then, he stood up again and looked around at his vast lack of support.

"Sheriff, apprehend that squirrel and that dog and that cat!" Carvile pointed at Anthony's pocket and the panting Ichabod and Dante. Savannah bared her rarely seen but wickedly sharp and tiny teeth.

"Umm, Sir, she scares me," the sheriff admitted. "Her friends scare me, too."

He bit one side of his lower lip and watched warily Ichabod and Dante, both wild-eyed with the excitement of finding their inner-hooligan.

"Oh, for Heaven's sake. Aa shall do it," Carvile lunged for Anthony's pocket and Anthony's hand stopped him.

"I would not do that, Sir," Anthony spoke for the first time in what seemed like a year. Savannah was shocked. "This squirrel has done nothing to offend you or your King. She loves her Britain, this I know."

"Step aside, boy," Carvile ignored Anthony and reached for Savannah with his other hand. Anthony grabbed it, too.

Carvile now stood shackled by Anthony's strong hands. Savannah's nose peeked up through them to look up at Carvile. She could smell the evil on him.

"Do you jest? Are you manhandling me, son?"

"I am not your son or your boy," Anthony stated solidly with eyes like marble.

"Clearly, you are a slave run amuck. Are you not worried aa could have you arrested, too?" Carvile was without a soul, his speech as fast and sharp as ever, but now much deeper in tone.

Anthony cleared his throat, blinked twice, tightened his grip on Carvile's wrists, "Owww", and spoke clearly and strongly, enunciating each and every word for Lord Carvile, Snake-Man.

"I am not a slave. I am Romulus. My brother was Remus. He was murdered by men such as yourselves," he pointed a long finger in a wide swath over the mob. "For nothing more than to seek his brother and live the life with me I promised but never gave him. For nothing more than seeking freedom, he was hunted like a wild animal and left to die outdoors." Anthony stood up proud and tall. "No, Lord Carvile. I am not a slave. I am my own man and I am free," his voice began to tremble. "My mother was a slave, my brother was a slave and I was a slave. My baby brother was kidnapped from me and taken to a life of Hell. Fortuna did not spin her wheel kindly for him as she did for me. But I am free, and if you do not mind, I have a play to see with my friend," he patted Savannah's head and turned toward the theatre.

Carvile shouted to the sheriff, "Arrest that man!"

The sheriff made a motion toward Anthony, but could swear he saw Anthony's eyes glow red. He stepped aside. Carvile then jumped in front of Anthony, trying to physically block him. Anthony breathed in deeply through his nose and stared even deeper into Carvile's squinty eyes. When Carvile wouldn't move, Anthony walked on anyway, hitting Carvile's left shoulder with his right, toppling Carvile out of the way.

"Stop him! He is a criminal! No one may see that play! Anyone going into the theatre will haaaang! Aa shall see to it personally!" Carvile was panicking.

A member of the mob, a large rice farmer from Gloucester, moved up to stop Anthony.

"I shouldn't do that, my man," came a firm voice from below, Dante.

The farmer looked into Anthony's eyes and saw this was probably good advice. He stepped aside. Savannah ran up Anthony's coat and stopped on his shoulder. She gave him a huge squirrel hug and staved off her own stream of tears building inside. Then, she jumped onto the nearest branch to go back and face her ordeal.

"I shall be fine, my friend. Thank you," she said in a whisper.

The tears let go and Anthony no longer tried to stop them. They flowed in continuous streams and down his neck, eventually soaking the chest of his crisp, white, summer, linen blouse. A path opened for him as he made his way to the theatre. He did not stop, nor did anyone else try to stop him. He walked in through the gates, into the lobby, down the center aisle and took a seat in the front row. He sat politely and patiently, his head held high, his hands folded, his legs crossed and his eyes straight ahead. Tonight, he would see Savannah's first play, his friend's hard work created, he knew, all for his baby brother Remus. There he sat, in the footcandles of a stage awaiting its actors and waited, and cried, alone.

"Aa am not through with you, Miss Savannah. Aa shall gather whatever forces are necessary to imprison you in the Williamsburg gaol, then watch you hang by your pretty, little, flower-stemmed, odd choice for a necklace by the way, neck," Carvile was starting to sound mad. Not angry-mad, but insane-mad. "Your friend in there, the slave boy, shall be the next one to hang and after him aa shall hang your strange cat and dog friends! What kinda cat wears a wig, anyway? Aa shall hang him for that if aa so choose! Another thing aa shall do is aa shal. . ."

"Lord Carvile, I should stop if I were you," a stern but dignified voice stated calmly from above.

Carvile whipped his head around to see Gooch sitting atop a giant, chestnut horse. Gooch looked down his nicely proportionate nose at Carvile's gleaming scalp. Carvile had been so enthralled listening to the sound of his own voice that he had not even heard Gooch gallop up to the tree. Yet, there he stood. He and his horse, Buca, stood in the very middle of the entire fuss. Buca was at least seventeen hands tall, a Dutch Warmblood standing just under six-feet in height at his withers. With the nearly six-foot Gooch on top of that, even in his funny gardening clogs, he posed a menacing force as he hovered above Carvile.

"Royal *Lieutenant* Governor Gooch," Carvile snickered. "Aa was just thinking about you. Maa good man, aa fear you are out of your jurisdiction here. I shall be writing to VanKeppel tomorrow and he shall be dealing with you thusly. So in short, aa may say whatever aa like. Aa know my raaghts."

The crowd, it seemed the entire town, gasped. Nobody spoke to the governor like that! Nobody, except maybe the King!

"Ahhh, VanKeppel. Good man. He is currently hosting my niece, Prudence."

Savannah clapped her hands, excited that her middle name was the same as Gooch's niece. Dante thought that was a weird thing to be excited about and wriggled his nose.

"She is living with his family for the year whilst she stays in London to study her pianoforte and singing. Fine, fine family the VanKeppels."

Carvile's already squinty eyes were growing tighter and tighter as his face grew more and more red, his sharp, high cheekbones becoming more and more prominent, his teeth grinding with more and more aggression.

"Yes, let us write to VanKeppel together. Why wait until tomorrow? Let us have a letter writing party tonight! What do you say? What fun!" Gooch beamed and turned his body toward the sheriff. "Sheriff, bring Lord Carvile to the Palace. Let's place him in one of the first floor waiting rooms, shall we? The guards will escort you," Gooch gestured to the twelve, armed men that stood in perfect formation directly behind him.

The apprehension of Carvile and the presence of the guards caused the mob to disperse pretty quickly. Within moments they were all mingled with the theatergoers and lots of nervous grins were being exchanged. Gooch watched Carvile and waited for his explosion. Carvile was indeed highly placed in London and was indeed a powerful man with powerful ears at his disposal, but he was not powerful enough to speak to a royal governor that way and he was not powerful enough to hang some of Williamsburg's most beloved citizens. Miss Savannah Squirrel for one. Gooch understood power and what it could bring, for good or for bad. Those whom had been troubled before they attained power, must be closely regarded. As Shakespeare wrote, "Madness in great ones must not unwatched go." Astride Buca, Gooch watched this great one called Carvile.

"You have no power here!" the ranting began the second the sheriff grabbed Carvile's upper arm. "You have no power anywhere, unless you count this, this. . ." he made a disgusted face as he glanced around the dark town and its people, "burg, this hamlet of yours. Aa am from Lon-don!" he continued patronizingly to Gooch. "Do you understand that, *Lieutenant* Governor William Gooch? My governor is your superior, the real royal governor!"

Clearly, Carvile was going mad. Even if he believed these things, in his right mind he would know to keep it an inside-thought. It was as though he snapped. He began to distrust even his own mob.

"You never supported me! None of you! You never believed in me! You're no better than Judas!" he ranted to Daniel Ray, Mr. Blair, anyone around him. "We coulda stopped this! We coulda stopped her! You'll be sorry! All of you! Just watch, you'll fail! All of you! The slaves will taak over, you'll all be deaaaad! Remember Bacon's Rebellion? It shall be laak thaaaat, but the slaves will revolt on the government! The landowners will daa again, but this taame at the hands of your own slaaaaves! Mark my woooords!"

Carvile searched the crowd for some support, but found no one even looking at him. Nobody but Savannah, Ichabod, Dante, Sterling and Rebecca were making eye contact. He was a mad dog and everyone knew that was a dangerous situation. Everyone except these four and Governor Gooch avoided his mad gaze. The five friends just watched him and actually came to pity him. Where he was going was not to be envied.

Gooch was a good man and would not just ship him off to prison for threatening him. But, he would most likely have him observed by the court physician, Dr. Gerstl. A longtime, familiar face working for the Crown and Council in Virginia, he had recently been appointed as Royal Physick to the

Royal Governor, a position he found paid very well, which in turn made him very happy. If Dr. Gerstl found Carvile suffering from maladies of the head, he would recommend Gooch send him to a hospital for the mad, not prison and not death. But, those locked in asylums would quickly tell you death would be easier to endure than London's homes for the insane.

Everyone watched in silence as Carvile raved and ranted and was dragged off to the Palace by the York County Sheriff and twelve well-armed, quick-stepping, military-trained guards. Savannah watched the guards and hoped they were not coming back later to take her to gaol. While Carvile may be insane and stepped over some lines, it was still possible Gooch also felt her play was seditious. She approached Gooch gingerly with that very question in mind. She hung her head just a little, in deference, clasped her paws together in front and walked slowly toward his towering persona atop his towering horse. She strained her neck and looked up to ask her fate. Before she could utter a word, however, Gooch spoke to his secretary.

"Beddoes?"

"Yes, Your Excellency?" he showed up instantly at Buca's side and waited.

"Do you have that declaration you were preparing earlier this evening?"

"Yes, Sir. I anticipated you might need it. Right here, Sir," Beddoes handed up a rolled parchment tied with a fluffy, pink, silk bow.

"No, no. Please, hand it to Miss Savannah."

"Yes, Sir." Beddoes did just that.

Savannah accepted it, stunned but pretty certain it was something good, considering the gorgeous bow. Grand Jury indictments weren't served with pink bows, were they?

"This is lovely!" she smiled up at Gooch.

She untied the bow very carefully and slung it around her neck and shoulders like a shawl. She looked to Rebecca whom also found it very pretty and nodded in accord. The parchment was tiny, squirrel-sized, but still a little big to handle once all unrolled.

"Shall I?" Sterling bounded up to Savannah and offered to read it for her.

"Oh, please!" she handed it over to Sterling and she pet her ribbon as he prepared to read.

Always the consummate showman, Sterling straightened his tricorn, adjusted its feather, checked all his scarves to be sure they flowed properly, pulled up his boots, tugged down on his coat and shot his cuffs. He unfurled the parchment, one arm stretched high and the other low. He then placed one foot out at a dramatic point whilst planting the other firmly at a right angle under his hip. Now, he was ready to read aloud. Dante smirked and rolled his eyes. Ichabod found it all very stylish and appreciated the effort. Savannah just wanted to hear what the parchment read.

Presented to Miss Savannah Prudence Squirrel of London and Williamsburg

A Royal Grant and Proclamation

It is hereby granted by Royal Lieutenant Governor William Gooch, extended by royal grants from Virginia Royal Governor Willem Anne VanKeppel, 2nd Earl of Albemarle and His Royal Highness King George II, that "The Mysterious Silence Dogood" is given with great pleasure a three-month summer run at Levingston's Theatre, also known as The Play House, Williamsburg, Virginia.

Savannah had been quietly clapping non-stop ever since the phrase 'Royal Grant'. She was making that funny, toothy smile she did when she was really excited and her eyes were all bugged out as she clapped her tiny paws over and over. Finally, Sterling stopped, bowed first to Savannah, whom curtsied back, then to Gooch and Buca whom both nodded regally, then to Miss Rebecca Lane because he thought she was pretty.

"Governor Gooch," Savannah curtsied again. "Thank you so much. I never expected a royal stamp of approval. Really," she looked sideways at Ichabod who had understood fully the real goal of her play in the first place.

"It is a fine play, Miss Savannah. Mr. Franklin is a notable man. We know of him well in many circles. He is a fiercely loyal British subject. No one would ever question his or your loyalty to the Crown. He and you are both inspirations to auto-didactics the world over."

"What's 'auto-didactic' mean?" a lingering mobster whispered to another one.

"Means you make your own bread," he answered.

"Hey! I make my own bread! That means I'm auto-didactic!" the first one beamed, proud to be like the play's main character. He was going to have to see this play.

"It means 'self-educated'," Phil the Bruce commented as he walked by with Beauregard. He gave the man a sidelong glance within a look of general disgust. "I've got to get back to the woods," he said loudly to Beauregard. "These people make me sick." Bruce had had about all the human contact he could stand for a very long time.

Pretty soon the crowd was abuzz with chatter and whispers about the royal proclamation. The mobster merchants, farmers, watermen and planters remained suspicious of the play's motives. Yet, based on Carvile's rather embarrassing dispatch and, far more importantly, the fact that the play had just been validated by no less than the King himself, if they had reservations they now kept them to themselves, or at least to dark, quiet, smoky tavern corners.

As Gooch turned his horse's reins to head back to the Palace, he leaned over and said privately to Sterling, "We don't need to make a big, public show of this, but I'm going to need you to come with me."

Sterling's heart dropped like a bag of corn. His ears wilted and his tail fell slowly and settled flat on the ground. This was it. He had helped a friend and that was good, but now, he was ruined. He looked to Gooch for some sort of elaboration, but he had already clicked his heels on his horse and they were off down the Green. Beddoes waited for Sterling, to escort him back to Gooch. Sterling looked around to say good-bye or hug someone or something, but the crowd was already dispersing and Savannah was in such a state of glee, he just didn't feel right bothering her. There would be time later to say good-bye, wouldn't there be? Dante and Ichabod were busy congratulating each other on their attack on Carvile and laughing with Miss Lane. The whole scene had turned to a party. There was no place for Sterling and his heartbreaking, cheerless life. With his head very low, he turned toward Beddoes, who smiled sympathetically at him and held out arm, inviting him to follow him back to the Palace. Today, not even Sterling's favourite red clogs made him feel good. He took them off, held them in one paw and shuffled sadly across the Green to a very uncertain, yet strangely very certain, and probably very short, future. He glanced back one last time at the happy scene and saw Savannah scurrying back up her tree branch, her smile visible even from where he stood. He then faced forward again and followed Beddoes to his doom.

"Alright then, people!" she addressed the crowd as loudly as she could. "Cast, crew, we still have a play to put on! Back to the theatre! Let's shake this off, relax a bit, get ourselves back into the right frame of mind and regroup. Folks, we shall have a special, command performance tonight. A late showing. . .curtains up at midnight! Spread the word!"

Those whom were still crowded around the tree cheered *Huzzah! Huzzah! Huzzah!* What was more fun than a midnight event?! Mr. Levingston ran a hand through his thinning hair and immediately thought about the implications of such a late show. Certainly something bad was bound to happen. Levingston was a worrier and even the best of news brought him premonitions of the worst outcomes. Then, as he usually did, he saw the bright side. Not only did this mean outstanding box office receipts tonight, but most likely amazing profit all summer long! Then, as he usually did, he saw a problem again.

Levingston had negotiated, or rather Ichabod had negotiated for himself and Savannah, rather high box office percentages. Levingston agreed to the ridiculously significant share when he thought it was a simple, one-week run nobody would attend. Why had he agreed to such numbers? Darn it. Still, profit for them was profit for him and he then realized how many hungry people were standing about with nothing to do for almost two more hours. Nobody was getting a share of The Kitchen receipts! Naturally, as Levingston jogged toward The Kitchen, he then found a problem with too large of a crowd and how would he accommodate them, and so forth and so forth fortune and disaster. That was Mr. Levingston. That was how he functioned and it appeared to work for him. Suddenly, he stopped mid-jog and like a coyote howling up into the night sky, he shouted, "The Kitchen is now open!" His voice was squeaky and weak, but the message was carried over and over by the crowd and within minutes the crowd started moving toward The Kitchen in one giant mass, like a patch of algae floating across a windswept pond.

As the crowd descended upon The Kitchen, Mr. Hopkins, who was washing the last of the *avant*-crowd dishes, and happy to have a couple hours' break before the *après*-crowd appeared, looked out one of the many paned-glass windows and saw the onslaught of patrons headed his way. He tossed his dishrag over his shoulder in total defeat and, grumbling all the way to the metal coffeepot which hung in the stone fireplace at the far end of the building, he took his personal mug down from the wooden mantel and poured himself a giant helping of his special Viennese-Turkish espresso blend and waited for the crush of customers. Watching the mass of people, Mr. Hopkins really hoped his country-boy waiter was coming back with them.

CHAPTER THIRTY - NINE

"Motion for a Struck Jury granted," New-York Supreme Court Chief Justice James DeLancey banged his gavel. "The Honourable Frederick Philipse concurs?" DeLancey nodded to the Province's Second Justice whom nodded back.

Being the first business of the day, the courtroom held only a few men in these early hours: DeLancey and Philipse high upon their bench, overlooking the New-York City Hall courtroom; Mr. John Chambers, Esq., defense counsel for Mr. John Peter Zenger; Mr. Richard Bradley, Esq., Attorney General and prosecutor for the Crown; and Mr. John Peter Zenger himself.

This was actually a good morning for Mr. Zenger who was hopeful that since his jury was to be pulled from a book of random names, this could be very helpful to his defense. Surely, when the common folk of New-York heard of the ridiculous charges and accusations against a common man like themselves they would stand in his support. A jury of the people was clearly better than a jury of two judges, which was what the case had been until Mr. Chambers appealed to DeLancey and Philipse for a jury of men. Surprisingly, they had granted his motion: Zenger was entitled to a Struck Jury. Maybe they were fair-minded men after all. Maybe they were realizing this whole tryal was unfair. Yes, this was a very good sign indeed. The only issue now was that tomorrow was the tryal. Could they pull a jury, a fair jury, that quickly?

"You are each and everyman here to arrive at the Office of the Clerk of the Court this evening at the chime of five bells," DeLancey spoke loudly and with perfect enunciation which echoed through the empty and vast courtroom. "The Sheriff of the Province of New-York will also attend. After both sides have finished striking their jurors from the Freeholders Book, the final list of jurors shall be handed over to him. In this evening, he shall then go to the homes of said jury and apprise them of their roles and recommend they be ready for duty in the morning next.

Tomorrow morning, before the tryal commences, the Sheriff shall go back into the City and pull the new jury from their homes, thereby providing Mr. Zenger with his Struck Jury as decreed by my approval."

DeLancey banged his gavel once more, dismissing all participants. Zenger smiled cautiously at Chambers whom showed no reaction but a blank stare. He was not happy about this assignment and was not a fan of Zenger anyway. He was, in fact, a political ally of Cosby. However, his ethics and legal training pulled at his conscience and he knew, friend of Cosby or not, he needed to present the best, strongest and truest defense possible. He was not happy today, but he was pleased his motion was granted. A Struck Jury was a fair thing for a man in Zenger's position. So far, Chambers' conscience was clear.

Outside Andrew Hamilton's carriage the forests were as black and spooky as a Carpathian hillside, it was very possible vampires and wolves lurked behind each and every tree. Only three days into the month and August was already in full, disgusting swing along the colonies' seabord. Nevermind it was two o'clock in the morning amidst the heavily canopied New-Jersey woods, being in the carriage was as muggy and uncomfortable as riding in it during midday. The iron and wooden wheels rolled over the fertile and mucky roads; the trees' leafy blankets drooped hopelessly in the night without any promise of breeze for at least another month. Those trees and plants that lined the main thoroughfare from Philadelphia through New-Jersey and into New-York were fortunate enough to catch the momentary breezes that came from passing coaches and carriages jostling along at full speed. Andrew Hamilton's vehicle was absolutely at full speed. As Hamilton looked out into the blur of black woods, he saw the blinking eyes and scampering moon shadows that betrayed the silent, nocturnal activities of New-Jersey's shy, woodland creatures.

"*Rap rap rap!*" Hamilton tapped impatiently on the carriage window behind him with the knob of his walking stick, signaling "Faster faster faster!"

to his driver. On cue, Hamilton heard the snap of the coachman's reins and was pitched forward on his bench seat as the horses obeyed and jerked into action, spiriting the coach and its important passenger closer to New-York City. Without hesitation, urged only by the relentless stings of the coachman's whip and reins, the two great horses pushed themselves near the brink of exhaustion. They had been running at a full gallop for what seemed like twenty-four hours straight, but it mattered not. They had a task, a very important task, the very task that could very well prove to be the pivot of freedom.

Each time their flanks ached or their hooves twinged they remembered their part in this play of justice and snorted and wheezed anew as they cut through the Witching Hour fog. Their breathing became more laboured and painful with each step as tearing through this vile summer air was akin to a fly swimming through porridge. Their noses filled with a visible humidity, their mouths and throats became caverns of mucus, proving the simple act of swallowing too difficult to accomplish without distress.

"*Rap, rap, rap!*" sounded another wordless urgency. Inside the stifling carriage, Hamilton checked his pocket watch as he listened to his page read aloud bookmarked, courthouse histories and legal precedents from a tattered copy of *Institutes of the Laws of England* and *Coke's Reports*: both popular and common text utilized in all English, legal education, *Coke's* being the ultimate source.

". . .for what greater scandal of government can there be, than to have corrupt or wicked magistrates to be appointed by the king, to govern under them?" he read with a bouncy voice as he was jostled up and down on the bench seat opposite Hamilton.

The next hour passed without exception or surprise as Hamilton and his page, Satchel, cited, argued and memorized elements of English law stretching all the way back to King John's *Magna Carta* of 1215, the very foundation of all Western civilization's common law. If someone was unsure as to how important Hamilton's task was, all one needed to do was to eavesdrop into that three a.m. carriage ride.

As Satchel and Hamilton debated the dangers of quoting the *Bible* in a legal case, their books suddenly flew off their laps and onto the floor, Satchel and Hamilton following. Outside, some very serious and horrendous sounding *cracks* and *snaps* reverberated through the sticky, misty early morning. The carriage careened off the road, steadily, but frighteningly so. The ride was violent and jerky but strangely slowed as the carriage gently guided itself into a roadside ditch and rested there at a most undesirable tilt.

"My God! What is happening up there?" Hamilton fell out of the carriage, unharmed, as the door flung open after the crash.

Looking up at his coachman, he saw him trying to stand upright after having been tossed to the ground from his high perch on his driving seat. It was clear by his pained attempts and unnerving groaning that he would not be standing anytime soon. He had broken his leg.

"Radoslav?! Are you okay?" Hamilton ran to his coachman.

"Oui, M'sieur. I shall be fine, M'sieur Hamilton, Sir. Just an uncomfortableness. Nothing a physick cannot fix for me," Radoslav downplayed his injury with his usual, unexcitable, Swiss professionalism and decorum.

"What on earth happened here?" Hamilton patted Radoslav gently on the shoulder and immediately regarded their two white horses, both of whom displayed the same calm as their driver.

They stood near the wreckage, outwardly uninjured and nuzzling each other in what looked like an emergency meeting of the equine minds. One stamped his feet as the other shook her head, jangling and rattling their hardware and bridles in disagreement. Hamilton yelled out to Satchel, whom he knew was alright, but double-checked to be sure.

"Satchel? Are you well?"

"Yes, Mr. Hamilton, Sir," he answered in a high, stressed, panicked squeak. "Just gathering up all our books and notes, Sir. I've lost my place in *Coke's*, Sir. I have no idea what page I was on!"

Hamilton smiled in relief. Everything, except Radoslav's leg, seemed to be fine. Everything except the carriage. As he walked around the right side of the conveyance he saw it. A wheel was broken, a pretty important item where carriages are concerned. Scanning the road behind him he saw the culprits. There in front of a large pothole lay a larger rock, the rock which had ripped a strip of wood off the outer wheel and bent two of the iron spokes like Chinese noodles in water. What a disaster.

Whilst they were all very lucky the accident had not been more horrific, it was all still very, very bad luck. It was three in the morning and black as ink. Stranded there, somewhere in the New-Jersey woods, were three fancy men, two upset horses and a useless carriage. Miles from home in Philadelphia and still miles to their destination, they waited and wondered who might happen along the trail to help them, and when. It was too much to ask fate for a wheelwright and far too much to ask for a physick. Yet, someone would show soon. They were all sure of it. This was a highly travelled road and dawn was not more than a few hours away. Each, however, had his own, immediate concerns.

Hamilton's first and foremost thought was getting back on the road. The carriage was no longer a possibility, but there were two horses. He marched to where they stood stamping their feet and snorting in a very serious argument. He grabbed the bridle of the larger horse and pet the horse's nose in an attempt to calm him, but he would have none of it. Instead, he backed around and tossed his head up and down, his back hooves prancing around and around, his front hooves taking small steps and pivoting his entire body in a continuous circle. Seeing that the pleasantries of a nose nuzzle was doing no good, Hamilton attempted to just jump on. But the surly equine would have none of that either. His back legs began to kick and buck and his head tosses became ever more thrashing and wild.

"Satchel! Get out here and help me mount this creature!" Hamilton yelled to his page.

Radoslav, while his pain was just a bit dull, tried to stand and offer some assistance.

"Radoslav, you stay put!" Hamilton yelled out, knowing he would try to help. "Satchel, quickly!"

Satchel tumbled out of the carriage and ran to Hamilton's aid, but he was even more frightened of horses than he was of the dark woods. He tried, sort of, to grab the flinging reins and leathers, then ran around somewhat aimlessly and frantically trying to stop the bucking. It was laughable really, except it wasn't.

"Oh, nevermind, Satchel," Hamilton appreciated the half-attempt but knew he was worthless here. A great legal mind he had, five languages he spoke, but just worthless at anything outdoors-related.

Hamilton tried to tame the other, smaller horse. Being a female horse, he figured she'd be much easier to handle. Not a chance. She bucked even more wildly and never even let Hamilton near her reins.

"M'sieur Hamilton?" Radoslav called out. "They shan't allow it, Sir."

"Say again?" Hamilton began to sound breathless as he ran around both horses, trying to grab whichever one he could, his silky, white wig now bouncing so wildly atop his head that it was now sitting askew, nearly covering one eye completely.

"They are pulling-horses, Sir. They do not like anything, or anyone, on their backs. You'll never get them into position. If you were so fortunate, they'd throw you off in an instant, Sir."

In a way, this was a relief to Hamilton. He was already exhausted from chasing the petulant beasts. In the immediate moment, he was happy to have a valid reason to stop. Then, as quickly as the relief set in, the dread did so. Now, he really had no means of continuing his journey. He was stranded. Surrounded by men of the finest intelligence, etiquette and attire and it was all totally useless. He eyed the naughty horses with contempt, but being the great, thinking and noble man he was, realized they were no better suited to the task of carrying riders than he was to wrangling horses or Satchel was to, well, much of anything outside. He watched with a mixture of amusement and pity as Satchel swatted himself repeatedly, trying in vain to rid himself of the blackflies that plagued this region in the summer.

Now settled down but still snorting furiously, the horses turned their argument from blaming each other about driving right into the pothole, to how insulted they were that this Hamilton fellow tried to mount them. They didn't care who he was, nobody tried to mount Gavin and Gwendylyn. Nobody. Hamilton listened to the jingling and jangling of the feisty horses and thought only of his task, and how he was clearly going to let down a lot of people. Satchel stood with his back to the carriage, slapped his arms, face and legs and stared out into the woods, his eyes giant and ears attaining supernatural hearing with every crack of a branch and hoot of an owl.

Jennifer Susannah Devore

Satchel did not like the woods and did not like country roads for this very reason. He was imagining his soft mattress and his small, brick townehome centered smack dab in the middle of Philadelphia's financial district, far from any wolves, snakes, panthers, bears, vampires, whatever it was that lurked in the Jersey woods. Business and legal predators he could handle; the furry, clawed and scaled kind he could not. Moreover, he thought of the ghost stories his brother had told him as a child, always meant to scare him into being a better help to their mother: the terrifying tales of The Jersey Devil. Was she out there? Was it out there? What was it, exactly?

"What was that?!" Satchel shrieked and scrambled back into the carriage, falling on all fours and bumping Radoslav's leg as he passed him in the process. He heard what he was sure was a low, rumbling growl in the trees. "Oh my God! What *was* that, Mr. Hamilton?!"

"'Tis the sound of injustice, Satchel. Injustice is coming for us, my friend and it shan't be pretty."

The Clerk's office was rather full this night. At least ten men stood hovering around the Clerk's vacant desk, all watching their pocket watches and listening for the City Hall's bell tower to chime five of the clock.

John Chambers was there, Attorney General Richard Bradley was there and Zenger was there under the guard of the Sheriff. Also present was a large number of Morrisites, friends of the defendant John Peter Zenger and there to assure Chambers selected a fair and unbiased jury. The prosecution had no friends or supporters in the office. They needed none. AG Bradley was utterly confident in his ability to choose a jury. Clearly, it was Zenger whom needed moral support. Neither Bradley nor the Clerk objected to the preponderance of Zenger's friends in the room. What did Bradley or the Clerk care? As far as Bradley was concerned, the tryal was all over but the details. Tomorrow's court case was merely but an errand in his day. As far as the Clerk was concerned, this was a job. His main concern was doing his job properly, not getting into any trouble with his superiors and getting out of here as soon as possible. Mrs. Clerk of the Court was making crayfish soup, broiled Maryland rockfish, and corn chowder for dinner. He had missed lunch and only eaten half a sourdough roll with bitter coffee, no cream, for breakfast. He couldn't finish this fast enough.

The Clerk then entered the room. He was a supremely average man. He was of average height, sported an average haircut of an average brown colour and wore average clothing of an average quality and an average style. He spoke with an average voice and possessed an average temperament. He was an average citizen with an average job and he was here to work in an average capacity, filling in his day with his prescribed hours of duty: never a minute late in the morning and never a minute over in the evening. The fates of anyone involved here mattered very little to him except where they interfered with the end of his day. To Zenger, however, this meeting was a deciding factor in his very freedom of life.

Bong! Bong! Bong! Bong! Bong!

"Right then. Let's get this done with," he called the group to order around his table without salutation or greeting of any kind. "Per motion granted by Chief Justice James DeLancey in the matter of *The Attorney General of our Sovereign Lord the King, for the Province of New-York versus Mr. John Peter Zenger*, we are present this evening of August the third in this year of seventeen and thirty-five to strike and agree upon a jury of twelve men for the aforementioned tryal, convening tomorrow morning, eight o'clock."

Also present was Linus. Zenger employed him to follow the tryal, certain that no matter the outcome, it would be something of import for years to come. Plus, Zenger could print and publish a small booklet on the event to help recover some of his monies lost throughout the ordeal. Linus received a notice by messenger that morning from a member of the Morrisites that the Striking of the Jury would occur that evening. Unsure of what a Striking of the Jury exactly was, Linus used his journalistic skills that day and cornered a lawyer in a coffeehouse to learn exactly what he would be covering tonight. A Striking of the Jury, otherwise called a Struck Jury, meant very simply this.

First, a book of names titled the Freeholders Book was produced by the Clerk of the Court. This is a book filled with the names of adult, male, New-York, taxpaying landholders eligible to sit on a jury.

Second, a list of forty-eight names is taken from the Book.

Third, each side is presented with the new list and given the opportunity to scratch off, or strike, one name at a time. The list is handed back and forth as each side, defense and prosecution, strikes names off one by one until there are only twelve names left.

Fourth and finally, those twelve men are officially listed as jurors. A jury is struck.

This seemed pretty simple to Linus and was the one thing in this tryal that appeared totally objective and fair. Linus readied his journal to mark the event and write the final list of jurors.

"Right then," the Clerk continued. "Who shall strike for the King?"

"I shall strike for the King," Attorney General Richard Bradley, Esq. stepped forward and procured one quill pen from the triple-quill holder on the Clerk's desk. The Clerk already plucked one from it. One was left for the defense.

"Who shall strike for the defense?"

"I shall strike for the defense," Mr. John Chambers, Esq. stepped forward and pulled the last quill from its brass nest.

"Very well. Let us begin. I have here a list of eligible names. Who shall strike first?"

"Please, the King grants first strike to Mr. Chambers," Bradley bowed to Chambers.

Chambers looked at the list and knew right away something was wrong. He took off his glasses as he addressed the Clerk and the prosecution.

"Mr. Clerk, Mr. Attorney General, I am sorry, but this is a fake list. Where is the Freeholders Book? We are ordered to strike a jury from the official Freeholders Book," Chambers scrunched together his eyebrows in concern, making two tiny, vertical wrinkles above the bridge of his glasses as he replaced them.

"These names are all pulled from the Freeholders Book, Mr. Chambers. I have seen to it myself. There are forty-eight names taken directly from the Book," the Clerk held out the sheet for Chambers to view.

"May I?" Chambers looked to Bradley and the Clerk before taking the paper in hand.

"Please," Bradley answered first, then the Clerk handed it to Chambers.

Chambers began to peruse the panels of names as the Morrisites gathered around and looked on. They pointed, mumbled and nodded at each other as they looked over the whole of the list. Zenger watched from behind the small cluster of gentlemen and Linus stood in the back of the room writing in his journal, certain this was a very interesting twist in the story. If he could just get hold of the list. He walked closer to take a peek, but just as he stretched up on his toes to look over one gentleman's shoulders, the group broke up as Chambers stepped forward to speak.

"With all due respect, Mr. Clerk, Mr. Attorney General," Chambers began with a slight crack in his voice; he hadn't planned on such an immediate conflict. "It is of the considerable and learned opinions of Mr. Zenger's acquaintances, as well as my own opinion, that a good many of these men listed here are indeed not eligible men. Their names could not be from the Freeholders Book for they are well-known not to be landholders and some of them presumably not taxpayers."

Bradley pursed his lips a bit and cocked one eyebrow as he replied "Really?" He then turned to the Clerk of the Court. "Is this true, Mr. Clerk? Are these not properly selected from the official Freeholders Book?"

The Clerk shot a look of surprise up at Bradley. His eyes grew large and unblinking and without realizing it he dug his front teeth into his lower lip, purely astounded at Bradley's query.

"But, I. . .you said. . ." he started to respond and Bradley's eyes grew darker and tighter as he nonchalantly pulled a silk hanky out of his pocket and began to polish his cuff buttons, never taking his own unblinking eyes off of the Clerk. Message received.

"Um, yes, well, the list is indeed pulled from the Freeholders Book," the Clerk stammered. "If you have objections, show them now and show them clearly," he said to the defense as he quickly regained his confidence.

There was instant grumbling and flustering in the office and Chambers asked that they quiet themselves so that he might give a proper argument.

"In fact, Mr. Clerk, Mr. Bradley, besides the many questionably eligible names where landownership and taxpaying is concerned there are also, more dangerously so, names of persons holding commissions and offices at Governor

Cosby's pleasure." A great murmur of agreement rose behind him. "In addition, there are listed the very names of magistrates and officials featured in the very publications in question." A greater murmur rose. "Surely, gentlemen, those men shall have the greatest resentment and bias of all toward my client."

Zenger walked a little closer to the Clerk's desk, feeling oddly more confident as he grew less confident. Clearly, the cards were stacked against him and even the Clerk of the Court had it out for him. The whole tryal was looking more and more rigged as the minutes ticked by; but as these elements made themselves apparent, it also became apparent his attorney actually had a real interest in protecting his client. Chambers actually appeared to be fighting for him! This is something for which attorneys are not well-known.

"Mr. Clerk," Chambers continued, "it must be clear even to you that some of the men on this list are in the official employ of the governor. His baker, his tailor, his shoemaker, his candlemaker? This is neither fair nor balanced, gentlemen." A great Huzzah! erupted from the group standing around Chambers and Zenger.

"Please, please!" The Clerk was growing irritated, and evermore hungry. Crayfish soup was sounding so delectable that his mouth was beginning to water. "Mr. Chambers, do you find every man on the list objectionable?" he kind of smirked with Mr. Bradley who had moved on to polishing his front buttons. "Surely, you must see some names you approve."

"Indeed, there are but a few and those I fear shall be struck by Mr. Attorney General, leaving us no one impartial."

His crowd started to cheer again, but Chambers and Zenger both turned around and warned with their eyes to please be quiet. Cheering was not going to help the situation.

"It is our request that you produce the actual Freeholders Book from which we may choose forty-eight, random names."

"The list is set, gentlemen. The court has neither the time nor the inclination to produce a new list as your tryal commences in a mere," he looked at his pocket watch, "fifteen hours. Less even."

"Then it is our request that you hear our specific displeasures with each and every questionable name on this list and you replace them with impartial and unbiased men."

"Again, Mr. Chambers, the list is set."

The crowd booed loudly for almost a full minute as the Sheriff and the Clerk tried to settle them down. At this point, Chambers and Zenger figured rowdy Morrisites or not, their goose was cooked.

"What you may do," the Clerk said as the gentlemen quieted themselves eventually, "is to strike any name you like from the list, even beyond your allotment."

"This is a generous attempt, Mr. Clerk, and we thank you. However, once we strike every objectionable name we shall have no jury. There shall not remain twelve names. I fear we must appeal to Chief Justice DeLancey for a new motion to produce the Freeholders Book."

"This is your right," the Clerk acquiesced. "You may call for an emergency motion. The Honourable DeLancey should still be in the courtroom. Should he grant your motion, you may return here by the chime of six and I will produce the Freeholders Book, but only on a judge's order."

In a shot, Chambers was out the door, down the stairwell and down a long hallway to seek DeLancey, papers flying out of his portfolio and nearly losing a loosely tied shoe in the process. Fortunately for Chambers, and Zenger, the Clerk's office was in City Hall and equally fortunately DeLancey and Philipse were still in the courtroom. Loading papers into their leather folders and cases and removing their white wigs and black robes, they were obviously on their way out the door.

"Your Honours! Please, may I be indulged a mere moment of your time?" Chambers panted as he ran into the courtroom and stood catching his breath in front of the high bench, papers still spilling out of his portfolio.

DeLancey and Philipse enjoyed their superior positions, physically as well as administratively, and looked down on Chambers for a moment before speaking.

"What is it, Mr. Chambers?" Philipse asked.

"It is the Struck Jury, your Honours."

"What of it?"

"We are asked to strike from an illegitimate list. The Clerk has produced a sampling of Zenger's enemies and no Freeholders whatsoever." Philipse and Delancey just stared at him. "Your Honours, we ask for a new motion. A motion to produce the official Freeholders Book and to toss out the current, sham list."

DeLancey and Philipse stood still on their perch of authority and said nothing. Chambers knees began to shake and he moved his portfolio to his front to keep them hidden. It didn't hide his knees at all though, and merely produced a smirk from Philipse and a full laugh from DeLancey. Chambers was starting to worry.

He had been appointed by DeLancey personally, on behalf of Cosby. They expected him to bury Zenger. They never expected him to actually fight for his client. Chambers never expected it either. He hadn't exactly gone into the case planning to bushwack Zenger, but he hadn't planned on exerting much energy for him, either. Yet, as the days had gone on, it was clear to him the whole thing was an ambush, a joke of justice.

Chambers didn't particularly care for Zenger as a man. He found him less than intelligent, sloppy, and his thick German accent bothered him to no end. Moreover, Chambers was a proud Cosby ally and supporter. He never did like Zenger's paper and found his Animal Stories particularly childish and objectionable as a friend of the government. Nevertheless, he was an attorney first and actually believed in the law. He was charged with the title of Defense Counsel in this case and his legal education and ethics would not allow him to railroad an, as yet, innocent man.

Still, as he watched DeLancey and Philipse watch him, he began to see flashes of a doused career, poverty, trumped up charges, imprisonment, death, whatever Cosby and DeLancey chose for him as punishment for defiance. Chambers gulped loudly and some more papers fell out of his portfolio. He was sweating so much his glasses kept slipping off his nose. As he pushed them up on his bridge for the countless time, DeLancey laughed at him.

"Motion granted," he said with a chuckle. "Go strike your jury from the Freeholders Book, Mr. Chambers."

"Thank you, Your Honour. Thank you," he bowed to both justices as he kneeled to pick up the papers which had fallen.

After gathering all the papers as well as his glasses, which had fallen twice during the process, he smiled tentatively at the bench and turned to run back to the Clerk's office. As he turned, he tripped on the leather lace of that loosely tied shoe and dropped his entire portfolio. He scrambled to clean up his papers again as quickly as possible, his face burning fuschia with embarrassment, his heart beating in his mouth and his head throbbing with panic. His glasses slipped off again. He had to get out of there; he was growing less and less confident by the second. DeLancey and Philipse smirked and went back to organizing their cases and folders to take home. They whispered something to each other and both laughed simultaneously. Chambers just wanted to get away from them and back to the Clerk's office. He finally gathered everything, tied his shoe, replaced his glasses and was headed out the door and down the hallway when DeLancey offered a snotty good-bye.

"Have a restful night, counselor. See you on the morrow."

Philipse pulled on a linen coat and stifled a laugh as he shook his head. DeLancey just grinned and Chambers bolted down the hallway, up the stairwell and into the Clerk's office.

An hour later twelve new names from the Freeholders Book had been finally selected and agreed upon. Starting at the top of the list, names had been struck off one by one by both Chambers and Bradley and what remained were twelve names, now set at the bottom of the list. It would be these twelve men whom would make up the jury. In the morning, the Sheriff would present to the court his *venire*, or official summon for all twelve men. He would then be sent into the town whilst the court recessed to retrieve the twelve jurors as approved by the court.

As Chambers left City Hall and Zenger was returned to the gaol in the custody of the Sheriff, both men thought the same thing. There was nothing more to do now except go through the tryal itself. The jury list was a good start, but they clearly had a steep and muddy hill ahead of them. Chambers wondered what he had gotten himself into. He had made his stand tonight in front of DeLancey and Philipse. They now knew his true mind and would most likely react to it very unfavourably. Chambers needed a good night's sleep, but there was little possibility he would get one.

Jennifer Susannah Devore

Zenger was not happy, but he contentedly ate his dinner of bread and hambone soup. He knew the tryal was set against him and he knew not whether Chambers would continue to fight for him. He also knew he and Chambers had a little something up their sleeves. Whilst this gave Chambers no peace this night, for he understood a great deal more about the legal process and all its pitfalls, it gave Zenger, in all his blissful ignorance enough hope that he at least slept better than Chambers.

Linus stayed up very late. He wrote in his journal well into the night. He also read over and over what he had previously written. He was having a hard time grasping the Struck Jury process. If he was going to cover a trial, he needed to understand all aspects. In the end, he realized he had gotten all out of the day he could. He was not an attorney, had no desire to become one and was very tired. The day was over and he could do no more. He needed a good night's sleep, he needed to be fresh tomorrow. As Linus drifted off to sleep in the early-morning hours of August 4th, 1735, he dreamed about what was truly a complicated, unsual and utterly, exceptionally important case.

"Satchel, what are you doing?" Hamilton had grown irritated with his page.

Since the carriage crash, they had decided to walk the road, certain that as morning came somebody would have to travel this route. Satchel had wanted to stay put and wait for help. Hamilton laughed at this and stated empirically that this was a ridiculous option and that as long as they were walking in the right direction, they'd be making progress. At least there was a chance, even if the odds were astronomical, that they'd make their destination. There was zero chance if they sat and did nothing. They had brought along Gavin who was more than happy to carry their satchels and books. Other than that, he made it very clear there was no way in Hell he was going to let anyone ride him, especially a couple of counselors from Philadelphia.

Currently, it was after four in the morning and while daybreak was not too far off, Satchel was certain death by claw and fang was lurking around every tree. The dark stillness seemed magnified by the crunchy *clip-clop* of Gavin's hooves. Satchel figured though, if he was scared of Mr. Hamilton, which he was terrified, the beasts might be, too. So, for the past half-mile, he'd walked so closely behind Hamilton that he kept stepping on his heels. This latest step had caused Hamilton to step out of his shoe completely.

"My Heavens, son. Please. Give me some room," he snapped as he stopped to put back on his shoe. He then stood up and saw the sheer terror and apology in Satchels's eyes and felt a wave of pity for the young man. "Listen to me, Satchel," he said much more gently. "you've nothing to worry about. We are in New-Jersey. What safer place is there than New-Jersey? Especially at dark? And we're headed into New-York. It's even safer there in the dark. For now though, we are safe. The only things out there are raccoons, mice and squirrels."

"Squirrels?" Satchel looked around frantically. "I had not even thought about the squirrels. Squirrels give me the heebee jeebees, Sir. They skitter. That word doesn't even sound like a real word. They move too fast. It is not natural," Satchel skittered behind Hamilton as he heard rustling in a nearby bush.

"I shall protect you from any rogue squirrels, I promise," Hamilton laughed. "For now, why don't we focus on our task at hand. Why don't you recite some precedents for me. It would be a true help to me. I fear I cannot remember all of English law on my own."

A smart man, Hamilton needed no help to recall English case law, but he knew this would take Satchel's mind off the squirrels and, more importantly, off his heels. With a wary eye still on the noisy bush, Satchel swung his rucksack around so it hung in front of him and began to dig for a book.

"No, no," Hamilton shook a finger. "Recite. Declaim. Narrate from memory. No books, no notes. Let us walk and you tell me all about, oh, I don't know. How about Brewster's Case? And why don't you hang your rucksack on the horse?"

"I like to have it close-by, just in case. Um, Brewster's Case. Yes, well, um. Let's see."

Satchel closed the flap back over his rucksack and slung it around his back. He thought hard, visibly so as his eyes rose skyward and squinted and his mouth twisted all the way to the right.

"Yes! Brewster's Case!" He had located the precedent within his little grey cells. "1664, *That the subjects might defend their rights and liberties. . .in case the King should go about to destroy them. . ."* he looked to Hamilton for validation of his recitation.

"Excellent. But, what is the twist? What is the next case that brings us a surprise?"

"Um, surprise. Twist?" Satchel mumbled to himself, then found the answer and recited dutifully. "A Dr. Sacheverell was later sentenced in the highest court in Great Britain for publicly stating such resistance as *illegal*! He went to gaol for actually trying to stand up for the Crown!"

"So how can we extrapolate this, string it out to apply it to our situation?"

Satchel thought for a few minutes and came up with what he thought was a pretty good answer.

"That the laws of England have progressed with great changes for the good of man, and so should the laws of her colonies in America."

Satchel walked with a bit of a spring in his step now. He had forgotten about his fears and the sun was starting to peek over the horizon. New-Jersey never looked so beautiful, really. He and Hamilton went on for another half-hour or so and whilst they made good conversation and Satchel did a fine job of case law recitation, Hamilton's mind was never fully within the moment. He was certain he was just hours away from letting down scads of people, not to mention the entire future of Western law. Oh my, but Ben was going to be upset.

As Hamilton reached for one of the rucksacks hanging off Gavin, the horse suddenly kicked up his front legs and bucked all the way around so that he landed facing the way from which they'd all come.

"Damn horse," Hamilton thought.

It was a wonder they'd been able to even get him to carry their books. There was no way Hamilton and Satchel could carry all those books and notes and walk to New-York. Gavin seemed capable of carrying their sacks, but sad to leave Gwen behind to watch after Radoslav. Until now, he'd been relatively cooperative, only a few outbursts. This one, however, was a bit much. Hamilton was about to reach into the sack for a bisquit again when he saw what Gavin saw. Another horse! And rider! There was help! Galloping at a full and fast pace behind them strode a magnificent creature.

Standing nearly twenty hands high, far taller at the withers than a large man standing perfectly erect, the horse was a Dutch Warmblood and as black as onyx. His fur and mane shined almost blue they were so black and he glistened all over from what looked liked hours and hours of running at this same pace. Both horse and rider were soaked to the skin with perspiration and summer humidity, and the horse's mouth was dripping foam, his nose snorting frothy phlegm. The rider was a young boy, maybe a young man, of sixteen or seventeen. He was of small-to-medium height and build, fair-haired and fair–skinned, but looked quite capable astride this beast. Together, they cut through the Jersey woods like a low-flying dragon and his conquering, young knight. As fast as they came down the road, they came to a halt, a mere snout's length from Gavin as the rider yelled a hearty "Whoaaaaa!"

"Thank goodness, young man! Serendipity is busy this morning!" Hamilton slapped Gavin on his flanks and he snorted right in the face of the new horse. "Show off," he thought to himself.

"We saw your carriage wreck. Your coachman told us of your situation. Do you still wish to make your destination?" the boy jumped off his steed and patted his flanks, too, thanking him for his general magnificence.

"Yes! Absolutely! Have you options for us? Do you have colleagues coming this way soon? Do you know of a carriage coming?" Hamilton asked excitedly and took charge of the situation.

Satchel just stood gleefully, thrilled that another human being was now part of their group and that hope and help were on the way. In an instant Satchel's fear of nature kicked in again and he was ready once again to get out of there.

"No, Sir. But, I have a horse for you, Sir," the boy patted his horse again and beamed with pride. "He is all yours, Sir. I can run back for the other horse and take her to find help for your coachman."

The boy waited for gratitude and Hamilton and Satchel offered very little. It wasn't that Hamilton wasn't grateful, he was just a little skeptical, not of the boy, but of the horse. In truth, his horse was a fascinatingly strong-looking creature and clearly more willing and spirited than Gavin, but frankly he looked like he'd been worked over for far too long to be of any assistance. Not to mention that he was slung with more bags and rucksacks than Gavin was. He must have been a workhorse of some kind, but no horse was that sturdy. He was snorting and puffing as hard as Gavin was, except that Gavin's exertions had nothing to do with exhaustion, he was just being jealous and snitty to this new horse. He was glad Gwen wasn't here to see him. Oh, wait a minute, Gwen had met him earlier. So what? Nobody really likes a horse who's that showy. Gavin was sure he had much more substance than this guy.

What Hamilton did not understand was that this was no ordinary horse and that he was not snorting out of exhaustion, but out of excitement. He was not used to standing still. He was ready to go anywhere, do anything.

"Actually, Sir," the boy leaned in to whisper, "I was wondering, why is it that you are not riding this horse? You know, you'd make better time."

"Thank you, son," Hamilton was a little embarrassed but played it off. "This, we know. Not only would it be unhealthy and unfair to ride him, but in truth," now he leaned in toward the boy, "he would not let us anywhere near him when we tried."

"What about that other horse back there?"

"She's ridable, but with a really bad attitude. I couldn't get anywhere near her, either. Anyway, Radoslav said she needed to stay put. This one here was the stronger of the two."

Hamilton didn't want to seem unfriendly, but he needed to stop the horse chat and figure out what to do. Surely he couldn't ride this new horse. Maybe the boy had some other ideas.

"Now, do you have any knowledge of other carriages making this route this morning?" Hamilton asked.

"No, Sir. I know this route very, very well and I am the only one on it before about seven o'clock," he pulled a pocket watch from his thin coat. "'Tis not even four-thirty, Sir." Hamilton sighed and the boy wrinkled his brow. "As I said, Sir, you may take my horse. I shall tie up yours here, run back to your other one and ride her to get help for your coachman. You must hurry, though if you want to make New-York by eight as your coachman said was your goal." He anxiously dangled his horse's reins in Hamilton's direction.

"But, son. He looks absolutely beat. Besides, we have all these books.

They must go with us and he is already laden with his own burden."

"Trust me, Sir. Do not worry about him," he winked at his horse whom winked back, his long, black lashes releasing a distinct sparkle from his left eye. Hamilton and Satchel both saw the sparkle and looked at each other. "Please, Sir. Hurry!" he dangled the reins harder.

"How will we get him back to you?" Hamilton asked as he and Satchel worked quickly to load up their bags on the new horse's hindquarters.

"Worry not. I shall bring your mare tomorrow night to the Wooden Horse Tavern at Fort George, New-York. We shall meet there."

"What if we miss each other? We don't even know where this place is!" Satchel panicked.

"Do not worry yourselves. It's a popular tavern. Anyone can tell you where it is. Besides he knows where it is," he patted his horse and he stamped a hoof three times. "Mr. Phillip Geraerdy's Wooden Horse Tavern near Fort George. Right, pal?" The great horse stamped his hoof three times more and nodded just as many. "We go there often. 'Tis an official mail stop."

"So in these bags?" Satchel patted the leather sacks hanging off every inch of the horse's hindquarters.

"Official, royal mail. Some colonial news-papers," the boy stated with no excitement whatsoever. Satchel found it very exciting.

"What about Radoslav and our horse here?" Satchel worried.

"Again, worry not. I shall get help for both of them. You shall all be reunited soon, healthy and happy. Now you must go!" he insisted as Satchel looked terrified as he watched the black horse.

Hamilton helped push Satchel up on the horse's back. This took three tries for Satchel had never sat atop a horse in his life and was clearly scared to death. The boy walked over and gave Satchel one big nudge on the rump and pushed him on for good. Hamilton was next and took two tries. This was a big, big horse. Very tall. But there they sat astride an almost wild creature, a spooky but friendly beast laden, to a near-supernatural level, with human and paper weight.

"I said worry not, my friends," the boy smiled mysteriously as he saw Satchel's terror and Hamilton's doubt. "He can handle it. He can handle anything," he beamed. "He knows how to get you there, in time."

"Well then," Hamilton interrupted from atop the horse. "I am loathe to be impolite, and we thank you profusely, truly, but we must be off. I am still not sure we can make it to New-York City by eight o'clock."

Hamilton double-checked all their bags and slapped Satchels' hands whose nails were digging into his merely linen-sheathed rib cage.

"Yes, yes. Go, go. You will make it. Worry not," he smiled mysteriously again.

Hamilton clucked his tongue twice and pulled the reins toward the left to point the horse in the proper direction. The horse danced in place, all fours prancing up and down like a ballerina and just waiting for the universal heel taps on his flanks to bolt out of there. Hamilton looked down at the boy on the ground and asked him one last question.

"I am sorry, son. What is your name? What is your horse's name? I do not how to properly thank you or find you later if need be."

"Do not worry about thanks. We understand the importance of your task," he and his horse winked at each other again. "My name is Samuel and he is Merlin."

CHAPTER FORTY

The morning got off to a rocky start but by nine-thirty, the courtroom was full. Zenger had come to court in relatively good spirits, for he and Chambers alone knew something the rest of the court did not. Chambers had definitive plans revolving around this shocker and Zenger was counting on it to retain his freedom. They both looked at their watches and saw it was nearly ten o'clock.

In addition and much to their chagrin and after the belief that their jury had been finally and securely selected at last night's late session in the Clerk's office, they entered the courtroom this morning to find that the Sheriff's list of names, his *venire*, had been written incorrectly and instead of the final twelve names being submitted to DeLancey and Philipse for approval, the *first* twelve names scratched off last night were submitted! Exactly the names they did not want!

"I move, your Honours," Chambers objected first thing, "that we may have justice done by the Sheriff and that he may have the list of jurors that was correctly and fairly struck last night."

"How is that? Are they not so returned?" DeLancey asked innocently, his eyes blinking and his eyebrows arched high.

"No, they are not. For some of the names that were last set down in the panel are now placed first."

"Make out that this is true and you shall be righted," DeLancey offered to correct the situation if Chambers could prove it.

Chambers, being well-prepared and very paranoid by now, kept a copy of the original list struck last night in his notes. DeLancey dismissed it with a flick of his wrist and gestured for Chambers to present it to the Clerk of the Court.

"Clerk, is it so? Look upon that copy. Is it a true copy of the panel as it was struck last night?"

"No, Your Honour, I believe it is different," the Clerk accepted the list from his small desk near the judges' bench then passed it along to the Sheriff.

"How came the names of the jurors to be misplaced, written incorrectly in the *venire*?" DeLancey asked the Clerk.

"I know not, Your Honours."

Chambers was stunned. This was a circus. He didn't know who he could trust at this point. Was the Clerk in on it? Was DeLancey toying with them? Was the Sheriff setting them up for defeat? What in Heaven's name was going on?

Zenger was getting really anxious, too anxious for his stomach's pleasure. Every minute that ticked by he grew more and more panicked and felt like vomiting more than was normal. Ironically, he had nevertheless appreciated the jury mistake for this bought him time. Had the tryal actually started when it was supposed to, they'd really be in hot water by now.

"Your Honours," the Sheriff addressed the court after a few minutes, "I have returned the jurors in the correct order now, the new order in which the Clerk has given me. The twelve men agreed upon by both sides last night are the correct jury."

"Let the names of the jurors be ranged in the order they were struck, agreeable to the copy here in court." DeLancey proclaimed. "Sheriff, please read aloud the names of the true jurors."

"Yes, Your Honours," and he read them to the courtroom.

"Harmanus Rutgers, Stanly Holmes, Edward Man, John Bell, Samuel Weaver, Andries Marschalk, Egbert van Borsom, Thomas Hunt, Benjamin Hildreth, Abraham Keteltas, John Goelet and Hercules Wendover."

Upon hearing the names read aloud, it occurred to Zenger that they were largely of Dutch and German ancestry, perhaps forming a supportive jury. He felt a little better. He had heard the names before obviously, but now as they were read aloud, it all seemed very positive. Surely the Dutch folk would recall

Cosby's fight with Rip VanDam, a fellow countryman. The Germans might find some solidarity with Zenger. It had also not gone unnoticed by many in the courtroom that many of the jurors were men with ties to the Morrisite Party, including the jury foreman, Thomas Hunt.

Just over an hour later, these twelve men were assembled in the jurors' box. As DeLancey called the courtroom to order everyone stood. Zenger wiped his hands on his pants as he stood. Chambers and the opposing attorneys stood with their hands at their sides. As the tryal's opening words flowed out of DeLancey's powdered face, Zenger began to feel dizzy and the words soon turned into a dull hum, making as much sense as a sheep's bleating. He glanced at the main doors, worried, then faced front again. He steadied himself by leaning forward on the defendant's table, resting both palms flat in front of him. His mind began to race as the Chief Justice droned on and on about the Crown-this and His Majesty-that. By the time everyone was ordered to sit, Zenger landed so hard on his wooden chair that it called the attention of the entire courtroom.

Sitting was definitely better, but now it was the Attorney General's turn to speak and as he stood up to straighten his frock coat and take a sip from his teacup which sat near his open portfolio, Zenger was sure Bradley's opening statement wasn't going to be any shorter than DeLancey's. Richard Bradley stood to deliver his opening statement just before ten o'clock in the morning.

Barely ten and the New-York City, August, morning heat was already causing great discomfort. Along with the rest of the courtroom, the cravat-choked professionals, the bewigged judges, the standing-room-only public gallery of citizens, Zenger sorely wished he was fishing on a lake or lounging in a park somewhere and sipping a cool tankard of a nice, German, white wine. Maybe a Riesling.

The sun was perfectly positioned to stream in through the tall windows of the second-floor, City Hall courtroom. The room's east-facing windows made up most of the wall and this made for a very hot, very suffocating feeling inside. Everybody was already stewing in their own juices and the tryal had only just begun.

Linus, having been there since the very beginning at eight, was leaving sweat stains all over his journal. He was so hot that he kept running his hand over his forehead, through his sweaty hair and then wiping it on his pants, which were becoming oily from this process and seeping onto the open pages of his journal. Even the leather binding was getting a little moist. Everything was getting sweaty and dangerously close to becoming inky.

Yet, Linus had been scribbling away too frantically to really notice how gross that all was. If last night's issues at the Clerk's office were interesting, today's were even more so. He was feeling a little guilty about getting excited by all the twists and turns of this tryal. After all, it was his friend and boss at the end of the proverbial rope. However, the innate journalist in him recognized this was going to be a fascinating story in the end, one way or the other.

"May it please Your Honours and you gentlemen of the jury," Richard Bradley started pacing and facing the judges' bench and the jury box, "the defendant John Peter Zenger has pleaded 'Not Guilty' against an Information for printing and publishing a false, scandalous and seditious libel in which His Excellency, the Governor of this Province, the King's immediate representative here in New-York is greatly and unjustly scandalized."

Zenger shifted in his seat and felt his linen knickers and blouse stick to his chair. He lifted up and out slowly and felt the cloth on his back and his bottom peel thickly away from his skin. How could such a light fabric become so heavy with mere saltwater? He was so hot that his entire suit, chosen specifically for its bright, crisp and clean look (Zenger's attorneys, former and current, had advised that white was a positive colour and would make him look more sympathetic to the jury.) had become no more than a pile of sweat-soaked rags. Ick.

"Be it remembered that I, Richard Bradley, Esquire and Attorney General of our sovereign Lord the King, for the Province of New-York, who for our said Lord the King in this part prosecutes, in his own proper person comes here into the court of our said Lord the King. . ."

For nearly forty minutes Bradley would say quite a bit of nothing as he repeatedly reminded the courtroom of the God-given and unquestionable authority of the King of England. Zenger's eyes closed a number of times, dreaming of that big fish and cool wine; then, he'd sit bolt upright, shake his head and try to focus. No matter how hard he tried, his mind was too occupied to hear even the formal charges being brought against him. He looked back at the main doors again. Nothing. This was not going well at all.

The ferry pilot looked through squinted eyes at the strange group that had barely made the last boarding call before pulling slowly, excruciatingly slowly, out of its slip. Not his fault. He should have never allowed these folk on his periauger. Sure, it was a sturdy little sailboat, but it was a sailboat nonetheless and who ever heard of a horse on a small sailboat? Especially this beast! His bags of books and papers alone were enough to sink the whole lot of them. Clearly, the nervous boy thought it was all a bad idea. But, the old one, the poncy one in the fancy, blue frock coat wasn't going to take 'No' for an answer and, happily for the captain, offered him more money than he'd make in a month of passengers, just for this one, half-hour crossing. Good thing, too. He was forced to toss off the boat, at the last minute, more than few very angry men. He promised to come back for them as soon as possible, and at half-price. This assuaged some of the grumblers, but as they sailed off, he was sure he heard some language even bluer than the poncy man's coat. The captain wasn't going to waste time fretting over it too much. He was a private businessman, running a private service. The polite and diplomatic "First come, first served" would eternally be supplanted by the fiscally-friendly, capitalist "Sold to the highest bidder!"

He'd pay for such business, though. This ride was going to be a sketchy one; the boat was already bobbing and waggling from side to side. One just didn't put a horse in a tiny periauger. Certainly not one like this. Strangely enough, this horse seemed to understand and stood perfectly still, his black, pearl eyes locked on the horizon, as if aware that should he shift his gaze even a fraction he could topple the whole boat.

He made eye contact once with the captain and it scared him a little, the captain was scared, that is. Merlin had a spooky way about him if one didn't know him well. The trip was a short one and while his pocket watch read just past ten o'clock, far later than he would have preferred, Hamilton felt hopeful and relieved. Not half an hour to the ferry landing at Whitehall Street on Lower Manhattan's tip, another ten minutes' gallop straight up Broadway, past Wall Street and Trinity Church and he'd reach his destination. New-York City Hall.

Hopefully, the tryal won't have progressed too far. If Hamilton knew his court patterns, and he did, two things were always true: judges were always late, and prosecutors loved to bloviate. Court might be scheduled to convene at eight, but it was more often than not that the judges would arrive just after nine, if not later. After they conferred with their sheriffs, bailiffs, fellow judges, assistants and pages, got some coffee and the tryal got underway, a prosecutor's opening statement could go on for what felt like days. Hamilton laughed, drawing attention from the suspicious ferry pilot. One upside to all this, Hamilton thought, is he wouldn't have to listen to this Richard Bradley blather on and on. Hamilton looked at his watch. Ten-fifteen. He could be there by eleven if there were no problems and if Merlin could make it up Broadway in record time. Having come this far, what could possibly happen?

As Hamilton watched the horizon and the oncoming village of New-York, it occurred to him what a marvel that such populace had been built into and carved out of this vastly wild and frightening landscape. To his right, floating like a large bisquit rising out of the Hudson and East Rivers' meeting point, emerged *Noten Eylandt*, or Governor's Island. From the periauger, he could see the relatively unimpressive Fort George.

Fort George was large, by colonial standards, but rather boring in architectural detail. Surrounding it stood some clustered, private homes and businesses. All of this was laughably protected by a simple, flat-topped, brick wall. Fort George was, in essence, a medieval city trying to fit into the 18th Century. Around it breathed the true life force of this region, a spirit and soul that could not be barred by a mere wall: the Native Americans, the forests they respected and its animal inhabitants they revered.

Hamilton wondered as he turned to look straight ahead at a somewhat similar landscape on Lower Manhattan how long it would take for this city to either encompass and subjugate the original residents, or be pushed back themselves to the Mother countries across the Atlantic. New-York was an impressive colony, but Hamilton wondered for how long?

"Mr. Hamilton, Sir?" Satchel asked nervously and tentatively from behind Merlin.

"Hey! Keep that blasted animal still! This isn't a Spanish Galleon! He shouldn't be on here as it is! Now keep him still!" the pilot yelled at Satchel as the small, two-masted sailboat began to rock back and forth. "Besides, I can't swim."

"Yeeeees?" Hamilton didn't like the tone of Satchel's voice one bit, but glanced at the pilot. Who ran a ferry service for a living but couldn't swim?

"Mr. Hamilton, Sir? I think we have a problem, Sir."

Hamilton dropped his head, sighed deeply, "What is it, Satchel?"

"I think you have to come over here, Sir," Satchel braved.

Very carefully, Hamilton stepped over two bench seats to get to the other end of the boat and see the source of Satchel's concern. The boat stopped rocking as Merlin balanced himself perfectly on three hooves. The other, he held back for Satchel. Now, neither Satchel nor Hamilton were horsemen, but it didn't take a caballero to see that this was bad news. Merlin had thrown a shoe. There was his back, left hoof: totally bare.

"He must have lost it on the trail," Satchel stated the obvious.

"Yes, I see that," Hamilton said dryly. "We shall have to walk the rest of the way when we land. He'll destroy his hoof if we ride him like that."

Merlin slammed down his hoof and the whole boat shifted side to side again and the pilot began muttering insults and profanities. Neighing and snorting, Merlin shook his head aggressively side to side in time with the boat and uttered his own insults and profanities right back at the pilot. Merlin's eyes had grown darker and he stamped his shoeless hoof three times on the boat's wooden floor, very nearly stamping a hole right through it.

"Keep your damned animal still or we'll all drown!" the pilot screamed.

"I think he doesn't want us walking," Satchel translated to Hamilton, ignoring the pilot, and instantly Merlin mellowed and nodded his head up and down slowly but strongly. Satchel stroked Merlin's mane and patted his cheek. "See, he wants to help. He wants us to ride him."

Merlin snorted and stamped his hoof three more times, bringing on some rather blue language from their pilot. Hamilton regarded his watch for

Jennifer Susannah Devore

372

about the fifteenth time since they boarded at the *Staaten Eylandt* St. George Ferry slip. It was so late. Who was he to deny anyone's help. If Merlin wanted to help they would accept. Hamilton tipped his hat at the mighty Warmblood whom nodded back in kind. Within minutes they'd be at the Whitehall Ferry slip and, as long as Merlin could carry them, he and Satchel should be standing behind John Peter Zenger's defense table within half an hour.

". . .whereupon the said Attorney General of our Lord the King prays the advisement of the court here, in these premises, and the due process of the law against him, the said John Peter Zenger, in this part to be done, to answer to our said Lord the King!" nearly an hour after court finally convened, Bradley finally finished his opening statement.

Linus dropped his pencil in his journal as soon as Bradley finished and rubbed his palm and fingers vigorously. Ouch. That was ridiculous, Linus thought. Bradley had said nothing. He just repeated the same phrases and titles over and over: "Our said Lord the King" and "His Excellency the said Governor" and "blah, blah, blah". No wonder adults had so many running jokes about lawyers and the government. It was as though Bradley knew he had a wobbly case, so he figured if he just said a lot of royal and official-sounding mumbo jumbo, he might sound more viable. At this rate, this case should go on until Christmas. At the thought of Christmas Linus smiled, closed his eyes and imagined making snow angels. Then he opened his eyes, was reminded how icky it was right now and assumed with every movement in his seat he was probably making sweat angels.

"Mr. Chambers? Your response?" DeLancey asked Chambers to rise and speak to the court.

"Thank you, Your Honour, " Chambers stood and walked to the central area in between the judges' bench and the jury box. "The defendant, John Peter Zenger, has pleaded *Not Guilty* in this 'Information' and we are ready to prove it." He then turned to the judges. "If I may, Your Honours, I would like to explain to the jury why my client is charged by an 'Information' rather than an 'Indictment'."

"Objection!" Bradley rose quickly. "Zenger is charged. Period. It serves no purpose to explain how he got here."

DeLancey and Philipse whispered to each other. Then DeLancey spoke whilst Philipse marked in a notebook and snickered openly.

"We think there is no way this can hurt us, I mean, the case. Objection denied. Carry on, Mr. Chambers."

"Thank you, Your Honours," Chambers turned to the jury and proceeded to explain the difference.

Linus was grateful for this and he opened to a new page in his journal and waited with pencil ready.

"Gentlemen of the jury, an 'information' is indeed similar to an indictment, except that an indictment is brought by a Grand Jury, gentlemen like yourselves whom agree there is enough evidence to go to court at all. When no Grand Jury can find enough evidence, a prosecutor takes the law unto himself and charges the individual anyway, regardless of justice."

"Objection!" Bradley howled. "He's leading the jury!"

"Objection denied," DeLancey said calmly.

"History shows us in the past year that two," Chambers continued and held up two fingers, "New-York Grand Juries have found no such evidence in the case of my client. Today though, he is here based purely on the tyrannical vindictiveness of Mr. Richard Bradley and his supporters!" Chambers swung around and pointed his finger at Bradley to emphasize the end of his statement.

"Objection!" Bradley nearly screamed.

"Objection sustained," DeLancey said strongly and leaned forward in his bench. "I suggest you watch yourself, Mr. Chambers. I notice your predecessors, Mr. Zenger's former attorneys, here in the gallery today," he pointed with his gavel to Smith and Alexander whom sat directly behind the defendant's table, but behind the bar that separated the legal staff from the viewing gallery. "I had them removed from this case and I can do the same to you, Mr. Chambers. Now," he leaned back and smiled at Philipse, then back at Chambers, "I suggest you get back to the business of protecting your client rather than bringing him more harm."

That was clearly a threat and it did not miss Chambers, Zenger or anyone in the courtroom. It was now so quiet one could actually hear bottoms releasing with sweat as they peeled off the benches, as people shimmied in their seats. Simultaneously Zenger and Chambers looked at the courtroom doors. Where was he? This was suicide. They'd never make it through the day.

"Mr. Chambers! What on earth are you waiting on? Are you expecting someone? Is your nursemaid to bring you some milk before continuing? Shall she bring you some bisquits and cocoa?" DeLancey derided the young Chambers and the whole courtroom laughed hysterically.

"I apologize, Your Honours," Chambers capitulated to DeLancey and winced at the laughter. "I thought I heard something. I am sorry. Yes, well, I, well," he stuttered, "we mean only to present the jury with every bit of evidence available to them. Gentlemen of the jury," he turned away from DeLancey and Bradley and back to the jury box and took a deep breath, "it is our intention to prove the very nature of a libel.

We intend to prove that Mr. Zenger is not guilty of *false, scandalous and seditious libel* because in order to commit a libel against a person, the law states that in a libel there must be no doubt as to the specific person or persons mentioned in the offensive material. We shall prove that no person, no magistrates, officials or governors were ever named in these alleged libels."

Chambers looked to his left and saw the courtroom's side entrance. There in the doorway and all dressed in their finest attire, stood Zenger's two sons, his journeyman and a host of other men, most subpoenaed by Bradley. They were the material witnesses in this case, brought together by both sides hoping to give evidence that would aid either the prosecution or the defense, depending on how they were examined. Both the prosecution and the defense were given the chance to question not only their own witnesses, but also those of the opposing side. An attempt at fairness.

Chambers looked back at the main, double-doors one last time, then back to the side door where the witnesses stood waiting. It was time. Chambers heaved an audible sigh and faced the judges.

"We would ask at this point for Your Honours to bring forth all witnesses so that we may prove our innocence and thereby disprove the prosecution's charges of *false, malicious and scandalous libel.*"

Chambers plopped back down at his table and waited. He didn't even try to hide his defeat. He had all but given up. Zenger just dropped his head on the table and imagined the rest of his life in that wet, dank cell. DeLancey and Philipse whispered some more things to each other and giggled like schoolgirls before turning to address the courtroom.

"Fine then," DeLancey said. "First witness for the prosecution?" DeLancey motioned to the bailiff to bring forth the first name called.

"In the name of The Sovereign Lord King George the Second, the prosecution calls forth. . .," the bailiff began.

At that moment, a flash of muggy heat exploded from the main doors and travelled throughout the courtroom like smoke blown into a glass. There in the doorway stood Andrew Hamilton and Satchel. They both looked like they'd spent the night in Hell: smudged faces, rumpled coats, messy hair. No matter, for like the gentlemen they were, they smoothed themselves and walked into the courtroom as if they were King George himself. Even Satchel, who loved the law but was scared to death of courtrooms held his chin high and followed Mr. Hamilton with great pride.

Satchel carried all their papers except one portfolio which Hamilton held under his arm. With the sharp and determined *clicks* of his heels, Hamilton walked rapidly but elegantly to the defendant's table, set down his portfolio and approached the judges' bench with a few more *clicks*. DeLancey and Philipse could do nothing but stare at him, their mouths hanging open like codfish. They said nothing.

"Good morning, Your Honours. I apologize for my appearance and that of my page," he gestured back to Satchel whom was trying to keep his bags and sacks from falling onto the floor as he spread them out on the table.

DeLancey and Philipse still said nothing. Andrew Hamilton, Esquire? *The* Andrew Hamilton, Esquire of Philadelphia? Good Heavens! How did he come to be here? This was a huge stick in their spokes. Amazed and stunned, the codfish still stared and said nothing. Zenger couldn't contain a huge smile and sheer giddiness; Chambers leaned all the way back in his chair and released a sigh as his body slumped into total relief.

"May it please Your Honours, I am here on behalf of Mr. Zenger. The information against my client," the courtroom buzzed as Hamilton labeled

Zenger *his* client, "was sent me a few days before I left home. Regarding this matter, let it be known I am in agreement with the prosecution that my client did indeed print and publish those news-papers referenced in the information. Further, I shall save Mr. Attorney General the trouble of examining the witnesses."

The courtroom buzzed again. Were they hearing what they thought they were hearing? Zenger and Chambers both sat bolt upright in their chairs. Were they hearing Hamilton correctly? Had he just admitted that Zenger was indeed *guilty* of the charges of printing and publishing the news-papers?! The jury shuffled in their seats and spoke to each other through silent but astonished faces. DeLancey, having regained his speech banged his gavel and called for quiet.

"Silence in the court! Silence in the court! Mr. Hamilton, please state your business more clearly."

"Yes, Your Honour. I cannot think it proper for me, without doing harm to my own principles, to deny the printing and publishing of a public complaint. This, I think, is the right of every free-born subject to make, especially when the complaint so published can be supported with the truth.

Therefore, I do confess for my client that he did both print and publish the two news-papers set forth in the information, and I hope in so doing he has committed no crime."

Hamilton walked back to his table, sat in a chair that the ex-attorney James Alexander had rushed to provide for him, and patted Zenger on the back and shook hands with Chambers, both of whom now stared like codfish themselves.

"Then if Your Honour pleases, since Mr. Hamilton," Bradley bowed with true respect to the legendary attorney, "has confessed the fact, I think our witnesses may be discharged. We have no further occasion for them."

"If you brought them here only to prove the printing and publishing of these news-papers, we have acknowledged that and shall abide by it," Hamilton stood at his table.

A few moments passed as the bailiff formally dismissed all the witnesses. Most left, but Zenger's sons found seats in the gallery and stayed to watch their father's tryal. His journeyman left as quickly as possible as he still had a news-paper to run in his boss' absence. The jury talked amongst themselves and some began to pack up any belongings they brought with them. Some members of the gallery started buttoning their coats and donning their hats to go. This couldn't possibly last any longer. Zenger was guilty. Hamilton admitted it. Linus scribbled frantically in his journal, then sat upright and tried to discern what was going on at the judges' bench. Bradley had gone up there, but neither Chambers nor Hamilton had been invited to approach. That seemed unfair. Should the prosecution get to share secrets with the judges? Something wasn't right. Linus waited, pencil at the ready.

DeLancey and Philipse conferred and whispered with Bradley, all out of earshot of Hamilton, and realized they had no choice but to allow Hamilton to stay. Chambers could stay on as second defense. Hamilton saw them discussing him and whispered his own secrets to Chambers. Hamilton wasn't worried; he knew his reputation preceded him. They weren't going to dismiss him and he was right.

Philipse argued that Hamilton was no simple lawyer. He was a legend, well-respected throughout the colonies, nearly sixty and, most importantly, had many friends in places much higher than the New-York Supreme Court. DeLancey, barely thirty years old would never be swayed merely by Hamilton's age. He had no respect for the elderly. In fact, he thought them a nuisance and to be retired from most professions. Youth was king. What DeLancey did respect was Hamilton's reputation and his link to some of England's and America's most wealthy and powerful. He wasn't about to step on these toes. Besides, this was all over except the paperwork. He'd just buried his own client! Legendary? Legendarily stupid, maybe.

"Well, Mr. Attorney. Will you proceed?" he admitted Hamilton by saying nothing to him, but directing his question to Bradley.

"Indeed, Sir. As Mr. Hamilton has confessed the printing and publishing of these libels, I think the jury must find a verdict of *Guilty* for the King."

Zenger threw his head back down on the table.

"Supposing they were true, these libels," Bradley continued. "Even better! The law says they are no less libelous for that. Nay, indeed the law says their being true is an even greater aggravation of the crime. The truer the libel, the greater the crime!"

"Not so, Mr. Attorney," Hamilton retorted. "I hope it is not our bare printing and publishing that will make it a libel. You will have something more to do before you make my client a libeler, for the words themselves must be libelous. That is false, scandalous and seditious or we are not guilty."

Hamilton sat down and the courtroom noise mounted again. Those whom had buttoned their coats now unbuttoned them and those in the jury whom had packed up their portfolios or rucksacks now set them back down on the floor. Linus grinned from ear to ear. This was by no means over! This man was indeed clever. He had a plan, a fantastic plan of some sort. Zenger and Chambers breathed sighs of relief together. Zenger didn't understand exactly what was happening, but he knew he had a chance now. He knew that Alexander and Smith had been very smart in arranging with their secret Philadelphia friend for Hamilton to join the defense team. Chambers was just relieved he didn't have to face the, now finally apparent to him, corruption of the New-York courts alone.

For the next hour or more, Hamilton and Bradley argued back and forth about the special rights of the men in power and their need for extra protection in the law. If they are men chosen by their very King to protect and govern His Majesty's subjects, should they not be afforded better protection than average to prevent anything that might bring them harm? Must not the greatest care be taken to prevent anything that might tend to scandalize these officials, especially the highest magistrate, the governor? Must not they be protected from all evil and scandalous words, true or not, the truer the worse, that might endanger their position of authority? Should they not be safe from awful tales which could bring contempt from the community? Yes! These were men of a superior position, with superior duties than the average farmer, salesman, shopkeep, maidservant, waitress and, yes, even a mere lawyer. These men needed superior protection and therefore a different standard of the law. Bradley was no stranger to legal studies and pulled from his bags the same books Hamilton did. From *Coke's Reports* they both found citations to support their arguments.

The day was growing hotter and hotter and the courtroom smellier and smellier. The people were growing grumpier and grumpier and Zenger sleepier and sleepier. Linus was just as sticky as could be. All that aside, it was a fascinating case being presented and those with the inclination to doze found themselves unable to close their eyes for more than a few seconds. It was surprisingly exciting, this mundane law of libel. Of course, libel was, in a nutshell, gossip.

Be the gossip true or not, humans loved hearing private, shocking and outrageous information about other humans. For now, this case was the most exciting thing in the New-York courts since last year's Shankly vs. Shankly in which a Brooklyn woman ran her husband through with a foil for bringing her the wrong colour dress back from Paris. He sued her and recovered nicely. She was hanged. Bradley finished a round of arguments by citing *Coke's* legal description of a libel.

"A libel is a malicious defamation of a person, expressed either in printing or writing, signs or pictures to asperse the reputation of one that is alive or the memory of one that is dead. If he is a private man the libeler deserves a severe punishment. But if it is against a magistrate or other public person it is a *greater* offense."

Some members of the jury nodded silently as if they agreed; but most crossed their arms and grimaced. These were all private men, not a magistrate or public person amongst them. Why should their reputations be regarded as less valuable than a public man's? Linus wrote this legal definition in his journal and put a star next to it. Zenger, Chambers and Satchel noticed the generally negative disposition of the jury after this statement and all were made a little happier for it.

Then, Bradley brought out a Bible from his leather bag. He held it up high, with both hands and slowly spun around to show the whole courtroom, as if it was a precious new infant or a rare diamond brought from hinterlands of India. He was now going to use the fear of God to sway this jury. If they weren't going to listen to the legal definition of libel, they would surely listen to God's definition of it.

"Libeling is an offense against the law of God!" he drew out the last word and raised his voice as he did so, just like a preacherman. "For it is written here, in the New Testament's Acts of the Apostles, Chapter twenty-two, verse five:

'Then Paul said, I wist not brethren that he was the High Priest. For it is written thou shalt not speak evil of the ruler of the people!' "

Bradley spun around one more time with the *Bible* now open, showing the words to the people of New-York. This would work on some of them, many actually. But, not all. Linus wasn't buying it. He also put a star next to that quote. If a man is evil, a man should be called evil, regardless of his position, especially if he is supposed to be caring for a great many men under him.

"So clearly, gentlemen of the jury, it is clear by both the law of God and Man that it is a very great offense to speak evil of those in authority over us. Mr. Zenger," he turned dramatically to point at Zenger, "has offended in a most notorious and gross manner in scandalizing not only the governor but both the council and assembly in his Animal Stories and in dangerous reports of the governor aiding French ships in our harbour."

"What an excellent speech, Mr. Attorney," Chambers spoke this time, slowly as he stood up and walked around his table to address the court. "But, it seems to me you have left out an important matter of your own charges: Man's law. You have not pressed to the jury the pivotal nature of the word 'false'.

Mr. Zenger is charged with printing and publishing *false, scandalous and seditious libels.* We have admitted to the printing and publishing, that much is true. You, Sir, must now bear the burden of proof for the label of *false.* You also must now bear the burden of proof that Governor Cosby and his officials are indeed the persons in questions. Prove my client's words were false and he shall be a libeler. Prove the persons are Cosby and his friends and he shall be seditious. Yet, if his words are true, which they are, and if the subjects of the Animal Stories are nameless, vague similarities to any government monkey, then my client is innocent," Chambers concluded and sat down, leaning on the back two legs of his chair to listen to Smith and Alexander whisper something in his ear.

"Your honours," Bradley approached the judges' bench as he smirked at Hamilton, like a big brother running to Mom to tattle, "I do not know why we are entertaining any further discussion. Mr. Zenger and his counsel have all confessed to the charges against him. The charge is printing and publishing a libel. He is guilty by his own admission, by his counsel's own admission for him. I request you instruct the jury to find the defendant guilty so we can all go home," he ended with a high-pitched whine.

"Mr. Hamilton, Mr. Chambers. Attorney General Bradley is right. This tryal is over. You have confessed. What more do you dare say?" DeLancey was growing bored with the whole thing and really wished Hamilton hadn't come in to stir up the pot.

"With all due respect," Hamilton took this one, "we have confessed to the charges of printing and publishing. This is 'Part One' of the charges. We are now in the process of defending against 'Part Two': the charges of libel. I have witnesses prepared to testify as to the truthfulness behind the alleged libels. Again, we have never confessed to libel because everything my client printed and published was true. I shall appeal to the jury to find *two* verdicts."

DeLancey and Philipse leaned into each other and whispered some more, always returning to the same conclusion. It was just good politics to indulge Hamilton at least a little while longer. He was just too well-known and celebrated to toss out of the room. What DeLancey could do was prevent him from making his case.

"Continue then, Mr. Hamilton. If you can, show the truth of your libel in evidence. But take advisement, I cannot allow you to call any new witnesses to prove your 'Part Two' of this case, because technically there is no 'Part Two'. The jury will find one verdict and one verdict only."

Linus had made two columns on one page of his notebook: "Printing and Publishing" headed one column; "Libel" headed the other. It had never occurred to him before that there should be two charges. Of course! Just because something is printed, doesn't make it wrong, especially if it is true.

"Take very serious note, gentlemen of the jury," Bradley spoke to the jury box now, "it is your duty only to find a verdict of *Guilty* or *Not Guilty* whereas regards the printing and publishing of the issues in question. Chief Justice DeLancey and Second Justice Philipse shall decide in a 'Special Verdict' whether or not it was a libel. The libel shall be none of your business."

"If it pleases your Honours," Hamilton argued, though stunned by this latest statement, he handled it with all the calm and grace that were his hallmarks, "it was my hopes that Mr. Bradley would not have attempted to set up a Star-Chamber here, a terrible court long ago laid aside as one of the most dangerous to the liberties of the people of England."

"What is your meaning, Mr. Hamilton?" DeLancey didn't like Hamilton's inference.

"In times past it was a crime to speak the truth and in that terrible court of the Star-Chamber centuries ago, many worthy and brave men suffered for doing so," Hamilton turned now to the jury. "And even in those bad days, a great and good man once said, 'The practice of Informations for libels, instead of Grand Juries, is a sword in the hands of a wicked king and an errant coward to cut down the innocent."

"Pray, Mr. Hamilton," DeLancey leaned far over his bench and hissed at Hamilton, "have a care what you say, don't go too far neither. I don't like those liberties you take with me."

Hamilton bowed and sat down to think of another approach. Bradley did not rise right away, but searched through some papers in his portfolio. Hamilton and Satchel perused some books and for a while, maybe ten minutes, the courtroom was very quiet. Linus took the few minutes to go back through his notes to see if he'd noted anything that needed further elaboration. He also took a moment to shut his eyes, lift his arms slightly and let whatever air he could get flow under his arms. This was highly offensive to the woman sitting next to him and she made a face to tell him so. It wasn't his fault. The air was stifling. There was no breeze outside and it was making the courtroom unbearable. Still, nobody would leave. This was just too exciting, even if it was a bit boring at the same time.

Linus stretched his arms across his chest, rolled his head, then re-opened his journal and made a short note about the Star-Chamber at the bottom of his columned page. He knew only the basics about it; ironically, it was Zenger who told him about it one day over the printing press.

These were terrible courts utilized primarily by the English Kings James I and Charles I in the early 17th Century. It was a mechanism used to prosecute political figures whom had legally committed no crimes, but had in some manner offended the king or his administration. There were no rules, no legal procedure, no juries and no due process; but there was plenty of torture, coerced confessions and arbitrary verdicts, Special Verdicts.

This was a verdict in which judges could decide Guilty or Not Guilty without any evidence or input of a jury. Zenger's tryal wasn't really being conducted as a Star-Chamber, but the instruction of Bradley to the jury that the judges 'shall decide in a 'Special Verdict' whether or not it was a libel' and that 'the libel shall be none of your business' was bothersome.

A regular fixture in Star-Chamber cases was *seditious libel* and many of these cases were still used in current, 18th Century courtrooms as precedent and examples. Bradley had, in fact that day, cited some Star-Chamber cases in this tryal. A Special Verdict was the very thing someone like Zenger feared. English law clearly granted him the right to be judged by a jury completely: not half by jury and half by the judges. Yet, that didn't mean the law would always be upheld.

After the brief and quiet respite, with only the sounds of skirts and trousers shuffling in their seats and the outside noises of New-York in the summer, Bradley and Hamilton started up again. More cases were cited from *Coke's*, Thomas Wood's *Institutes of the Laws of England* and John Lilly's *Practical Register*, not to mention more *Bible* quotes from Bradley. He continued to argue that libel was libel and it did not matter if it was true or false. Hamilton, on the other hand, kept trying new ideas, high concepts and abstract thoughts to bring his point home.

"If truth be an issue in this case, than there is no libel," Bradley had oddly argued.

"Exactly! Must a man be a libeler for telling his true sufferings to his neighbor? Has he not a legislature? Has he not a House of Representatives to whom he can complain?" Hamilton rebutted.

"We are not discussing a man and his neighbor. We are discussing a man and his news-paper, which he used to complain to the entire colony about a very important man," Bradley replied.

Satchel handed a Hamilton a piece of paper which he read, then stuffed in his pocket. He would try a new tactic.

"Do you not think it a strange doctrine to press everything in the law here as it is in England?"

"Pardon?" DeLancey quipped.

"Did you know that in England if a man strikes another in Westminster Hall, in the presence of a judge, that man shall lose his right hand and forfeit all his land and goods for the crime?" Hamilton finished with raised eyebrows.

"What? What are you speaking of?" DeLancey looked to Philipse who looked just as perplexed.

"Did you know that in England a man has right to bring action against his neighbor for suffering his cow or horse to come and feed upon his land or corn, even though land in England is more open than not?" Hamilton continued. The judges stared and began to speak but Hamilton went on. "And yet I believe it would be strange for a man to bring the same legal action here, because most of the farms here in New-York and all the colonies are indeed fenced, and not generally left open wide."

"Mr. Hamilton!" DeLancey had had enough of all this.

"What on earth has this case to do with Westminster Hall or a cow on some man's unfenced land? The case before the court today is whether Mr. Zenger is guilty of libeling His Excellency the Governor of New-York," Bradley was sick of these word games, too.

"May it please Your Honours and Mr. Bradley, there are numbers of instances like this that might be given to show that what is good law at one time and in one place is not so good at another."

"Your point, Mr. Hamilton?" DeLancey said with a tempered anger that he was trying very hard to keep in check.

"My point is that laws which have been used for centuries in our Motherland may not be appropriate or even applicable in a new land so far away and completely out of her sight. America and its people are both vastly different from that of England. Should not our American laws reflect this difference?"

The courtroom cheered and the jury sat straighter in their hard chairs, refreshed and visibly inspired by such a revolutionary idea. DeLancey banged his gavel numerous times to quiet the court.

"Mr. Hamilton, I have had enough of this all. Your arguments are nonsense and shall not be considered by anyone in this room," DeLancey looked directly at the jury, but they had all already considered them very well. "Mr. Hamilton, the court has delivered its opinion and we expect you will use your good manners and judgment to argue no further against said opinion. The jury shall find a verdict of *Guilty* and allow us get on with our Special Verdict."

"I will say no more at this time," Hamilton turned to the jury. "The court, I can see, is against us in this point. I hope I can say that in this court."

"Use the court with good manners and you shall be allowed all the liberty you desire," DeLancey said calmly.

Hamilton paced for a few minutes, then stopped at his table, smiled at everyone there, took a deep breath and turned back to the jury as he straightened his finely embroidered, yet still dusty frock coat.

"I thank Your Honours," he bowed to the bench and then faced the jury again. "Then, gentlemen of the jury, it is to you we must appeal. Witnesses to the truth have been denied. We are not allowed the liberty to prove our *onus probandi*, our proof of a negative, which is inherently impossible and would therefore make this tryal worthless. As Mr. Bradley himself said, 'If truth be an issue in this case, than there is no libel'. We are not allowed to prove that the statements in Mr. Zenger's paper are not false but true." Now, his voice began to rise, his chin as well. Now, he began to speak like a preacherman.

"You are citizens of New-York!" Hamilton suddenly bellowed. "You are what the law supposes you to be: honest and lawful men! If a libel is understood in the unlimited sense described by Mr. Bradley, there is scarce a writing I know of that may not be called a libel!

Men who injure and oppress the people under their administration provoke them to cry out and complain. They then make that very complaint the foundation for new oppressions and prosecutions! The question before the court and you gentlemen of the jury is not of a small or private concern. It is not the cause of the poor printer or of New-York alone. No!" Hamilton pounded his fist on his table and it resounded through the room with his belting, full-throated passion.

"No, gentlemen! It may in its consequence affect every free man that lives under a British government on the main of America! It is the best cause!" his voice continued to escalate. "It is the cause. . .of liberty!" his head hung, as if exhausted from such a lofty theory.

"I will make no doubt," he raised his head and his fist again, "but your upright conduct this day will not only entitle you to the love and esteem of your fellow citizens, but every man who prefers freedom to a life of slavery! You, as men who have baffled the attempt of tyranny, and by an impartial and uncorrupt verdict, have laid a noble foundation for securing to ourselves, our posterity and our neighbors, that to which nature and the laws of our country have given us a right and a liberty, both of exposing and opposing arbitrary power, in these parts of the world at least, by speaking and writing the truth!"

Hamilton ended by quietly taking his seat. The courtroom was in an uproar of cheer. Satchel, Zenger, Linus and Chambers all couldn't believe what had happened. Hamilton had essentially turned the entire case around. His message was clear. These men of the jury had to do the right thing and not even allow DeLancey and Philipse to get hold of Zenger to enforce their Special Verdict. DeLancey was not amused or impressed by Hamilton's drama.

"Gentlemen of the jury," DeLancey spoke with such contempt that it instantly smothered the good cheer in the court. "The great pains Mr. Hamilton has taken to show how little regard juries are to pay to the opinion of the judges is done, no doubt, with the design that you should take very little notice of what I am about to say. I shall therefore only say to you that whether the *words* set forth in this case make a libel is none of your business. That is a matter of the law which you may leave to the court."

Delancey continued in his final speech by quoting Chief Justice Holt in a 1704 case: the tryal of John Tutchin. In this speech he argued that a corrupt government is no good for anyone and that how could the people and their monarch be expected to exist in harmony if those officials in between are not virtuous. He argued that only a government kept in check and one that endeavoured to right any wrong was the life link to a good society. He stated that to imply that those appointed to such high offices did not understand the importance of integrity was a grave insult and that those who think differently are ignorant. In short, Governor Cosby was a good man and would not think to harm his people of New-York. In closing, DeLancey did not like Hamilton's closing argument and took it all very personally as a high-official himself. He instructed the jury to deliver a verdict of *Guilty*.

The jury was escorted to a separate and private chamber. The courtroom was now down to a quiet hum. DeLancey and Philipse were whispering to each other. Bradley was packing up his portfolios and straightening his books in one tall stack. Zenger sat alone with his thoughts, still consumed with the possibility of many years in gaol. Satchel and Chambers whispered quietly with Hamilton as Alexander and Smith leaned over the bar to join the conversation.

Linus was still writing in his journal. Hamilton's and Bradley's closing arguments had been long and at times confusing. He wrote as fast as he could in the beginning, but then decided to just capture key elements. Bradley's were easy. He had only one: Did Zenger print and publish the papers in question? Hamilton's were a bit more detailed. He had five-pronged defense.

First, the allegedly libelous articles were true.

Second, a truth cannot be a libel.

Third, there must be no doubt of the identity of the libeled person or persons. No names were ever printed in the Animal Stories. They were merely symbols of the government in general.

Fourth, the jury cannot allow for and must override the unfair Special Verdict: a practice taken back to the early days of the Star-Chamber.

Fifth, and finally, things are very different here than in England. Therefore, the laws must also be different.

The woman next to Linus watched him write and thought his journal looked a complete mess; but he understood his system. He knew what every star, symbol, asterisk, underscore and doodle meant. She looked more closely at some teeny-tiny writing that snaked around the whole border of the page: Linus' answer to running out of space on the page. If he had a compulsion to finish a thought, and if there was only a sentence or two left, he'd write on the same page instead of going to the next, full, blank page, even if that meant writing those last two sentences like a fence around the page.

The woman shook her head and was glad she didn't have to bother with frivolous things like reading and writing. Plain old gossip was good enough for her. She impatiently watched the door behind which the jury convened. She was hoping for a *Guilty* verdict. She loved her governor and hated foreigners, even though she herself had come here from Scotland. That was still the British Empire she told anyone whom would listen and by that fact she had the right to live anywhere the British ruled. She thought Linus looked like a foreigner and instinctively distrusted him. Linus thought she smelled like cabbage. They did have one thing in common, though. Neither could take their eyes off the jury door. Then, in what was a very short time, the door opened.

DeLancey and Philipse were not surprised by the quick return. Their point had been made very clearly. Chambers, Satchel, Hamilton and Zenger were surprised and Zenger flopped his head back on the table. This couldn't be good. The jury filed back into their box and took their seats. They all eyed Zenger as if he was the cause of something very disturbing.

"Has the jury reached a verdict?" the Clerk of the Court spoke his only words in the tryal from a small desk just below the judges' bench.

DeLancey and Philipse had smirks on their lips. Zenger lifted his head and glanced at Satchel whom was chewing his fingernails. Chambers and Hamilton remained utterly professional and unfazed, whilst Smith and Alexander leaned forward anxiously on the bar. Linus just sat on the edge of his seat and felt sweat drip down his cheek from his hairline as he waited, literally, breathlessly. Zenger's sons gritted their teeth and tightened their jaws as they awaited the pronouncement of their father's future.

A man in the jury stood up and brushed his hair back with a sweaty palm. The jury foreman, he was named Thomas Hunt and was dressed in olive linen today. He planted his old, leather shoes firmly on the floor and spoke loudly, clearly and plainly as he looked Zenger directly in the eyes.

"*Not Guilty.*"

"Huzzah! Huzzah! Huzzah!" the courtroom erupted into instantaneous pandemonium, clapping, cheering and dancing in the aisle.

Zenger flopped his head down again, this time in sheer relief. His two sons ran from the gallery and hugged him as they cried. Satchel, Chambers, Alexander and Smith were all stunned and just smiled huge, gaping smiles at each other as they patted each other on the back and shook hands, one over the other in a big mix of happy hands. Linus jumped up and down and hugged the woman next to him, whom pulled away and left the courtroom in disgust. He was right, she definitely smelled like cabbage.

DeLancey, Philipse and Bradley just watched silently, truly stunned into silence. The courtroom was out of control. It was like a circus or a festival, not a chamber of justice. Little children took the opportunity to run amuck and scream, young boys saw it as an opportunity to hug as many women and girls as they could, and ironically a few pickpockets took the opportunity to nick a watch or a coin purse here and there.

DeLancey banged his gavel over and over again, literally screaming for order; but, no one listened. He even threatened gaol time for anyone whom didn't settle down. Still, no one listened. The banging and the yelling proving futile, DeLancey huffed, tightened his jaw, grabbed his portfolio in a hard, jerking motion as if it was personally responsible for all this and stomped down his steps and out of the courtroom, his diamond-buckled heels making a sharp, angry cacophony as he left the courtroom. Philipse followed suit and gave the whole room a dirty look as he ran to catch up with DeLancey. Shortly thereafter, following some civil and professional handshakes with Hamilton and Chambers, Bradley gathered his things and went home.

After the cabbage lady left, and after he watched the courtroom's party for the next ten minutes or so, Linus opened his journal and wrote the final page of this adventure amidst the courtroom festivities that would forever live in his memory. On a new page he noted that Mr. Hamilton was right. This tryal had not been about a poor printer, or even New-York, but about the greatest cause of all: liberty.

CHAPTER FORTY - ONE

"Safannah, this is marfelous! You haf really improved," Ichabod admired Savannah's painting.

The summer heat had finally fallen off and what remained was one of the most pleasant months in a Virginia year. September was still warm enough to leave the coats at home, but the brutal heat was gone and the summer thunderstorms had mostly abated. The days were blue, beautiful and the perfect breezes quietly gossiped about the autumn days to come. Today was the perfect kind of day to lounge by a creek and do something like paint.

Early that morning, three friends walked a mile or so outside of town and relaxed for the day. Beside a trickling creek, amidst a lovely, grass clearing surrounded by a thinning forest Savannah painted. Sterling practiced his juggling with some small, wooden bowling balls he borrowed from Mr. Levingston's bowling alley. The bowling season was dying down and people were spending more time readying themselves for harvests and vendanges than playing at sport.

Ichabod read his latest book purchase: a collection of plays by Jean-Baptiste Poquelin, better known as Molière. Ichabod laughed and laughed at the satirical, comedic plays and they all brought back fond memories of his days in the French court of Louis XIV. Williamsburg, Ichabod mused, was certainly far, far away from France, in more ways than one.

Sterling couldn't have agreed more. Right on cue, Sterling's wanderlust, his need to travel the world and a general angst at being stuck in one town for too long, was beginning to kick into high gear. Life was good, really good now; but, he had been in Williamsburg for almost a year and it was all a pretty trying time. As lovely as the town was and as much as he liked Savannah,

Ichabod, Dante, Mrs. Pritchen, Anthony and the whole gang, he was ready to move along. Maybe he'd go to New-York for a while.

Gooch had surprised him that night he was escorted back to the Palace. Not only had his warrant had been lifted personally by Gooch, he was fully pardoned of all crimes and even officially sponsored by the governor himself. Sterling was truly free to explore the world at his leisure. He was so relieved to be done with the whole Vagabond mess. Of course, Dante, the one person in whom Sterling had completely confided his history, could never seem to get enough of the adventure. Dante had insisted on learning more details of Sterling's Vagabond struggle and last night had been as good a night as any.

It was rare for Dante to lounge in the Raleigh Tavern. Mrs. Pritchen never knew about his visits there, but he just liked a change of scenery and in truth, they served a great trout dinner. There he was last night when Sterling strolled in, looking for a change of pace himself. They spotted each other and as the ale flowed, so did the stories and it was then that Sterling told him the details of the Vagabond ordeal.

"What? I don't understand." It was the first thing Dante said after hearing the tale thus far. "You sang to a sheriff and he put you in gaol?"

Dante and Sterling laughed, thinking about a stern-faced sheriff.

"It all came down to having no sponsor." Sterling explained.

"What does that mean? A sponsor?" Dante took a drink and eyed a fish platter a barmaid carried by.

"Someone who knows I'm bloody brilliant and shouldn't have to spend my time working a job-job and stifling my talents. Someone to pay me so my gifts don't go to waste."

"So? Is that a law or something? So what if you're poor."

"I am not poor!" Sterling was offended. "That has nothing to do with it, at least in the eyes of English law. The English government does not look kindly on artists. They think we're a drain on the infrastructure, a blight to hard-working folks." Sterling leaned back and rested a boot on his left thigh.

"So, were you being a blight?" Dante got a boy-grin on his face, hoping for a good story.

"No, Mate. No blight. Just being me. Thing is, the sheriff asked me on the road, 'Do you have a proper sponsor' to which I said, 'I sponsor myself, Chap.', so, he smirks and tells me I'm no William Shakespeare and how Mr. Shakespeare had proper sponsors, to which I say, 'Mate, I know all about Shakespeare. I don't need you to tell me about the Bard.' He didn't like that," Sterling laughed and nibbled on a cheese stick.

"Shakespeare had sponsors?" Dante ate one, too.

"Absolutely! That's why his troupes were called official names like The Chamberlain's Men or The King's Men. This was proof to the authorities everywhere that they were legally allowed to travel and perform. Otherwise, Shakespeare himself might have never written or performed half the plays he did."

"That's fascinating!" Dante looked wistfully out into the dark DoG Street. "I've got to get out of this town. Nothing exciting like that ever happens here."

"Trust me, Mate. Nothing exciting about going to a London gaol."

"Right. Sorry. I didn't mean that," Dante apologized. "So how did you get here then?"

Sterling ran down the intricacies of the Vagabond Act, to which Dante compulsively shoved cheese stick after cheese stick into his mouth.

"Are you having a laugh? Is he having a laugh?!" adopting some of Sterling's vernacular, Dante asked no one in particular about the absurdity of the Vagabond Act.

Dante had no idea such stupid laws even existed. This was what the powers-that-be in London did all day? What a joke! You could own a slave, but you couldn't juggle and dance without a sponsor. Brilliant lawmaking.

Sterling leaned back and motioned for more ale to the tavernkeep. Dante was stunned. Maybe he didn't want to travel. Could he be picked up for just walking around Ireland or Denmark without a good reason? Of course, Williamsburg was a British colony, maybe he could be arrested here just for fishing. Then, a thought occurred to him.

"So that's why Ichabod was so insistent on everyone always referring to the play as being 'an Ichabod DenVries Production'. I thought he was just being poncy and arrogant."

"No, Chap. Ichabod knows his way around this globe. He knew what he was doing. That's why he's the impresario, the producer. Always trust the producer. They seem worthless, everyone says, 'What exactly does a producer do?', but you can't put on a play without them."

"So, how did you escape? I mean, you weren't hunted, I assume."

"Not likely, Mate. The minute they carted me to my destination and opened my cage, I ran like the Devil. They could never catch me. A fond farewell to thee! They saw only my fluffy tail and never a bit more. I was on the run south when I met Remus. You know the rest of the story, and here I am," he smiled, leaned all the way back in his chair and held his arms wide and high, as if the Raleigh Tavern was his. "Not a bad life after all, this vagabond life, eh, Mate?"

Sterling and Dante toasted each other and the vagabond life. Then, Dante thought of one more thing.

"What about your clothes? Your mandolin? If they took all that away, where did you get all this?" he gestured to Sterling's finery.

"Stolen, yeah?" he said plainly.

"Really?" Dante grinned.

"Lots of gypsies living near the bay on the Virginia side. Nothing to smile about, though. I've always felt guilty about it, but what could I do? Now that I've made a bit of money though, it's on my list of things to do when I leave here, is go back and pay the gypsies for the clothes. It's only right, Mate."

"What about the mandolin?"

"I actually did some gardening work for an old woman in Pennsylvania. She needed help digging up an area for a soup garden. I saw some instruments in her house and said I'd do it for a trade. I guess her husband was a musician and they were his. He'd died."

"Oh," Dante thought the stolen gypsy clothes were more interesting.

All in all, it had been a long, hard struggle for Sterling to get back on his feet, but he had and he knew he had a few people to thank for that. This Williamsburg gang to start with.

Indeed the year had been abysmal and Savannah had tucked away all her painting supplies. She'd never even broken out the gorgeous set of paints and brushes Anthony had gotten her from Italy. It was only this week she had done so and after nearly a full four seasons, she found that Italian blue, the Canaletto skies which had been so far out of reach before. Now they flowed from her brush like a new Beaujolais wine at an autumn wedding in Orléans. She was so pleased with herself.

"You haf finally gotten your blue skies of Fenice. . .here in Villiamsburg!" Ichabod pointed to her canvas and its blue sky.

"I know! It's just coming to me and I can't stop it! It's as though I had some mental block and now. . .gone."

"Are you shocked by this, Love?" Sterling looked over her painting. "It's been quite the year for everybody. Who can create when the mind is taken up by so much sorrow?" He leapt and snapped at a passing bird, then apologized, still unable to break the natural habit. "Sorry about that, Mate!"

They all said very little for a good hour. Only the sounds of the birds and the creek made any noise. Intermittently, Ichabod's page turning and Savannah's brush on canvas filled the air. More often than that, Sterling's juggling faltered and the *thud* of a bowling ball hitting the grass echoed through the silence. Then, there was a great ruckus of voices, twigs snapping and footsteps crunching across the soft forest floor.

Instinctually, the three stopped what they were doing and watched the outskirts of the woods. Ichabod chirped a little "Hallo? Who is it?" Nobody answered and the three waited, their ears perked up and fur on end, all ready to spring into the safety of the trees if necessary. Closer and closer the voices and footfall came.

"I cannot imagine a better location," Anthony stepped out of the trees first, followed next by William Parks, then Dante, who saw Savannah and his other pals right away.

"Greetings, all!" he left his present company and ran to the group. "I didn't know you would all be here today."

"Yes, remember I said I was going to try to finish my painting *en plein air*?" Savannah greeted him with a cheek-kiss.

"I thought you'd be back on the James River for outdoor painting."

"I needed some new inspiration. I like the trees here," she looked up at the dizzying heights of the mélange of pines, oaks and birch trees.

"VShat are you doing here?" Ichabod wondered.

"Mr. Parks and Anthony are going into business together, maybe. Parks asked me if I want to do some more work with him. I guess I did such a good job before, he thinks I'd make a great printer," Dante eyed a fish making its way down the creek.

"I thought you hated that work," Sterling said.

"I did. But, I might get to do more of the business-end of it, like travelling to Philadelphia and New-York if I want!!" Dante was as ready to travel as Sterling was.

He didn't really want to leave Williamsburg altogether, he could never leave Savannah and Ichabod. Yet, he did need to get out and see some of the world, that much was certain.

"You see, if we build it here, we have a ready and inexhaustible water source. The creek shall never run dry," Parks was giving Anthony a good sales pitch.

Anthony had survived the year. Barely. Still, with the friendship of Savannah and many others, he had gotten through it. His loyalty at the play that night and the allegiance, late as it had been in coming, he paid posthumously to his little brother, had earned him the respect of many in town. There had been many he angered by crossing the line and essentially supporting the message against slavery, but that mattered not. There were enough in town who believed as he did and as Savannah did and they brought him the business necessary to open that fourth store. Furthermore, Anthony had gone to great lengths to be as sure as possible, when possible, that his goods were coming from direct sources in India, China and Africa. He was doing his best to not use the East India Trading Company or any middlemen that knowingly and brazenly received their goods through the Slave Triangle of Trade. Still, he could never really get away from the slave trade if he stayed in retail. Even goods coming directly from India or China or wherever could still be the product of slave labour in those countries. So, today he was talking with William Parks about branching into a new area of business: paper.

"Unlike the retail concerns you have, Anthony, paper is a commodity we can create right here in Williamsburg, without any slave labour if we choose and sell it within the colonies for a fair price," Parks was gesturing to the land and the creek as he spoke.

"What is he talking about?" Savannah's nose was all twitchy at the idea of new business.

"A paper mill," Dante answered.

"See, I think it is time that Virginia had her own news-paper, and I am the man to print and publish it," Parks proudly stated. "I am doing very well with books, pamphlets, sermons and the like, but it is time to do something lasting, something revolutionary," he glanced around as he said this.

It was well known that Gooch was in fact a very printer-, people- and book-friendly governor. In fact a few years back when Parks first came to town from Maryland, he had printed a work known only as *Typographia* by one J. Markland. In this work, Markland had praised Governor Gooch in no uncertain terms by writing gloriously,

> *A Ruler's gentle Influence*
> *Shall o'er his Land be shewn;*
> *Saturnian Reigns shall be renew'd*
> *Truth, Justice, Vertue, be pursu'd*
> *Arts flourish, Peace shall crown the Plains,*
> *Where GOOCH administers, AUGUSTUS reigns.*

Gooch aside, Parks had been around long enough to know that words like "revolutionary" could make some people, the Carviles of the world, nervous.

Savannah dropped her brush into a cup of water and ran up to Parks.

"A news-paper?! We are going to have our own news-paper?! I don't have to wait for old deliveries of Maryland and New-York papers to get my London news?! Oh how exciting!" She ran up Anthony's shoulder and tugged on his shoulder pad excitedly. "Just think, we can read the paper every," she interrupted herself and looked to Parks, "How often will you print it?"

"Probably similar to the *Pennsylvania Gazette* or the *New-York Weekly Journal*. Weekly. Maybe Mondays."

"Every Monday! We can have a café or tea and get together to read our very own Virginia. . .," she interrupted herself again and asked Parks, "What will you call it?"

"Probably the *Gazette*."

"*The Virginia Gazette*," she said it lovingly, in the same way she might repeat the name of a perfume she really wanted. "We can get together on Monday mornings and take café and read our *Virginia Gazettes*. Oh how wonderful!"

"The problem is cost. A news-paper costs a lot to run, an awful lot to print," Parks took the romance out of the whole thing and Savannah's grin drooped.

"Why not sell advertising?" she suggested.

"Well, of course. But, there is still a great output for paper. That is why I am trying to build our own paper mill. Here," he gestured to the land and the creek, "not only can we save money making our own paper on a grand scale, but we can sell it to other printers amongst the colonies."

"Do you have other printers right now whom would buy from you, from us?" Anthony was getting closer to buying in.

"Indeed, my friend, I do. The news-paper business is growing strong, mostly up north. Down south, Charleston and Savannah," Savannah giggled as she listened to Parks, "are also good possibilities. But straight away, I have a very dear friend up in Philadelphia who will most certainly be our first customer."

"Who is this?" Anthony asked.

"Mr. Benjamin Franklin and the *Pennsylvania Gazette*."

The day was so perfect that Parks and Anthony stayed on the creek a little longer than business should allow and enjoyed a few laughs and some good cheer with Savannah and the gang. Soon though, as happens in September, the sun begins to set sooner than everyone wishes. Anthony helped Savannah with her easel and her brushes and everybody set off down the road, back toward town. As they walked, the beat of hooves could be heard approaching from behind. Curiosity turned everyone's head to see the oncoming horse. What they saw was no ordinary horse.

This was a beast. A giant, black horse thundering toward them. Astride him rode a boy of about sixteen, maybe seventeen, clad in a russet-coloured frock coat of velvet, black breeches and a black tricorn all of which set off his blond locks, even from far away. Sterling's ears stood sky-high and his tail wagged back and forth. His eyes gleamed brightly and his teeth glistened as he smiled so much it began to hurt his cheeks. He knew this boy!

"Good afternoon, friends," the boy brought the giant horse to an elegant halt, tipped his hat and smiled with perfect teeth. "Perhaps you can tell me if I am close."

"Close to vhat?" Ichabod stepped up to handle the situation, not at all intimidated by an equine which towered over his tiny, Pomeranian frame.

"I am headed for Mrs. Pritchen's Main Street Tavern," he patted two large saddlebags hanging off his horse's rump. "She is the newest stop on His Majesty King Geroge's Royal Mail Route."

CHAPTER FORTY - TWO

Mrs. Pritchen was beside herself with glee. A Royal Mail stop!

"Let's see how the Raleigh Tavern likes this!" she fondled her bag of mail as everyone sat in the gaming room of her tavern after dinner.

"Mrs. Pritchen," Samuel gently reminded her, "please do not forget these are official documents and *private* letters. The appointment of a Royal Mail stop is not to be taken lightly and when one is honoured as such, one must assume the responsibility of a royal appointment. No peeking."

Mrs Pritchen dropped her head like a child who'd just been reprimanded and locked the bag in an armoire near the front door.

"You must thank Mr. Franklin for me," Mrs. Pritchen whispered to Ichabod.

When Ichabod learned that Mr. Franklin was heading up the Royal Post Office for all the colonies, he wrote a letter, pulling what strings he could, and got Mrs. Pritchen on the route.

The night had drawn on late and Samuel was glad this had been his last stop of the night. As a mail courier, he was entitled to tavern lodging wherever he made stops and tonight was a good night to take advantage of that. He was exhausted and so was Merlin. Of course, Mrs. Pritchen would have put them up anyway. Ichabod decided to stay the night as well. He also made an announcement that night that he had decided to buy a small property in town. He had even hired someone to stay on the property to keep it safe.

Ever since Ichabod heard about the Custis Estate having an intellectual hermit, he'd been obsessed with the idea of having one on his plantation. Over the summer, he had become better acquainted with Beauregard and, over time, came to earn the trust, as had all the gang, of Beauregard's dear friend Bruce. Well, it only made sense and as the three of them discussed this one night over a late-summer dinner, outdoors on the Custis Estate, it seemed there could be no more perfect match.

"So, you want to hire me to be your hermit? To live on your plantation?" Bruce had squinted an eye at Ichabod, never having believed a fancy dog might one day be his employer.

"Yes," Ichabod said concisely.

"And where is this place again?"

"Outside town, about eight miles that vay," he pointed to the east with his walking stick as his leaned back on their picnic blanket.

"And there is nobody living there except you?" Bruce found this hard to believe as he popped an olive in his mouth.

"Just my serfants and me, all vell-paid, of course."

"You or your servants are well-paid?"

"Both, of course."

"Of course."

Beauregard just watched the exchange and said nothing, but ate blueberry muffins like they were going out of style. His stubby, little paws shoved cakey pieces in his tiny mouth as his stubby, little tail waggled wildly at the thought of living on Ichabod's plantation. Bruce was quiet as he weighed his options and, knowing his stint at the Custis Estate was over now that they had found him out, he realized he really had no options, but he did have pride.

"Alright, Herr Ichabod. I'll be your hermit, but I must be free to pursue other arrangements or jobs if I feel like it," Bruce leaned back, both palms spread on the blanket.

"It matters not to me vhat you do," Ichabod poured himself some more white wine, a German wine. "You may life on the plantation as long as you like, you may dine vith my guests and me vhen I hafe them if you like, and you may look for other vork if you vish to."

"Good. I may wish to dine and I may not," he was trying to keep the upper hand. "But, I am still free to look for other work?"

"Of course," Ichabod removed a leaf which had stuck to his shoe. "Vhat kind of job are you looking for? Maybe I can help."

"Well, I don't think I'd like to go back up to Harvard," he looked at Beauregard whom waggled his tail and stuffed another blueberry muffin into his mouth, "but, I think I might like to see about a professorship this autumn at the College of William and Mary here. Philosophy, ethics, something along those lines. There are some very interesting ideas coming out of Europe and the British Isles right now. Diderot and his *Encyclopedia* project? A verrrry fascinating look at new science and thought. And George Berkeley? Perplexing writings on the whole idea of consciousness as existence and sensory as reality? I like that."

Beauregard just blinked and stuffed a chocolate truffle in his mouth.

"Ah, yes. Berkeley. I haf read a number of his treatises and essays. 'Truth is the cry of all, but the game of few.' " Ichabod quoted the Irishman.

"That's right, my little fellow. That's absolutely right," Phil nodded his head and closed his eyes as if imagining a world of pure truth and real existence.

"I shall se vhat I can do," Ichabod offered his eternal social connections. "I haf a friend, a mouse-traveller named Bartholomew. He teaches mathematics and ethics-in-law," they all laughed heartily, then Ichabod regained his composure, "at the College, but travels to Svitzerland and France so often, he needs replacement professors to cofer him vhile he is avay."

"A sabbatical? I think I could manage that. I don't like the idea of a total commitment. A semester at a time would be perfect," he lay all the way back on the blanket and let the summer sun bathe his VanDyk beard.

Beauregard nodded, too, chocolate smudged on his nose. He wasn't really sure who this Berkeley person was; but, if people as smart as Bruce and Ichabod liked him, Beauregard did, too. He would try to find a book on this Berkeley man and learn more about him.

"Alright then, Herr Ichabod. You have yourself a hermit. Shake," Bruce bent down and shook Ichabod's paw.

Beauregard's tail waggled like crazy as Ichabod took a large, iron key from his rucksack and handed it to Bruce.

"What's this? What's that for?" his nose wrinkled up in distaste.

"It is the key to my home. It is so you can get in. I don't understand this qvestion."

"I'm to live on the grounds, little fellow, in a hut," he stated with dignity.

"Okay," Ichabod put the key back in the bag and Beauregard's tail stopped wagging. "You can life in a hut if you like, but the whole house is pretty much empty except for a few serfants and I shall be lifing in town more often than not. Vhy not take the big house? Vinter can be fery cold here."

Beauregard's tail wagged again as he looked up at Phil.

"Because I can't support your excessive lifestyle, little fellow."

"You are the philosopher. But did not Foltaire say 'The superfluous is very necessary'?"

"I don't like Voltaire."

"Oh don't be ridiculous. Eferybody likes Foltaire. Look, life in a hut, life in the big house. It matters not to me," Ichabod leaned back and sipped his lunch wine.

Beauregard tugged on Bruce's breeches but said nothing. He only shook his tail and looked with huge, pleading groundhog eyes. Bruce sighed.

"Alright, little fellow," he said.

Ichabod smiled tightly. He liked this Bruce very much. How could one not? But, he did not like being called 'little fellow' and yet he was too polite to ever say so.

"If I must, I shall live in the big house," Bruce capitulated. "But just to keep an eye on things for you," he added quickly.

"Of course. I vould be most appreciative if you 'keep an eye on things for me'. And you, Beauregard? Are you going to life there, too? You are more than velcome."

"Oh yes! Thank you, Herr Ichabod! I vill be, I mean, I will be the best houseguest ever! And I am going to learn all about George Berkeley and this Voltaire person also!" Beauregard's tail was going so wildly Ichabod thought he might burrow himself right into a hole if he didn't stop soon.

Beauregard had a lot to learn in the art of remaining cool and blasé. Ichabod resolved he might help him out with all that. He liked Beauregard, even if he was a bit eager. Not to worry, Ichabod could polish him like no one else. The three finished their lunch *al fresco* and enjoyed the fresh summer air and the anticipation of a wonderful new year and friendships to come. Ichabod also thought about a house for sale in town that he liked very much. He also thought about how it was right next door to that pretty little rabbit, Miss Onyx. Yes, this would be a very good year to come, he was sure of it.

A second home really did make sense. He was spending more and more time at Mrs. Pritchen's instead of going back and forth between his plantation and town. Besides, he had chatted a bit more with Mr. Parks and Anthony on the walk home from the creek and Ichabod was smart enough to see that the news-paper business could be a lucrative one. He was a little leery of being considered a revolutionary of any type, but he could help with the money issues behind the scenes and build himself a healthy profit. Besides, being a news-paper mogul couldn't be a bad thing when chatting up Miss Onyx, could it? Yes, Ichabod needed to be in town now.

Anthony had said goodnight and Savannah walked him to the door. She was so happy her friend was back. Whatever had happened over the last year was no longer spoken of, but always remembered. Anthony was a new man, a better man, a truer man. Savannah, though she would never see it herself, had probably grown up a little bit, too.

The tavern was mostly dark by now. All of Mrs. Pritchen's guests, some fifteen in all, had gone to bed and only Savannah, Ichabod, Dante, Sterling and Samuel remained in the gaming room. Merlin was out back in the garden enjoying a nice flowerpot of chamomile and lavender cuttings. They were so tasty and so relaxing, he eventually fell asleep mid-munch and swayed slightly, his tail blowing gently in the September evening breeze as he dozed standing up. Below him, two garden mice watched and laughed as they mimicked him. They swayed back and forth on all fours and made silly faces and faux snores as they pretended to be sleepy horses.

Back inside, Dante and Sterling finished a card game of Whist with Samuel while Savannah and Ichabod chatted about the news-paper industry as he read a slightly old *New-York Weekly Journal* about The John Peter Zenger

Tryal.

"It is unbeliefable," Ichabod said aloud. "Efen after Herr Zenger vas found 'Not Guilty', they made him stay in prison ofernight."

"What?! That's madness!" Dante was instantly incensed.

"It says here, Herr Zenger himself actually writes it, that DeLancey vas so angry vith the outcome that he left the courtroom before officially freeing him. Then, vhen he finally freed him the next day, he ordered that Zenger pay for all his costs vhile in prison before he could go home."

"His costs?" Dante was suddenly seething. "What costs?!"

"His food, guard vages, that type of thing," Ichabod said. "That is actually fery standard."

"So how did he pay it?" Savannah worried for the man whom she did not know but for whom she was extremely grateful.

"His supporters. No names," Ichabod scanned the paper. "He just says 'his supporters' paid his costs the next morning and by noon he vas a free man."

Ichabod folded his paper in half and set it on the tea table next to him. He then picked up his port glass and took a sip of wine. It was getting late and whilst everybody had pretty much said their good-byes earlier, it was always a little hard to say them again before one went to bed. Sterling would be gone by the time they awoke in the morning. He was headed back north with Samuel and Merlin.

Sterling had already said a fond farewell to Anthony. It was a quiet one and though not a lot of tears were shed, neither's eyes were dry. They had shared so much this year and while they knew they might never see each other again, that was okay. They shared a friendship that no one else could touch and even though it would only exist in one place at one time in history, it was theirs. Years back in London, a friend of Sterling's, a lively redhead named Kathleen, had once called such a friendship a soul contract. That's what Sterling and Anthony had: a soul contract. In fact, that's what all these friends had. Not many words needed to be spoken with a bond like that.

Sterling had also said his good-byes to Savannah and Mrs. Pritchen, both of whom had cried a lot, and to Ichabod whom had merely nodded and bowed deeply. They, too, shared a bond: a knowledge of the world, a comfort with travel and a strange ease of parting company, since sadly that's what travel and wanderlust bring. They might bump into each other again someday and when they did it would probably be somewhere in Europe and they would buy each other a stout and have a wonderful time making fun of Williamsburg together.

Dante's good-bye was a little more difficult. Sterling liked Dante a lot and even suggested he come with him and Samuel and Merlin back up to Boston. Dante said he couldn't; he had work to do with Parks now. Plus, he couldn't just leave like that. Sterling thought that was nice and it made him a little sad that he never really had good, old friends that made parting too difficult to do. It was never too hard for him to leave anywhere.

Still, he loved to travel, he loved to explore and, for good or for bad, this time was different. This time, it was hard for him to leave. Nevertheless, he was going; but, he was going with friends. The first friends he had made at the beginning of this journey, friends he was sure he'd lost as surely as he'd lost Remus. Sterling was going to be just fine. He was travelling and for the first time in his life, he wasn't doing it alone.

The good thing for Dante was that, unlike with the departure of friends in the past such as Tara, Connor and Louis, folks he had met years ago during that fabulous Age of Pyracy, he wasn't overcome with the sadness of corralled wanderlust and the knowledge he'd never see them again. Dante was going to travel and soon! Better yet, he already had a planned meeting with Sterling, Samuel and Merlin in Philadelphia in November!

They were going to meet with Satchel, Radoslav, Gavin and Gwen. Mr. Andrew Hamilton had been so grateful for Merlin's and Samuel's help, he had insisted on treating them to two weeks at his country house outside Philadelphia. Radoslav was staying there indefinitely until his leg fully healed and Hamilton thought Satchel needed a break from the city. He needed to face those squirrels he so feared, face-to-face. Dante hadn't asked yet, but he was pretty sure Savannah and Ichabod were going to Philadelphia, too!

The main reason for Dante's trip though, was because the paper mill business was moving forward and Dante was to be part of Parks' sales force. He was going to meet with Mr. Benjamin Franklin as soon as construction of the

Williamsburg mill was underway. After his meeting, he was to join Samuel and Merlin in the country. Hamilton said any friend of theirs and any new business associate of Ben's was welcome in his home. Dante was going to see the world! Well, Philadelphia, at least.

Savannah needed to get home, but Mrs. Pritchen told her she'd seen a rather large and intimidating sparrowhawk circling her back garden tonight and perhaps Savannah should stay here. A squirrel versus a sparrowhawk was not a fair fight. Sparrowhawks could destroy a fancy little squirrel in no time. They were quite the bullies. Mrs. Pritchen said she had a room for Savannah, a teensy linen closet actually, but then that was all a squirrel needed, wasn't it? Well, at least for one night.

"Well, everybody. I think I shall be off to bed. I've got to be on the road very early tomorrow. Four o'clock," Samuel tapped his pocket watch at Sterling.

"Yes, my liege! Before the glory of the sun opens her sleepy eyes, upon the road we shall gallop and the world we shall discover!" Sterling snapped his tail back and forth in a dramatic fashion and bowed from where he sat.

Samuel laughed to himself. What a ham. He would certainly be the talk of the town in staid, old Boston. Samuel walked to the kitchen window to check on Merlin and was relieved to see him sleeping. He was such a hard worker, it did Samuel's heart good to see him rest. Even the mice had fallen asleep.

Under a nearby rosebush, they curled up under a tiny, canvas, Medieval-style, striped tent that looked ready to host a Robin Hood archery tournament. The mice tucked themselves into teensy, linen sleeping bags and snored tiny mouse-snores. Under the cover of the rosebush and the Robin Hood tent and next to the giant Merlin, the wee mice slept a hard and deep sleep, knowing they were safe from that menacing sparrowhawk.

Samuel's boots *clunk*ed up the stairs, as quietly as he could he trod, careful not to wake the whole tavern. Boots and wooden floors are a noisy partnership. Savannah giggled as she watched him try to tip-toe up the stairs. Then, she turned back to the group and there were only Ichabod, Dante and Sterling. When she awoke, Sterling would be gone. Life would be back to normal in lovely, pristine Williamsburg. Another friend suddenly injected into their lives, then just as quickly, gone. She looked around the room and smiled an odd, tight-lipped smile, one in which her lips curled over her teeth and her eyebrows stood high, her eyes huge as they blinked back tears. She didn't want to go to bed.

"Shall we all play another game of Whist?" she asked hopefully, her voice unnaturally high and squeaky.

Nobody wanted to. Everybody was tired.

"Sure. One more game, Love," Sterling said and he moved across the room, sat down next to her and wrapped his tail around her tiny shoulders. And she began to cry.